SMOKE
Got In My Eyes

BRUCE RUBENSTEIN

**CALUMET
EDITIONS**

Minneapolis

**CALUMET
EDITIONS**

SECOND EDITION DECEMBER 2022

SMOKE GOT IN MY EYES,

ISBN – 978-1-960250-56-8

10 9 8 7 6 5 4 3 2

Book design by Gary Lindberg

This book is a work of historical fiction and it mixes fact with fiction liberally. Many of the characters were living people who did things very much like they are portrayed as doing - among them Charles Ward, Floyd B. Olson, Homer Van Meter, John Dillinger and others. Some would be flattered if they could read what I've written, others would be furious, but they're all dead so they can't sue.

Thanks to Julie Schaper and Steven Horwitz for commissioning the short story that was the germ of this novel. Paul Maccabee's book - *John Dillinger Slept Here: A Crooks' Tour of Crime and Corruption in St. Paul* - was invaluable as a reference.

SMOKE
Got In My Eyes

BRUCE RUBENSTEIN

PART 1

SMOKE

Floyd B. Olson's funeral cortege wasn't scheduled to leave the State Capitol for an hour, but a throng of thousands already lined University Avenue for a glimpse as it passed. The November sun wasn't doing much to warm them so they'd squeezed together instinctively, five deep, all the way to the police cordon at Rice Street. It gave them a huddled masses look appropriate to the occasion. A cynic might say that in this year of our Lord 1934, anybody who advocated redistribution of wealth could draw a crowd, even if he was dead. As for me, I voted for him once, and I'd have done it again if the iron crab hadn't taken him down. I wasn't there to freeze my toes for a peek at his corpse though. I elbowed my way to the door of The Criterion. It was warm inside, a few bar flies were clustered around their Manhattans, and somewhere in the murk a client was waiting.

Margaret Thornton had phoned me after a fellow parishioner of her's steered her to my uncle, who'd recommended my services. She said I'd recognize her by the black hat she was wearing, and there she was in a corner booth, with her veil pinned back over one ear.

The rest of her outfit echoed the darkness of the place as well. That didn't strike me as a good sign a year after her husband was iced, though she looked just fine in widow's weeds. Her face might have hardened a bit since it graced the front pages, but there was still a girlish softness about her.

I introduced myself. She nodded nervously. She had green eyes, raven-colored hair and pale luminous skin. A little spray of freckles around her nose was barely visible in the dim light. Her fingers fidgeted on the table. One of her nails was chewed to the quick.

I ordered a beer. She turned down a refill on a Presbyterian she'd been nursing. I felt like a heel for arriving late. The poor kid had probably never been in a joint like this before, at least not alone. I was 34 then, she was maybe ten years younger, so these weren't fatherly feelings I was having but I didn't stop to analyze them at the time. It wouldn't have changed much anyway.

She told me she was Thornton nee Gallagher, a St. Agnes graduate. You can bet that tugged at my heart strings. In fact, it put a face to the premier fantasy in my rich selection of largely hooch-induced fancies: Catholic school girls in Little Bo-Peep shoes, white knee socks, and those short, plaid skirts they wear for God only knows what perverse reason. When I was a lad me and my pals would sometimes get a glimpse of alabaster thigh as they walked away. Of course if we caught some Protestant or worse yet a sheeny doing the same, the gauntlet went down.

I managed to elicit a fair amount of personal information in the guise of professional inquiry. For example, why a proper young lady like herself married a rabble-rouser who'd published his wing-nut tabloid out of a storefront in Frogtown. It came down to this; after 18 years in the grasp of the nuns, and two more clerking at a department store, she wanted some excitement.

"Walter was always railing about something," she said, "and there were all these interesting people around. Some with beards even. I guess I just got carried away."

She chewed her fingernail and looked thoughtful for a moment. "He came downtown to buy some socks," she added. "That's how I met him."

She said she was living with her mother now. They made ends meet with help from their fellow parishioners at St. Andrew's, and from some Reds who'd admired her hubby. I told her that Jerk Madigan, who'd put her in touch with me, was my uncle on my mother's side; that I was unmarried (true) and an irregular confessor (a lie, well, quite an understatement anyway—I hadn't confessed in years and had no intention of ever doing so again).

Close to an hour passed thus pleasantly before we got down to business. Margaret Thornton wanted what I had a reputation for delivering, the truth about an unsolved crime.

"Walter's murder just gnaws at me," she said, and she nipped another bit of fingernail.

She had a notion of what the truth was, and she made it clear that she'd be gratified if I confirmed it. That's not unusual. Most of my clients want their theories confirmed. They've been clinging to them a long time when they come to me. Nevertheless, her problem was anything but routine.

"Walter was murdered because Charlie Ward wanted to stop him publishing," she explained, and her eyes lit up as she spoke. "I don't blame Governor Olson, you see. I blame the man who has everything but the respectability the Governor could bring him. I don't even care if he's tried for murder. I just want it on the radio and in the newspapers what a dreadful person Charlie Ward really is."

"That's all you want? Nothin' to it. Should be easy to get the goods on a defenseless guy like Charlie Ward."

"You can do it, Mr. McDonough. Your uncle says you never fail."

Her confidence was touching, but the prospect of going after Charlie Ward was daunting nonetheless. I'd heard rumors that he was behind Thornton's murder, everybody had, but those rumors had no legs because people loved the guy. More important from my perspective, even if they didn't love him they knew better than to cross him.

She brought up the matter of my fee. I said we'd discuss it after I nosed around a bit. I'd known her about an hour, and she already had me putting first things last.

I escorted her out the back, and opened her car door for her. There weren't many woman drivers then, and to me she looked brave and vulnerable seated behind the wheel, all the more so because I recognized her bucket. It was the same one that shared the front page with her the day after her husband's murder. They'd mowed the poor stiff down when he stepped out of this very automobile.

She gave me a little smile that faded quickly, and then she exited down the alley.

That spared her a demoralizing sight around front. Floyd B. Olson's cortege was going past and people were surging into the street, but not to say goodbye to the Governor. Charlie Ward was seated at the passenger window of the hearse, and whether they knew it or not they were crowding toward him because they believed in what he stood for —redemption. They practically trampled each other trying to touch his cashmere coat, as if some of that magic of his might rub off on them.

According to the story that every St. Paulite knew, Charlie Ward was born out of wedlock to a waterfront prostitute in Seattle. He'd spent his childhood scrapping for change on the docks, then took off for the wild west while he was still a teenager. He worked as a saloon bouncer in Arizona, and a gold miner in Alaska and Nevada, then dropped the pickax and picked up a rifle to soldier for Pancho Villa. It was in that latter capacity he made his first fortune, selling the hides of the cattle slaughtered to feed Villa's army, about 2000 skins a month, for $5 each in El Paso. Those hides were all he'd asked for in return for his services making deals for supplies in border towns, but he went AWOL pronto when Pancho realized what a good thing he had going.

Ward spent the next decade raising hell (his term) in the Southwest. That surely included some smuggling given his familiarity with the border country, but mostly it was one long party that ended when the G men fitted him up for a nose candy charge in Denver. He hired a lawyer who took his money, but didn't beat the rap. Ward was stone broke when he went to Leavenworth. That was where he met Herbert Bigelow of Bigelow Enterprises, a St. Paul calendar manufacturing company.

Bigelow, heir to a medium-sized fortune and a nice little business, was a pampered playboy who was in stir for tax evasion. He was terrified of the other inmates. Ward made a deal with him. He promised to protect Bigelow in prison if Bigelow would give him a job when he got out.

Ward held up his end. Bigelow tried to renege many times, but Ward had some kind of hex on him. He climbed toward the top of Bigelow Enterprises, and in 1930, when Bigelow died mysteriously, became president of the company. Since then he'd turned Bigelow Enterprises into the largest advertising firm in the country, and made himself a legendary figure in the process.

Like many a millionaire before him, Ward dabbled in king-making. He'd befriended Floyd Olson when Olson was the County Attorney over in Minneapolis, where he was known for his outspoken belief that the Depression made criminals of honest men. He routinely stood shoulder to shoulder with the defense attorney after a trial, and asked the judge to give the fellow he'd just convicted a break. That appealed to the ex-con in Ward, while the aspiring king-maker couldn't help noticing that Olson's pleas often landed him on the front page.

He'd bankrolled Olson's run for Governor and was ready do the same for his shot at the presidency on the Populist ticket. By then observers nationwide had recognized that Olson was political dynamite. He was tall and stately. His name smacked of Midwestern rectitude. His oratorical gifts were considerable, and his record as Governor indicated that he could parse principle and expediency with the best of them. He was so good at the latter that Huey Long, the huckster from Louisiana, had agreed to take the number two slot on his ticket. The smart money said that with the Depression on and Ward's bucks behind him Olson would beat FDR. Then the poor man took sick and died, just like that, in the space of a few weeks.

It was a sad day for many when that happened, but it came about a year late for Margaret Thornton's husband.

Olson was a prosecutor during the waning years of Prohibition, and his attitude toward bootleggers had been passive, to put it mildly. He'd grown up in a mockey neighborhood, and many friends of his youth had joined the Hebe bootlegging underworld. That didn't seem to end their friendship, even though he was sometimes required to prosecute them. Critics like Walter Thornton noted that those fellows were often the ones he stood with in the dock at sentencing.

You might say Olson had an interesting history by the time he became Governor, and began making the kind of deals he had to in order to govern. The way he got things done appealed to the voters, but it didn't sit so well with some of his fellow radicals, especially Thornton, who published a yellow sheet devoted to calling him a crook and a sellout.

Thornton was a pain in the ass who might've hurt Olson's chances to be President, but about the time he was getting worrisome a car full of mugs pulled up as he arrived home one evening and ended his career in journalism.

Shay Tilsen, a mockey gangster from Minneapolis, was tried for Thornton's murder. He was acquitted, but everyone figured he'd done it. There just wasn't enough evidence to convict him. My copper friends told me that the prosecutor offered Tilsen a sweet deal to rat on whoever hired him, and left it on the table right up to the moment the jury walked in but he never opened his mouth.

I had no skin in that game, so I didn't give Ward's possible involvement in the murder much thought. I could find out though. My clients think it's sorcery how I get to the bottom of things, but my reputation rests on two solid facts: One - the majority of murders go unsolved. The coppers don't mouth that around, and since most people don't know it, they're also unaware of fact two; the investigators usually know who did it, they just can't prove it.

The rest of the equation is pretty simple. I'm second generation Irish, I know most of the bulls in town, and I can usually get the information I need by dropping into Tin Cup's and buying a few rounds.

My first stop wasn't Tin Cup's, however. Next morning I headed for Kuby's Place, on Front Avenue. Kuby's served as a parlor for many a retired St. Andrew's parish fellow, and sure enough, there were about ten of them gathered around the wood stove, warming their ale on the firebricks.

When in Kuby's do as the Kubans do. I pulled up a stool, ordered coffee and brandy, and put my nose to the crossword puzzle.

It wasn't long before I felt a sharp tug on the sleeve. They don't call him Jerk for nothing. He was freshly shaved and nattily attired, the picture of contented leisure. I don't know how he does it, I thought. By rights he should be in a bread line.

"How's my blue-eyed handsome nephew?" Jerk said.

"He's in need of a four letter name from Shakespeare that epitomizes cunning."

"I'm proud to say I've never read a word that limey bastard wrote, Martin. - How goes it with the widow Thornton? Quite the example of lace curtain womanhood, isn't she?"

"She is indeed, Jerk, and a welcome respite from the kind of dames I generally consort with. But why did she come to you of all people?"

"Ah - give me a moment to count ... Yes, a 15 letter name that epitomizes cunning. Martin McDonough."

We both knew why Margaret Thornton was steered Jerk's way. Four years ago, when Jerk was still an investigator with the St. Paul Police, a bootlegging operation he was looking into with little or no enthusiasm led him straight to the late Floyd Olson. That piqued his interest, and when Jerk got interested he had a way of finding things out. He'd always clammed up about it, but he must have known plenty. That had to be why Eternal Tommy Brown, our Police Chief for Life, summoned him one day and told him an early retirement was called for. No scandal, he assured him, just a health matter (Jerk will outlive me), a Patrolmen's Benevolent Association benefit and a civilian again at age 50.

A lesser man would have been devastated. Not Jerk. He lived with his wife and youngest son in a plain frame house on Oxford Street, apparently lacking for nothing. True, they were a mere two doors from the tracks, but Jerk claimed that the sound of the Great Northern put him to sleep at night. I think it's a nip of the Irish that does it, but be that as it may, retirement agreed with him. I don't know how he maintained their standard of living, but it was no mystery why Margaret Thornton was sent his way. He was an authority on Floyd Olson's affairs.

"What do you think," I asked, "was Ward behind it?"

"Nahh. That husband of her's was preachin' to the converted. All that Commie crap would've helped get Olson elected."

He looked as serious as any guy with a puss like Jerk's can - squinty eyes, big lump of a Mick nose - but he was shoveling malarkey.

"He was also repeatin' rumors you're familiar with," I reminded him, "rumors you could verify."

He waved that off. "Nobody cares about that old bootlegger stuff," he said.

"Oh, a guy in bed with gangsters can get elected President?"

"Anybody who can end this Depression can get elected, Martin." He shook his finger under my nose. "FDR has my vote. What about yours?"

A few of the old geezers pricked up their ears at that, but I didn't take the bait. "I've got other things on my mind," I said. "Like who hired that mockey to drop Walter Thornton? And now that I'm thinkin' about it, what kinda Jew is named Shay?"

Jerk smiled. "I don't know, but I can tell you how to find out. Go to a place of worship over in Minneapolis called Adath Jesherun Synagogue. Tuesday night. It's the men's social evening. The business guys talk business, the religious nuts talk some Sheeney hocus-pocus, and a bunch of radicals argue with each other so loud it drives everybody else nuts. I hear Shay Tilsen comes around. I wonder who he discusses things with. So should you, Martin."

Jerk rarely disappoints me, but I still have to crack wise. "Maybe I should ask him why he dropped Thornton. He wouldn't tell the prosecutor, but I suppose he might unburden himself to me."

He grabbed my sleeve, jerked me in close and slipped me the whisper. "I was you, I'd talk to one of the Reds. Name's Lou Rothman."

According to him this Rothman and his buddies had Margaret Thornton's interests at heart. They took up a collection every week and sent it to her, in honor of her dead husband.

"Maybe you can find out somethin' from them," he said.

I agreed, and stood to leave "When was the last time you talked to your ma?" Jerk asked. A week ago Sunday, I told him. "Well, I have a message from her," he said.

I should've seen that coming. I was out the door before you can say home and hearth, but he shouted after me: "GET MARRIED, MARTIN - SOON. AND IN THE CHURCH GODDAMIT!"

Jerk stepped in after my dad drank himself to death. Sometimes Jerk did the impossible. He made me miss the old man. I was only 12 when he croaked, but he'd already made it clear that he didn't give a rat's ass what I did and never would. Jerk had plans for everybody.

I spent the rest of the day in the usual half-hearted attempt not to follow in the old man's footsteps, which meant stopping for a late breakfast at the Town Talk Diner, wandering around downtown, reading The Dispatch early edition the minute they started hawking it (**Thousands Turn out To Bid Governor Farewell; Ward Seeds Memorial Fund With Generous Grant - Nazi Putsch To Seize The Saar Reported**), shooting the breeze with one fellow and another, all the while watching the clock until it ticked off a decent hour for my daily trip to hooch city. November is one of my favorite months in that respect, the others being December and January. A man who finds himself on the horns of a dilemma at 5:00 P.M. on a sunny June day feels no conflict at all in the dark days of winter.

I hung around Rice Park a while, and listened to the Wobblys who'd set up camp there after the trucker's strike over in Minneapolis. They took turns haranguing passers-by about the evils of capital, the martyrdom of the Ludlow muckers, and the virtues of various bundle-tossers and silent agitators who'd gone to that big union hall in the sky. It was a pleasure to hear them sling their lingo, but the wind had a bite. I walked over to the library and took shelter in the entry.

The town scribe, John Howell, was there as well. He was deep into his greatcoat, puffing a gasper.

"How's it goin, John."

"Can't keep up, Martin. Scribblin' dawn to dusk."

John must've been seventy by then. He'd been writing letters for the illiterate in St. Paul as long as anyone could remember. He was such an institution that the library had recently set him up with a desk. About five years past he'd fretted that the compulsory education laws would render his trade obsolete, but the Great Depression saved him. There were so many shoeshine boys and flower peddlers out hustling instead of going to school that John's business would surely thrive as long as he could push a pen.

Sporting gals from Nina Clifford's place were his mainstay. They dictated tall tales about their jobs as shop girls and seamstresses, and slipped a few bucks into the envelope for posting to the hinterlands from whence they came. John picked up gossip from them (his memory was such that he could recite the more interesting letters verbatim), and sometimes shared it with me. The real dope, the kind I had to pay for if he was willing to part with it at all, came from the letters he wrote for the host of illiterate gangsters who hid out in St. Paul. For some reason they treated John as if his services came with the clerical privilege.

I asked him about the Thornton murder.

"Never heard a word about it," he said. "Gotta run." He stashed his butt and ducked into the library.

I stopped by the St. Francis Hotel to waste some time. A ring was set up in the lobby but nobody was sparring. I went over to the cigar counter, where a dice game was in progress.

It wasn't a spirited affair, just a few punters standing around: a double-jointed contortionist named Bones Schwartz, who tumbled in front of oncoming vehicles, blustered about a lawsuit, then jacked the driver up for a few bucks; Damper Shackleton, a man of many skills all related to robbing banks; Blanche Schuh, a lovely gal with an unlovely name and a long list of suitors, which occasionally included me; Jimmy Brennan, who walked a beat on the east side of the Loop when the spirit moved him; and Dave Swindeman, proprietor and stick man.

My presence failed to stir any action. I busied myself thumbing through a penny dreadful off Dave's rack.

"How's it goin', Martin," said Bones.

"So so."

"You datin' anybody?" asked Blanche.

"I have so many girlfriends I beat 'em off with a stick, but there's always time for you. Should I talk to the desk clerk?"

"Not me, ya big lunk. Viv Mathis. She's lookin' for some excitement."

"No kiddin'? I guess she's incurable."

Viv was the recently-departed Charlie Harmon's squeeze, and you'd think she'd had a lifetime of excitement in the year or so they were an item. Charlie was murdered in the aftermath of a botched kidnaping he'd planned, not more than two weeks past. Normally I'd have been intrigued by a date with Viv. She was a typical gangster's moll, loose in her ways, sexy-looking - in need of comforting. Right up my alley. But when I pictured her another widow popped into the frame.

Dick Pranke walked in. Pranke hung around the fight game. I heard he sold used cars for a living. That was a brand new occupation in those days, and you never knew who might be good at it. He was, judging by his snappy threads and the diamond stick pin that held his choker in place. His presence stirred some action.

"Cover me?" Shackleton inquired. He laid two bucks on the counter.

We all threw in. Swindemann raked off his cut, and handed the dice to The Damper, who rolled a seven. Goodbye deuce. I shelved the penny dreadful and bid farewell to all.

I stopped by The Real McKay's dingy little office. Information was his business too, but unlike me he had to connive to get into it.

Back when Jackie McKay was still Jake Mackovich, the Associated Press decided to open an office in St. Paul, and advertised for a reporter with the standard caveat; "Jews and Colored needn't apply."

Jackie wanted that job. It so happened that applications were being taken during the run-up to St. Patrick's Day. He walked in with a paper shamrock in his lapel, introduced himself as Jack McKay and said he had a way with words, which was true. They hired him. When it got around what he'd done, some of my fellow North Siders became irritated. My pal Joe Rogers called him a phony.

"Jackie?" said one of the sharp-tongued Delaney sisters, who was soft on him. "Uh-uh, he's the real McKay."

That tickled Joe's funny bone, and since he has a big mouth, it stuck.

Tape was spooling out of The Real McKay's machine and passing through his fingers when I entered. He swore he read it all, but he must've been a speedy reader. There were yards of it on the floor.

I asked him what he knew about the Thornton murder.

"What's the mystery?" he replied. "Shay Tilsen killed him."

"Why'd he clam up? Who was he protecting? Was it Charlie Ward?"

McKay was forever writing articles about Ward and they were buddies, so it didn't surprise me that he had a different theory. I just wanted to hear what it was.

"What makes you think he was protecting someone?" he asked.

"Could've taken the deal. He risked life in prison."

"Maybe he'd rather spend life in prison than back down in public. That's what I think, but it's just a thought. As far as any investigative reporting, no one took an interest."

"Why's that?"

He peered at me as if I were a bit thick.

"Because of what happened to the reporter that the trial was about. Remember?"

I said goodbye and walked toward the river, considering the matter at hand. Margaret Thornton thought Charlie Ward paid to have her husband murdered. Jerk said he didn't believe it. Margaret claims she wants the truth and nothing but the truth, but what she really wants is Charlie Ward's head on a platter. In any case, if the truth was obvious I'd be out of business. Sometimes the best you can hope for is a glimpse of something elusive, and the gift to describe it.

There wasn't much doubt about the trigger man. But who hired him? In order to answer that question I'd have to find out if Thornton was really murdered to further Floyd Olson's career, or if something else was going on.

I walked out on the Robert Street Bridge to watch the sun set. A cold wind blew down the Mississippi gorge. Far below, in the scrub between the railroad yards and the bluff, a bunch of bindle stiffs were huddled around a pathetic little fire. They'd have done better to jump the blinds. Winters are cold here, and the only migrants we welcome are gangsters on The Layover.

GUILT

Jerk thought it unlikely that I'd find a bride at Tin Cup's, and upon reflection I had to agree. Frails started coming in unescorted after Prohibition - some shanty-Irish gals, a few Kraut dames from St. Albert's - but they weren't the kind you'd bring home to mom.

There was a likely-looking bunch sitting near the Wurlitzer when I walked in, Maggie Quinn among them. She looked up from a pig's foot she was gnawing and gave me the eye, but I paid her no mind. I was on the clock now, the rationale for my nocturnal routine. Inebriation was an occupational hazard that I'd decided to live with.

My plan was to find a counter to the theory that Jerk and the Real McKay shared, in order to test Margaret's. It had just dawned on me that Jimmy Brennan, the beat copper, was the man of the hour in that regard. I could've talked to him back at the St. Francis if I'd had my wits about me, but lo and behold there he was, on the inside curve of the second horseshoe, right under the bar man's nose. Before I could approach him I felt a tap on the shoulder.

"Say there, Martin," said Billy Powell, "been a while."

Billy was a friend from sandlot days. He was a sure-handed second baseman, I was a catcher with sufficient natural padding to withstand some punishment and enough arm to throw a base runner out from time to time. We'd shared some triumphs, Billy and me.

It took us most of a whiskey and water to catch up. By then John O'Connor had joined us.

John was a copper. His father had been the chief until bootleg rye rendered him dysfunctional, a sad thing in many ways, not the least of which being that it ushered in the reign of Eternal Tommy Brown. John Sr. had negotiated the original Layover, before the bottle got the best of him. John Jr. functioned as a go-between with the Minneapolis police when jurisdictional scuffles arose regarding that arrangement. It was a legacy from his old man. He once got Machine Gun Kelly released from the Mill City pokey when that fool punched some Swede in a bar across the city line. The Minneapolis coppers were about to dial up Hoover when John arrived and talked them out of it.

John had good connections across the river. When I brought the conversation around to the Thornton killing he asked the same question I always get from coppers, even an old friend like him.

I assured him that my client was not the sort to take revenge.

"Good," he said. "I wouldn't want anything I tell you to get somebody killed, Martin. You know that."

Of course I knew, because I'd been told so many times. The cops claimed that was because it's their duty to prevent violence, not facilitate it, which is true but not the whole truth. They were forever putting things right as a favor to people that mattered to them. They liked to think their superior sense of justice made it ok - its' own form of corruption in my opinion, and far worse than the money they took.

"Check out the murder of Howard Godfrey a few years back," John suggested. "Same motive, same M O, same palookas doin' the dirty work."

"No conviction?"

"Nah, those Sheeney bastards are too slick to leave a thumbprint. It was Shay Tilsen and his mob though."

"I'll be ... So how did this Howard Godfrey - excuse me..." I waved down the bartender, who was a little slow. "Drinks around," I said.

He poured straight into our empties and we touched glasses before continuing. That's how it was done on Rice Street back then.

"To the memory of your fathers," I said to my companions. "Yours as well," John replied. "My dad gave up drinking," said Billy. "Then he's not dead?" I inquired. "No, but he wishes he was," Billy responded.

We all laughed about that.

"So John," I asked, "how did this Godfrey get himself killed?"

"Shootin' off his big mouth. Had a radio show, and he was no friend of Floyd Olson, who was about to run for Governor at the time. Godfrey went after him over the bootleggin'."

John allowed as how this Godfrey may have been less exercised about bootlegging than the bootleggers themselves, because most of them were mockeys. I asked if he knew any Minneapolis investigators I might have a word with.

"I do, but they won't say much. I'll tell you somebody who will though. Name is Erick Klawitter. He used to be a vice president at Bigelow Enterprises. He'll tell you some interesting things."

Well, there we have it, I thought. The shank of the evening and I've already done a good night's work. John told me how to reach Klawitter. We continued to chat about this and that, but our eyes began to stray toward the women. Mine met Maggie Quinn's when I glanced her way.

I excused myself and nodded toward an empty table, where she was pleased to join me.

"Jeez, Martin, thought you'd never ask," she said.

"You know I work nights, Mag. Drink?"

"Nah, I've had plenty. So've you."

"How do you know?"

"Bitter experience."

She cracked her gum. LOUD.

"How do you do that?" I asked.

"I suck a bubble instead'a blowin one, then I bust it with my teeth, like this."

SNAP!

She knew it irritated me, so she sat there with a defiant grin on her mug. She had hazel eyes, and a wicked smile. Her upper lip looked swollen, like she'd been stung by a bee. It was oddly appealing.

"Let's get outta here," she said.

I drained my glass. Her girlfriends giggled as we walked past them.

Mag was thirtyish back then, with some hard years behind her. As a child, Mag, her mother, and her 12 sisters and brothers lived in a shack among the shop ponds. They'd survived by the grace of the Great Northern Railroad. Their home was fashioned from an old wooden boxcar, and heated with coal the boiler men threw off for them. What little money they had came of selling scrap iron they picked up around the tracks. I went to school with Mag's brother Tommy, who coughed himself to death before he was 20. The first time I ever noticed her was at his funeral. She was only 15, but she had that same wicked grin on her face when we got to spooning behind the church. It was still there when she unbuttoned my fly and went to work.

Where'd you learn that? I asked.

From Tommy, may he rest in peace, she replied, and she crossed herself with sticky fingers.

Mag and I continued to have a soft spot for each other over the years, although sometimes we'd go months without bumping into one another. Our meetings had become more frequent since she'd been coming into Tin Cup's. They'd taken on a familiar pattern. We'd walk to her place, a furnished room over a grocery store on Jessamine, and quickly draw the curtains. She'd pull the Murphy bed out of the wall and stick her gum on the rail.

We both wanted a poke, but she was bold and uninhibited and I needed a snoot full because Holy Mother had drummed it into my head that sex outside marriage was a sin, a belief I apparently still held. Between that and the hoocher's curse, Maggie often had to resort to carnal stratagems. One thing would lead to another, and sometimes we didn't get to pleasing her at all, which must've left her questioning what was in it for her.

It was obvious what was in it for me. The sight of Maggie shucking her drawers was enough to rouse the dead, if not the dead drunk. Her ample figure had a way of jiggling a bit after she moved, then falling in place again. It drove me nuts.

That night we got to talking after we'd finished, and Mag told me what she and her girlfriends called what we'd done - "Vatican Roulette." I laughed, but she said it wasn't funny.

"What would'ja do if I got pregnant?" she asked.

The very thought of it struck me dumb.

"C'mon Martin. What?"

"I don't know, Mag. Why? You aren't gonna -"

"We're not talkin' about what I'm gonna do. We're talkin' about what you're gonna do."

She broke the ensuing silence by informing me that we'd been sinning, and it was time we sanctified our relationship.

She broke the subsequent silence by informing me that we'd just committed our penultimate sin. The next time we climbed the stairs would be the last unless we began making plans forthwith.

She had the consolation of faith. All I had was some warmed over guilt. I knew this day was coming, but I'd put it out of my mind.

I knew there was an institution called marriage too, but I hadn't given that much thought either, despite the best efforts of Ma and Uncle Jerk. Margaret Thornton just made a complicated matter even more bewildering. I stood and began putting my pants on.

Where'ya goin'?" Mag asked.

"To have a drink."

She put her gum back in her mouth, and chewed while I buttoned my shirt.

"Coming?" I said.

"Naw. Why don'cha go up to Mooney's or somewhere. If ya go back to Tin Cup's they'll think ya just stepped out for a poke. Ok?"

"Yeah, yeah," I mumbled on the way out the door.

"Father Finnerty 's gettin' tired'a tellin' me to say some Hail Marys and it'll be alright," she hollered after me. - "Martin! Did'ja hear me! He's gettin' tired of it. I can tell by the tone of his voice."

JOHNNY'S JOHNSON

ormally I could sleep late and still find a parking place right in front of the Town Talk Diner, but there wasn't a space to be had next morning. The Paramount was playing a special 11:00 A.M. matinee: Fashions Of 1933, five cents for the movie, a soda and box of popcorn. The line was three blocks long, and mingled at the tail end with another line facing the other way, toward the Office of Migrant Services.

Both crowds were queuing for the same reason, to put something in their bellies. The women in the movie line were gabbing excitedly, looking forward to some entertainment I suppose, but the men looked bored, and the kids were glum. They stamped their feet to keep warm, and swiped their runny noses with their mittens. One of the many indignities of the Great Depression was all the crap people had to put up with - lines, sermons, insufferable movies about what the hoi-poloi were wearing - all for a bite to eat.

I found a space on Fifth Street and hurried through the lightly falling snow, stopping only to buy a special edition of the Dispatch. It had big headlines trumpeting a shooting in Minneapolis: **MOTORIST GUNNED DOWN IN FRONT OF HIS HOME!**

I grabbed a stool next to a friend of mine, officer Jack Moylan. Jack was a first generation fellow with a big belly, a big ruddy mug, and fists the size of Hormel hams. He acknowledged me with a nod but stuck to the task at hand, a plateful of eggs and hash browns.

I spread the paper out on the counter, and skimmed the headline story. The victim had gotten into a traffic squabble with a man in a black Hudson. That party took offense, tailed the victim to his home yelling threats, then drilled him when he stepped out of his car. The victim was in the hospital with life-threatening wounds.

It seemed a bit severe to sort out a fender-bender, unless of course the guy in the Hudson was one of the psychos who chill out in the Saintly City. They were forever resorting to extremes to remedy trifles, but usually amongst each other.

Jack mopped up the last of the yolk with a crust of toast and washed it down with a swallow of coffee. He asked me to accompany him on a chore he'd be doing for Eternal Tommy in the next few days, and indicated that it had to do with the very murder I was reading about.

I often rode with St. Paul's finest when they stuck their courage to the sticking place and set forth to do their duty. It was helpful for them to have a civilian along in ways that were incomprehensible unless you understood The Layover agreement. Odd, how the past lurks in every detail of the here and now. I spent a year at St. Thomas before tiring of higher education, and I've retained a few odds and ends, among them a term used by a Jesuit philosophy teacher who referred to secular history as 'meaningless intellectual necrophilia.' Something about the eternal present being an instant that lasts forever in the mind of God.

I'm always reminded of the sheer, otherworldly goofiness of that theory when I consider the great historical events that shape our times, as well as the small ones that affect everyday life.

The little chunk of history that had the biggest impact on my life occurred in 1918, just a few blocks from where I was sitting that morning. It was there, at the Green Lantern Saloon and Restaurant, that Dan Hogan, a big harp gangster who owned the joint, met with John O'Connor, the St. Paul Police Chief. The two of them formalized the Layover agreement, which was elegant in its simplicity.

Gangsters on the lam got police protection in St. Paul if they followed three simple rules: check in with Hogan at the Green Lantern; pay the required monthly gratuity, in full and on time; commit no crimes within the city limits.

The Layover gave Dan and his gang a monopoly in our town, and they held up their end by sparing us the violence that plagued other cities. That was especially true after Prohibition was repealed, and the bottomless well of ready cash that bootlegging provided dried up. For a few years bank robbery was practically the national pastime, but it was only at the tail end of that brief era that banks in St. Paul started getting hit. By then everything was falling apart, and such was the anarchy that the St. Paul Police were on the verge of going straight. But I'm getting ahead of myself.

The east coast mob took over crime in just about every city in America in the 1920s. Most of those places had been home to thugs like Dan Hogan and his gang. There was usually a brief battle between the local outfit and the outsiders, which the outsiders won. But by the time the mobsters were ready to make their move here, Hogan was dead and enforcement of the Layover had fallen by default to a well-armed, well-organized gang called The Police. Worst of all from the mob's perspective, The Police were incorruptible. They were already thoroughly corrupted by the Layover, and doing quite well.

Again, history had spared us. Chicago was practically next door by rail, and once in a while you'd hear that Capone's gang was trying to penetrate St. Paul in small ways, mostly dope and street prostitution, but nothing much came of it as far as I could see.

Plenty of cities had rackets like The Layover during the Depression, but ours was unique in its long history and the open way it operated. The police chief and a few other coppers got rich, but everyone down to the lowliest jail guard got a little something. Ordinary citizens did ok as well. They got the security that the system brought them, plus the cheap thrill of knowing that at any given moment five or six of the ten most wanted men in America were walking their streets.

Daring young couples would amuse themselves by frequenting certain hangouts -The Green Lantern, Wabasha Caverns, The

Stahl House - where they could rub shoulders with mugs like Al-vin "Creepy" Karpis, Homer Van Meter and John Dillinger. Some-times the gals got tipsy, hoisted their shimmy skirts, and asked one of the gangsters to autograph their thighs. Karpis actually earned his nickname by the look on his face when he knelt down to sign that creamy Midwestern flesh. He always made a great show of crossing his eyes, lolling his tongue out, and licking the tip of his pen before he affixed his signature. His colleague Fred Barker, a mama's boy who frowned on such lewdness, was once heard to mutter "creepy" when witnessing Alvin en flagrante graffito, and it stuck.

The year I met Margaret Thornton was the heyday of the lay-over. A steady stream of roscoes took refuge here, which left the G-Men in a state of constant frustration. The protection the police offered the likes of Dillinger, Baby Face Nelson, the entire Barker-Karpis mob, and a host of lesser known but equally lethal mugs, was so effective that the feds couldn't nab them. After a while they didn't even try. If they managed to discover the whereabouts of a wanted criminal they simply organized a hit squad and attempted to kill him. But those guys shot back, so St. Paul was the scene of some spectacular gun fights.

The most notorious one had happened earlier that year, on an unseasonably warm spring afternoon. 1934 was the hottest summer of the dust bowl era in our neck of the woods, and in retrospect it had already begun on March 19th. The temperature topped 70 de-grees. The spacious lawn surrounding the Lincoln Court apartments was bare and brown, but a few piles of snow, lightly crusted with topsoil, hung on in the shade of the north facing wall.

There were three of us in the nondescript Chevy the coppers used on such occasions, officer Jack Moylan, a lieutenant with the unlikely moniker of Swede Pandowski (both in plainclothes), and myself. We'd parked in a driveway off Lexington, where we had a view of a certain first floor window.

Pandowski had risen in the ranks despite his ethnicity, mostly because of his demeanor. He was one cool cookie, but I noticed his jaw drop as he gazed upon the proximate cause of the impending fuss.

Out in the back yard of Lincoln Court, a moll named Billie Frechette was gathering undies from a clothesline. Her dark hair was bobbed and styled in what they called a 'page boy' in those days, but only a blind man could've mistaken her for a boy. Billie was one curvaceous babe and dressed to show it, in a red halter, and short red shorts. She had a heart-shaped mouth and sleepy eyes. Her rear end jiggled pleasantly as she plucked her panties off the line and gave them a shake. She turned her face so dust wouldn't get in her eyes.

"Will'ye look at the arse on that dame," said Moylan, as she headed for the back door.

"I've always said if you want to see beautiful women check out the visiting room at a prison," said Pandowski. "Not a jail, mind you. A pen. Tomatoes love those gangsters. Why?"

"They lead exciting lives," I said.

"Uh-oh. Some excitement is about to enter hers," said Pandowski.

Two boyish looking G-Men in pin-striped suits and snap-brimmed hats had just parked, and were striding purposefully toward the Lincoln Court Apartments.

"Where is that fookin' Van Meter?" was Moylan's rhetorical query, because this scene was scripted tightly, and at that moment how it would play out was up in the air.

It had all begun the day before, when a woman named Daisy Coffey called the St. Paul office of the Bureau of Investigation.

Another odd consequence of the layover was the role property managers played in law enforcement. Daisy belonged to a network of landlady/snitches who'd been encouraged to report suspicious activities among their new tenants directly to the feds. Hoover's boys had to conscript those biddies because the sources of information they relied upon in other cities were so close-mouthed here. As a result some remarkably minor transgressions came to their attention - illicit romances, drunken parties, tardiness with the rent. But every once in a while the Gs got lucky.

Daisy had taken umbrage at the way Billie, who'd registered under the name Florence Hellman, flounced around in her scanties. She'd made a project out of spying on her. She'd been peeking in

the window of number 103 the day before, and had witnessed Billie in the throes of fornication with the tenant of record, one Carl P.
Hellman. The act itself must've been a federal case in Daisy's book,
but what really scandalized her was an anatomical peculiarity that
marked one of the participants. She'd managed to explain, in words
I can scarcely imagine, that Mr. Hellman was hung like a donkey.

That rang a bell with the feds. John Dillinger had been arrested
and strip-searched twice in the past year. He'd escaped both times,
but not before the arresting officers took note of the same thing the
landlady noticed. Word about Johnny's johnson had gone out in law
enforcement circles, and the moment Daisy mentioned the crucial
measurement our local BI agents (there were only two because the
St. Paul office was staffed commensurate with its productivity) knew
who they were dealing with. They'd suspected Dillinger was in town
because he'd dropped off the map a few weeks earlier, after robbing
a bank just over the Iowa line. They began having visions of glory.

They were typical G-Men, clean-cut recent law school grads
of the sort Hoover recruited. They'd probably been wearing lamp-
shades at a frat party about this time last year, but they had enough
sense to look for back-up. Under normal circumstances the local
police would have gotten the call. Not here. In desperation they'd
tried the Minneapolis coppers, who'd promised them some men,
and then informed their St. Paul counterparts when the assassination
was scheduled to take place.

Duty called. Moylan and Pandowski answered. They'd come
to help Dillinger get away, or to be precise, they were there to su-
pervise me while I helped him get away. They were ready to take
it on the Arthur Duffy and leave me holding the bag if the feds
twigged to the set up. That was the price I paid for the information
I relied on to make a living.

The G-Men paused at the door and consulted their watches.
They were probably wondering where the Minneapolis coppers
were. They'd be arriving late, per arrangement with their fellow officers in St. Paul, but they'd made it clear that once they got there
their goal would be the same as the fed's, to kill John Dillinger. The

burning question was, would Dillinger's henchman Homer Van Meter get here before the coppers did?

Eternal Tommy had tipped him about the ambush, after failing to
reach Dillinger himself. Johnny had the phone off the hook, the moron.

The theory was that Dillinger and Van Meter could handle
Hoover's boys, but once the Mill City buzz arrived the likely result
was two dead gangsters. That would be bad publicity indeed for The
Layover. It was white knuckle time in our car.

"Five minutes and counting," I said.

"That's him," said Pandowski. He pointed down Lexington toward a man who was strolling our way. "That's Van Meter."

"Jayzus," said Moylan. "What's his hurry?"

Van Meter was whistling as he approached, so melodiously you
almost expected him to break into a two-step. He was a hawk-nosed
Kraut, with dark, slicked back hair, and a mean squint that belied his
otherwise cheery demeanor. He was wearing an overcoat despite the
balmy weather. It seemed to take him eons to reach the car.

"What's up, fellas?" he asked. "Must'a been a stick-up or somethin, all you coppers around."

"Those are the Gs," Pandowski replied, with a nod toward the
Lincoln Court apartments.

"No kiddin? I'd best tell Johnny."

"They won't let you in."

"I'll figure somethin' out."

"Don't hurt 'em" said Pandowski. "Scare 'em, but don't kill 'em."

"Me? Kill a G-man? You must be thinkin'a somebody else, Sta-
shew. I'm a sweetheart."

He opened his arms, and burst into song. "I'm the SWEEET-
HEART - of SIGMAA - KI... Hold the applause now boys, don't
wanna draw any unnecessary attention."

He bowed, and ambled off toward the apartment building, hands
in his pockets and an aw shucks grin on his mug.

Pandowski's eyes narrowed as he watched him walk away. Van
Meter was a weird combination of cornball prankster and cold-blood-
ed killer. A former singing waiter from Ft. Wayne, he'd once told the

citizens of an Indiana burg that he was a Hollywood director in town with a crew of actors, then managed to pull off a bank robbery while the police and a crowd of gawkers watched what they thought was a scene being shot for a movie. Van Meter had killed two coppers the past year, and rumor had it he'd iced several more law men between stints in the Illinois prisons. The St. Paul coppers didn't find that amusing. They would've gladly double-crossed him, but Eternal Tommy had his back. Van Meter paid a small fortune for protection. He had thousands on permanent deposit at The Green Lantern, and he made regular contributions to Eternal Tommy's slush fund.

The feds stopped him at the door of Lincoln Court. A conversation ensued. We couldn't hear, but things didn't appear to be going too badly. Nor were they going too quickly. The Mill City buzz were due any moment.

Van Meter and one of the feds abruptly headed back in our direction. Van Meter was talking loudly, to keep us apprised. His hands were still in his pockets.

"Why do I hafta show'ya my samples?" he was saying. "My car's half a block away. It's hard enough sellin' soap door to door without you guys makin' more problems. There's a Depression on, y'heard about that?"

"Just show me your wares," said the G. "Get going." They were about 20 feet away.

"Yeah, ok, I'll show'ya," said Van Meter. He whirled suddenly, arms out in front of him. A .45 had materialized in one hand, a .38 special in the other. He leveled both guns right in the startled fed's mug.

"JOHNNY," he bellowed, "IT'S THE GEES!"

Then he turned his full attention to the G-Man. "RUN FOR YER LIFE, SHIT-BIRD ! MOVE IT!"

The kid took a tentative step backward. Van Meter bounced a shot off the sidewalk in front of him. We heard it whistle past his ear. He shot again. The kid turned around and ran.

The other fed dropped to one knee on the apartment house steps, took aim and fired. The bullet hit the fender of our car.

Van Meter unleashed a fusillade with both pistols in return. Chunks of brick flew off the apartment building. Holes appeared - one two three - in the pebbled glass door.

The fed was in a terrible position, with nowhere to run. He flattened himself on the sidewalk and fired a wild shot. A car going by on Lexington jumped the curb, and smacked into a tree on the boulevard. The driver leaped out, and hit the ground running.

"OH JOHNNY-BOY," yelled Van Meter, as he reloaded. "TIME TO AMSCRAY! OUT THE ACKBAY!"

Remarkably, he began whistling again as he chambered rounds. From down the street came the sound of a woman screaming. In the distance, but fast drawing nearer, sirens could be heard.

The fed who'd been accompanying Van Meter had run most of a block before stopping. Then he got down on one knee, the same as the kid on the front steps. It must be a posture they teach on the BI training range. It made for a steady weapon, but not much maneuverability. Van Meter's extended arms caused his overcoat to hang wide at his sides, and the kid's first shot put a hole right through it.

Van Meter, who'd trained exiting banks, knew the value of a salvo. He blazed away with both guns.

"AGGGHHH" - the kid fell backward, screaming in pain and fear.

"Jayzus," muttered Moylan. "He hit him."

Van Meter retreated down the block. He wasted a few more shots on the fed in front, who'd abandoned all pretense of firing back and was concentrating on making himself as flat as possible.

A rag sheenie emerged from a side street, then halted his horse and wagon on Lexington when he saw what was going on.

The sirens reached a crescendo, then whined to a stop. A squad car full of Minneapolis coppers screeched to a halt in the alley.

"Uh-oh. Dillinger'll be comin' out that way," said Moylan.

"Get back there, and tell those cops to come around front," Pandowski said. "Hurry!"

He meant me.

I exited the bucket on the run, knocking my hat off in the process. My heart was banging at my chest like it wanted out. I didn't blame it. I crossed the street and ran past the prostrate fed, all the while gesturing wildly toward the front, and tried to yell. My voice wouldn't work.

The cops got the picture though. They bolted toward Lexington, guns drawn, and as soon as they did, John Dillinger and Billie Frechette came out the back door, not ten feet from me.

Frechette made a B-line for a nearby garage. Dillinger followed, walking backwards slowly and cautiously, a Thompson Gun in his mitts. He was in his shirtsleeves. His big glittery eyes darted in all directions. The thin mustache he was sporting as a disguise was shiny with sweat. I dropped to the ground and started crawling.

One of the cops glanced my way, and spotted Dillinger. "OUT IN BACK - IT'S HIM!" he yelled.

He fired, and Johnny let go with a burst in their direction. I sat down in a snow pile and plastered myself against the wall.

Bullets whined past. A puff of dust exploded off Dillinger's leg, and wafted away on a zephyr. Johnny grimaced, dropped one hand to the smoking hole in his pants, then steadied that Tommy Gun and fired again. The cops hit the ground and kept shooting. Dirt flew. Bullets tattooed a car parked out in the street.

A blue Oldsmobile emerged from the garage behind Lincoln Court, and backed toward Dillinger with the passenger door wide open. He fired a final burst and got in. The Olds peeled away, turned the corner and disappeared.

I tried to stand but my legs were too shaky. I just sat there for a few moments watching the cops pick themselves up, dust themselves off, and head for their squad car to give chase.

As soon as I could walk again I joined the crowd that had gathered out front. It looked like a disaster scene in a low budget film - a car crumpled against a tree; a bunch of stunned-looking people standing around; a few kids snickering at a woman who was hiccuping little sobs.

The fed who'd been flat on the steps had raised himself to sitting position. He had his head in his hands.

Van Meter clip-clopped past on Lexington in the rag sheenie's wagon, wearing the rag sheenie's battered straw hat. He nodded at us affably as he went by.

I walked down the block to where Pandowski was standing over the G who'd been shot. He was comforting the kid.

"You'll be alright," he said. "It's just a flesh wound. An ambulance is on the way, and someone must have called the police."

"The Police?" The kid looked genuinely frightened. "They'll probably kill me."

Pandowski patted him on the shoulder. "Oh, I doubt it," he said.

We tried to be as unobtrusive as possible as we walked back to the car.

"Now what?" I asked.

"The Town Talk," said Moylan. "I'm hungry enough to eat a nun's arse through a convent hedge."

"Why not, our work here is finished," said Pandowski.

Off we drove like thieves in the night, past the rag sheenie who was standing on the corner of Goodrich and Lexington with a smile on his face, and a wad of notes in his hand. Why Van Meter decided to pay him instead of shooting him to death for his wagon I'll never know.

Dillinger got clean away, but his luck was running out. A few months later the feds shot him dead outside a movie theater in Chicago. They say the mob fingered him because of the heat mugs like him brought on businessmen like themselves.

The coroner severed Dillinger's dick and had it sent to the Smithsonian for observation. Something about its freakish size relating to the man's criminal nature. I know that to be true because it's recorded in the annals of meaningless intellectual necrophilia. According to some off the record scuttlebutt I heard, Hoover made a plaster cast of Johnny's johnson to use for a dildo, but I can hardly believe that, can you?

As for Van Meter, he'd overstayed his welcome in St. Paul. Later that summer the buzz chased him up an alley, and shot him down like a dog.

DISHONOR

Erick Klawitter wore a bow tie for my visit. First thing he did when he opened the door of his one bedroom apartment in the Crocus Hill neighborhood was point out a three story brownstone down the street.

"Dat is vhere ve used to live," he said, "and make no mistake; Dis is vhy I am talking to you. Am I a man spills his heart to strangers? Look vhat dat son of a bitch did to us, pardon my language, and my motives become clear. - Sit down Mr. McDonough."

He took my hat. "Can ve offer Mr. McDonough some tea, darlink?" he said, addressing himself to an elegant-looking woman of 40 or so who was sitting in a small parlor a few feet from us.

"Hilda?"

She just sat there, hands on her lap, staring out the window at the falling snow. The demoralized look on her face didn't quite mask its' loveliness.

"Uhh..." said my host, "maybe I could ..." His voice trailed off into a vague gesture toward their little kitchen.

"Nothin' for me, thanks," I said.

Klawitter, it soon became clear, wanted to get even with Charlie Ward. A few years back he'd been the golden boy of Bigelow Enterprises. At least that was his claim, which I took with a grain of salt because he had the demeanor of a crackpot. And he certainly spilled his guts to strangers.

He explained that he'd once caught the eye of the late Herbert Bigelow, the man who'd gone to Leavenworth for tax evasion, and met Charlie Ward there. Ward's climb to the top of Bigelow Enterprises had taken place over a period of several years. It began with a menial job maintaining presses, and Klawitter, a German immigrant, had been his supervisor.

"I didn't like him," he said. "Mr. Bigelow did though. Dey say Ward took care of Mr. Bigelow in der koop."

According to Klawitter, Ward's inexorable rise was well underway a few years later when Bigelow decided to buy a state of the art lithograph machine from a German manufacturer. He got the bright idea to use Klawitter to negotiate the purchase in his native language. The deal worked out so well that Bigelow decided to stage a little award ceremony for his maintenance supervisor. He told him to come up to the executive lunch room for his moment of glory - a short speech, a hearty handshake, a free calendar - and he could bring his family.

The day after the ceremony, Klawitter was summoned into Bigelow's office.

"He pulled out of his drawer a bottle, dis vas Prohibition mind you, and poured for me a drink. He said he'd been thinking about a better position in da company for me, but dere vas some conditions."

Klawitter proceeded to describe those conditions in a normal tone of voice, which must have carried into the parlor. There was no way to tell if his wife registered what he said or not. Despair seemed to be molded so thoroughly into her delicate features that the expression of anything else would be impossible.

Apparently Bigelow's proposition was pretty straightforward. He said he had a fishing cabin in the northern part of the state. He wanted Mrs. Klawitter to accompany him there the following weekend, and depending on how things went, perhaps again in the future. In return - and of course in consideration of the excellent job he'd done purchasing the lithograph machine - Erick Klawitter would become a vice president at Bigelow Enterprises at a salary of $19,000 per year.

"I vas making $300 a month as a machine supervisor. Mr. Bigelow told me, 'Erick, dere's going to be some belt-tightening here, but you von't have to worry.'"

There was, and he didn't. Hilda went up north with Herb Bigelow a few times, and Klawitter's job appeared secure.

"I remember da day ven everything started to change," he said.
"By den Ward vas a vice president, like me, but not like me. I vas
in charge of da machines. Ward vas in charge of every damn thing.
Every department in da company vas full of his people. You know,
his convicts."

I did know. I couldn't help knowing. Charlie Ward was constantly being lauded in the newspapers for his policy of giving ex-
cons a job at Bigelow Enterprises. It was one more feather in that
cap full of plumage he sported, but Klawitter explained something
about it that had never occurred to me. According to him, Ward rose
by squeezing out the men above him one at a time, using the ex-cons
as one half of the pincers. His protégés sabotaged his target's department while he badmouthed him to Bigelow and the board.

"But dere vas a few of us didn't have to worry," Klawitter said,
glancing in his wife's direction. "So vun day I'm over by Ward's
office, and his door vas open. I heard some laughing, and naturally
I'm curious, because everything dis man does makes us curious by
den. So I valked by. Inside I see Ward and another fellow. He's tall,
maybe as tall as Ward, black hair mit curls. Good looking fellow, but
not kind looking. And loud. Ward is laughing. He's laughing louder.
I stopped to see better, and Ward spots me. 'What're you looking at,
buster!' he says, and he slammed da door, but not before da other
fellow gave me a look makes my blood run cold. Blue eyes he had.
Big, crazy-looking eyes."

According to Klawitter, the incident made enough of an impression on him that he remembered it, despite the much more dramatic
event that took place one day later. Herb Bigelow, a fishing guide
and the wife of one of the other vice presidents all drowned when
their canoe capsized on a lake in northern Minnesota. The board immediately named Ward as President of the company.

"About a year passed," said Klawitter. "I vas in da executive
wash room one day, and who is standing at da porcelain convenience
next to me but da same man, same blue eyes, same crazy look. Shakes

off his shvontz, doesn't even vash his hands, and da very next day dis fellow you're interested in, Howard Godfrey, is murdered."

Ah, here's something I'm familiar with, I thought; the conflation of coincidence into conspiracy. The thread that stitched it all together had yet to be revealed, but that was surely coming. My task was clear. Ask the right questions to hurry this process along, make a polite exit, and look for somebody with some information. Like a bent copper. I cursed myself for not cornering Jimmy Brennan when I had the chance.

"So, did you connect this fellow with Godfrey's murder?" I asked.

"No, not right den, but I marked da occasion, because I knew about Godfrey, listened to him on da radio. So critical he vas of Floyd Olson and his Jew friends. I hadn't heard Ward vas backing Olson yet, but it made me feel badly dat such a fine fellow like Godfrey is kaput, so I remembered."

He glanced over at his wife, who was still gazing out the window. "And den, presto, everything changed," he said.

His lip began to quiver when he described what happened next.

"Ward called me in, and told me I vas finished. Just like dat. 'Get out.' One of his convicts had my work da next day." - He paused, and heaved a sigh.

"All of us vhat got our jobs dat vay vere fired, as soon as one of Ward's men learned our positions. Da only one Ward didn't get to fire vas da man whose wife drowned mit Herbert Bigelow. Dat fellow didn't show up for a few days after da murder, so da police vent to his house and found him hanging in da basement."

"He hangs himself after Godfrey is shot? Why?"

"No, no. After his wife and Mr. Bigelow vere killed."

"But they drowned. - Y'think that was murder too?"

"Of course it vas, don't you see! Da man who killed dem vas the one in Ward's office. He killed Godfrey. He -"

"Wait a minute. Why him?"

"Because murder is his business."

Klawitter explained that after his dismissal he'd taken to scouring the newspapers front to back, as people at loose ends will do. One day he'd read a thumbsucker about Murder Incorporated, a term that was unknown to him at the time. It explained that Murder Inc. had come into being when rival bootleggers needed to hire killers to rub out the competition. It speculated about the future of that organization now that Prohibition was over. Who would require its services, and why?

"Murder Incorporated is run by a bunch of east coast Jews," said Klawitter. "Dere pictures vas in da paper, and one vas da fellow I saw mit Ward. His name is Siegel. He has some nick-name, Antsy or -"

"Bugsy?" I said.

"I believe dat's correct sir. So, you've heard of him?"

"Yeah, I've heard of him. But look here, I have it on pretty good authority that Godfrey was murdered by a Minneapolis gangster named Shay Tilsen, and his mob."

"Sure, sure, dat's how dey do it. Da New York kikes make da arrangements, da local kikes do da dirty work."

Now I had to backtrack. There was some logic to what he was saying.

"So you believe Charlie Ward hired Murder Inc. to rub out both of'em?"

"Vhy else is dis crazy man coming to Bigelow Enterprises before each of dese crimes? Vhat is he doing here tell me?"

"Ever heard of The Layover?"

"No."

"It could explain why Bugsy Siegel was in St. Paul."

He stood up, clearly agitated, and paced around the little living room.

"Does it explain vhy he's in Charlie Ward's office?" he asked.

"Ward met all sorts'a roscoes at Leavenworth. Maybe they're friends."

He stopped pacing directly in front of me, and leaned down so his mouth was six inches away.

"Does dat explain vhy Ward gave dis crazy man $150,000?"

"How do you know that?"

"Believe me. I know."

"But how?" I persisted.

"I cannot say. I'm sorry."

Another all too familiar occurrence in my line of work - the casual drop of the unattributable gem, the implication being that it's my job to find out what the source already knows. Often, because the source has no real interest in the investigation, I have no leverage. But not this time.

"Well, thanks sir," I said, and I stood to leave.

"You'll make sure Ward gets vhat he deserves?"

"I'll keep in mind what you've said, but to be honest, unless you can tell me what makes you think Ward gave Bugsy Siegel $150,000, and convince me it's true, the information you've given me isn't worth a plugged nickel."

"My hands are tied, sir. Dis is something I cannot do."

His wife stood, and framed her self against the wan light from the window. Her movement had a startling effect, as if a statue had come to life. It added impact to her words.

"Tell him, Erisch. Or I will."

"But -

She seated herself, and resumed her study of the falling snow.

"All right," said Klawitter, after a few moments of silence. "But you must never tell anyone vhere it is you get dis information. I need your promise."

"You have it."

"But I can trust you?" he asked.

"Listen Klawitter, I get all sorts of information on the Q T. I rely on it. I'm no double-crosser. If word ever got out that I betrayed a confidence I'd have to sign up for the WPA, so don't worry about me keeping my mouth shut. Convince me."

He proceeded to do so. He described an organization of fellow Krauts he belonged to, called the German-American Bund. It sounded like a counterpart to the Marching Hibernians. By virtue of his former title at Bigelow Enterprises he'd become a member of the upper echelon of the Bund that met after oompah band practice. His buddy, the glockenspieler, was the chief operating officer of a bank in the Midway, and one evening Klawitter had unburdened himself to that gentleman by way of soliciting the position he presently held, that of a $200 a month bank teller.

He told the man the whole sad story; his wife's shame, which he apparently shared at the drop of a hat, and his curt dismissal at the hands of Charlie Ward, which was way more difficult for him to discuss. He'd been on the verge of tears when he told me about it. He said he actually cried when he told his buddy, but he must have composed himself by the time he described Bugsy and opined about the murders of Godfrey and Bigelow. It prompted his pal to recount a run-in he'd had with the feds, which had scared him half to death.

"Ward does business at my friend's bank," Klawitter told me. "Company money, his own money. Vhen I told him about Godfrey's murder and my suspicions, he asked me vhen it happened. I knew da very day. 'Ach, then listen to this,' he said, and he told me dat da day before Godfrey vas murdered, da same day I'd seen that kike in the Gentlemen's, Ward came in da bank and made a request. He vanted $150,000 cash sent over to his office by courier that afternoon. So dey put da money in a brown envelope, the kind mit a string wrapped around a metal ring and sealed mit wax. Dey labeled it, bank's name, officer's name, date, amount, and sent it over."

"Yeah, that's intriguing, but what makes you think he gave it to Siegel?"

"Because later, maybe two months, into da bank comes da G Men, and dey show my friend da very same envelope. 'You better explain this,' they say, or else they'll bring him in to see this chief of their's, this Hoover. My friend tells them exactly vhat it is. Vhy should he lie? 'Den how come it is ve find it in Ben Siegel's apartment in Miami, Florida?' dey ask. 'Explain dat mister!'"

He couldn't explain it, nor when push came to shove was he required to. That was down to Charlie Ward, and whether they ever followed up with him or not Klawitter couldn't say.

His theory wasn't perfect. The going rate for a drop was a fraction of the sum the banker sent over to Ward. On the other hand, most drops don't facilitate a candidacy for President of the United

States. Klawitter had made his point. Ward was connected to Bugsy Siegel, and through him to Murder Incorporated.

Good information, especially since it came from a source I found distasteful enough so I'd have preferred discrediting him. I assured him I'd follow up.

I tipped my hat to Hilda on the way out. She didn't acknowledge me. There goes another guy who knows I screwed Herb Bigelow to get my husband a job, she must've been thinking. And he got fired anyway.

* * *

It rained the next night, a cold rain that turned yesterday's snow to slush. I couldn't find a parking spot in front of the synagogue with the unpronounceable name. When I'd first taken the wheel of a Model A, ten years before, that never happened. Now it was something you half-expected. "An inconvenience of modern life," some egghead called it. I had to park a block away and soak my brogans.

As I slogged through the slush I had time to reflect on how doggedly I was pursuing Margaret Thornton's case. You'd have thought there was some money in it, but I'd decided it was on the cuff.

Inside a bunch of men were gathered in an overheated room that was thick with cigarette smoke. I took off my hat out of decent respect for an alien faith, but soon noticed that everyone else had theirs on. When in Hymietown. I put mine back on, wet as it was.

The room was too small to hold everyone comfortably. There must have been fifty or more guys in groups of eight or ten, yakking amongst each other. I stood around until an old gent in a black skullcap offered me a glass of disgustingly sweet wine, and asked what brought me there.

It turned out he was some kind of facilitator. I told him who I was looking for, and he guided me to a knot of fellows dressed like laborers. They were all wearing little corduroy caps.

We waited around for a pause in their heated conversation, but it just got louder. Pretty soon one guy grabbed another by the collar and twisted. "Stalinist bastard!" he said, and he almost burnt the other guy's nose with a gasper he had stuck in the corner of his mouth.

I thought the brawl was on, but a medium-sized, olive-skinned fellow about my age stepped in. He had a square jaw, and a short, dark beard. He didn't say much, but whatever he said worked. The disputants separated and rejoined the discussion. A moment later I thought I saw one of them launch a sucker punch, but he was just talking with his hands, a common mode of discourse here I realized, as I looked around.

A few more minutes passed, then the old gent called out "Lou," and the guy who'd short-circuited the donnybrook turned our way. His flat gaze came at me from behind fragile, wire-rimmed specs, but he looked hard nonetheless. When I told him my name and said I'd like to speak to him, off came the goggles.

He moved right up close, and squinted at me.

After a few moments he said, "Lou Rothman," and we shook hands. He had a grip like a teamster.

The face mirrors the soul and my profession often requires me to make distinctions between one soul and another, so I pride myself on characterizing faces. Rothman's map puzzled me in that respect until a few years later, after Jerk's son Danny became a Lincoln Brigadier in a fit of youthful idealism. Spain cured him of that, and when he came home he said it wasn't the Falangists who'd scared him. It was some of the characters who were nominally on his side. Rothman, it occurred to me, had a puss you'd see in a doorway in Barcelona just before the bomb exploded.

He was personable enough that night though. He laughed when he heard my first question.

"His name is Isadore," he said. "'Shay' is short for 'shaygus.' It's Yiddish for a certain kind of eastern European bully that picks on Jews."

"So he beat up mockeys?"

Rothman gave me another long look, best described as bemused. A couple of other Reds were within ear shot, which meant real close. The din of conversation and coughing in that room was something, but suddenly it got quieter on our end, and the whole bunch, must've been a dozen of them, were looking at me. The collar-twister edged my way.

"No," Rothman finally said. "It's an irony. When Isadore was a kid he beat up goyim who picked on Jews. You could say he took pleasure in kicking their Mick asses."

"Hey, I didn't mean anything by it."

"OK, neither did I," he said. The rest of his group resumed arguing, to my great relief.

It was my turn to lean in close, so I could hear him. "What brings you here, McDonough?" he asked. "You didn't come all the way from St. Paul to find out how Isadore Tilsen got his nickname."

"I'm here on behalf of someone you know. Margaret Thornton."

He looked surprised. "Sure. We collect money for her."

"So I hear. But why? I thought you fellows, you know, you lefties, liked Floyd Olson. Margaret Thornton isn't so keen on him, and she really despises one of his pals."

"Floyd Olson and Margaret's husband were both Farmer-Laborers," he announced, as if he were making a funeral oration. "They stood squarely with the working man, and whatever differences they might've had didn't matter to us. Olson's widow will be well taken care of, and Thornton's shouldn't go begging either."

I was impressed. When it came to improvised malarkey he was right up there with any Tin Cup's hoocher. His little speech inspired me to boldness.

"Margaret thinks Charlie Ward paid Shay Tilsen to murder her husband. Me, I hear Olson had a lot of friends in this part of town. Maybe one'a them paid him."

He didn't seem shocked by the suggestion.

"Olson grew up in the neighborhood," he said. "Some of the men in this room knew him personally. They liked him, they liked his politics. You could ask around if one of them hired somebody to kill Thornton, but it couldn't have been Shay. The jury found him not guilty. What's the matter, you don't you trust our legal system?"

We were nose to nose, but nobody seemed to be taking any notice. In Tin Cup's and other venues with which I'm familiar nose to nose is the penultimate gesture before fists fly, but Rothman didn't seem belligerent. He was just making a point.

"Can't stop people thinking, though," I said. "Tell me - and this is another thing I'm just curious about - why did those two fellows you broke up almost come to blows?"

"They were arguing. Trotskyism or Stalinism."

"What's the beef there?"

"Trotsky doesn't compromise on world revolution. Stalin talks about Socialism in one country. No question he's warped the Soviet workers state to fit his own ideological deformity, but some of us wonder if that's what's required to fight fascism. The question is - what does history demand? That's why Meyer almost punched Sherman."

"Doesn't seem worth fightin' about."

"Some of us think it's the only thing worth fighting about."

"You should hear what gets us Micks brawlin'. Nowhere near as elevated. - Is Tilsen here?"

Rothman pointed him out through the smoke, a tall guy off in a corner conversing with a few hard cases I took to be his brunos.

"What group is he in?" I asked. "I see some religious looking fellows here, you and your bunch seem pretty political, those younger guys over by the door, they're probably talkin' about dames. Is Tilsen one of the business men?"

He allowed himself a bit of a smile. "Yeah, he's involved with a big corporation."

"Fallen on hard times, I hear."

"Just like everyone else," he observed.

"Right, but working stiffs have some advantages. The bigs can't make a buck without labor, so if laborers look hard enough some of'em can find work. Murder Incorporated... I don't know. They used to sit and wait for the phone to ring, but now things are different."

"Different how?"

I explained that the high demand for droppers during Prohibition had slacked off since repeal. "They're casting around," I said. "They need a new strategic plan."

"You think now that Prohibition's over nobody wants to kill anyone?"

The way he put it, it sounded kind of silly.

"No, it's just that in my line of work you tend to see how complicated things have become. A few years back, if a pretty young widow asked me to find out who hired Murder Incorporated to kill her husband, odds are hubby was a bootlegger trying to muscle in on somebody's turf. The only question was, whose? Now I hardly know where to start."

"Margaret Thornton thinks Murder Incorporated killed her husband?"

"No, but I do. That's who Tilsen works for, isn't it?"

He rubbed his stubbled chin, and gave that some thought. While he was doing so a guy with a broad-brimmed hat, a long black coat, and a little pigtail hanging over one ear, approached him and put his hand out. Rothman gave him a coin.

The guy said something that sounded like, "I'll pray the T'fillin for you." - "Oh, please do," Rothman said. "And ask God to put the means of production into the hands of the workers."

"God doesn't meddle in such things," the guy replied.

"Then gimme my fuckin dime back!" said Rothman, with an excellent show of mock outrage.

The moocher just smiled, and moved over to the business types, where bills, not coins, were quickly produced.

"You pretty sure Murder Incorporated rubbed Thornton out?" Rothman asked.

"Just one of several leads I'm following up," I replied, in my best professional tone.

"'Following up?' What's that supposed to mean?"

I cupped my ear and stalled a bit, as if the noise had made me unsure of what he'd asked. He repeated himself.

"Well, I'm lookin' into it," I replied. "I'm, uh, scrapin' around. Tryin' to get some more information."

The specs came off again, and he was up close, squinting.

"So you think Isadore works for Murder Incorporated, and you're 'scraping around' here at the synagogue."

"Well, yeah."

He stepped back and put the glasses back on.

"I'll tell you something I've discovered in my line of work, McDonough. Sometimes the more information you get, the more confused you become. Stop and analyze things, you see you have all the information you need."

"What is your line of work?"

"I'm in the trucking industry."

"Let me guess. You load freight."

He stopped just short of the specs off squint-in-the-face treatment, and gave me the flat stare before replying.

"Labor of the kind I sell is required at the point in the distribution chain where cargo is taken off freight trains and loaded on to trucks," he explained, in the tone one employs with a dull-witted five year old. "That's how I make a living. But it's not my work."

I was genuinely puzzled. "Then what is?"

"Finding ways to break capital's stranglehold on distribution," he said. "That's what this Depression is about, McDonough. Distribution. I spend ten hours a day six days a week on a loading dock, and I can tell you there's no shortage of goods. That's not the problem."

In other words, he was a Red, which was no surprise. The distinction he drew between work and making a living was a new one for me though, and I said so.

"Of course that's never occurred to you," he said. "It's not supposed to. My back is for sale because I have to eat. My mind belongs to me, and that's what I work with. My comrades and I used to spend our time gathering information about who owns the trucks in Minneapolis, how they live and where, how much money they make. Lately I've decided that gathering information about local distributors is a waste of time. What's important is analyzing the distribution sector. And if you really believe Murder Incorporated killed Walter Thornton, you should analyze the murder for hire business. Then you'll realize that nobody in our community could be behind it."

"Explain," I said.

"Think of Murder Incorporated as a small partnership in New York that grew into a large national enterprise. They call on their local contacts to take care of business in other cities. I've heard rumors they call on Shay Tilsen around here, because they know he can handle it. He doesn't work for them, though. You could just as well say that they work for him. They find a job and take a cut. He does it and takes the rest."

"So you're admitting he -"

He raised a finger of caution. "I'm not admitting anything. Let's just assume for the sake of analysis that Isadore kills people for money. If someone who's a stranger to him wants to get rid of somebody they can't go to him directly. He'd say, 'I don't know what you're talking about, get outta here.' Murder Incorporated gives that person a way of approaching him. Through one of the partners."

"Maybe Bugsy Siegel."

"A word to the wise, McDonough. If you ever meet Ben Siegel, don't call him Bugsy. Some Teamsters from Chicago tell me he doesn't like that name."

"I'll keep that in mind, although if I ever did run into him it would be in St. Paul, and he'd be the one mindin' his Ps and Qs."

"Ah yes, St. Paul. - So, do you still wonder whether anyone in this room hired Isadore Tilsen to kill Walter Thornton?"

I glanced through the smoke over in Tilsen's direction, wondering where this was going. He was still chewing the fat with his palookas.

"Don't worry, this is between you and me," Rothman said. "My comrades and me wish Margaret Thornton the best, and if she wants to know who's behind her husband's murder I want to help you find out. The point I'm making is this. The men here all know Isadore Tilsen. In fact anyone from this community who took exception to Walter Thornton's attacks on Floyd Olson either knows Isadore personally, or knows someone who does. They don't have to call New York to make an arrangement, any more than Isadore has to report to Murder Incorporated if he takes a job here. That isn't how the business works."

"Well, I suppose you have a point. Maybe Margaret is right. Maybe it was Charlie Ward."

He shrugged. "Everybody knows Ward's story, that he supported Floyd Olson, that he did time in Leavenworth. It'd surprise me if he ever met Isadore, but I bet he knows how to reach Murder Incorporated."

"Could be," I said. "Makes sense." - I glanced at my watch. "I oughta get going."

I didn't say why. Tin Cup's closed in four hours.

Rothman walked me toward the door, nodding at the mooch with the pigtail on the way, cracking wise to a guy with a full beard and a tiny beanie on his head.

He stopped, and introduced me to one of the business types, a tall, black-haired guy with flaring nostrils and intense, dark eyes.

"Meet the head of the Midwest scrap metal cartel," he said. "Howard Kravetsky, this is Martin McDonough. - Howard once offered me a job. Nine hours a day at a dime an hour more than I'm making now. Correct me if I'm wrong Howard, but wasn't I supposed to pull the rag man's cart after his horse died?"

"Yeah, Lou, you were supposed to pull the cart, and holler 'rags' too. That way I wouldn't need a rag man HA-HA!" He barked.

"I've known Lou forever," Kravetsky told me. "Lou wants to change the world."

I nodded. Rothman was a Red alright, but he was also the sort of fellow whose company I sought in those days. The kind that likes to banter.

"Nice meeting you," I said, when we got to the exit.

"Likewise. Come around again. Tell me how your investigation is going. I'm interested."

We shook hands. He gave me a comradely pat on the shoulder.

I felt pretty good about my night's work. I'd observed Shay Tilsen and took note of who he talked to - his yegs and nobody else. That, plus what Rothman explained, made Charlie Ward my best bet. That should make Margaret happy, I thought.

Later, when I had a chance to reflect on the strange turn things took, I wondered when the object became making Margaret happy. Probably about the time I decided it was on the cuff.

Meanwhile, I looked forward to talking to Rothman again. He knew some things I didn't, and he was a mockey to boot, which made it more interesting in an odd way.

It was cold and windy out, but I didn't mind so much after the heat and the smoke inside. They were turning out the electric street lights at nine P M to save money in those days, so driving was difficult. I almost ran over a dog in downtown Minneapolis. The streets were deserted except for a few men sleeping in doorways, their boots out in the slush.

I got lost for a while, but finally reached the river. I drove along the bluff on a winding road full of icy spots and potholes, looking for a bridge. The only light was my bobbing headlamps, and a little shaving of moon haloed in haze.

The darkness was so profound I began to project a fantasy out there, a dazzling vision of Margaret Thornton in her St. Agnes uniform. While I watched in wonderment she kicked off her buckle shoes, unbuttoned her blouse and dropped it, slid her skirt and underpants down and stood before me naked except for her white knee socks. She averted her gaze demurely, but there was a faint smile on her lips. Her pale shoulders were lightly freckled, her small breasts firm, her nipples rose-colored and erect. Her slender forearms rested on her hipbones, and her hands, which were clasped beneath her smooth belly, partially obscured her maidenhair, which wasn't hair at all, more like a bouquet of flowers and - CLUNK!

An axle-cracker of a pothole jarred me out of my trance, and I realized I was most of the way back to my Rice Street haunts. That must have been how the Crusaders made it to Jerusalem.

Jimmy Brennan wasn't in Tin Cup's. I cursed myself yet again for not talking to him when I had the chance, and looked around for Maggie. She wasn't there either. I bolted a shot, excused myself, and made for her place straightaway. She opened the door a crack when I knocked.

"Yeah."

I was momentarily puzzled. Then I remembered our last conversation.

"Lemme in, we can talk -"

"Talk out there. We'll see if I let'cha in."

"Well, I - uh, - y'know..."

"You haven't been thinkin' about what I said, have'ya?"

I admitted I hadn't. "I've been busy," I explained.

"Yeah, well, I'm busy now." SNAP! went the gum. "S'long."

She closed the door. The bolt slid into place.

Worse yet, Jimmy Brennan didn't show up either, a first in my experience. Strong drink was my only solace.

* * *

Next morning I made it to Kuby's while they were still airing the joint out. The odor of stale beer and cigarette smoke wafted out the front door. That clean north end air, lightly flavored by the sulfurous bouquet of the coke plant, blew in the back. The wood stove was lit and crackling. I warmed my hands while they set up for business. After the floor was swamped and dry the doors were closed, and the sawdust was spread. I ordered a coffee and brandy and waited for Jerk.

They were trying out a brand new Mighty Wurlitzer. According to the bar man, Kuby was hoping to draw a younger crowd.

"I hope it doesn't work," he confided in a whisper. "Let'em go over to Tin Cup's with their noise and their fights. I like these old gents."

He nodded toward the door, which had opened a bit more than a crack to let in the first regular of the day, a bag of bones in an army surplus overcoat that was way too big. If not for the shock of white hair protruding from the upturned collar and the way the hem dragged across the floor you'd have never known there was a living soul inside.

"THEY

 ASKED ME HOW I KNEWWW

 MY TRUE LOVE WAS TRUUUE," crooned the scratchy voice from the box.

Jerk walked in a few minutes later. "What brings you here?" he asked. He took off his hat, fussed with the brim, put it back on.

I told him I'd been thinking about marriage. I had it in mind to explain my conundrum, Maggie or Margaret, but he was two steps ahead of me as usual.

"Good," he said. "It's time you got serious with somebody suitable. Now listen t'me. Take it slow. Make sure the widow's mother gets a good impression. Stay on the right side of her. She's the key. Do a good job on this murder, then speak from your heart to her daughter. And bring roses. Hear me?"

"Yeah, yeah."

"Whats'sa matter?"

"I just want ma to know I'm thinkin' about it is all."

"Ok, I'll tell her. - Better yet, you tell her."

"I don't like talkin' to her about that kinda stuff."

"Well, I'm here to help," he said, with a little edge, a little hardening of the twinkle in his eye. "How's that investigation coming?"

Just then up walked Kuby himself. He was a husky fellow, with bristly black hair. I'd never spoken to him, but I knew him by reputation as one ballsy bar owner, because he was a St. Albert's guy doing business in St. Andrew's parish. He gave Jerk a perfunctory nod, but it was me he wanted to talk to.

"How'ya like the music?" he asked.

"Just here to see my uncle," I said. "Wasn't payin' much attention."

"Yeah? I'm gonna try somethin' a little bouncier. Maybe that'll get your toe tappin.'"

"At eight AM? You must be kiddin'."

We all laughed at that, but Jerk cut it short the moment Kuby turned his back.

"That Hun cocksucker," he said. "Let him go over to Rice Street with that music crap."

"It's his joint," I observed.

"Bullshit, it's my joint. Tommy Scanlon over there," he gestured toward the bag of bones in the overcoat, "it's his joint."

Tommy Scanlon seemed to be using all the strength he could muster to haul a mug of ale slowly toward the wood stove. The hem of his coat left a trail in the sawdust.

"Time marches on, Jerk."

"Yeah, in the direction it gets pointed."

He took off his hat and pulled the feather out of the hatband.

"Know what kind of bird this feather came from, Martin? A Passenger Pigeon. Know how many of'em are left?" He made a circle with his thumb and forefinger. "Zero. That's how many. - Jesus, will'ya listen to that!"

"It's not the end of the world, havin' some music in the joint."

"It's the beginning of the end, mark my words. - Where were we?"

"I don't know. Pigeons? - I got a tip about a murder that might be related to Thornton's. Howard Godfrey."

"Who's Howard Godfrey?"

I explained, and told him what Erick Klawitter told me. He listened carefully.

"That's a lotta mazuma to get somebody snuffed," he said. "Even if it is Bugsy Siegel doin' it."

"Point taken, but I'm gonna look into it. What else is Bugsy doin' here?"

"Just pokin' around, lookin' for some cooch, or maybe a way to peddle some flea powder."

"You know as well as I do the coppers won't sit still for that."

"Nature hates a vacuum, Martin. What the coppers sit still for isn't the whole story. Anyway, go ahead, check it out, be thorough. - So this Godfrey was another newspaper guy?"

"Radio. But he went after Floyd Olson, same as Thornton."

"Hundred and fifty Gs. Oughta be able to buy the radio station and cancel his show for that kinda money."

"Maybe Ward was sending a message."

His eyes were twinkling again. "Oh. A message. - Thornton didn't get it, apparently."

"Well, I told'ya, that cash covered two murders according to Klawitter."

"Yeah, Herb Bigelow. Except, best I can recall, he drowned in the middle of a lake. What'd Bugsy do, swim out there and tip the canoe over?"

"That isn't how that racket works, Jerk. Those east coast mock-eys hire people to do the deed."

"Who'd he hire up there at - where was it? Bear's Ass Lake? - This Meyer Lansky, I've heard he's a guy who delegates. Bugsy is hands-on. Gets his kicks that way."

"I don't know. Jesus! I told'ya, I'm lookin' into it. First thing, I'll check the papers when Bigelow drowned, see if it sounds square."

"Well you're right to do that."

He asked if I wanted to go with him to ma's right then, and the two of us would tell her I was courting.

"No can do. I'm meeting Jack Moylan down at the Town Talk. Going on a little errand with him."

I told him it was about the shooting in Minneapolis. I could tell the way he reacted that he already knew. Once, years earlier, I got into a brawl outside a speak and came home an hour later with a shiner. Jerk was in the living room with ma, and before I could open my mouth he told me who I'd been scrapping with and why, then chastised me for taking offense at such a minor slight. - "It's the hooch, Martin," he said. "Don't let it get the best of you."

It was good advice. But I never could figure out how he knew what happened. We didn't even have a telephone back then. It's like Jerk's wired to the source or something.

I told him I'd stay in touch, and headed downtown.

* * *

There was a big crowd milling around outside the main Post Office and spilling into the street. Traffic was snarled for blocks. I crawled down Kellogg wondering what the problem was, until I spotted my friend Tim McKenna standing on the curb. Tim was a mail sorter, and a Tin Cup's regular. He was trying to organize the mob into orderly lines, without much luck. I rolled down my window.

"What's this about?" I shouted.

"Hey, Martin. Whynt'cha step outta the fliver and help me out here. These people are nuts."

A guy he was herding toward the line turned around. "You're nuts, mister," he said. "I got six dimes here, and in two weeks I'll have sixteen hundred dollars. Then we'll see who's nuts!"

Tim shrugged. I moved slowly past him.

"It's the chain letter thing," he said. "The banks are runnin' outta dimes. Human nature, I guess."

Funny term, "human nature." It comes up all the time, and rarely to describe anything edifying. Instead it's employed to excuse everything from foolishness to pure evil.

Thank God for human nature. I'd be out of work without it.

Jack was done with his breakfast, and anxious to get going. He was in full uniform. His size 12 brogans were polished and shined, his gray twills pressed. A paddy-whacker hung from his belt, alongside his .38 special. He loosened the belt a notch, told the waitress the food was "lovely," and motioned for me to follow him, a big smile on his face.

Jack was a man who liked his work, and he was good at it, although you'd have to understand what it was before you could make that judgment. He was a copper in name only. Jack was actually a mob enforcer, a role the police were required to take on due to another link in the chain of meaningless intellectual necrophilia. It began when Dapper Dan Hogan, who'd negotiated the original layover and made sure that visiting gangsters lived by its terms, turned on his ignition key one morning.

When the smoke cleared, Dapper Dan was in bits and pieces and Harry Sawyer owned The Green Lantern.

Sawyer was a gifted money manager, more interested in acting as a banker for our town's many well-heeled visitors than in reminding them of the rules. It was a conflict of interest that resulted in an enforcement vacuum.

Some downtown boosters eventually took Eternal Tommy to task, claiming that St. Paul was fast changing from a place where the crime was organized to one in which anarchy reigned. High profile kidnappings were the proximate cause of their concern, but many

lesser transgressions had occurred by then. The citizenry was beginning to grumble. Unless things change, Tommy was told, the layover
and his tenure as chief would soon be history.

At the time Jack Moylan was still a beat cop. He'd spent most
of his working life in speaks, drinking with people he was supposed
to bust. Tommy spotted Jack's incipient gift. He assigned him a task:
Impress upon the tough guys, whose natural inclination was to do
what they pleased in our town, that there was a price to be paid for
misbehaving.

"Whose bucket we takin, Jack?" I inquired.

"Squad car, Martin. We're showin' the colors today."

He used his siren to get past the Post Office. It was slow going
anyway, but eventually we crossed the Third Street Bridge, and pulled
into a gas station on Maria Street. A guy seated on an overturned pail
was shooting the breeze with a grease monkey, but he rose when he
saw us and walked over to the squad car. It was Dick Pranke, the Hun
I'd been rolling dice with at the St. Francis a few days before.

He nodded to me, and handed Jack a slip of paper with an address written on it. "He's there now," he said, and gave Jack a wink.
Off we went.

"How do you know Pranke?" I asked.

"He finks boyo. Keep it under yer hat."

"Small world. I see him around the fights."

"Find out which way he's puntin' and do th'same, that's my advice."

"Naww. None'a our guys take a dive. Krauts maybe."

Jack just smiled and shook his head. He enjoyed playing the
knowing copper.

"So he corrupts'em, does he?"

Jack rolled his eyes at that. He had the typical copper attitude -
original sin, taken to its' logical extreme. Every bull in St. Paul got
something from the layover, Jack more than most.

"Some guys'll go in the tank, some won't," I opined. "Either
way, somebody's gotta tempt'em."

"That'd be our Dicky," he said.

A few blocks later Jack put the siren on. We turned down Reaney street, shattering the silence as we came, and parked behind a black Hudson. The siren slowed to a hum, and died.

Jack pulled a riot gun off its mount above the windshield, laid it on my lap, and stepped out. He commenced strolling around, whistling loudly and melodiously, making a show of his officially clad presence. I stayed put in the squad car.

The sun gleamed off puddles of melted snow in the yard of the fourplex in front of which we'd parked, one of those old East Side mansions that had been split up in deference to hard times.

A bird that was splashing around cocked its ear in Jack's direction, trying to make sense of his song.

Soon the door opened, and out sauntered a tall, rail-thin peckerwood, with an ugly goiter bulging at his neck. It was "Beanstalk" Powers, an Okie who'd honed his unique skills with the Barker-Karpis gang, and now employed them with the remnants of Dillinger's. Despite his buzzard-like demeanor (or was it because of it?), Beanstalk was said to have a gift for hitting it off with bank managers. He would put on a suit, and pretend he was a business man contemplating a large deposit. But first he wanted a tour of the security system. He had a photographic memory, and when he left the bank both the robbery and the escape route had been meticulously planned.

"Ah heard yez comin'," he said to Jack.

"Did'ye now, Mr. Powers."

"Yup."

"And might Mr. Gillis be about?"

"He assed me to see what'chu wanted."

"I'd like to speak with him. If I may."

Beanstalk flipped a lick of stringy hair out of his eyes with a jerk of his head.

"He ain't dressed yet," he said.

Jack stepped up close, a big smile on his face.

"Tell him it's time to be gettin' dressed. Tell him Officer Jack wants to say good mornin'." He bumped Beanstalk with his belly.

"Would'ye mind obligin' me in that regard, Mr. Powers?"

Beanstalk's goiter bobbled. "Uh, shore," he said. He turned and sauntered back toward the house.

A face appeared in a second story window next door, and a few people began gathering in nearby yards. The presence of onlookers was part of the plan. This was to be an unpublicized but well-documented police action, word of which would spread quickly through all the circles that were meant to get the message - yegs, hoi-poloi who worried that they were on the kidnappers' list, nervous neighbors - especially the latter, and the neighbors here had every right to be nervous. Due to an accident of history called The Layover, they were living in proximity to one of the trigger-happiest metal pumpers who ever robbed a bank. Jack later told me that "Mr. Gillis" been wandering around the neighborhood drunk a few days past, taking potshots at squirrels with a .45 revolver.

"Oh, and Mr. Powers?" said Jack, just as Beanstalk reached the door. "Would'ye be so kind as to tell Mr. Gillis to leave his guns in the house? Tell him I'll be pattin' him down when he comes out, and if I find him to be armed I'll step aside, and my friend over there will blow his fookin' brains out. - Show him your weapon, Martin."

I raised the shotgun. Beanstalk took note, and went inside.

Jack paced around, twirling his paddy-whacker and whistling, nodding now and then to the neighbors, who were moving closer.

Soon Lester Gillis emerged from the house. He was a diminutive fellow with a putty nose, rosy cheeks and the smooth skin of a newborn. I was astounded to see that he was wearing the same jaunty cap of Harris Tweed that he sported on the many posters adorning the walls of our nation's federal buildings. In the few short minutes we'd waited, he'd also managed to put on a starched white shirt, a maroon necktie and an expensive looking brown suit coat. His slacks were pressed and his shoes were shined. These guys were rarely seen in public without the accouterments of respectability.

"Dere a problem, officer?" he said.

"Indeed there is Mr. Gillis," Jack replied. "Put'cher hands on the car."

He motioned toward the Hudson. Gillis complied. Jack patted him down.

"Turn around," he said, when he finished.

Gillis complied, but not cheerfully. "You coppers are supposed to be polite. Tommy Brown told me I was welcome in St. Paul."

"Did he now." Jack moved closer. He towered over the diminutive yeg by a foot. "Don't ye go by another name, Mr. Gillis?"

"Yeah, my friends call me Big George. Big George Nelson."

"Really? But yer a just a wee speck of a man. I thought they called'ye 'Baby Face.'"

His eyes narrowed to slits. "I don't like dat name."

Jack glanced over at the Hudson. "This your bucket, Baby Face?"

"Yeah, what of it?" he snarled.

Jack started whistling again. He walked around back of the Hudson, and prodded at a wrinkle in the bumper with his paddy-whacker.

"Got a bit of a dent here," he said.

"So dat's what dis is about?"

"Now what would'ye be referrin' to by 'dat,' Baby Face?"

"Dat accident I had da other day."

Jack scowled. He pulled a notebook out of his pocket, paged through it, then pretended to study something intently.

"Doesn't sound like an accident. Says here you drilled that man four times. And you was rat-arsed drunk when ye done it."

"Maybe it was more of a misunderstandin."

Jack tucked the notebook back in his pocket, and punched Baby Face a terrible blow to the stomach.

His cap dropped where his feet had been, and he landed in a heap a few feet away.

Ahhhh, the little crowd that had assembled sighed in unison. The neighbor who'd been looking through his window raised it and leaned out. Jack grabbed Baby Face by the necktie and jerked him to his feet.

"Listen to me, you wee piece'a shite," he said. "Get yer skinny arse behind the wheel'a that boiler'o yers, and get the fook outta town. If I ever see you in St. Paul again I'll wring yer neck."

He leaned down and put his nose right close to Baby Face's. "Any misnderstandins'?" He hawked up a gob and spit in his mug. "Get outta here. Now."

"B -but, I need, I need -

"Yeah, I know. Y'need yer wardrobe, yer hardware, yer dough. Too bad! Have yer friend Mr. Powers forward it t'yer next address, which better be far, far away I might add. Yer leavin' here with the clothes on yer back. Got'cher keys?"

Baby Face nodded yes.

"Then what're ye waitin' for!"

Baby Face slouched around to the driver's side, spit clinging to his cheek. Jack rapped the roof of the car a few times with his paddy-whacker to hurry him along

The neighbors cheered as he drove away. Jack smiled and waved.

They say character is fate, and Baby Face Nelson was living proof of that - for about one week longer. He'd been comfortably ensconced in a quiet neighborhood in the safest town in the U.S.A. for the likes of him, but he had to go and lose his temper. He headed for Chicago after Jack gave him the boot, and acquired some new weaponry.

Somebody down there must have fingered him. A copper made him behind the wheel of that black Hudson out in the north suburbs somewhere, and phoned the feds. A gunfight ensued in which two G men died, and Baby Face was mortally wounded. His body was found the next day at the gate to a suburban cemetery, where his wife had dumped him.

Traffic was backed up across the Third Street Bridge as Jack and I headed back downtown. Jack turned on the red light. We moved over to the left side of the road, passed the long line of idling cars and horse and wagon rigs, then came to a dead stop almost a block from the Post Office. The street was full of people. There must have been a thousand or more by then. They were waving their arms, shouting, moving in surges toward the entrance, then retreating as some coppers repelled them.

The mob backed off from a show of force near the building, and closed around us. An elderly woman, a Swede by the look of her, peered in the window on Jack's side. Suddenly her features flattened as the weight of the crowd pressed her against the glass. Then the rush the other way released her and she fell backwards, leaving naught but a smear of face cream on the window.

"Jayzus!" said Jack. He opened the door, reached down and pulled her to her feet.

"You okay, darlin?" He straightened her cloche hat for her.

"Yahsureyoubetchatankyou." she replied.

She brushed herself off and rushed forward again, clutching an envelope in one hand, and stiff-arming her way toward the entrance with the other.

A mounted cop who was using his horse to part the crowd spotted us. "TOMMY'S LOOKIN FOR YOU," he shouted.

"HE KNOWS DAMN WELL WHERE I AM," Jack replied.

"NOT YOU. MARTIN. - TURN ON THE SIREN AND I'LL LEAD YOU THROUGH. HURRY!"

Thus began my descent into the pit of celebrity.

MONSTER

The moment we reached headquarters I was ushered into the Chief's office, a first for me. Eternal Tommy was seated behind his desk waiting, with a glum look on his normally inscrutable puss.

"Leon Gleeman's daughter has been kidnapped," he said.

I'd have been glum too, if I was in Tommy's shoes. No single crime could have been better calculated to expose the logic behind the apparent capriciousness of law enforcement in our town. Leon Gleeman was a 'fixer,' a title he'd earned during Prohibition, when he was the biggest bootlegger in St. Paul because all the mom and pop operators ended up dead or on his payroll. Once he attained monopoly status his only problem was mollifying politicians. He'd become a master of that. A little hush money here, a little favor there, a whisper in the ear about a past indiscretion. Whatever it took.

Gleeman used his talents to keep his bootleg operation running until Prohibition was repealed. Then fixing became his sole occupation. He had every official in St. Paul in his pocket, which was a constant source of irritation to City contractors. They had to pay him to get those contracts, then keep paying if they wanted them renewed. But it was the wealthy who really hated him. The fact that a mockey ran the show stuck in their craw, and Gleeman knew it. He'd ordered the coppers to feign helplessness during the recent rash of kidnappings, which meant several ritzy families had been forced to beg our local G men for help. Now the worm had turned.

"Let me guess," I said to Tommy. "If your gumshoes find Glee-man's kid, the Bremer family will wonder why the feds had to find their Otto."

"Worse. I got a call from a congressman's aide. Told me if we got involved in the case he'd have Hoover send every G-man west of Chicago here, and put us all in jail."

I smiled.

"Very funny."

"What does Gleeman say?"

"This is his eight year old daughter we're talking about."

"So he wants the boys out in force."

"He's a little more understanding than that. 'I don't care how you find her,' he told me, 'but do it, and fast.' I don't blame him. That pervert Goiffon signed the ransom note."

"Why didn't he pay? He's a millionaire fr'Christ's sake."

"He came up with $10,000, the frog son of a bitch changes his mind, wants twenty. Tries to give him that, and Goiffon doesn't even show up to collect. Calls and says he thinks it's a trap. Gleeman's afraid he's goofy about little girls."

"Ah, and where do things stand now?"

Tommy explained that some careful nosing around had turned up a bindle stiff who claimed that Goiffon and the kid were hiding out in a cave in the bluffs near downtown. In exchange for twenty bucks and a bottle of hooch a meeting had been set up so he could guide someone there.

"And that would be you," said Tommy. " Carry a rod?"

"Uh-uh. You guys are always tellin' me to make sure nobody gets hurt."

He handed me a little snub-nosed .22, and a bulging envelope.

"There's $30,000 in there. If he'll take the dough hand it over, but not until you've got the kid. If he has any more demands, game's over - understand?"

I didn't bother to answer, just took the gun and the cash and left.

I understood alright. Tommy Brown made a career of playing both ends against the middle, but he was in the middle now and he didn't like it. Tommy knew I depended on the information his men gave me. He thought he could order them to clam up any time, so ipso facto I depended on him. I never saw the percentage in straightening him out. Sure he could make trouble, but his coppers didn't know how to clam up, at least not in the venues where I rubbed shoulders with them.

It was common knowledge that Gleeman was rich, so it made sense that his family would be targeted for a snatch, but I'd never heard Jean Goiffon was a kidnapper. Not that it was beneath him.

Goiffon was a nasty piece of work from Little Canada, out near White Bear Lake. There was a colony of French-Canadians up there, and he was proof that the gossip about them was true. I'd seen him once in a speak; sloping forehead, big lumpy nose, about five and a half feet tall, maybe six feet across the shoulders. He looked like something it took generations of inbreeding to produce, and his reputation was as grotesque as his mug - rape, short-eyes, knife fights - but not kidnapping.

What rotten timing, I thought, as I turned the crank and climbed into the bucket. This was the day I was going to put on the push to pin Thornton's murder on Charlie Ward. I wanted to wrap up the case and hand it to Margaret along with a bouquet of roses later that week.

I hadn't given much thought to what came next. I tried contemplating marriage, home and family on the way to the hobo jungle, but strange to say I had no words for it, nor could I get a picture of it in my mind. At least not one that included me.

All I could see was my ma, fretting. Dad was down at the saloon.

I finally quit and took out my mental frustration on Goiffon. That baby-raping freak would rue the day he crossed Martin McDonough. I think I might actually have been looking forward to gunning him down.

It was a short drive from the heart of downtown to the hobo jungle, but once you turned on to a pair of ruts called Industrial Road you were in the wilderness. The thick brush and stunted trees of the Mississippi bottomland were leafless now. In the rear view mirror I could see the top of the Bremer Building through the branches, which only served to accentuate the remoteness of the place.

The city had grand plans for this area before The Great Depression. They were going to bulldoze the flood plain bare, make a levee out of the debris, and turn it into a manufacturing zone. The so-called road I was on was all that came of it. The place was still a haven for deer, fox, birds, and a seasonal colony of bums who found it quite habitable despite the mosquitos. Their ranks thinned when the snow flew, but some hung on. They had plenty of wood for lean-tos and campfires, but their only real comfort was the rotgut they purchased after a day bumming nickels downtown. They'd trudge back, wrap up in their bedrolls and hooch off to dreamland.

I parked the bucket and proceeded on foot. According to Eternal Tommy, my informant would be waiting on the shore, directly across from the barge terminal.

At first it appeared that he wasn't around, but he was there alright. I spotted him when the crackling of branches under my shoes disturbed a flock of crows gathered around something on the sand.

There was a splintered two-by-four laying a few feet from his caved-in head. The blood looked fresh, but the crows had already eaten his eyes.

The hair on my neck stood on end. I took the pistol out of my coat pocket, and kept it in hand for the trudge back to the car. You can bet I was scared, but I jazzed myself thinking of the pleasure I'd take in rescuing the kid, and leaving that repugnant frog dead in his cave.

The crows had begun circling and cawing when I approached, but they settled back on the corpse the moment I left.

Needless to say, Tommy found this development disheartening.

"We oughta get the meat wagon down there and give that bum a decent burial," I told him.

"You lost your senses, Martin?" he inquired. "If Goiffon spots a uniform or an official vehicle there'll be another stiff to deal with. I'm trying to get the Gleeman kid back, not get her killed."

"Any suggestions?" I asked.

He rose from his chair, red-faced and sputtering. "Do I have any suggestions? Listen to me GODDAM IT - I know what you think! You think my men'll give you the low-down on the sly if I tell'em not to. BUT DON'T COUNT ON IT! You mess this up and I swear it'll cost'em their job to give you anything! So YOU better come up with some suggestions. SOON!"

That took me back. He knew my mind. Nevertheless, I stood my ground.

"Maybe you're willing to fire half the force to put me out of business, Tommy. You might even be ready to spend a few months wiring their replacements up on the fine points of The Layover, but I don't see how that gets us any closer to finding Gleeman's kid."

He sat down again, and rested his chin in his fists. "I can't help you," he said.

"Hey, I don't need any uniformed back-up. Hows'about a little reconnaissance? Whatta'ya think that hobo was gonna show me? Any idea where the cave is? There must'a been some coppers down there sometime, for one reason or another."

He shook his head. "Cinder dicks, maybe. They get to roustin' bindle stiffs when they got nothing better to do, but they go back to the railroad yard when they're done. They don't hang around looking for caves."

"Well, who does?"

"Now you mention it, let's see...."

He rustled around in his file drawer, and pulled out a folder labeled "Hamline University," the Methodist college we despised when I went to St. Thomas because they had the temerity to win a few football games.

"One time a couple years back there was this professor wanted to go down there," Tommy said. "The president of that Protestant shit-house where he teaches called, asked me to give him an escort so the bums wouldn't bother him. He wanted to map the area for historical purposes. Some big event happened there, way back."

He peered at a typewritten sheet. "Professor Ian Jack. - Maybe he can help."

* * *

The egghead with two first names had an office in an old brown-stone mansion that served as Hamline University's history department. He had a ruddy complexion, gray hair, and a walrus mustache that might have been gray too, if smoke from the pipe clenched in his long yellow teeth hadn't stained it an unpleasant shade of brown. I told him what I'd come for.

"Perhaps I can assist," he said.

He bade me take a seat across a cluttered table from him, and told me more than I wanted to know about his work as he sifted through the junk.

If the old Jesuit crank at St. Thomas was too dismissive of history, the prof was too enthusiastic about it. His head was firmly planted in his specialty, local history from the arrival of the first explorers through the 19th century. That left him with the makings of his own little world - barely a living soul with any firsthand info, but a ton of written material to pore over. Judging by the hodgepodge on the table he spent most of his time doing just that.

He sorted through the mess, pausing to retrieve some arrowheads and a few feathered aboriginal gew-gaws that were scattered among the books and manuscripts. "I've been looking for these," he mumbled.

Finally he extracted a hand-drawn map.

"This is the area you're talking about. The so-called 'Industrial Zone.'"

"Junkyard is more like it," I observed.

He wagged a pedantic finger. "But that's better than the alternative. More enlightened generations than ours can pick up the junk, but restoring the area once the city has destroyed it would be a more daunting task."

He took off on a long-winded tale about an historical quirk of some interest, simply because of its uniqueness.

"It was there, in 1771," he explained, "that the explorer Jonathan Carter sat down with the Chiefs of the local Dakota clans, and purchased their land. He left with a deed to hundreds of square miles, including the entirety of St. Paul and Minneapolis. It was probably written on birch bark, but the Historical Society has the parchment replica that was filed with the state. And for all that land, Carter gave the Chiefs a few dozen blankets, some mirrors, some iron pots, maybe a musket or two."

"Same old story, noble savages selling their birthright for a handful of trinkets –"

"Aha," he exclaimed, with a smile so broad it tugged the ends of his mustache, "one might think so. But one would be wrong. It turned out quite differently."

According to the prof, the Redskins had spotted Carter paddling upriver in the grand limey style, a flotilla of underlings strung out behind him half way to St. Louis. They knew it was only a matter of time until he offered them the standard deal, everything they had for a canoe full of wampum. They held a quick pow-wow and agreed to offer him all the land they could legitimately claim, sweeten the pot with some more land that belonged to the Ojibway, take as much as they could get, then deny it ever happened.

That was their story, and they not only stuck to it, they passed it on. They called Carter's deed a forgery. They told a court of inquiry that they'd laughed and walked out when he made his offer.

"Carter's descendants were still hauling the Chiefs' descendants into court 50 years later, trying to assert their claim," said the prof. "Carter died in an insane asylum. The fact that he'd been the victim of a confidence game pulled off by red Indians drove him crazy."

"Very interesting, but what's it got to do with the cave I'm looking for?"

"The trade was negotiated in a cave, and Carter went to great lengths to describe its' location accurately when he was trying to prove his claim. It's one of only two caves in that immediate area, and it is located about two hundred yards from the place where you say that hobo was murdered. Not so long ago, when the appreciation of our common heritage was considered as important as the concept of progress that those know-nothings in government espouse, it was called Carter's Cave, in honor of the great palaver that was held there. To the best of my knowledge, the mouth of the cave and some of the tunnel back to the inner cavern has been filled with scrap metal in the last few years. Disgusting really."

"You pretty sure that's the cave I'm looking for?"

"It must be. The other one was sealed up when the brewery that was using it went out of business."

"Well, the know-nothings down at city hall would be in your debt if you could point it out on that map of yours."

He obliged, and even drew up a little guide. I tipped my hat and hit the road.

Finding the cave was easy. Getting into it would have been easy too. Somebody had moved just enough junk to create a narrow corridor. I stood off in the trees, and looked things over. There was no sign of anyone that I could see, but I was peering down a passage through a pile of scrap iron. Goiffon could easily be in there, but blundering in with a torch in one hand and a pistol in the other seemed ill-advised. So did standing around and cogitating while that pervert molested the fixer's kid.

Soon I'd been standing still long enough that I was part of the scenery. A deer tiptoed by with its nose to the ground, maybe twenty feet away. I could see its breath. It was a nose breather. A curl of smoke rose from the woods, probably the hobo's jungle. I wondered if they'd missed their pal yet, and indulged in a brief daydream: walk down there, tell them about his demise, hang around for a few snorts of Night Train, throw in on the next bottle....It was a lot easier to picture than marriage, and it took my mind off the problem just long enough to untie the knot.

It was mid-afternoon when I pulled up in front of the synagogue. I told a lady in a musty office next to the sacristy what was on my mind. She directed me down the hall to a nook the size of a broom closet, where the old gent with the beanie hung out. File this under useless but interesting; he's called a "shamus," just like a gumshoe. He gave me a careful look-see.

"So why should you wanna find Lou?" he asked. "He owes'ya money?"

"Nothin' like that. He's a - a friend."

He continued to look me over. He had a cup of tea in his hand with a round slice of lemon floating in it.

"You're the fella was here last night."

"That was me."

He sipped his tea, and scratched his beezer.

"Ask Bessie Rothman where her son is. She's a few blocks from here." He gave me the address.

I tipped my hat, which may have been bad form in the house of their Lord, but I meant well.

Mrs. Rothman was a plump woman about my ma's age, wearing an apron. She had thick grey hair tied in a bun. She gave me a quizzical look at the door, but invited me in without hesitation. I sat down in her neat little living room and told her I was looking for her son.

"You're with the Red squad?" she said.

"Cross my heart, I'm not a copper."

She considered that for a few moments. The house smelled vaguely familiar, like something my mother used to make, long ago.

"Who d'ya like, Stalin or Trotsky?" she asked.

"Maam, everything I know about those two I learned from your son last night, and it wasn't much."

"He'd be glad to teach you more, believe me. Why do you wanna find my Louie?"

"I need a favor."

"You wanna borrow money?"

"Not that kind of favor."

"Tea?"

"I'd love to maam, but I'm in a terrible rush."

She nodded as if she understood. Chicken and dumplings, that's what it smelled like.

"What did you say your name was?"

"Martin McDonough."

"You seem like a nice enough young man, Mr. McDonough. Let me give you a 'voonk,' - a whatchamacallit. A tip. In the home a gentleman takes his hat off."

I whipped it off. "Yes, maam, but I was just at the synama - uh, your house of worship, and...."

"Ahh. So here's the rule. In the synagogue, hat on. In the home, hat off."

"My apologies."

"Mox nix. Next time you'll know. You could find Louie at M & A Cartage, Fifth Avenue North docks, at the end of Seventh Street."

I made my way through a sprawling dinge neighborhood along the tracks, turned down a street lined with honky-tonks and hash houses, and crossed into the freight yards at the edge of downtown Minneapolis. Fifth Avenue was clogged with trailer-trucks and horse-and-wagon rigs, all jostling with each other to get to the railroad docks. When I tried to squeeze past in my Model A they assumed I was jumping the line. A couple truck drivers with tire irons in their hands got out to confront me. I rolled down the window and explained that I was looking for someone.

"Then leave that bucket here," said one of them.

"Yeah," the other one agreed. "So's we know yer levelin' with us."

I had no choice but to bump my car up over the tracks, park in the yards, and hoof it. I dodged between horse drawn carts and idling trucks, stepping over horse pats and bumping into wagon wheels.

The horse-drawn conveyances had an advantage. They could maneuver between trucks, straddle the rails, do a lot of things that the giant motorized vehicles couldn't. There was a phalanx of them at the head of the line, but their empty wagons were stopped short of the docks by a mass of jostling, shouting men who were boldly making deals for goods that had been snatched before they could be hauled away.

"SACK'A POTATOES," I heard someone yell. "EIGHTEEN CENTS," came the reply from somewhere in the crowd, then "NINETEEN," and the throng began to converge toward a big mug holding a bushel of spuds over his head. - "HEY," came a cry, "OVER HERE, I GOT A CASE'A CANNED MEAT" - "CLOTHES

- ALL KINDS'A SHIRTS AND PANTS!" - "TWO BUCKS FOR THE MEAT" - "TWO AND A DIME."

I squirmed through the crowd toward a cement dock elevated to the height of a freight car door. Rothman was up there with a bunch of other freight handlers, all seemingly oblivious to the noise and confusion around them. They were watching a train inch past. As I approached, it came to a squeaking halt. The cars banged together, shuddered, and the doors of the cars at the dock opened.

The crew rose as one man, and began off-loading cartons of freight.

Rothman spotted me.

"YOU TAILIN' ME McDONOUGH," he hollered. - "OOF." He jerked a box off the car by the ropes that held it together, and flung it toward another handler, who was piling them up.

"I NEED A FAVOR," I yelled.

"ANOTHER ONE? I ALREADY SOLVED YOUR CASE."

"YEAH, THANKS, BUT THIS ONE'S GOT NOTHIN' TO DO WITH THAT. - I'M NOT KIDDIN. KNOCK OFF A MINUTE AND LISTEN."

He nodded, threw one more box, and climbed down.

"What now," he said.

"I gotta borrow a truck full of junk, scrap, any damn thing. But I need it right away."

He whipped off the specs and gave me the once over.

"I won't ask." He put his glasses back on. "Scrap is money. People I know don't give it away."

"I just need to borrow it, but I can put some money down. For like a guarantee."

"HEY ROTHMAN,' yelled the straw boss. "GET'CHER ASS BACK UP HERE."

"YEAH YEAH. - Go see Kravetsky," he told me. "The guy I introduced you to last night. He's over on Washington. Mid-States Rag and Scrap Metal. Tell him I sent you."

"I owe'ya," I said.

"Damn right," he replied, as he climbed back on the dock.

"I'll buy'ya a drink. You a drinkin' man?"

"A little bit. Now and then."

"You got one comin," I assured him.

Kravetsky's business was about a mile down the tracks, on Washington Avenue. He was skeptical, but "why not?" was his rhetorical query when I peeled off one thousand of Leon Gleeman's dollars and laid them in his hand against the return of a load of scrap and an ancient pick-up truck.

The sky was turning the murky gray that augurs the hoocher's hour when I rumbled down Industrial Road again. A prudent driver would have slowed to a crawl, but I stepped on it to maximize the bang-crash as I approached. Tree branches scraped the cab. The truck bottomed out in a low spot, and jolted the load. The brakes squeaked as I came to a halt.

I slammed the door hard. The sound echoed against the bluffs. Off in the distance a train whistle blew. There was a faint stench in the wind, emanating from the corpse on the river bank.

I crammed my hat down on my head, picked up a rusty flywheel from the bed of the truck, and lobbed it into the heap of metal in front of the cave.

"ANYBODY IN THERE," I yelled. "I'M CLOSIN'ER UP." I threw a few more pieces of junk on the pile.

"Eh - by God," I heard a voice shout from back in the cavern.

About a minute later a creature emerged the likes of which I'd never seen. When someone had pointed out the fabled Jean Goiffon in that speakeasy years before, I'd glimpsed a misshapen but snappily-dressed fellow who hid much of his hideous mug under the wide brim of his lid.

The brute that pawed his way through the junk toward me now was clad in naught but patched corduroy pants, and a ragged sweater with sleeves far too short for his long, heavily-muscled arms. His tangled locks partially obscured his forehead, but the rest of his grotesque mush was visible, and a frightening sight it was. As he drew nearer I could see the web of burst vessels that criss-crossed his huge, pitted beezer. Hairy warts erupted from his craggy cheeks. He had to turn sideways to maneuver his massive shoulders through the narrow lane he'd cleared through the scrap.

He walked right up and gave me a shove. It wasn't much of a push, but I could feel the power behind it. I was eight inches taller than him but he'd have torn me apart in a fair fight, that was certain. I patted the equalizer in my overcoat pocket for reassurance.

"Hey, take it easy," I said. "I'm gettin' rid of a load here. I yelled to see if you was in there, didn't I?"

"Tek zat crap away from here!" he said. He glowered at me from behind his bushy brows. "G'wan!"

"Hey, hey, I'm on my way."

I held my empty hands out, and turned toward the truck. I could feel him right at my back as I opened the door, but once I had a foot in the cab it was easy to pull the gun without him noticing. I made sure the door was partially closed between us before I showed it to him.

"Jig's up Goiffon," I said. "Where's the kid?"

He went for his boot in a flash, and had the hilt of a knife in his hand before I squeezed the trigger. The little pistol made a big noise that echoed so emphatically it sounded as if I'd shot again. The bullet rattled around the scrap pile.

"I'll kill'ya," I told him. I drew a bead on his huge chest.

"Zat's not much of a gon."

"Got a lotta bullets in it though."

A few seconds passed, then he tossed the knife aside. I kicked the door of the truck open, and stepped out carefully.

"Turn around," I said. "That's right. Now keep your hands straight out in front of you." I approached cautiously and put the muzzle of the pistol against the back of his head.

"Lead the way. Walk slow and careful. One wrong move I'll shoot."

I instructed him to make sure his head stayed in contact with the nose of the pistol, but I pulled back a few inches as we got underway. I was trembling so badly I figured he'd feel it, and be emboldened to make a move. It was a combination of things - the dank darkness, the eerie flickering light that came from somewhere inside, and the monstrous creature in front of me.

I had to duck in order to make my way, but Goiffon fit nicely into the passage - vertically. Horizontally his shoulders almost filled it. His knuckles practically dragged on the soft sand beneath our feet.

The passage turned, and all at once we were in a chamber filled with dim light emanating from a dozen or so candles placed around on boulders. Icicles of limestone hung from the ceiling. It was noticeably warmer than the outdoors. A candle sat in a pool of wax on a huge round of log that served as a table.

A child with a round face, a button nose and curly bangs sat on a rock alongside the table. She had a crayon in her hand, and there was drawing paper on the makeshift table. I'd imagined her running to me with tears of joy on her face. Instead she gave me a slightly reproachful look.

"Why are you pointing that gun at Uncle Jean," she asked.

"Is ok," said Goiffon. "Your papa send zis guy."

"Did this man hurt you, darling?" I asked.

"No," she replied, with surprising poise. "Why are you asking me that?"

"Just wondered."

She began drawing again. "Uncle Jean plays scissors paper rock with me," she informed me. "We're hiding."

Goiffon walked over to a niche in the wall of the cavern. He grabbed a bottle he had stashed in there, took a swig, and sat down in the sand. "So, what now?" he asked.

"What's in the bottle?"

A smile crossed that ugly mug of his. He passed it over.

I sat down in the sand, which was deep enough so I sunk right into it, and took a snort. It had a hint of sweetness, not the sour burn of the stuff I was used to. When I think back on this whole strange episode with the fixer, that's the thing I remember best - the several new tastes my shanty palate encountered. I held the bottle up to the light.

"What is this stuff? Where do you get it?"

"Brandy," he grunted, and shook his head. "I don't get it no more. Mike LeDoucer, he make zis." He looked over at the little girl, who was concentrating on her art. "Zat bastard her papa had him killed," he whispered.

That seemed a terrible waste of talent. "Why?" I asked.

Goiffon shrugged. "Mike, he sell what he make. Her papa say no more you sell speakeasy, no more you sell your friends. Sell only me. Mike say no. One day, bang. Zat's it."

"That why you snatched the kid?"

He nodded. "I tink maybe I'm gonna kill'er... he shrugged, and passed the bottle over.

I took another taste. It was mellow and smooth. And this had been a long, long day.

"Do me a favor, Goiffon. If I relax, don't try to grab this pistol. You'd only get yourself shot and that would upset the kid."

"I don't shoot nobody. I stab'em."

"Cave their heads in with a two by four too, don'cha?"

I told him about the 'bo who was ready to turn him in for twenty bucks. He denied doing it, although he owned up to a few run-ins with the bums, which had left him with a dim view of their life style.

"Ze wans wiz some brain, zey're gone for winter. Zese wans, zey're too fuggin' stupid to leave. Too dronk. Look in zat dead wan's pocket, I'm bet zere is no twanny buck. Zey kill each other quick for less."

Sounded reasonable to me. Whatever visions I'd had of marching him downtown to face justice were fading. Our conversation rambled, as hoochers' will. He told me about life in Little Canada, which sounded like paradise. All the wine and brandy you could drink, good food, though I had to take his word on that because I couldn't understand the names of the dishes. Best of all, he said, the girls out there were so warm-hearted they even slept with a clunk like him.

After a while the kid put her head down on the log and bunked. Goiffon walked over to a pile of blankets, grabbed a few, and made a little bed in the sand for her. He put her down, and wrapped her nice and snug.

"You should get outta here now, Goiffon," I said. "I'll let her sleep, doze myself for a few hours, then bring her downtown. You can be long gone by then."

A big grin spread over his homely map. "I knew you wouldn't bringin me in."

"How?"

"You got kind face."

"This hadda end some time."

"Tell ze troot, I'm glad is over."

He gathered up a few things, including a foot long dagger that was ducked in the same niche where the bottle was sitting.

"Look at zis, he said, and he flung it end over end at the log table. It stuck and quivered, about six inches deep. "Could 'a hit'chu when I got ze brandy, eh?"

"Yup. We spared each other." - I noticed some marking on the log where it penetrated. "How'd you get that log in here?"

"Was back in ze cave, half bury in sand."

He pulled the knife out, tucked it into his boot, took one more sip of brandy, and gave me the dregs.

"Good lock," he said.

"Good luck to you, Goiffon."

His back spanned the width of the passage for a moment, and he was gone. I heard the junk at the entrance clanking faintly as he made his way through. Somebody told me he showed up in St. Paul again in the 40s, but I heard about it after the fact and far away, so I don't know if it was true.

Well, I'm rescuing a maiden, I thought, but there goes my chance to slay a monster. I'd been thinking about capturing Goiffon from the moment Tommy uttered his name. Frustration at not being able to work on Margaret Thornton's case was part of it, but his ugly puss was probably the real reason. He must've spent half his life dealing with people who wanted to do him dirt for that same reason.

Such were my thoughts as I drifted off in Carter's Cave.

⨍AME

It was still dark when I pulled up in front of headquarters."I've got somethin' for Tommy," I told the copper at the desk.

"Best leave it with me. He won't be in for quite a while."

"Can't do that. How's about givin' him a call."

He explained that waking the chief was a bad career move. I didn't doubt it. Given the moral balancing act Eternal Tommy performed every day, he either wrestled with insomnia until the wee hours, or used a big dose of Dr. McDonough's elixir to summon the sandman.

"Believe me, he'll want to hear about this," I said.

"You call him then. Here, be my guest." He handed me the receiver.

"Got his number handy?"

He wrote it out and excused himself to go to the men's room. I think he expected the phone to explode. It rang about ten times before Tommy picked up. He didn't say hello. He said; "This better be important."

"It's Martin. You should come down here to headquarters. I got something you're gonna wanna deal with personally."

"Jesus! Dead or alive?"

"Alive, but dead to the world. She's out in the front seat of a truck I borrowed - never mind. Just come on."

I don't think ten minutes passed before he arrived. I was back behind the wheel by then, and the Gleeman kid was sitting up beside me rubbing her eyes. Tommy was effusive in his congratulations as we bundled her into his office. We kept her wrapped up so the underlings wouldn't see her. I gave him the pistol, and told him about the truck and how I'd drawn Goiffon out of the cave.

"I knew you could do it, Martin," he said.

I knew he was lying, but that's the drill on such occasions. I had a chip to call in, the only important thing from my perspective.

"You've done yourself proud, m'boy," he said. "Anything I can do for you right now?"

"Nah. I gotta grab a nap before I take the truck back and collect my jalop." I handed him the envelope. "There's twenty nine large in here. I hadda leave one for a deposit in order to get the truck and the junk. I'll get it back later today. You gonna call Gleeman?"

"In half an hour or so."

"Ok then, see'ya around."

"Thanks, Martin. I'll remember this."

As would I.

Dawn was breaking when I rattled my way down Ivy, and parked in front of Mrs. Dunn's rooming house. The paper was on the porch. I didn't bother bringing it in. I picked my way through the clutter in my little room, and flopped on the bed.

Sleep came immediately. And so it seemed did the insistent knock on my door that woke me. When I opened my eyes the sun had risen just high enough to shine through the window.

"YEAH YEAH!

It was Jack Moylan, smiling like he'd just done over Al Capone. His expression sobered when he saw my place.

"Jayzuz, Martin, it looks like the bottom of a hoor's handbag here," he said. "Tommy wants'ye."

"Tommy! Jesus Christ, what does he think, I work for the department? Every time I turn around it's Tommy this, Tommy that."

"Ah, but it's the great Leon Gleeman requires your presence this time. First thing he's gonna do is tell you to keep the cabbage you put down for the junk. C'mon, it'll be worth your while."

That woke me up. "What time is it?" I asked.

"Nine-fifteen. - Up with'ye now. It'll be over in an hour or so, and you'll have a pocket full'a cash."

I went down the hall and made myself presentable, slapped on an overcoat and a nice felt lid. The day was so bright it hurt, with the low November sun pouring through the leafless trees unimpeded. We sped down Rice Street, siren blaring, a grin a mile wide on Jack's face. You'd have thought he was the one collecting a thousand berries. I assumed we were headed for headquarters, but we pulled up in front of the St. Paul Hotel, which made sense when I thought about it. Gleeman ran his domain from a suite he kept there.

"You comin' in?" I asked.

"No, Tommy said no coppers. The press'll be there."

Press? That didn't quite register. It was too early. I passed through the revolving door with the vague intention of asking the desk clerk where Mr. Gleeman's rooms could be found. There was a hullabaloo in the lobby. A mockey with a big cigar in his puss grabbed me.

"McDonough?" he said, and before I could answer he took my arm and guided me through a mob of fellows, several of whom had cameras hung around their necks.

"I'm Jake Silverman," said my escort, "Leon's drumma' - hey, watch it now! Lemme troo!"

We slipped between a bellhop and a woman in a big fur coat, both of them gawking at me, past the registration desk and into the lobby proper. An impeccably dressed, middle-aged fellow with fleshy cheeks, crinkly eyes and a dimpled chin, rose from a leather chair. He put out his hand to shake mine.

"Leon Gleeman," he said. "I can never thank you enough, Mr. McDonough. Never."

Gleeman was about five foot five, and built like a little bull. A neatly folded handkerchief peeked from the breast pocket of his tailored blue suit.

"Let's say something to the press, then we can talk alone for a few minutes," he said.

"C'meah, c'meah," said the drummer to the reporters. "Mistuh Gleeman has a few woids."

The reporters gathered round, notebooks in hand. Flashbulbs popped. The fixer cleared his throat. He reached up, and draped an arm around my shoulders.

"Gentlemen, this is Mr. Martin McDonough, the best private investigator in St. Paul, in the whole world maybe. Without him our little Frimme, who is upstairs right now, wouldn't be with us to- to-day ... excuse me, pardon me."

He pulled the hanky out, dabbed at his eyes. Then he stepped back, and looked up at me.

"I could kiss him," he said.

"Need a glass'a watah or somethin', Leon?" asked the drummer.

"No, I'm fine." Gleeman beamed up at me, and resumed his speech.

"I asked you fellows to come over here because I want you meet Mr. McDonough, and I want your readers to know that if they ever need any help of a personal nature, something that requires discretion, and smarts," - he tapped his noggin with his finger - "somebody who's tough as nails when that's necessary - well, you fellows know that I have friends in high places, that I can get things done." - He paused. The reporters laughed nervously. - "And I'm here to tell you that I asked around for the very best, and I was told 'Martin McDonough', and isn't it something that in this America of ours, a Jewish fellow like myself can call on an Irisher, and what a team, eh? The Jews and the Irish!"

He grabbed my hand and raised it.

"Was it Goiffon who kidnapped her?" shouted a reporter.

"Mmm, I don't know." I replied.

"Didn't you see the kidnapper?".

"Well, I was there to get Mr. Gleeman's daughter back, and -"

Gleeman nodded at the little drummer, who stepped quickly between myself and the minions of the fourth estate. "We're done here," he said. "Tanks for comin."

He shooed them toward the door like so many flies.

"You a drinking man, Martin?" asked Gleeman, when they'd all disappeared.

"Well -"

"A little early, eh." He motioned toward a leather sofa, and took his seat in the chair again. "So, what did happen with Goiffon?"

I shrugged. "He got away. I was concentrating on -"

"Forget it. We got Frimme, that's the important thing. My darling wife Helen May is upstairs right now holding our daughter in her arms"- tears welled up again, but he pulled himself together. - "Chief Brown tells me you had to make a deposit on the truck you used."

I nodded in the affirmative.

"That money is yours. Don't say no, I won't hear of it."

"Thank you."

"It's the least I can do. I'd like to have you up for dinner, Martin, you and your wife."

"Uh, I'm not married."

"Family is a great comfort, Martin, a harbor in the storm. Bring a lady friend. Tomorrow night. What do you say?"

"Well -"

"Please. My wife wants to meet you. She hates situations like this or she'd have come down. We'd be honored. Six O'clock tomorrow evening sound alright?"

I looked at him carefully. Button nose, round cheeks, big mutable eyes. His expression flicked from disarming to disconcerting moment to moment. His disappointment that I didn't bring him Goiffon's scalp was just as obvious as his gratitude, and those who knew him said a quick temper and a brutal nature lurked beneath his cordial exterior. I'd have just as soon taken his scratch and left it at that, but the moment he uttered his invitation the wheels started turning. I'd call Margaret, tell her I wanted to drop by to give her an update, and invite her to come along for a fancy dinner. More or less as an afterthought.

"Ok Mr. Gleeman," I said.

"Call me Leon. Please. Now, if you'll excuse me, I have to mind the store." He winked.

He put an arm around me as he walked me toward the door. "You know, I'm considering running for Mayor. What do you think?"

What I thought was, it's unthinkable. He was crooked enough, but he wasn't Irish. I mumbled some pleasantries and we shook hands at the door.

I walked over to the Town Talk. The morning crowd was gone, leaving me alone at the counter with a coffee and a newspaper someone had left there.

"GERMANY ARMING, ENGLAND WARNS" was the headline. According to the limey Prime Minister, a fellow named Churchill; "A reign of terror exists in Germany in order to keep secret the feverish and terrible preparations they are making."

Jack Dempsey had made his de facto retirement official. It was front page news. Queried who among the challengers could lick Max Baer, he replied that the title belonged to Maxie as long as he wanted it. "As a fighter he could rule for twenty years," Dempsey said. "The only thing that can beat him is the forced inactivity that comes with being a title holder."

Who forces it? That was my question. Jimmy McLarnin, the welterweight champ, had taken two out of three fifteen rounders from Barney Ross that past year. As soon as they finished one fight, they went into training for the next. What a team, the Jews and the Irish. Between them they probably needed an army of unemployed smokes to haul their cash to the bank. Jerk claimed all three bouts were fixed. For argument's sake I asserted the view that McLarnin took a dive once, and beat Ross fair and square twice.

"CHARLIE WARD HELPS FORMER CONVICTS MAKE GOOD" blared a headline in section two.

Further down the page was a little item about federal Marshals serving 54 subpoenas to prospective witnesses in an investigation of tax evasion by Mr. Leon Gleeman, "a downtown business man."

I tipped the waitress generously, and basked in the glow of her gratitude as she handed me my coat. Everybody was grateful to Martin McDonough today.

As soon as I walked out I encountered the unemployed. They broke into two groups during the Depression, those who faded apologetically into the woodwork and those who displayed their poverty in order to leverage a mooch. The street was crowded with the latter as I made my way to the trolley stop. There were men standing on the corner with their pants' pockets hanging inside out in silent supplication - "Hoover flags" in the parlance of the day. And making their slow way down Wabasha Street was a line of "Hoover Carts" - automobiles hitched to horses for lack of gas money.

I obliged a few flag-flyers with some change, and waited in a doorway out of the bitter wind for my trolley. The sky was clouding up.

I couldn't tell whether Kravetsky was happy to get his truck back or not. He handed over the cabbage with a sigh, graciously accepted the ten spot I offered for the junk I'd tossed, and we parted on good terms.

Margaret agreed to a meeting at her house at 5:30 that evening. It was a little later than I'd hoped - I'm usually bellied up to the bar by then - but I was satisfied nonetheless.

The theme of the day continued to be my heroics. The egghead with two first names almost fell out of his chair when I dropped by and told him about the big round of log in the cave.

"It was rough-hewn," I told him. "Not done with a saw. Thought you might be interested."

He speculated that it could be the very table that the Indians and Carter used when they drew up their agreement. Seemed a bit of a stretch, but what really surprised me was the fact that he'd never been in the cave.

"One investigator to another," I told him, "you need to get your hands dirty."

A little tip from the man of the hour.

I was back at Mrs. Dunn's by noon, sleeping the sleep of the just. When I awoke I had 45 minutes to shave, shower and get to Margaret's. The wad of bills I'd all but forgotten tumbled out when I picked up my pants. I stuffed it behind the radiator with the rest of my ready cash.

I pulled a new shirt out of the drawer, dropped the cellophane packaging on the floor, put it on, grabbed my topcoat, and headed for the Hatch Street home of the Gallaghers. Snow was falling, lightly, but it didn't melt when it hit the pavement.

* * *

Margaret greeted me at the door with an announcement that explained her look of mild alarm.

"Mom's not home yet. She knew you were coming, so she shouldn't be long."

"Should I, uh -"

"Of course not. Sit down right here," she said, and pointed to the dining room table. "I'll get us some tea."

She headed straight for the kitchen, while I surveyed the spotless and neatly appointed surroundings. There was time for a good long look because it was clear that Margaret wouldn't be joining me until mom arrived.

Pictures of Jesus, FDR, and a solemn-looking man with a dark moustache whom I took to be the late Mr. Gallagher, hung on the wall. A winged sofa and two overstuffed chairs with doilies on their arms were arranged around the Philco. A grandfather clock with a gleaming brass pendulum ticked off the seconds. Lace curtains were pulled away from the front window, and tied neatly to the side with white satin sashes. Nary a smudge besmirched the view of the falling snow.

The kettle began to whistle. I could see Margaret through the kitchen door, bustling over to the counter where a teapot was waiting, and bending to pour. Her dress molded to her slender hips, and hitched up high enough to drape around her svelte calves. She was lean and curvy, like a rotogravure flapper.

"Looks like winter's here," I said.

"Looks that way," she agreed.

"Do you mind if I call you Margaret," I asked, impulsively.

"Sure. Just don't call me Maggie. At least not in front of mom. She thinks it's common."

The front door opened. In strode mom, newspaper in hand.

"And who've we here," she said. "Could this be th' celebrated Mr. McDonough?"

Before I could reply she held up the afternoon paper and pointed to a front page picture of myself looking sheepish but snappy, hat at a rakish angle. Gleeman beamed up at me.

I'd never been famous before, but I sensed an advantage in acting as if it were nothing special.

"Margaret, are ye about fetchin' tea for th' gentleman!" said Mrs. Gallagher.

"Yes I am, mom," she replied, and in she waltzed, tea pot and cups in hand.

Mom took off her coat, and plopped herself down at the dining room table, leaving Margaret the option of seating herself next to me or mom. She sat down next to mom, and poured tea with a demure smile. She looked at the paper, as if to reassure herself that the mug in the picture and the mug at the table were the same mug.

Mom was a stout version of her daughter, raven-colored hair with a few streaks of silver, porcelain skin, fine features. The same slightly buck teeth made for a similarly fetching smile when Margaret introduced her. Meaghan was her name.

"We've not had such a famous and well-connected fillow in our home, have we dear," said Meaghan.

Margaret glanced at me conspiratorially, as if to say all the fuss will soon be over and meanwhile a man of my stature would surely know how to deal with it. Mom summarized my heroics for her daughter. She offered me biscuit and jam, which I turned down politely.

She told me that my reputation had preceded me in the Gallagher home, even before I hit the front page. She'd heard of me through the grapevine at city hall, where she worked. She didn't say what she did there. Cleaning woman, I guessed. Parish connections after the mister died.

"How's the investigation coming?" asked Margaret. "I'm on pins and needles."

"I'm making some progress. Your suspicions about Ward are well-founded. Not that I've confirmed'em to my satisfaction yet, but..."

I let it ride, and nodded meaningfully.

"Gosh," she said, "it would be so, so great if you could - what did you call it? 'Get the goods on Charlie Ward.' I'd be the happiest girl in St. Paul."

She put her elbows on the table, wove her fingers into a cradle to rest her chin, and looked right into my eyes.

"I'm not joshing, Martin," she said. "<u>The</u> happiest."

My groin stirred. I was on the verge of inviting her to dinner at the Gleeman suite, when Meaghan addressed me.

"There's talk iv a quare thing down t'city hall. They say that fillow there" - she pointed at Gleeman's picture in the newspaper - "might be runnin' fr mayor."

"Yeah, I heard that rumor."

She shook her head slowly, as if she were contemplating something sad beyond words. "A Sheeney in th' mayor's office," she said. "What's th' world comin' to."

"Oh, mom," said Margaret.

"Hushhh now, don't ye be 'oh mommin' me. Don't ye agree, Mr. McDonough -"

"Martin," I interjected.

"Don't ye agree now, Martin, that Jews and the like are steppin' in everywhere our kind belong."

"Mom!" said Margaret.

"Hush!" said mom. "Margaret's a headstrong girl," she informed me. "Ye can't tell her a thing, niver could. I said runnin' off with a Protestant would come to no good, didn't I? And politics is somethin' th' likes've Gleeman would do well to stay out've. Don't ye agree, Martin?"

"Well, I've never given it much thought."

"But now that ye've considered it, don't ye agree?" she persisted.

"Well, yeah, I guess - "

"Do ye know him well?" she inquired.

"No, just met him. I'm having dinner with him tomorrow night though." I glanced over at Margaret. "He wants to thank me."

"Well he should," said mom. "Ye saw to his dotter. He's some-thin' of an unsavory character, but I s'pose ye meet plenty'o them in your line of work. We don't envy ye that, do we Margaret?"

Margaret didn't reply. I think unsavory characters intrigued her. Nevertheless, and with Jerk's counsel firmly in mind, I decided not to invite her to dinner. It made me a little uneasy that mom was asking all the questions, but maybe this was how dames like Margaret acted in situation like this. Mom had to give her the green light.

"More tea?" said Margaret.

"No thanks. I have to leave. I'm meeting someone."

"A lady friend?" said mom.

"Business. I do a lotta work at night."

That appeared to satisfy her. She made some inquiries of a practical nature about my work (I assured I was well paid for my services), and even asked a question I get pretty regularly.

"Did'ye ever kill a man, Martin?"

I assured I hadn't. She nodded, and asked if I could give them any details about Ward's possible involvement.

"I guess it wouldn't hurt. A radio broadcaster who criticized Floyd Olson was murdered too, and I've discovered that Ward was discussing things with an east coast gangster around the time he was killed."

They both caught their breath at that revelation.

"Do you think you're in any danger?" Margaret asked.

"Well, there's some danger, but I'll be ok."

"Ye're a brave man," said mom. Margaret nodded her agree-ment.

"Could'ye be tellin' us who this gangster is?" mom asked.

"Name Bugsy Siegel mean anything to you?"

They shook their heads no, then gazed in wonderment as I filled them in on Murder Inc., and the Charlie Ward/Bugsy connection. I was surprised to discover as I spoke just how intertwined their lives were. It sounded as if Bugsy should've been best man at Ward's recent wedding.

"Ha!" said mom, when I finished connecting the dots. "Ward passes himsilf off as a respictable fillow an' he's nothin' but a common highwayman. And as fer this Bugsy, it goes to show!"

I wasn't sure what it went to show, but agreed nonetheless.

"I have to excuse myself," I said. "Nice meeting you, Mrs. Gallagher. Nice to see you again, Margaret."

"Been a plisure," said mom. "See him to the door now, darlin'."

Margaret walked ahead of me, affording me one more opportunity to ogle her lovely figure. She grasped my hand in both of hers at the door.

"I know you'll come through for me, Martin," she said. "Your uncle told us you never fail."

"Jerk's my biggest booster." I tipped my hat.

Night had fallen. Snow was still coming down. I was oddly relieved to be out of there. It was slow going on the side streets, which gave me an opportunity to review what had just transpired. At first I passed off my discomfort to the imperious mom, but it wasn't that simple. I think it was something about the ritual I'd plodded through. It made my skin crawl.

Margaret was beautiful alright, but Mag was a lot easier to talk to. She never did ask me down to the boxcar to meet her mother. Of course it was apples and oranges. The thought of marrying one or the other made me want a drink - real bad.

The snow was falling harder by the time I got to Rice Street. It was hard to see, but the Tin Cup's sign, which featured two light bulbs that had burned out the day after Prohibition was lifted, guided me. A throng of cheering hoochers waving newspapers greeted me when I walked in. I couldn't pay for a drink. Jack Moylan was especially effusive in his praise. He led a chorus of congratulations that rose again each time I tried to retreat toward the table where Mag was seated.

At one point Jimmy Brennan walked by and patted me on the back. - "I need to talk to you, Jimmy," I said. "You know where to find me," he replied. I did indeed. - Inside curve, second horseshoe, right under the barman's nose.

I never got to him that evening, though. When the frenzy subsided I found myself in a position to cut Maggie out of that flock of frails she ran with, and guide her to a quiet corner.

"Whatta guy," she said. SNAP went the gum. "Gonna buy me one?"

"Yeah, if you can get the waitress back here. If I go up to the bar again we might not see each other for a while."

"YOO-HOO!" She pointed to her empty glass. "Geez, Martin, everybody thinks you're the nuts. I was shoppin' with Sheila Dunn before I come in here and all she could talk about was Martin Martin Martin. I was pretty proud'a ya too."

She put her hand on my leg. Had fame earned me a reprieve?

"C'mon, let's get outta here," she said, after she finished her drink.

THE LATE MANFRED GOTTFRIED

A fellow called a "valet" offered to park my car when Mag and I pulled up in front of the St. Paul Hotel next evening. I was confused.

"It's a free service, sir," he said. "When you check out you just give us the receipt and we get your car for you. That way you won't have to walk through all this snow."

"We're not checkin' in. We're dining with Mr. Gleeman."

"Doesn't make a bit of difference, sir. Would you like me to park it for you?"

"Uhh, yeah."

Maggie was impressed by the service. I figured it was about fifty-fifty he was a car thief, but what the hell. I'd had that bucket for a long time and I could buy two more just like it for the cash Gleeman had given me.

We were met at the door to the fixer's suite by a guy with a prominent bulge under his suit coat. He was stocky with porcine features and elfin ears. He motioned us to enter with a sweep of his bowler hat, revealing a totally hairless head.

Gleeman himself took our coats. His wife was a little, round, doll-like creature, barely five feet tall, with a nose that was small and buttonish like her husband's. She threw her arms around me, buried her face in my starched white shirt, and cried warm tears of thanks. Then she took Maggie off to the far end of an elaborately set table. Within moments the two of them were gabbing like they'd known each other forever.

Our host sat at the head of the table. His bruno pulled out a chair for me on his boss's right, where I had the view.

The suite looked on to Rice Park and the library building, which shone white as the fallen snow in the moonlight. Baldy stationed himself right behind Gleeman, back to the wall, bowler in hand. I could hear someone fussing in the adjoining room. Soon a woman in a waitress's uniform came out and gave us each a highball.

"You have a real treasure there, Martin," said Gleeman, nodding toward Maggie. "Such a dumpling. She's lovely, friendly, sweet. Helen May took to her immediately, and my wife is an excellent judge of character."

The two of them were giggling about something. They'd certainly hit it off.

The evening before I'd spent the night at Maggie's place for the first time, which pleased her. When we awoke I told her I'd been invited to Gleeman's for dinner, and I'd like to bring her with me. That made her so happy that she forgot to bring up her ultimatum. I'd almost put it out of my mind, but now my host reminded me.

"Marry her, that's my advice," said Gleeman. "Forgive me, but I feel so strongly about this, Martin. Marry her and love her. That's what makes life worthwhile. I worship the ground Helen May walks on. I love to wrap her in furs, and drape her in jewels. Every time I look at her I want to kiss her."

She was bedecked alright. Whenever she moved, something sparkled.

"A terrible thing, this kidnaping business," said Gleeman. "That bastard Joe Schaefer and his pal whose name escapes me kidnaped my Helen May, two years ago."

"I didn't know," I said, although I'd heard a rumor.

"We kept it quiet. I was out of my mind with fear and anger, Martin. It could have gone badly."

I could see he wanted to confide, so I prompted him.

"This Schaefer called two days after they snatched her, said he wanted twenty thousand dollars. He wouldn't tell me who he was, of course, but by then I'd found out who had her. I didn't know where though, just as it was with our little Frimme, so I went along. I had Slobo bring the money." He jerked his thumb back over his shoulder at baldy.

"You had a message for Mr. Schaefer, didn't you Slobo."

"Hed messich," he agreed.

"Tell Martin what it was."

"Tell him, 'I kill you if you don't show me right away where is Mrs. Gleeman.'"

Gleeman smiled. "And what didn't you tell him?"

"Thet I kill him anyway."

Which confirmed the rumor. When Joe Schaefer and Hector Cummings were found dead in a car near Sunfish Lake, the official story was a falling out among roscoes, perp unknown. But the talk around was of a kidnaping, and the wrath of Leon Gleeman. Nothing remained mysterious to Martin McDonough very long, not in those days.

"They say kidnaping will become more frequent now that Prohibition's over," I said. "Lotsa hard guys with nothing to do."

"There's only one way to stop it."

He spotted my empty glass and called for another.

"It's a slow process," he continued, "but it works. You pay what the kidnapper wants, get your loved one back, then you find the sonofabitch and take all his money away. You take what he stole from you, plus any other cash he has, then you take everything else of value you can get your hands on, car, jewelry, burn his house down if he has one."

Gleeman leaned toward me, warming to his topic.

"When you get through with this rotten bastard he has nothing left. Then you cut off a finger or two, or maybe his balls, for good measure, and you send him out into the world to tell his friends about it. But we couldn't do that with Schaefer and his pal, could we Slobo?"

"No. Too bed."

"Tell Martin what happened."

"Him and other zeggert, they run away like girls. What I can do? Hef to shoot both. Then I drive out in country in their car, in woods, and leave'em." He threw up his hands, which required a bit of juggling with the bowler.

"Then I walk, three four kilometer beck. Is hard."

"Slobo is from Rumania," said Gleeman, as if that explained everything.

Slobo smiled broadly, and winked. He was smiling at us, but I believe he was winking at Mag.

"Schaefer thought he had a deal with me," said Gleeman. "I never said so, mind you. I told him 'I want my wife back, and I'll give you anything you require in order to get her.' We never discussed what would happen after that. My intention all along was to kill him and make an example of his partner. That's what I advised the Bremer woman to do, her and that Kraut chauffeur of her's. She looked at me like she'd stepped in a pile of horseshit. You can't tell those people anything. Let me ask you something, Martin. Just out of curiosity. You must have had the drop on Goiffon. How did he get away?"

He saw the look on my face, and immediately reassured me.

"I want you to understand something. You protected my family. I tried but I was helpless. They told me that monster had my darling Frimme in a cave somewhere. What cave? I was a kid when I came to St. Paul, and my friends and I used to play in the caves over on the West Side. There are hundreds of them. I was at a loss. I went to Chief Brown, he told me had a man for the job, and that was you, Martin. You found the cave, you found Frimme, God knows how, I won't even ask. You have your secrets I have mine, but there is nothing that could make me feel anything but gratitude and comradeship toward you. So tell me, how did he get away?"

I told him. He seemed to understand, even allowed how a person who isn't in it for the ransom presents a different problem revenge-wise, lesson-wise maybe, but a problem nonetheless. That seemed to be his attitude.

"As for Goiffon's friend, LeDoucer, I tried to do business with him," he said, with an expression that summarized eloquently the cost of refusing to do business with Leon Gleeman.

About then the bell on the dumb waiter rang. Soon the waitress wheeled a cart in, and the feast commenced. It began with little two-handled cups of broth that you picked up and slurped. The broth had a winey, meaty taste.

"They finally got it right," said Gleeman, which launched his wife into an explanation of the difficulties inherent in teaching a hotel chef traditional cooking.

"You tell them how many bones to use, they don't believe you," she said. "Me, I don't see the problem. The stockyard is a few miles from here. You can smell it when the wind is right. Buy bones, I keep saying. Pounds and pounds of bones. Bones are important."

"Oh yeah," said Maggie. "My mother, may she rest in peace, used bones. Sometimes that's all we had for stew. Bones and water."

"Poor dear. Tonight you'll eat. Martin, do you feed this girl right?"

"I do indeed," I lied. That was the first time I'd ever eaten with her.

"Martin bought me this dress," said Maggie.

"He's a treasure," said Helen May. "Such a hero."

The next course was bone-on rump roast, a little rare for my taste, but moist, and with a spiciness that I couldn't identify. When we'd each been served, Slobo approached the table. The bowler was on his head for this operation, which began with him stripping all the remaining meat off the knuckle bone. Then he took a little silver hammer out of his pocket, held the bone up, and rapped it sharply.

Plop! Out came a big blob of marrow. He dished us each up a small portion. It had the consistency of pudding, and a taste somewhere between blood and char. Maggie devoured her's like she'd been waiting all her life to get her hands on it. I couldn't help wondering how Margaret would've handled this unfamiliar entrail.

Wine was poured, broiled potatoes were served, then cabbage that was both sweet and sour, something I'd never tasted before and I thought I'd eaten every form of cabbage known to man.

The fixer held his knife like a pencil. He cut precise little pieces of meat and chewed them carefully. The wine kept coming until dessert, which was some kind of sticky pastry. When we'd polished that off he asked me to join him at a table that had been placed by the window. We drank coffee and brandy and talked.

"So, tell me about your work, Martin, if you don't mind my asking."

I wondered momentarily about the wisdom of confiding, but I'm rarely circumspect. I told him about of a few of my early triumphs, and quickly brought him up to speed on Margaret's problem. The possibility of Ward's involvement intrigued him. He folded his hand and thought about it.

"Charlie Ward is a very ambitious man," he said. "It must have broken his heart when Floyd Olson died. But murdering a journalist? There are other ways to shut people up. Pay them off. Threaten someone they care about."

"This Thornton was a fanatic," I explained. "There was no shutting him up, that's my impression. And Ward, of course, had motive. I think he had another journalist killed for the same reason."

"Really? Who?"

"Howard Godfrey."

He smiled. "Ah yes, Godfrey," he said. "His real name was Manfred Gottfried, you know."

"No, I didn't."

"He was from Germany," said Gleeman. "Strange people the Krauts. They have a real gift for the technical, the mechanical, but socially they're malignant half-wits."

He rose from his chair. "The coincidence is too much. I have to show you something, Martin."

He instructed Slobo to take care of the ladies, and informed them that we were going to his study. Helen May had taken out her jewel box. She was wowing Maggie with an array of brooches that she'd laid on the table. The two of them hardly noticed our departure.

We took the elevator to the basement. Gleeman led the way down a dimly lit corridor to an old storeroom. He opened it with a key and turned on a light to reveal a desk, a bookshelf, and boxes containing what appeared to be documents and records. He opened a locked cupboard built into the wall, pulled out a little machine with two sprockets - it was about the size of a Depression lunch pail - and plugged it into a socket.

It immediately began to emit a menacing hum.

"This is an example of Kraut ingenuity," he said. "It's called a magneto-graph. Are you familiar with recording technology?"

"Can't say that I am."

"You may want to give it some study. I imagine it could come in handy in your profession."

He pulled a crate out of the cupboard, sorted through dozens of spools of what appeared to be metallic ribbon, and selected one.

He placed the spool on a sprocket, unwound a foot or so, threaded it through some slots, wound a few inches on to a second spool, and flipped a switch. The ribbon began to snake through the slots. A scratchy voice came out of the box.

"Manfred Gottfried," said Gleeman.

"I am neither Democrat nor Republican," Howard Godfrey proclaimed, in a tinny screech. "Nor, fellow citizens, am I a poooisonous liberal Bolshevik! I AM a God-fearing, militant American vigillannnte, and an enemy of Jew internationalists who have NOOOO country, and therefore cannot be patriots. And I am the eternal foe of those TWO-FOLD more children of hell, the gentile traitors who betray country and race, among them the bootleggers' bootlicker, Floyd B. Olson, a man whose greed for the sheeney shekel debases the state he governs! Yes fellow citizens, every day that he sits in the Governor's chair is another day of shame!"

Godfrey's voice, despite being scratchy and at times barely audible, was bursting with rage. Gleeman was visibly pained listening to him.

"To those whose minds are not closed, our real enemies are NOT far to seek," said Godfrey. "Their own words confess their treason. Talmuuuudic quotations say Jewry is living in a state of war with all other peoples, and the Zionist Herzl admitted publicly that Jews regard the gentile as the common enemy of their cursed race! So we are not aggressors, fellow patriots, we are DEFEND-ERS!"

He was spellbinding in a disturbing way. It wasn't what he was saying about mockeys, which, truth be told, I couldn't follow very well. It was the passive way you were required to take it in due to the mode of communication, coupled with the aggressive way he was blabbing it out. I could imagine that with any volume behind it that effect would have been multiplied. You'd turn off the radio and go look for a fight.

"... nor is our fair state the only repository of the Jew sickness. The origin of the sinister spirit that today animates the White House proves unmistakably that the Roosevelt administration offers patri-ots a BIO-logical as well as a political problem - " He shifted into a droning incantation - "Roosevelt Rosenberg Rosenbaum Rosenblum Rosenthal -"

"Heard enough?" asked Gleeman.

I nodded yes, and he flicked it off.

"See what I mean," he said. "Every Jew in the world had motive to kill the bastard. Now as far as this Thornton is concerned, I don't know. I never heard he hated Jews, but these rabble-rousing bastards, I don't want to say they're all the same..."

He had a point, which I contemplated on the way back to the suite. I'd neglected something fundamental in Thornton's case. I'd never read a word he'd written. I was already contemplating a visit to the library to look up the newspaper stories about the drowning of Herbert Bigelow. There was probably a stack of Thornton's yellow sheets that I could peruse at the same time.

Helen May was hanging a brooch on Maggie's neck when we got back. Gleeman complimented her on how beautiful she looked, while Helen May beamed.

"It's a little wedding present," she said. "Because I'm sure this fine young man will do the right thing."

Apparently Maggie had been confiding. She blushed. I said we ought to get going, but Gleeman wouldn't hear of it.

"I've already reserved a room," he said. "One floor above us, looking out on the park."

We spent the night between linen sheets with a down comforter to warm us. Maggie took off everything but the brooch. Next morning we lingered in the coziness and talked, laughing and enjoying ourselves without even mentioning tying the knot. It might've come to that eventually, but breakfast arrived with a knock at the door, sent by Mr. Gleeman. Afterwards we got to snuggling, and pretty soon we were playing Vatican roulette. Then we napped a while.

* * *

It was getting on toward eleven A.M. when we woke again. Time to get to work. I sent Maggie home on the streetcar, which was still running despite the snowfall, and walked across Rice Park to the library.

John Howell was sitting at his desk, biting a thumbnail.

"How's it goin', John."

He came out of his reverie long enough to nod.

"What'cha thinkin' about?"

"My sex life, Martin, if you must know. I'm reviewing it. Now that it's over."

There was a frightening thought. I'd have left without another word but I didn't want to be impolite.

"So how was it?" I inquired.

"Adequate, Martin. Sufficient unto the day was the fucking thereof."

The newspaper article about Herbert Bigelow's drowning was even sketchier than I'd remembered, a paragraph on page four. That was in sharp contrast to the front page spread the next day, when the board of Bigelow Enterprises named Charlie Ward president. The only facts I could glean were that Bigelow died, along with a fishing guide and the wife of one of his executives, when their boat over-turned on Basswood Lake, in northern Minnesota. The guide and the woman went unnamed. The woman's anonymity might have been to spare her family, but it had to be either laziness or a deliberate effort to suppress information in regards to the guide.

The Ely Observer, a weekly from up near the scene, mentioned that there had been thunderstorms in the area the day of the mishap. You couldn't tell from either article whether the bodies had been re-covered.

A few days later a cryptic obituary for Herbert Bigelow made no mention of a funeral.

Thornton's rag, The Midwest American, was full of richly de-tailed attacks on both Floyd Olson and Charlie Ward. One article was an analysis of some real estate deals between Ward and the State. Thornton claimed they were arranged by Governor Olson.

The buildings, located near the Bigelow Enterprises main plant, belonged to Ward. The Highway Department rented one of them for $4000 a month. Thornton quoted real estate experts who called that four times market rate.

"Charlie Ward, who receives more than $70,000 annually for the rental of his previously empty properties in the Midway, once served a term in the Leavenworth federal penitentiary," Thornton wrote. "There he met the late Herbert Bigelow, head of Bigelow En-terprises, who had been convicted for income tax violations. When he was released Ward came to St. Paul, where he became a manager at Bigelow Enterprises and Bigelow's trusted confidante. When Bi-gelow drowned on a fishing trip he left most of his estate to Ward. Bigelow's relatives are contesting the will, which may come up for final adjudication before the largely Olson-appointed Minnesota Su-preme Court."

Beneath the article was a picture of one of the buildings the State rented from Ward. According to the caption, it was assessed at $110,000. - "But the state pays an annual rent of $40,872, more than enough to buy the building in a few years."

I figured the buildings must have been part of Bigelow's estate. More motive to get rid of Bigelow. And having this muckraker put the whole bunco on the front page couldn't have been too pleasing either. Nor could the relentless drumbeat of invective against Olson. There was hardly an issue of The Midwest American that didn't attack him, dating back to when he was still the county attorney. The theme was always the same; Olson was a phony radical who played ball with bootleggers, and toadied to the rich.

"Eastern Publications act as if Olson will be the next president, but hundreds of thousands of progressives from all over the country wonder if he is all he's cracked up to be. Skeptics who've been in the Farmer-Labor Party since it was formed point out that he didn't begin to press for passage of reforms 'to go to the root of capitalism' until after election returns showed him that the next Legislature would be safely conservative."

I skimmed article after article full of the same allegations - appointment of ex-bootleggers to Liquor Control Commissions, lots of talk and no action on pro-labor legislation, sweetheart deals between the state and Charlie Ward - before I stumbled upon a few lines of doggerel penned by Thornton to fill some space in a 1933 issue:

"Ten thousand jews
are making booze
in endless repetition
to fill the needs
of a million swedes
who wanted prohibition."

Would some mockey take such exception to those lines that he'd want to ice the author? I didn't know, but as usual I knew someone who did.

***

The snow began to fall again. It kept falling all night and all the next day. Soon it was ten inches deep, and everybody was on foot or on horseback. Just like old times.

The second day of the storm I trudged over to Maggie's and staked her and her shopping partner Sheila for a feed. It was a tough slog. The two of them normally threw in a nickel each and split a pound of hamburger twice a week, but that night we had corned beef and cabbage.

"Shay-la," as she called herself, refused to go into Tin Cup's, so Maggie stayed home with her while I went down in hopes of running into Jimmy Brennan. He never showed though. Not many did.

"The snow has discouraged all but a determined few," said John O'Connor, as we touched glasses. "You talk to Klawitter about the Godfrey murder?"

"Yeah, isn't he somethin'? Sent his wife over to screw Herb Bigelow, and tells me about it like it's all in a day's work. Right in front'a her. Only thing bothers him, Ward didn't stick with the deal. But he does make a case that Ward had Godfrey killed."

I told him about Gleeman's magnetic recordings. John nodded. "Me old biddy (meaning his maiden aunt) sits by the radio and listens to that priest from Detroit. You should hear him go on about the kikes."

"Kinda nuts, if you ask me.

"Well, yeah," John agreed, tentatively.

The bar man asked if we wanted another round. We did.

The door opened and in walked Tim McKenna, looking like he'd been rolled in confectioner's sugar. He stomped his feet, shook his arms, and left a scattering of snow on the bar room floor that quickly turned to muddy water. His spectacles fogged so's he didn't spot us, but I called him over.

"One more here," John told the bar man.

"How'd that chain letter thing work out?" I asked Tim.

"The mob finally dispersed." He shook his head in wonderment. "People are desperate."

We discussed hard times for a while. Tim was of the opinion that the Jews were behind it. John might've agreed, being an agreeable man generally, but our previous conversation must have given him pause. - "What do you think, Martin?" he asked.

"I'd say distribution's the problem. There's no shortage of goods, but they aren't bein' distributed properly."

The two of them mulled that over. "What the hell does that mean?" Tim finally asked.

"It means there's plenty'a stuff, but people can't get their hands on it."

John asked why. I couldn't explain. The bar man put a nickel of the bar's money in the Wurlizter.

"Miss Otis regrets she's unable to lunch today," sang a tomato with a husky voice. She made it sound like a tragedy. Something - that empty chair for lunch, the whiskey, Maggie and Margaret - made me melancholy. But only momentarily.

"They're puttin' a Wurlitzer in at Kuby's," I announced.

"Take more'n that to get me into that Hun's joint," said John.

"Right," said Tim.

We'd reached an impasse vis a vis the Jews, but Huns were something we could agree on, although later in the conversation it did come out that Tim was soft on a Hun named Trudy, who, he claimed, was a friend of Maggie's.

"She comes in here sometimes," Tim said.

"Frails, now that's a different story," said John.

"A different kettle of fish," I agreed.

We got off on many a tangent as the evening progressed; the proper place for women - clearly not in a joint, although each of us was entangled in our own way with a gal from the bar; the upcoming election and the terrible duplicity of the Republicans; the relative pugilistic skills of Jimmy McLarnin, Barney Ross, and a Rice Street kid named Myron Sullivan. Tim said the local boy would lick both of'em.

"On the same night," he said, and he stood to demonstrate Sullivan's style, which required some footwork he wasn't agile enough to duplicate.

John helped him to his feet. About then I decided I'd had enough.

It must've been close to midnight when I climbed Maggie's stairs, looking forward to a warm bed and the now familiar mix of real flesh and dazzling fantasy featuring the widow Thornton, but alas, twas not to be.

"Sheila's here," Maggie explained, in a whisper. "You've gotta go home."

"You'd turn a man out in this weather?" I was genuinely incredulous.

"You'll be alright." She had an amused look on her face. "You got plenty'a anti-freeze in your radiator, I can see that."

"Aw, come on -"

"G'night." She closed the door softly, but firmly. I slunk down the stairs like a rat.

It was hard going through the snow. My head was beginning to hurt already, For a while I considered cooling my throbbing temples by burrowing into a drift and spending the night like an Eskimo's dog, but good sense overcame that impulse.

PREZ

My fame had spread as far as the synagogue. The Reds grinned and nodded when Rothman announced that I was the dick who'd found Gleeman's kid. Meyer the collar twister got close enough so I could hear him, which meant the fag in the side of his mouth almost burned my cheek.

"Good woik," he said.

Rothman agreed to have a drink with me after the social hour, and disappeared into the smoke and the crowd.

The Meyer and Sherman show was on again. Without Rothman around to mediate I was sure they'd come to blows, but they didn't. "THAT'S NUTTIN' BUT BONAPARTIST BULLSHIT!" Meyer shouted, loud enough so everybody in the place must have heard, but nobody took any notice.

I moved into a more advantageous position, and watched Tilsen and a couple palookas yakking with each other on the far side of the room. They were positioned between the mooches in the broad-brimmed hats and some more worldly-looking fellows, among them Rothman's pal Kravetsky, who was six inches taller than the rest and wearing a big coon skin coat. His coal black hair glistened with melted snow, and his distinctive laugh cut through the noise like a knife. HA-HA!

I was concentrating so hard on peering at Tilsen through the haze that I didn't notice Rothman approach me from behind. His voice in my ear startled me.

"Want to meet Shay?" he said. "I'll take you over, come on. I can tell you're dying of curiosity."

I could hardly turn him down. I tried to think of something to say when we were introduced, but nothing came to mind. We picked our way through the crowd, Rothman nodding to some, edging by others so's not to interrupt.

Tilsen was a big guy with sloping shoulders and a thick neck. He was pushing fifty, I guessed. Rothman tugged the sleeve of his suit coat, and said something in his ear.

Tilsen pulled out a wad, counted off some bills and handed them over. Rothman pocketed the cash and motioned for me.

"This is Martin McDonough," he said. "Martin, meet Isadore Tilsen."

His yegs kept their hands in their pockets, and their eyes on my hands. Tilsen had big, hairy knuckles, reddish hair going gray at the temples, gold teeth. He didn't offer to shake, just nodded.

"You know Louie?" he said. "Louie wants to change the world."

"Well, uh, it needs changing," I replied lamely.

"You think?" He nodded again. "Nice meeting you, Mr. Mc-Donough."

I was dismissed.

"He's a man of few words," I said, on the way back to the radical caucus.

"He's short with the goyim, doesn't trust them," Rothman replied. "He's a big puppy with his fellow Jews though. When he was a kid he used to beat up the local shaygus for a favor. He wasn't much of a scholar, so that was how he earned respect."

He seemed in a forthcoming mood so I popped the question.

"What was that business between you and him, if you don't mind my asking?"

"Not at all. My comrades and I usually collect ten or twelve bucks for Margaret Thornton, but we like to give her thirty. Isadore makes up the difference."

"Why? Does he feel guilty?"

"You'd have to ask him."

"No thanks."

Rothman smiled. "Howard wants to come with us for a drink. He knows a place not far from here, ok?"

It was more than ok from my perspective. I could run Thornton's little poem by both of them.

Rothman rode in Kravetsky's bucket, a Cadillac with big red lights on behind, which made it easy to follow. We wound our way through the snow-clogged side streets. The Caddy made ruts. I stayed in them.

We bumped our way over the tracks into smoke-town, and parked in front of a tar-paper shack between two sagging clapboard houses. It looked like just another broken-down dwelling except for the blue light in the window, which shone mysteriously through the snow that had drifted over the sill.

Cigarette smoke and the sound of a saxophone poured through the crack between the door and the frame. A big black guy at the door shook Kravetsky's hand, and let us in.

The joint was dimly lit, full of shifting shapes and strange smells; burnt fat smelling of something fruity and piquant; tobacco smoke mingled with another, more acrid smoke; the cloying scent of perfume that came off the dusky shoulders of a dark-skinned tomato in a sequined evening dress, who led us to a table.

Couples danced in front of a little stage where a band played slow jazz. The piano inserted a line here and there. A drum roll could be heard - constant but nearly inaudible except for an occasional th- thump on the beat of some otherwise indiscernible measure - but the real music came from a saxophone. I tried peering through the crowd to see the player, and caught a glimpse of a reddish-brown darky, hat on his head, eyes closed. He was seated on a stool with one foot on the floor and the other on a rung, with a saxophone sticking out of his mouth at a ninety-degree angle, the weight of it resting on his raised knee. A mist of low-hanging fumes off a grill that sizzled and popped next to the stage quickly rendered him invisible.

A coffee-colored dame in tight red dress slid a chair in next to Kravetsky, sat down and laid her head on his arm. "What'chu been up to, How-wood," she said.

"Lurene, meet my old friend Lou. He's a left wing nut. - And this is Martin. He's famous." His free hand swept out toward me, as if he were throwing dice.

"You rich, baby" - a smile slowly parted her heavily-lipsticked lips - "or jus' well-known?"

"My fame is but fleeting. I'm a humble working fellow."

An arm reached over from the adjoining table, and held a hand-rolled cigarette in front of Lurene. She took it, dragged deeply and passed it over to How-wood, who did the same. He blew the smoke out through his nose. It spread across the table, and billowed up toward me.

"That gage?" I asked."

"We calls it tea," said Lurene.

Rothman took a tentative puff and passed it my way. I took in enough to make my eyes water, stifled a cough and handed it back to Lurene. She held it to How-wood's lips for another drag before passing it back to the other table.

Drinks appeared. I tried to pay, but Kravetsky shook his head.

Rothman winked. "When you're with Howard, it's on him," he explained.

The band shifted abruptly into something upbeat. This tune featured the piano playing a big hit from '33, It's Only a Paper Moon. Some couples near the stage began jitter-bugging. The door opened, and a blast of cold air blew the smoke away from the bandstand. I got a quick look at a flapping banner that said "The Young Family Band" before the haze blotted it out again.

Rothman nudged me, and passed the gage, which had reappeared at our table. I sucked the smoke in more carefully this time, and passed it to Lurene.

"How come you're famous, honey?" she asked.

"He rescued a little girl who was kidnapped," said Kravetsky.

"Good for you. I was famous one time. I ever tell'ya 'boutthat,

How-wood? The chief of the Terre Haute po-lees left his shoes under my bed. Poor man was so delirious with joy he done walked out in his stockin' feet. Next day the headlines read - 'Po-lees Chief Bewitched By Lurene Rose Carter, Loses Shoes.'"

HA-HA! barked How-wood.

I found it funny as well. Rothman grinned his wry grin, and shook his head. The music stopped, the couples left the dance floor, and soon another chair slid up to our table. The saxophone player seated himself. "Duh wa-zeer is here," he said.

He was tall, wearing a suit, and a silver tie. There was a little Homburg hat perched on top of his head with a red ribbon tied around it a couple times, but it was long enough so it dangled by his ear anyway. In later years I would see photos of him in which he looked thin and haunted, but back then his eyes sparkled and his features were round. He nodded to each of us, kissed Lurene's hand, then reached over and ran his hand along the fur of How-wood's coon skin coat as if he were stroking a baby's head. - "I've had eyes for such (he said 'thutch', but in a way that told you it was a rib, not a speech defect) vines to wind about me for, oh - eons. Be-bop-za-ree-bop, dig?"

How-wood nodded, as if that made perfect sense to him. "Lester Young, meet Martin McDonough, private eye," he said.

"Don't shoot, I'm unarmed," said Lester.

That really tickled me. Lester could tell the gage had taken a toll. He also read minds. "Howard's daddy gave me violin lessons," he explained, in answer to my unspoken question. "Thus have we been knowin' each other for, oh - lo these many. The Oxford Gray are generally reluctant to attend my performances - perhapth due to the venues - but Howard has always been a noble exception."

Kravetsky waved for the waiter, and nodded in Lester's direction.

"What's your pleasure, Mister Young?" said the waiter.

"Vin rouge, garcon. Or failing that, the domethtic equivalent."

"Sure glad we got to hear that last number, Lester," said Lurene. "Cuz we ain't stayin' for the next one. Are we How-wood." She laid her head deep into his furry shoulder.

"Your music presents then cannily solves the problem of glis-sando in a minor chord progression," said someone in a voice that sounded eerily like my own. I had no idea what he was talking about, but Lester must have thought it was perceptive, or at least rational. He winked - the kind of broad vaudeville wink the interlocutor gives a straight man when he arrives late at a conclusion, now that I think of it.

"You thir, have done me the courtesy of addressing me in the language of my art," he said, "I am honored my shamus friend, and promise to play a number for'ya soon's as I'm back on the stand. - Keep that eye'a yours private, dig? Be-bop-sha-bam."

He didn't ask what my favorite song was. I don't know what I'd have said if he did. Everything that came to mind that evening came from some part of it that I was unfamiliar with.

The waiter returned, bearing a glass of wine on a tray. Kravetsky handed him a bill, and waved him off when he began to make change. Lester took a sip, licked his lips appreciatively. He stood glass in hand, and bowed to each of us spilling nary a drop.

"I must away. Thanks for coming."

"And thank you," I replied into the void that was left in his ab-sence.

There was a pause in the conversation after that, and addled as I was, I had the presence of mind to pull a scrap of paper out of my coat pocket and get down to business.

"I'd like to read a poem, in the social realist tradition," I an-nounced. "Bear with me, the light's dim." I smoothed the paper out, held the crumpled edges down, and began.

"Ten thousand Jews, are making booze, in endless repetition" - I paused to assess their reaction. How-wood's brow tightened a bit. Rothman took his specs off and leaned toward me. "to fill the needs of a million Swedes, who supported Prohibition."

I nodded to indicate that the reading was over.

"You write that?" said Lurene.

"No. Walter Thornton did, a few weeks before he was bumped off. And I have a question I'd like you gents to answer. Would anyone of the Jew persuasion take such exception to that they'd drill him for writin' it?"

Rothman sat back and put his glasses back on. "For a few verses about how people were duped into acting against their own interests? I doubt it."

How-wood shook his head in the affirmative.

"I don't know, somebody writes a poem about Mick hoochers, puts it on the front page of a paper and hands it out on Rice Street, he's askin' for trouble. Maybe you Hebes aren't so quick to anger, but - "

"It's not a slur, it's an observation," said Rothman, "an accurate one at that. Walter Thornton didn't have a bigoted bone in his body."

"You and your comrades know that," I said. "How's about some'a your gangster countrymen?"

"Uh-uh, you got it wrong. Tell him Howard."

"Nah," said Kravetsky. "He didn't even say 'Mockey,' or 'kike.' Ten thousand? He's overstating the case maybe..." - "Poetic license," Rothman interjected. - "Whatever," Kravetsky agreed. "You're wondering did somebody knock him off because he wrote it? No."

I folded the poem and put it back in my overcoat pocket. "Makes sense to me, but you can't blame a guy for askin.' Isn't unheard of for a Jew to knock off a loudmouth who's casting aspersions on the race."

I could tell the word "race" unsettled Lurene. She snuggled deeper into How-wood's coat with a glum look on her face.

"What do you mean?" Rothman asked.

I recounted the fate of Howard Godfrey, complete with Leon Gleeman's suggestion that I look into Thornton's writings, and in conclusion, quoted Gleeman. "'Every Jew in the world had motive to kill him.' - That's what he told me."

"But only one Jew did kill him," said Kravetsky, "and his name is Leon Gleeman."

"Naw. Really?"

"That's right Sherlock. Another drink?"

"How-wood!"

"Ok, ok." He patted Lurene's hand, after removing it from where it rested, in the folds of his coat. "The lady says it's time to go. - Join us for a night cap, ok? Lou, you ride with Martin, so's he won't get lost." He thumbed a few bills off a thick stack, and placed them under an empty glass. The waiter noticed and came over.

"Don't leave jus' yet," he said. "Red's playin' a number for this fella." He nodded at me. "This here's your favorite song."

So we stayed and listened - me especially. He twisted notes in a way that sounded like moaning. The tune, which I sort of recognized but not really, was mellow and romantic despite all those bawdy sounds. A few bars of the melody seemed to float over the piano lines, then dissolve before I could identify it. Nor did he exactly play. He alluded to it. So did the piano player, in a more straightforward way, but not enough so I could to place it.

"C'mon," said Rothman, as the song ended. I was still trying to figure out what it was as How-wood slipped the big guy up front a bill. He held the door for us as we departed. I was dumfounded by the beauty of the blue light on the moonlit snow, and when the door closed again I felt as if I'd left another country, another world.

"I've never been in a joint like that before," I told Rothman, as we seated ourselves in my bucket.

"Wait till you see where we're headed next," he said.

His remark echoed in my mind, slowly replacing my favorite song, as I followed the hypnotic trail of the Cadillac's red lights. A fat white moon's reflection off the snow made the night brighter than the night club, which struck me as paradoxical in the extreme. I tried to put my finger on why, failed, and realized that we'd been silent for - how long?

"What'd you say?" I asked.

"Huh?"

"Where we goin?"

"To Howard's love nest in the junk yard."

I found that extremely funny. So did Rothman. He had a grin a mile wide after he saw me laughing.

"What's the matter, you don't believe me?" he said. "Wait'll you see it."

The red lights turned into an alley where I lost them briefly, but Rothman guided me around an L-turn to an open iron gate in a brick wall that must have been ten feet high. He got out and closed it behind us while I parked next to the Caddy.

How-wood and his squeeze were already making tracks through the snow, along a sidewalk that led between two mountains of scrap iron, toward a low shed.

It was chilly inside. Enough moonlight came through a window to reveal a row of work benches full of gears, wiring, shafts, and big greasy springs.

Another door opened behind the shop, and we stepped into a pasha's redoubt. It was only one room, but a big one, well-heated, built on three levels. Dim, reddish light emanated from recessed fixtures in the walls.

How-wood seated himself behind a mahogany desk up on level three. He looked on with obvious pride as we surveyed his domain and Lurene poured drinks. There were three overstuffed chairs with ottomans on level two, along with a huge leather couch and shelves full of fancy whiskies and wines. There was a Persian rug on the floor, and another one, I noticed, under How-wood's desk. Other shelves held glasses, nut bowls and cups, and whatever space was left between those items was filled with shiny, sculptural contraptions made of polished car parts, one of which must have been plugged into the wall. A worm-gear mounted on a silver cube turned, whirring softly, as if it were looking for something to burrow into.

Rothman and I seated ourselves. It was warm, cozy and slightly damp. The reason for the humidity was revealed when How-wood played with a switch on the wall, and illuminated what could have been characterized as either a small tiled pool or a very large tiled bath, set into the lower level. Rose-colored steam hung over the water and evaporated before it could fog a mirror fixed to the ceiling.

"For my sinuses," he said. "HA-HA!

We didn't stay long enough to finish our drinks. A few sips and Rothman hustled me out the door. Lurene wasn't sorry to see us go, but I could tell that Kravetsky would sooner we'd stayed awhile. He liked putting on the dog, although he probably liked what came next better. They were preparing to take the waters as we left.

The landscape had a marshmallow quality as Rothman directed me back to his neighborhood. I'd entered the night club with the thought to get back to Rice Street before last call. That goal had since faded, but now something, maybe the faint taste of whiskey on my tongue, reminded me. I realized I had no idea what time it was. I was about to ask Rothman when he said, "here," and we were in front of his house.

"Hey, I still owe'ya a drink," I said.

"Well, we won't take Howard along next time. Can't buy when he's around. - We straighten you out on that poem?"

"Huh? - Oh, yeah. Right. An accurate observation."

"I just wouldn't want Walter to be thought of that way," he said. "He was a good man. See you around, McDonough."

"G'nite."

I drifted off through the quilted streets, and tried to keep my mind on driving, although it didn't matter much. There was no traffic, and enough cars had been through since the storm to make well-worn ruts on the main routes. River Road was covered in a few spots but I broke through the snow easily enough. I was sailing toward the bridge, trying to reconstruct those bent notes that Lester played and fit them into some tune I recognized, when I spotted a big La-Salle angled across the road up ahead. It looked as if it had skidded and gotten stuck. Its headlamps pierced the woods that rimmed the bluff. A man in an overcoat and a snap-brim hat was standing by the driver's door.

I stopped and rolled down the window. He walked up to my car. I was about to offer assistance, but he spoke first. - "McDonough?"

I looked at him quizzically, but didn't deny it. He poked a .45 in my face.

"Get out," he said. I complied, feeling a little dazed by the sudden turn of events.

He marched me to the LaSalle. The curtain over the back window slid aside, revealing the bald head and thick-nosed mug of Charlie Ward, instantly recognizable from dozens of newspaper photos.

"Go 'round to the other side and get in, sport," he said. "You and I need to have a little discussion."

HISTORY

Ward's bruno put his piece away and assumed the role of chauffeur. We headed south on River Road, tires crunching over the snow, powerful engine purring. I was having a tough go processing the sudden turn of events, but it soon began to dawn on me that it might be fatal.

"Uh - wha - what's gonna happen - - to my car?"

"You've got bigger worries than your car, bub," said Ward. He peered at me carefully. "You aren't a tea head, are you?"

"Me? - I - "

"Jesus H. Christ." He shook his head. "That pretty young widow hired herself a tea-head, and told him to go get Charlie Ward."

I was just mentally organized enough to be mad. "You tailin' me around?" I demanded, with the highest dudgeon I could summon.

"No, sport. You're tailing me around, and that's what we're going to talk about. Relax. This'll take a while.

"Don't worry," he added. "You won't get shot unless you do something stupid. We can't dismiss that possibility given your record so far, but I'm hopeful things can be resolved peacefully. - We usually resolve things peacefully, don't we Broderick?"

The chauffeur nodded. "Usually."

"What do you mean, 'resolve'?" I asked.

"Don't play dumb with me, McDonough. You're trying to pin that newspaperman's murder on me and I don't like it."

He gave me another once over. - "Yup, you're a tea head. I know that look well. Old Pancho's Yaquis had those juju eyes. Nothing sleepy about'em when the shooting started though. Those Indians were some tough sons of bitches."

That was my first clue that I was dealing with a kind of man I understood; all business until the opportunity to tell a tale arose. Then the raconteur took over. My curiosity quickly overcame my fear. After all, this was the great Charlie Ward.

"That true, what I've heard? You rode with Villa, made all that dough sellin' cow hides?"

"People say a lot of things about Charlie Ward, sport. Some of it true, some not. I don't mind you asking. I'll give you the straight dope, and when we're done you'll realize I didn't kill that nosy twerp. I'm not that kind of fellow. - And of course if you don't see the light - what then, Broderick?"

His man turned around and made a slitting motion across his throat with his finger.

"Oh, I see. You didn't kill Thornton because you're not that kinda guy, but you'll kill me if I don't believe you?"

He sighed, as if to say he spent way too much time dealing with people who didn't get the picture.

"If I wanted to kill you, you'd be dead already, McDonough. Just get off my case or you'll make an enemy of me, and believe me, you don't want Charlie Ward for an enemy. Your sources will dry up, people will stop calling you with work. Then you'll try to get a job, but nobody will hire you...." He shook his head in sad contemplation of the fate that awaited me... "So. You wonder about Pancho, eh? That's what most people are curious about."

He sat back. A faraway look settled over his face, and he was silent a few moments.

"Pancho was a hard man but I cried like a baby when I heard they'd ambushed him. I'd still ride to the gates of hell for him, stiff and old as I am. All he'd have to do is send one of those pigeons of his... That's how he let us know where to meet him, you know. Homing pigeons. He kept coops of'em, in Juarez, in Villareal. He'd send one over to Harry Dreben's place in El Paso with a message: 'Get the gringos and saddle up!' Had'em trained to fly all over northern Mexico. Every place his 'muchachos' were holed up. He'd turn those pigeons loose, and pretty damn soon he had an army gathered."

Ward told me he served as quartermaster for Villa, which mostly meant bargaining for guns and ammunition in Texas, and riding shotgun on the railroad train that hauled them back. He met many newspaper reporters on those trains, he said.

"Americans, Brits, a Frenchman or two, an Italian. A guy named John Reed. Ever hear of him? He went to Russia a few years later, and they made a hero of him. They were all lefties, McDonough, just like your client's husband. I thought they had crazy ideas then and I still do, but I had a soft spot for'em because they wanted to talk and they spoke English. It broke up the monotony. They thought it was pretty romantic running guns. Well, it was damned dangerous because we carried thousands of dollars in gold into the U.S., and thousands of dollars worth of arms out, but mostly it was just hour after boring hour riding the 'ferrocarril.' You ever been on a Mexican train, sport? You don't go to the club car for a drink, or hang out on a leather chair in the smoking lounge. You sit on a hard wooden bench, and if you're me you keep your hand on your pistol because half the hombres on that train hate your gringo guts, and a few of'em are there specifically to rob you. Twenty, thirty straight hours with your finger on the trigger. I've killed men, McDonough, but I never have killed a reporter."

"Yeah, yeah. Saint Charlie. What kinda guy was Villa? That was the question."

He feigned irritation, as all storytellers will if you jerk them off a tangent. But he was back on track quickly.

"He was a quirky bastard, impetuous, ruthless, but he loved those Mexicans and they loved him. Not the Grandees, mind you. The little fellows, the pelados - the ones those reporters were always talking about, but never bothered talking to. Well, Pancho talked to'em. He'd gather'em all up in the zocalo, and give a speech. 'When I was a young man four ranchers owned all the cattle in Durango," he'd tell them, "and if Carranza had his way they'd still own'em. And you, my friends would be fighting with the cattle for grass to eat. But now we fight the ranchers, and we fight that dog Carranza!' Then he'd make a big show of slaughtering ten or twelve steers, and we'd all have a fiesta, and get drunk and shout, Viva Madero! - Jesus, Mc-Donough. Those were the days. Yessir, Charlie Ward has had quite a life."

He told me he'd hooked up with Villa in Juarez, when his troops were camped there before a big battle. He and his buddy Jim had come down from Nevada with a stake they made mining gold. They'd heard money could be made selling supplies to the rival armies in the revolution that was going on across the border.

"They wouldn't let the combatants into Texas," he explained, "so an American could buy cheap on one side of the Rio Grande and sell dear on the other."

The day they arrived they spotted a team of burros pulling two station wagons across the river, amid a great hullabaloo. The wagons were deposited right outside Villa's tent, and Ward and his pal watched while Villa's purser paid off the car dealer in gold.

"Then Villa himself walked out, looked at a bunch of us gringos who'd gathered around, and said; 'Whoever can turn these station wagons into armored cars, I'll pay him well.' Now Jim was a damn good mechanic. He said we could do it. Pancho gave him the go-ahead, and pretty soon we'd done a job with sheet metal and cotton wadding that looked like the real thing. Pancho asked what we wanted. Jim answered first, which gave me a minute to think. Jim said, 'six ounces of gold.' Pancho didn't even blink, just told the purser to weigh it out. Then it was my turn. Well, right then I did the second smartest thing I've ever done, McDonough, and that's saying something."

He glanced over to assess the effect of his braggadocio, but I kept a stone face.

"I said I wanted the hides of all the cattle he slaughtered to feed his army, and told him that I'd serve with him any way he pleased as long as I could have them. Pancho, he looked at me kind of strange, and I do believe my life was on the line for a moment, because he thought I was insulting him some way, making a joke. But let me tell you, the opportunity I'd spotted was no joke. Well, he finally laughed and said he'd take us both on, Jim as an armored car driver and me as a quartermaster."

Ward told me he salted those hides down and sold them for five dollars each in El Paso. As many as a thousand a month when they were on the march. He claimed he had seventy grand in the bank the day a bullet went through the sheet metal they'd called armor, and killed his pal Jim.

"Luckily Pancho wasn't in the car at the time," said Ward. "He'd have executed me on the spot when he realized how safe he'd really been in those cars. I jumped on my horse and didn't stop until I got to Texas. That wasn't the end between Pancho and me though. He sent word to Harry Greben a year or so later that all was forgiven. He wanted me back as quartermaster. No more hides though. He'd been asking some questions, and now that was his department."

He paused, and knitted his bushy brows in contemplation.

"You know, I've often wondered why I went back. I was a young man with money to spend, and I'd had some hard times. I grew up dirt poor on the Seattle docks, McDonough. Left home at 16 - what home there was, my mother being a whore and us living in a shanty next to a fish-gutting shack - God, the stink of that place! I can't eat fish to this day. I rode the rods, slept in haystacks, punched cattle in Arizona, worked as a seaman out of Frisco for two years, and a bar bouncer for two more years in Skagway, then in Reno. I lived in a tent and mined gold in Tonopah for the best part of three more years, and there I was in El Paso with a pile of dough and a yen to spend it, but Pancho says come back and risk your life again and back I came. The only way I can explain it, I guess loved the guy. Just like those little Mexicans did. He was cruel and unpredictable - why, once I saw him lose his temper and shoot a man to death for some trifle, then weep over his body - but he had a way of making you believe you were part of some grand thing. You'd listen to him, and you'd think that history wouldn't take much note of the brutality and the double-dealing, but these Mexicans will have a better life, and that will be remembered."

He snuffled back what might have been a tear, and directed his bruno to cross an upcoming bridge to St. Paul. I had no idea where we were headed or how I'd get my car back, but it was fascinating listening to him.

"But you know what, sport," he continued. "I never was a man of the people. Love of the masses is well and good, but Charlie Ward was always uppermost on my mind."

He told me he tired of the revolution again after a few months, headed back to the U.S., and commenced to have himself a party. A long one.

"I'd get up late, have some breakfast, read the papers, take a little horseback ride up in the mountains - I was spending a lot of time in Denver by then - and all the while I'd be consulting my watch, because I didn't want to take that first bump of whiskey too early. Remind you of anybody, sport?"

"How do you know so much about me, Ward?"

He laughed. "What's the matter? Don't you like people snooping around in your life? Sounds like you can dish it out ok, but you can't take it."

"I'm not a snoop. I'm a detective. I help people with their problems, and I do good work. Don't you read the papers?"

"Oh yes, I read about you and that little girl. You can be proud of that, but it certainly wasn't Leon Gleeman's finest hour. A man who lives the way he does ought to take more precautions. If somebody tried to kidnap me, or my wife, or the children we plan to have - I just married recently, did you know that, McDonough?"

"Yeah, a lovely woman about half your age. I read the papers."

He ignored the dig, and drew the picture.

"Somebody tried to kidnap my family he'd be damn sorry. If my police dog didn't kill him Broderick would. But I digress. I was telling you my life story. So you'd know what kind of man I am."

"Naw, you were telling me your life story because you like tellin' it."

He smiled, and picked up his tale where he'd left it, in his early thirties with lots of swag and developing some bad habits ala Martin McDonough.

He said he'd made a few half-hearted stabs at business, a stage line in Arizona, a race track in Colorado, but they fizzled. The people he hung out with in Denver were fugitives from justice and soldiers of fortune like himself. The feds had him tagged for a smuggler, which he adamantly denied, and offered up his shrinking bankroll as proof.

But he didn't pretend to be faultless. He told me he gambled, chased women, bought drinks for whoever wanted to listen to him brag about his Mexican bonanza, and got into drunken fist-fights, including one with a Hawaiian stool pigeon called Pineapple who played a part in his downfall.

"I can't blame him, though," he said. "Pineapple may have been a weasel, but I was fool. I was just about broke, but they were still tailing me around like I was public enemy number one. The Denver papers were writing editorials about people like me. They called us 'border riff-raff.' Said we stood squarely in the path of progress in the great Southwest. They never named names, but they had me and my compadres in mind alright, Harry Dreben, Tom Mix - Tom rode with Pancho, but when the heat came on he had sense enough to head for California and get into the movies - Two Gun Tracy Richardson - now I'll admit they had a point with Tracy. He was a highwayman, no doubt about it - but they called us all highwaymen and desperados, and I was nothing but a red-blooded sport, McDonough, too damn busy drinking and whoring to see the end sneaking up! I knew they were tailing me, but I didn't care. I was actually kind of flattered, and I thought if I didn't hurt anyone but myself I had nothing to worry about. They arrested me in a flophouse on Curtis Street one morning, summer of 1918. Fed reached behind the dresser, and pulled out a sack of cocaine. "Now what have we here,' he said. Well, one look at that room and you'd know the occupant didn't have ten cents worth of anything. Pineapple lived down the hall. He put the dope there. Took'em two years to bring me to trial they had such a shaky case, but they got me. They got me good. I was thirty-three years old when I went to Leavenworth. They gave me a number. 15716! That's who Charlie Ward was. A cipher. I thought about going over the wall. I knew the odds were they'd shoot me, but I didn't think it mattered. The judge said I was 'beneath contempt,' and you know, for a while I thought he was right."

Ward told me he kept sane the first year by viewing imprisonment as retribution for an earlier moral failing of his, "high-grading," in the parlance of time. I'd assumed he'd mined a claim of his own in Tonopah, but he told me there was no such thing. The gold vein was in a mountain called Radiator Hill, and a mining company owned it. They hired men like him to risk their lives blasting tons of rock loose and throwing it into hoppers.

"It was hard, dangerous, low paid work," he said, "and every damn one of us were 'high graders,' meaning we pocketed as much as we could. For a while you could just walk out with pounds of likely looking ore. Then they began searching us, so we devised all sorts of plans. They had a portable privy in the tunnel and we took to ducking rock in with the crap, and then retrieving it when they hauled it out to dump it. They soon discovered that, and quit providing a privy. Instead they had us dig a ditch along the wall, and every once in a while they'd run some water through to flush it out the entrance into a pit. We'd drop all manner of packages into that foul muck as we came off shift, McDonough - tins, rag bundles, Bull Durham sacks full of rock. After the guards left we'd come back with iron rods and fish in the pit for our prizes."

He said the money the mining company paid him barely covered food, but he left Tonopah with a small fortune, more than five thousand dollars. It was theft any way you cut it, but he told himself it was ok because he'd been treated as if his life and his labor were worthless.

"But I knew it was wrong," he said. "I began to think that the money I took to El Paso had a curse on it, and that was why I went to Leavenworth."

I rolled my eyes at that one.

"Laugh if you want. It kept me going until Herb Bigelow came along. I took one look at him and said to myself, 'grab this guy Charlie, he can pull you out of the muck.' Herb was in for tax evasion, and he was the kind of rich, arrogant fellow the other convicts took pleasure in tormenting. I made him a deal. I told him, 'I'll see to it no harm comes to you as long as you're here, and you give me a job when I get out.' Well of course he agreed. The man was scared to death."

Ward told me that once the fear was removed from his life, Bigelow's true nature came out. He was bone lazy. He was still the president of Bigelow Enterprises, and he was supposed to be running the business by corresponding with his executives from prison, but he turned most of that chore over to Ward as well.

"I wrote his letters and answered theirs," he said. "I knew more about that business than he did by the time I got out."

I let him go on about his rise to the top at Bigelow Enterprises, waiting for a chance to drop the bombshell. I figured if I slipped it in at the right time I could judge his guilt by his reaction. He told me the proudest day of his life was the day the board of directors named him president, but it was ruined because the death of his old friend Herb Bigelow precipitated it.

"Lotta people think you killed him," I said.

He glared at me. "You one of 'em?"

"It crossed my mind."

"Herb Bigelow saved my life. If it wasn't for him I'd be a drug store cowboy. I'd be telling tales in saloons."

I shrugged. "It's possible to be grateful to someone and kill him anyway. Sometimes it's a motive."

"What's that supposed to mean?"

"You don't strike me as the grateful underling type."

He snorted and shook his head. "Now you sound like a damn newspaper reporter," he said. "That's how they have me figured. 'Ex-con Makes Good Under Guidance of Wealthy Patron.' I'll tell you something, McDonough. The board would've made me president anyway, probably sooner than later. Herb didn't have much of a head for business. We were barely breaking even when he died, and now we're the biggest advertising company in America. That's no accident."

"Speaking of accidents."

"Yeah, yeah. How am I supposed to counter something like that?"

"You have to admit that drowning business looks queer."

"Herb had two bad weaknesses, McDonough, other men's wives and booze. One of 'em got him killed. I don't know which, but I didn't have anything to do with it. - What the hell do you care anyway? I thought you were investigating that Thornton kid's murder."

Bombs away.

"Same guy killed Bigelow and another journalist you didn't like. Probably had a hand in the Thornton murder too."

He frowned. "What are you talking about?" he said.

"I'm talking about Bugsy Siegel."

He sighed another long sigh, and addressed the chauffeur. "Never mind Rice Street, Broderick. Head toward St. Peter and the asylum. We have to lock this guy up for his own good."

I pressed on, undaunted. "A little birdy told me you wrote Bugsy a check for $150,000 just before Bigelow died. Same little birdy told me Bugsy kills people for a living."

He considered that for a while before responding. I glanced out the window and saw the Cathedral. We were nearing Rice Street.

"I'm impressed, McDonough. There might be more to you than meets the casual eye. Here I thought I was dealing with a common drunk who trades on coppers' gossip. Turns out I'm dealing with a drunk and a tea head who trades on all sorts of gossip - coppers, feds, disgruntled former executives." He paused for my reaction but I didn't give him one.

"Ben Siegel and I have some mutual friends," he continued. "He was here two or three times promoting a plan for a casino in the Bahamas. I invested $150,000. The FBI searched his apartment down in Florida, and found the envelope. My lawyers are working on getting it back. And that's the nature of my dealings with Ben Siegel."

I was incredulous. "You forked over that kind of dough to build a gambling hall in the middle of nowhere?"

"Where would you put your money smart guy, in the stock market? I prefer dealing with mobsters. You know where you stand with them." He shook his finger under my nose. "I'm a hard man if I have to be, McDonough. I know how to make life difficult for people, but I don't have'em rubbed out. That's a mark of desperation, and I made a vow that I would never be desperate again when I was in prison."

"You can't tell me that you didn't want Floyd Olson to be President."

"Floyd was a good man and he was interested in some of the same things I am - a fair shake for the underdog, helping the poor fellow at the bottom of the heap. I was ready to back him all the way for friendship's sake, but between you and me he'd have made a rotten President. My taxes would've gone up. Considerably."

"And you'd have a friend in the White House. But that muckraker Walter Thornton was throwin' a monkey wrench in the works, wasn't he."

"That's right, smart guy. He was telling the hundred or so radicals who read that rag of his that Floyd wasn't a good Bolshevik. And of course the American voters in their wisdom want only the most committed Reds for President."

We pulled up in front of Tin Cup's.

"Well, here you are, McDonough. None the worse. Hopefully a little wiser. And in plenty of time for last call."

I stepped out into the snow. "Thanks for the ride," I said, with what I trusted was conspicuous irony.

"Don't mention it. Hope you enjoyed our little chat."

"I learned some history."

"I am history, sport."

"What about my bucket?"

He nodded toward the other side of the street. Sure enough, there it was, in a carefully shoveled parking place. It looked like it had been washed.

"Mind your Ps and Qs, McDonough," he said, as he closed the curtain.

It was nice to be back in familiar surroundings, but I wasn't exactly pleased with the way things had gone. Sure, it had been interesting, but in the final analysis I'd spent the evening seeking clarity and wound up more confused than ever.

* * *

Nevertheless, some things were permanent - the two burned out light bulbs in the Tin Cup's sign, for example, and McDonough's Law: The coppers know who did it, even if they can't prove it. With that in mind, it came as a great relief to see Jimmy Brennan at his usual spot.

Jimmy was often the reason they couldn't prove it. He was a walking warehouse of concealed evidence, on the take from any number of local crooks - pimps, shakedown artists, fences, and probably some peter-men as well. At least they seemed to have great success blowing safes when Jimmy walked the beat.

His shrewd little eyes assessed me carefully as I approached. The road to his mouth ran through his wallet, so he knew that I saved him for special occasions. That gave him the upper hand in these matters.

I sat down and put a twenty on the bar. "What's your pleasure," said the bartender. "A nip of the Irish," I replied, "top shelf. And one for my friend here."

Jimmy nodded, as if to say it was a start, but only just.

The good stuff came dear at Tin Cup's. The change was less than nineteen dollars. I tapped my finger on the notes. "Give me some information and I'll leave these when I go, Jimmy."

He nodded again.

"Jerk doesn't think Charlie Ward paid for the Thornton hit," I said. "How's about you?"

He chuckled. "Lotta people think Jerk is retired, but I get the feeling he still has a job."

"Why's that?"

"He ain't goin' without."

"They held a benefit for him, remember?"

"Yeah, I was there. Must'a collected nine hundred bucks or so. You could live for a year on that if you was careful."

"What're you driving at, Jimmy?"

"Jerk carries water for Charlie Ward."

I can't say something of that nature hadn't crossed my mind, but blood is thicker than water.

"You saying Jerk is bent?"

"Hey, the man has to live. I'm puttin' two and two together is all."

"Four. I learned that in the first grade." I tapped the bills. "Information please. If all you have is theories I'll keep the cash, and if all you have is theories that insult my family we'll be stepping outside."

"Ok, ok. Relax. But that sheeny torpedo would've squealed unless he was paid to shut up. Somebody put a bundle down, and who besides Charlie Ward has that kinda money?"

"Another theory." I knocked back my shot, and picked up the bills.

"Hold it," he said. "Name Wicky Hanson mean anything to you?"

It did indeed. Most of the ex-cons Charlie Ward hired were nobodies, but Wicky's reputation preceded him when he came to work on the Bigelow assembly line. He'd been a hit man in Chicago for Capone's succesor, Paulie "The Waiter" Ricca.

"What about him?"

"He's another guy lives beyond his means. He's learnin' to crack safes, but he still works the old trade occasionally. He was in on the Thornton hit. Knows Ward, knows Shay Tilsen, maybe put'em together."

"Any chance he'd talk to me?"

"He owes me a favor. You could buy it." He glanced down at the bar. "Not for eighteen bucks though."

A fight broke out at the other end of the bar, but we didn't let it distract us and soon struck a deal. I'd be ashamed to say how much it cost in view of the fee arrangements on this matter. Jimmy said he'd be in touch.

* * *

Jerk and I stared transfixed as the seemingly empty overcoat containing what was left of Tommy Scanlon moved ghostlike across the floor, and came to a shaky stop in the glow of Kuby's brand new Wurlitzer.

A sepulchral hand protruded from the sleeve, and dropped a nickel in the slot. A bony finger stabbed at the buttons.

THEY...

ASKED ME HOW I KNEWWW...

"Ah fr' Christ's sake," said Jerk.

He sulked for a few minutes while I sat there listening to the song for lack of anything better to do. It's not as if I wanted to start my day this way. Why do I feel like I need to report to Jerk? I wondered.

Something was eating at Jerk, and it wasn't the Mighty Wurlitzer.

"Jimmy B says he can put me together with a dropper from the Thornton hit," I finally said, to break the spell. "And did I tell'ya? I didn't find out much over in Minneapolis."

"Didn't see who Tilsen talks to?"

"His palookas, that's all. Exchanged greetings with a few people, business type guys mainly, but no conversations. Only interesting thing, he gave Rothman some cash for the widow. Maybe he feels guilty. Oh - there's one guy he talked to briefly. Me. Rothman introduced us. He said, 'nice meeting you, Mr. McDonough.'"

Jerk sighed. "Press Wicky Hanson hard, Martin. He might have something."

"How do you know it's him I'm seeing?"

He laughed. "Jimmy B's helping Wicky with his schooling."

Not much gets by Jerk.

"How's the courtship coming?" he inquired.

"Still courtin'. Not sparkin'."

"Hey, I told you to go slow. I didn't tell you to go backwards."

We discussed the niceties of courtship for a while. Jerk thought the time had come for roses.

"Don't even think about the yellow or white ones," he said. "A dozen red roses. Not the kind they peddle in the bars either. Fresh ones from a florist. I know they cost a few bucks but you've got the cash. Your pal Leon Gleeman's running for Mayor, by the way. That's how bad things are breakin' down."

I dismissed the notion with a wave of my hand. "A mockey can't get elected, not in St. Paul."

"Don't be too sure. He was on the front page of the paper the other day with a well-known Irish detective. Couldn't hurt his chances."

"Don't tell me you're lathered because I rescued his daughter? Tommy Brown sent me after the kid."

"Yeah, I know, I know... He lapsed into another sulk.

"So what's botherin' you? Is there somethin' I'm missing here?"

"It's just that I remember the way things were. Now you see Jews and Huns stepping in -"

"You sound like Margaret's mother."

He shrugged. "Maybe all us first generation folks sound that way."

"Yeah, maybe. I gotta go. I'll let'cha know how things work out."

He nodded. "My blue-eyed handsome nephew. - Good job on that Gleeman case, Martin. You made us proud. Now find out who killed Walter Thornton."

I didn't work for the next few days, just waited for Jimmy's call. And planned my meeting with Margaret. Oh, and brooded a little about Mag.

I decided to surprise Margaret Sunday afternoon. I figured she and her mom would be finishing dinner around 3:00 P.M.. That left a few hours of daylight. We could drive over to Como Park if it was a nice day, maybe stop by the lake.

Our courtship was moving like a juggernaut.

I bought a dozen roses, and kept them in the icebox Saturday night. Jimmy B called early that evening, and said I could meet Hanson the next day. I told him I was indisposed.

"Christ, Martin, I thought this was important," he said.

"I've got something else going. What about Monday?"

"The guy works for a living."

"Blowin' up a safe is he? Killin' somebody?"

"I'm talkin' about Bigelow Enterprises and you know it, Martin."

"And you know I work nights, Jimmy. - Set it up Monday night. Anywhere he wants."

Sunday dawned mild and sunny, a September morn in November. Snow melt ran in the street. You could hear it gurgling down the gutters. Jimmy called about the time both of us should've been at Mass, and said to meet Hanson at Chan's, Monday at 7:00. I had to write it down I was in such a tizzy. This is very unlike me, I thought.

I started slicking up for the occasion about noon, and looked my Sunday best when I arrived in front of the Gallagher residence. I was about to step out of the bucket, when the front door opened, and Margaret walked out arm in arm with Lou Rothman.

I processed this as quickly as possible under the circumstances. All I could think of was ducking those roses before they spotted me, but that was unnecessary. They only had eyes for each other. They strolled past in the general direction of Como Avenue.

Margaret looked back when they reached the corner, probably to see if mom was watching, then kissed him on the cheek.

How did I feel? Double-crossed, I guess, but I'd have been hard put to say by who.

I felt like I'd put on a cheap suit and an ugly necktie to apply for a job that I didn't get.

I hardly remember the remainder of that day. I know I threw the roses out in the street and drove around aimlessly for a while, cursing the Sunday closing laws. Hours passed before I found myself at the back door of a blind pig, where an elderly smoke sold me a bottle of something like whiskey. I made good enough use of it that I had a terrible hangover when Monday finally came. Although our one-sided romance was kaput, my business with Margaret was far from finished. She still wanted to know who was behind her husband's murder. The best I could do was suck it up and come out with my reputation intact.

I gradually wrestled my hangover to the ground, then quelled the urge for a drink that came over me mid-afternoon. I walked over to Rice Street and bought an afternoon paper.

Leon Gleeman had decided not to run for Mayor. That fact was buried in an article explaining that the witnesses who'd been subpoenaed in the investigation of possible tax evasion by Mr. Gleeman had been told they wouldn't have to testify after all.

Around six PM I shaved and prepared to go to work.

Sorry as I felt for myself, I had some pity to spare for the late Walter Thornton that evening. He'd stepped out of his fliver anticipating his wife's welcoming arms. Instead the pock-marked mug of the man sitting across the booth from me ushered him into the next world.

"I could use a drink," said Wicky Hanson.

"So buy one," I replied.

"Jeez, I though you wanted some information."

"I do, and I already paid for it."

What he told me almost made me sorry I'd been so short. He cautioned that Tilsen didn't confide in the non-Jews he hired on such occasions. All he knew was what he overheard. But he had sharp ears, and a good memory.

He explained that the mood among the five torpedos was about what you'd figure, tense and silent on the way to the hit, relieved and talkative afterward. Tilsen was the wheel-man.

"There was this one mockey in the front seat next to him," Hanson said. "Wasn't no dropper, but he looked like one - hard guy, fag in the corner of his mouth - but there strictly to finger Thornton. So we're waitin' in the street, car pulls up, guy opens the door, finger man says 'that's him.' He jumps out, and motions us to follow. We step out and I overhear the mark say to the finger man, 'Meyer, what're you doing?' - 'Sorry, Walter,' he says, 'I'm an agent of history.' Then we start blastin' - his wife runs out screamin.' That's about it."

"You're sure his name was Meyer, and that's exactly what he said?"

Hanson nodded.

"Anything else?"

"Yeah. When we're drivin' away we're all laughing and crackin' wise, even Tilsen. He turns around and says, 'May not look that way, but we changed the world today, boys.' Then he nods to the finger man. 'Make sure you tell him I said that,' he says."

I put my head in my hands and thought hard.

"That it?"

"Well, Jimmy B says you want facts, not theories."

"From Jimmy. If you've got a theory, go ahead."

"The finger man wasn't the guy ordered the hit. Tilsen told him to tell somebody about this changin' the world joke he made. That's who was behind it."

I nodded, and motioned to the waitress. "Give this man a drink," I told her.

Tuesday morning, two three times, I was on the verge of calling on Margaret and telling her. But I couldn't. Not yet. I wanted to nail it down.

That night I drove over to the synagogue. They were all there, the radicals, the scholars, the business men, Tilsen and his palookas, the old gent with the skull cap. He smiled when he handed me a wine. "You're a reguleh reguleh around here," he said.

I sought out Rothman, pulled him off to the side and got right to the point.

"You'd have liked to see Floyd Olson become President, wouldn't ya?"

He knew something was up. He didn't take off the specs, just gave me the flat stare.

"Was he what the times call for?" I persisted. "Was he historically necessary?"

"That's a complicated question, McDonough. What makes you ask? Thinking of joining the Party?"

"No." I stepped in closer because even where we were, by the wall, it was loud in there. Everybody was talking at once, some shouting to be heard.

"I'm thinkin' of telling Margaret Thornton who put the hit on her husband," I said.

He rubbed his beard, and took that in. The air was so full of smoke I could hardly see.

"Let me show you something," he said. He grabbed my arm and pulled me into the crowd.

"Every kind of person you can imagine is here," he practically yelled into my ear. "Hard workers, lazy bastards, thinkers, doers, drunks, pious gentlemen, killers. These are the masses here, McDonough. They're all talking, and you can't understand a word they're saying, can you?" He paused and let the din make his point. "Somebody overhears a little snatch of something, passes it on the way he thinks he heard it, or maybe changed a little to suit his own interests. The guy he tells tells somebody else, and that guy passes it on, and so on, until sooner or later, who knows why, somebody does something that matters. Somebody acts."

"And then it's history."

"That's right. History is its own imperative. Anything can happen until something does, then nothing else was ever possible. - So, what'll you tell Margaret?"

"I don't know."

I turned and walked out to the bucket with goose-bumps all the way, wondering if someone was going to shoot me in the back.

I mulled things over for a while the next day, then decided to phone her. I didn't want to behold her disillusionment, which she made no attempt to disguise.

"I don't know who put the hit on your husband," I told her, "but I know who it wasn't. - Charlie Ward had nothin' to do with it."

"I thought you never failed," she said.

"I didn't fail. I progressed to a point where my skills are useless."

I explained that Shay Tilsen had organized the rubout, but the decision to do it was made in a situation I had no way of investigating.

"I find out what the coppers know," I told her. "Things they don't even tell each other they tell me. But the plot to kill your husband was hatched between a bunch'a mockeys who won't tell me nothin'. It happened at a place of worship in North Minneapolis, called Adath Jesherun. During the men's social evening. I'm tellin'ya this because maybe sometime you'll make the acquaintance of someone who can tell'ya what goes on there, maybe even has some firsthand information. Anyway that's the best I can do."

Actually, it was the least I could do, and that was exactly how much I wanted to do. I don't know why. Maybe it was the history lesson.

"Oh, and there will be no charge," I added, as much to break the silence as anything. "Good luck."

She said goodbye and hung up.

When I told Jerk he couldn't believe it. We were at Kuby's, standing at the bar, even though there were lots of empty stools. Jerk needed room to wave his arms. It was late afternoon. The old gents had departed, and a few of the younger folks who came there at night were just arriving.

Kuby was eying us warily because the harangue I was getting was so loud he thought we might throw hands.

"That was your last chance for a decent marriage and you blew it," Jerk said. "What the hell's the matter with you! You should'a - "

"Charlie Ward stopped me on the way back from Minneapolis the other night, Jerk. I can't figure out how he knew where I was, and what I've been doin.' Oh, and how'd you know about Rothman?"

"That's none'a your business."

"Really? I thought information was my business. Not clearin' Charlie Ward's name."

He brushed that off, and continued ranting about the Madigan's silk curtain aspirations. I listened politely as long as I could stand it.

"Gotta go," I told him.

"Where? To Tin Cup's? It'll still be there when we're finished."

"Thanks for all your help, Jerk. See'ya around."

Later I heard that Margaret and Lou couldn't find a clergyman of either persuasion to sanctify their relationship, so a Justice of the Peace did the honors. They have kids now, three I believe. Charlie Ward, of course, lived happily ever after.

Mag continued to hold out for the blessings of the Church until she saw how fruitless that was. Then she took up with Jack Moylan, and they got married.

Catholic school girls are still my fantasy. Classy ones. I've shortened their skirts and dirtied up their knee socks a bit over the years, but they're still walking away just as fast as their pretty legs will carry them. In my opinion, nothing else was ever possible.

PART 2

THE KEY MAN

After the Margaret Thornton fiasco I was in the dumps, but not for long. I started going to the movies on a regular basis, afternoon matinees. It was a comfort for a time, then it just got to be a habit. I'd buy a ticket and slide into the theater without bothering to look at the marquee. The film ended about the time I wanted a drink.

Sometimes Blanche Shuh came along. We disagreed about the plots—affably, but completely. It was a matter of perspective. For example, she thought the two big hits that winter, Gold Diggers of 1935 and Top Hat, were about gals finding the guy of their dreams. I thought they were about money, and how some lucky dog ended up with it—a topic of endless fascination during The Great Depression.

The only character I identified with in either film was played by Frank McHugh, a bit actor who'd have fit right in at Tin Cup's. He played the wayward son of a rich widow in Gold Diggers. The big question is whether he'll survive his run-ins with gangsters, gamblers and other hard guys, but he not only survives, he prospers. He falls for Dick Powell's fiancé, she falls for him, and the film ends with the two of them figuring how to spend mom's dough.

Blanche thought it was about McHugh's sister, played by Gloria Stuart, prying Dick Powell loose from his squeeze.

Top Hat was incomprehensible, although I picked up on an element of plot that was central to both films; the nefarious foreign weasel. I took that as a reference to current events. If there was any trouble in the world, those rats across the pond were causing it. A conniving Russian dance director tried to get his hands on the widow's fortune in Gold Diggers, but he was foiled. So was the Italian pansy in Top Hat. But before what's his name, the hoofer, finally outwits him, his dance partner almost marries the guy. Could this happen in real life? A down-to-earth Midwestern gal with legs to make a gentleman's groin stir comes within a whisker of getting hitched to a dusky-skinned deviant who can barely speak American?

Anything can happen in the movies, of course, but what usually did was a series of unlikely events leading to something predictable, if not inevitable.

I did see one tear-jerker that left me feeling like nothing else was ever possible. The poor production quality worked to its advantage. It was gray and scratchy, like something half-remembered that you'd prefer to forget completely.

It concerned an earnest young mother with an only son, and a dour, hard-drinking husband who speaks in an old country brogue when he speaks at all. Mostly he is moody and silent, even when you see him sitting in a turn-of-the century style saloon with the other Mustache Petes. The atmosphere in that joint is funereal, which is fitting, because they're all drinking themselves to death.

Many's the time mother and son go to the saloon, and drag dad out. Mom isn't allowed through the door due to her gender, so it falls on the kid. He pulls at his father's sleeve, and pleads with him—Dah, come home—but Dah stays put.

Mom goes to the priest for guidance on the Q T, and is advised to pray. It doesn't work. Awhile later, unbeknownst to mom (In movies you know things about the characters that they don't know about each other—isn't that cheating?), the kid goes to the same priest. He's maybe ten at the time.

Father, he says, I keep hopin' things'll get better, but they just get worse.—You must not despair, my boy, the priest replies. There is no greater sin than that.

So the Church is worse than useless, and the community isn't much help either. Mom's friends pity her, but they tell her that she not only has to stick it out, she's duty-bound to prolong it, by trying to save her husband from himself. Long-suffering mom doesn't have enough imagination to question the life sentence she's been handed, so she and the kid slog it out all the way to the grave with the old man. The kid is thirteen when they bury him.

From then on mom is a widow-on-the-make, but in the strait-laced, Church-approved, Hibernian fashion. This leads nowhere romantically, and creates many an awkward situation, in which the gentleman caller, the widow and the son sit around their shanty-Irish parlor like three strangers on an elevator, except the ride lasts an hour or so.

Might I call on'ye again, Mrs. McDonough? the gentleman inquires, upon leaving.

Cut to the kid's eyes rolling at that quaint anachronism. This is all told from his perspective, years later. Mom, eternally the widow, still lives in the shanty, but they don't see much of each other. As for the kid, he's grown up wary of the kind of involvements that lead to emotional responsibility. He's better-natured than his old man about drinking, but a lush nonetheless.

There weren't many films like that. Most of them were "light-hearted romps" in the parlance of the poster. The newsreels, on the other hand, were about history, which was being made a mile a minute over in Europe. Lots of Hun soldiers marching the goose-step, then a slow fade to some solemn Limey wringing his hands—Sir this, Prime Minister that—interchangeable worrywarts.

Meanwhile the Wops were fixin' to invade the Fuzzy-Wuzzys. That was supposed to concern us here, as if we didn't have enough to worry about—commies set to take over Detroit, kids dying of the dust pneumonia, a sheriff shot to death at a foreclosure auction in Iowa.

One newsreel had scenes of half-starved yokels staring in bewilderment at some neat little bungalows they were supposed to move into. They were starving Okies, being relocated to "Green

Towns" in upstate New York. There was some comic relief when pa tried to screw a light bulb into the ceiling, or ma used the flush toilet to wash the clothes.

A huge celebration was held out in the desert somewhere to commemorate the completion of a 750 foot high dam, but the only ones who looked they had anything to celebrate were the politicians. Four thousand men who'd had steady work for five years were out of a job.

Unemployment overall was down to just over twenty percent, however—"a sure sign of recovery."

One February afternoon Blanche and I sat through, "A Celluloid History of The Great Depression." It began on a note of pathos; Wall Street one week after the crash, crawling with well-dressed gents peddling apples. It was enough to make you weep, unless you hate the rich or like apples. Being lukewarm about both, I tried to view it as an attempt to re-establish distribution channels in a way that put cash in empty pockets.

It occurred to me that something similar had happened here. The downtown streets, the speakeasies, and then the saloons after Prohibition was repealed, were full of flower peddlers. Hundreds of them. That was something you never saw before the crash. I gathered that it didn't happen in other cities. It was unique to St. Paul.

Who knows how things like that get started? Time marches on, in the direction it gets pointed.

A few of those posie-peddlers were the kind of geezers who had the cush in '29, but mostly they were young folks who never had much and took the Great Depression in stride. They had various ways of hawking their blossoms. There was the winsome lass on the windswept corner, the plucky kid with the patched-up knickers, and my personal favorite, the bold lad who got right in your mug when you were sparking a frail and asked if you'd like to buy the lady a flower. That was mostly a barroom phenomenon, so I saw plenty of it. The going price was only five cents a bloom so it literally took a nickel-nurser to say no. I usually managed.

This came to mind one day that Spring, when I had three chances to buy a rose on the half block walk from the spot where I'd parked my bucket, to the Criterion, where I'd arranged to meet a prospective client. That might've been a record, but it was a balmy afternoon and love was in the air—outside. Inside was the usual fug of cigarette smoke and stale beer, not as aromatic as my evening headquarters at Tin Cup's, but a relief to my jaded lungs nonetheless.

The shades were drawn against the afternoon sun. I made my way past a knot of bar flies who were clustered around their Manhattans, and settled into a booth with my back to the door—stylishly late, but nevertheless first to arrive.

There must have been a pinhole in the shade, because a moving image of the traffic on University Avenue was projected on to the back wall. It looked almost like a movie, but in color. The flivvers stretched out and floated past upside down, as if in a dream. As I watched, I idly pondered the nature of peddling—apples, flowers, information—doesn't matter. The formula is the same; buy cheap, sell dear. The recipe for acquiring the information I trade in was still simple and inexpensive—have an Irish surname and a weakness for hooch. I patted myself on the back once more for the clever way I'd turned those liabilities into assets.

Marcella Kirkwood hadn't told me much when she called. She clearly wanted to size me up before we came to terms. Other than that I didn't know what to expect, but a odd skill I've developed gave me a clue just before I saw her. A certain solid sound her heels made on the parquet floor led me to believe that she'd be a real tomato. I'd honed the knack of hearing what dames looked like by dint of much trial and error, and was rarely wrong.

"Martin McDonough?" she inquired.

Right again. I stood and asked her join me.

She was tall and smartly dressed, in a pleated skirt, a linen jacket and a ruffled white blouse open at the neck. A pair of pince nez specs dangling from a chain around her neck rested on her bosom. She had long legs, big brown eyes and penciled eyebrows. Her chestnut hair was swept into a pile, tied into a thick braid and done up in a bun, leaving her lovely face framed by naught but her nibbly pink ears.

She was thirtyish, and she sported a monstrous diamond on the third finger of her left hand.

"Drink?" I asked, when she'd settled in.

"A little early, isn't it?" she replied, with a frown. "You a soak, McDonough?"

"Ah, that's harsh. But now'ya mention it, hooch is a professional hazard. I spend a lot of time loosening tongues. That's what I'm good at."

"So I've heard....hmm. Ginger ale for me."

I waved the waiter down. Dream buckets oozed across the wall behind her. We exchanged what one might call pleasantries. By the time my beer and her soft drink arrived she'd satisfied herself that we could do business.

"I want to know who murdered my father," she said. "He's been dead for a year, no arrests, nothin'. Seems like an easy case to me."

"Why's that?"

"I'm not tellin' you. I don't want to prejudice your inquiry."

That was a first. I usually have to discourage clients from actively steering my investigation, either to save money or serve some agenda. Things were going well enough professionally that I could afford to be principled.

"Your choice, but I charge by the day," I told her. "The more you tell me, the faster things usually go."

"That's ok, I've made up my mind."

I sighed. "Gonna give me the victim's name? I can tell by that manacle on your digit it wasn't Kirkwood."

She wouldn't smile but her eyes crinkled a bit.

"Robert Tuttweiler. Everybody called him Bobby."

"I'm gonna ask you to write that down, and a few other things—"

She immediately opened her purse and pulled out a pencil. "Got somethin' to write on?"

"—but first I want to know why you think the coppers aren't pursuing it."

"I told you, I don't want to prejudice your investigation."

"I'm not asking who you think the killer is. Why aren't the cops looking? That's what I want to know."

She put the pencil down, picked up her glass, squinted at it. That big rock of her's caught the flux of light coming through the pin hole, and the wall behind her went blank.

"It's not 'the cops,'" she said. "It's this one copper. Eddy Guilfoyle."—She jiggled her glass. The ice tinkled.

Evidently I was supposed to drag information out of her one piece at a time.

"Why isn't he pursuing it?"

"Because he's *corrupt*, that's why."

Of course he was corrupt, but she made it sound supremely disgusting, and she had a defiant look on her puss as she said it too, as if it were my fault. This was 1935, remember, the waning days of the layover, but gangsters were still allowed to take refuge in St. Paul if they paid off the police. That was what made life interesting in the Saintly City. How it affected the work of an investigator like Eddy Guilfoyle might make a fascinating inquiry, but in this situation it only confused things.

"As far as your father's murder is concerned, Mrs. Kirkwood, who'd want to corrupt Eddy, and why?"

"He's just *corrupt*." She wrinkled her nose as she uttered that awful word. "You can call me Marcie."

I took all of that under advisement. Being on first name terms with this lovely creature would certainly spice things up, but her theory was nonsense. The way corruption worked in St. Paul served to isolate it from ordinary people. If anything it made their lives more comfortable. The gangsters had to keep their noses clean while they were in town, and it gave the Krauts and other heathen an excuse to blame Mick coppers on the take whenever a crime went unpunished.

How did Marcie know Eddy was *corrupt*? She'd long suspected it, she explained, but about a week earlier she'd barged into the Rice Street Precinct House and demanded to know why an arrest hadn't been made.

"He couldn't look me in the eye," she said. That cinched it for her.

"Did you know that most murders go into the books unsolved?" I asked.

"No," she admitted.

"The coppers aren't exactly eager to get the word out. Fact is, they get enough evidence for a conviction in maybe three outta ten."

She was unmoved. "Most of'em aren't as easy as this one," she said.

Try as I might, I couldn't get anything more out of Marcie. I settled for the names of her mother, sister and brother, their address and phone number, and the advance on my fee. She extracted the promise of frequent progress reports in return.

"I want to see if you're getting the picture," she said.

I could hardly wait. I was half in love with every tomato I met back then, but I rarely encountered anything like Marcie. 'Classy' was an overworked adjective during the Depression, but it certainly fit her. Every head in the joint turned when she left. She had hips about as wide as her shoulders, and that long, lazy hourglass between.

I dug up a smidgin of dope about the murder that evening at Tin Cup's.

"Bobby Tuttweiler?" said little Mikey Bailey, a bull with a local beat that included a few blocks of Hun turf over in St. Albert's parish. "Some Mocky dropped him, that's what I heard."

I bought him a drink and prodded, but to no avail.

"Tell the truth it didn't make much of an impression," he said. "Mocky ices a Hun—so what? Didn't happen on my shift. Some dame comes into his shop early in the morning t'buy flowers, finds him dead. Talk to Eddy Guilfoyle. He was the investigator."

A fight broke out and interrupted us or I would've asked a few more questions. Fights are hardly a rarity at Tin Cup's, but I remember that as an especially combative evening. This particular tussle involved a Kraut posey-pusher who had the temerity to stick his nose in the door and holler "ROSES," and one of Slapper Doran's stable of young prize fighters, a middleweight named Harry Cassidy.

The Hun tried to put his bouquet in front of his face to protect himself, but this Cassidy had a quick straight left and he landed it hard.

The Hun dropped his blossoms, and commenced swinging, a ballsy move that those of us at the bar approved vociferously. It had the makings of an interesting brawl, but Doran broke it up. That was unlike him. Doran was a pushy, loudmouthed little guy who got in the fight business so he could surround himself with boxers and act tough, or so it seemed to me. He usually encouraged his boys to throw hands when an excuse presented itself. It saved gym expenses.

Doran sat the Hun down at his table, took a handkerchief out of his breast pocket, and dabbed at the Hun's bloody nose. He made Cassidy pick up the flowers, waved the waitress down and bought the kid a drink. Soon they were all getting along famously, as young guys will after they've expended a burst of energy in a wholesome way. Before I lost interest, I noticed Doran take his wad out of his pocket and purchase the flowers. Later on he was walking around giving roses to all the frails. The Hun was long gone by then.

Next afternoon I stopped by The Real McKay's office, and asked if he'd ever heard of Bobby Tuttweiler.

"Yeah," he replied. " A genuine Lothario. Sheila Delaney dumped me when she got involved with him."

"'Lothario?'"

He handed me a dictionary. His machine buzzed, and began spitting out tape.

WEEPING WIDOWS

A couple days later I met Marcie for an update. Not at a hot sheet joint as I'd been fantasizing. At the Criterion again. By then I'd spoken to mom and sis, who told me nothing, and a few of my copper pals, who were the usual fount of information.

The waiter said hello, and seated me in a back booth. He must've assumed we were lovers meeting on the sly. The Criterion had become famous for that since Prohibition ended.

Nearby sat another type of customer the joint was known for. Middle-aged women found it a comfortable spot for a solitary drink. They were treated respectfully, and gentlemen sometimes sent the waiter over with an offer to buy one, which could be accepted or politely turned down. Genteel ladies all, but not necessarily candidates for sainthood. Much of the scuttlebutt that spiced up everyday life in our little city, and occasionally found its way into the gossip columns, owed its existence to the peculiar acoustics of the Criterion.

"I know where you get your looks," I said, after Marcie turned down my offer of a drink.

"Oh? Where."

"Your mother."

"Bang-up, Martin." She placed her pince nez on her nose and peered at me intently. "You're a real sleuth."

"An observation, that's all."

"Any observations about dad's murder? Or am I here so you can look at me."

"Little of each."

She dropped the specs. Her mouth retained its stern line but her eyes crinkled again, and I couldn't help noticing she'd worn lipstick for the occasion. Hope springs eternal.

"So what 'd you find out?" she asked.

"That your father was the greatest flower salesman ever lived. That every florist in St. Paul bought from Midland Wholesale Flowers when he was their salesman, and a few months before he was killed, he quit, opened his own business and took all his accounts with him. Which made the owner of Midland pretty unhappy."

She raised a pencilled brow. "Bingo," she said.

I could see her point, but something her mother told me, a mere aside as I was leaving, led me to believe it wasn't quite so clear cut.

***

Bob had the most beautiful funeral," Betty Tuttweiler had informed me, but as she described it, she spoke caustically of a dozen or so sobbing women "hiding behind veils," who'd elbowed their way into the inner circle as the coffin was being lowered, and thrown bouquets of roses into the grave.

"There were so many weeping widows you'd have thought he was a bigamist," she said. "But I guess that was the nature of the business. Women do most of the buying for retail florists, so Bob saw a lot of them."

Marcie's sister Angie, who'd been bustling around putting the final touches on her makeup before going out for the evening, stopped in her tracks and gave mom a bemused look.

"What?" Betty asked.

Angie just shook her head.

I'd let their little interchange pass without further inquiry, but I decided to mention it to Marcie.

"Let me put this as tactfully as possible. Think maybe a jealous husband might be worth a look?"

"No."

"Oh. I'll keep that in mind."

I told her about Mikey Bailey's tip.

"Sounds like you're on to somethin' there," she said. "Don't pay much attention to mom and Angie. They're tired of the whole thing. Mom won't even talk to me about it."

I'd sensed as much, although they were gracious and friendly. Real friendly. Betty was tall, fifty or so, but quite the looker still. She knitted her hands as we spoke, more beleaguered-seeming than nervous. It made me want to put an arm around her, which wouldn't have been hard. The moment I walked in she seated me on the sofa and sat down next to me.

"Angie, bring the pictures," she said.

Soon Angie squeezed in on the other side, photo album in hand. Betty flipped through and showed me a photo of her late husband. He had that lounge-lizard look, right down to the half-smile and the curl of smoke from the cigarette gripped like a dart between his thumb and forefinger. He had a hawk nose, and eyes that you just knew were blue, even though the picture was sepia-toned; intense, snapping eyes, hooded under thick, dark eyebrows. A lick of hair hung over his forehead.

"Handsome, wasn't he," said Angie. She leaned in close to tap her finger on the photo. I felt her breath on my shoulder. My leg pressed up against Betty's. Heat came off both of them in waves. It was about seven in the evening of what had been a very warm day. The light from the lowering sun through the living room window shone red through a scrim of dust bowl haze. The air in the house hardly stirred.

"We're alone here now," Betty said. "Bobby Junior comes in late at night, sleeps all day. Oh, I don't know..." Her fidgety hands brushed against mine, which were braced against my thighs.

"Uh, do'ya feel, well...safe?" I asked.

"How can we?" Betty replied. "With Bob being shot and all."

"I do," said Angie. She gave me a quick smile. "Not that it wouldn't be nice to have a guy around sometimes. My brother is gone a lot."

"Oh sure, you feel safe," said Betty. "You don't sit here alone at night wondering where your children are, when they're coming -"

Angie leaned over me to put her hand on her mom's arm. "We're not kids, ma," she said. "We're fine, you'll be fine."

I was rigid and sweaty, trying hard not to cop a feel, wondering why I was trying so hard. Nobody else was. Angie braced her hand on my knee when she reached across me. I could smell her hair. She wasn't lean and statuesque like Marcie. More the round, scrumptious type.

"Hot, isn't it?" she said. "Want some lemonade or somethin', Martin?"

"Nah, I'm ok. Well, maybe."

"Get him some, dear," said Betty.

She brought me a glass of iced lemon drink, then continued to bustle about while her mother and I spoke, passing close enough for me to get another whiff of her perfume (nice but not subtle) and a touch or two from the fringe of her shimmy skirt. Her cheeks dimpled when she smiled. She was certainly easy on the eye, even if she didn't have legs to the chin like mom and sis.

"You ever hafta kill a guy, Martin?" she asked.

"Naw, never came to that."

"Marcie told me she wanted to hire you," Betty said. "I wish she hadn't. It's time to put it behind us, don't you think?"

"It's easier when y'know who did it. Or so they say."

"But that's not going to happen, is it." Her tone was resigned.

"We'll see. Marcie claims the investigator's the problem. Says he's bent. What do you think?"

"Eddy? He's a dear."

I knew Eddy. He wasn't a dear.

I got some idea of what the deceased was like from talking with them, but not much else. They made it clear who'd run the show in their family. Angie said her social life was more to her liking now that she didn't have to feign interest in various well-born stiffs just to please dad. Betty wouldn't discuss the murder. Angie seemed to take her cues from her mom.

I asked when I might find Bobby Junior home. Betty said call first and I'd catch him sooner or later. When I rose to leave, Angie asked if she could have a ride. She was headed down to Kuby's joint.

"They have live music there now," she said.

She was bubbly on the way. She told me she loved jazz music. I said I was surprised they had smokes playing at Kuby's. Only one, she explained, the rest of the band were guys she knew from the neighborhood. I gathered they were Krauts like her. Playing jazz music. Strange times we live in.

"Wanna tell me who killed your father?" I asked.

She shook her head. "You'll find out soon enough."

"Marcie tell you to clam up?"

She admitted she had, but explained that none of them, especially her mother, needed much coaxing. They were keenly disappointed that a case that they thought would be solved in a few days was a year old, and had apparently hit a dead end. Like her sister, she assumed I would draw the obvious conclusion once the facts were revealed.

"Thanks," she said, when I dropped her off. "You know how to get hold'a me. Say hi to Marcie." She squeezed my hand before leaving.

***

Angie says 'hi,'" I told her big sister, who barely acknowledged that she'd heard. She told me I should have gone into Kuby's with Angie if I wanted to talk to her brother.—"He spends most of his time there," she said.

"You worried about him?" I asked, just to keep the conversation moving. I didn't want her to leave.

"He took dad's death pretty hard."

"He into the hooch now?"

She shrugged. "Bobby's a poet or somethin'," she said, as if that answered the question.

Mom and Angie's feelings seemed a more promising line of inquiry anyway, so I inquired.

"Why do you want to know?" she asked. Her attitude was that I shouldn't let anything distract me from the obvious, but I persisted.

"It was a jolt when he was killed," she told me "but it was a relief to have him gone, if you must know. He had ideas about how we should live our lives, and he was kind of a tyrant about some things.—Buy me a drink. Put it on the bill if you want."

Needless to say, that was a welcome development. I assured her the drinks were on me. She ordered a Manhattan.

"I take it your father cheated," I said.

"Boy, did he." At long last she smiled for real. On top of everything else she had that sexy gap between her two front teeth.

"Who did he cheat with?"

"Every gal he could, till the day he died. That dame who found him? Guess what she came to the shop for."

"To buy flowers?"

"Ha!—Well, that's not fair. Most of his sweeties bought flowers from him. That was the excuse he used when him and mom argued."

She sloshed her drink around, took a sip.

"I loved my dad, but he *corrupted* us."

There was that word again. This time I asked her to explain.

"Everybody thinks about two-timin'," she said. "Doin' it, that's different. Dad turned mom into a cheat. It didn't come naturally to her like it did to him, but she's a number, always was, so she had plenty of opportunity. They pretended things were ok in front of us kids, then argued when they thought we couldn't hear. That's how I grew up. By the time Angie and me were in high school they didn't care if we heard or not. My brother was still a kid. We'd take him out and play with him so he wouldn't have to listen."

"Maybe your mom killed him."

"Not funny."

"Wasn't a joke."

I waited for her to react. She didn't.

"I still don't see why you're so sure a jealous husband didn't do it," I said. "Seems logical to me."

She shook her head. "You didn't know my dad. People loved him. We loved him, in spite of it all. Mom loved him, the gals he played around with loved him. Their husbands probably loved him. He was handsome, smart, witty, a great salesman, took the parish orphan kids on outings."

"Sounds perfect."

"But he wasn't. He used animal magnetism to get what he wanted. That was his flaw."

"It's human nature."

"But it's not much of an example. Dad was a liar too, lied like a rug. Not that he was ashamed. He just wanted to avoid scenes. Mom had her ways of findin' out though. She liked to catch him, then use it as an excuse to tell him about her latest romance. Me'n Angie lied all the time when we were kids. About school, about our boy friends. To the priests. I didn't make an honest confession until I left home."

"That wasn't a problem for me," I told her. "I just stopped goin' to confession. All those impure thoughts.—You said everybody thinks about playin' around. That mean you too?"

"Don't be coy." She swallowed some more of her Manhattan.

"Ok. You think about playin' around with me?"

"Sure. You're handsome, you have kind of an intriguing life, a reputation. But I'd never do it."

"Aww."

She laughed and patted my hand. "Don't take it personal.—What do you need me for anyway? You meet lots of 'dames,' have lots of rumble seat sex, don't you? I suppose you're quite the rogue, Martin, a real seducer. Just like dad."

I didn't know exactly where this was going, but I knew where I hoped it was going.

"From what I've gathered, I'm not in your old man's league."

"Huh." She fussed with her pince nez, and didn't say anything for awhile. -"So tell me about them," she said. "Your girl friends."

"Jeez, Marcie. They're all different. You know that."

"Ok. Tell me about one of'em."

"There's Blanche Schuh. Every once in awhile we get a yen just lookin' at each other. At least I do. She must too, because we go somewhere and—uhh .."

"God! She should restrain herself."

"Why?"

"Because nice girls—"

"Blanche isn't a nice girl, Marcie. She's a 'dame.'"

I told her about another gal, Jeannie Hallgren, former maid-in-waiting at the court of Boreas, King of the St, Paul Winter Carnival. Jeannie ran off with His Majesty a few years later.

"Quite the 'tomato' was she?" said Marcie.

She actually said 'tomato' in quotes, but I don't know who she was quoting. Not me. I'm careful how I talk around classy dames.

"You know how they choose those gals. The Snow Queen is somebody whose daddy has bucks, but the Princesses and Maids are there because they're lookers. Jeannie, well—how should I put it—Jeannie put the carnal into carnival. "

"Was she as good-lookin' as me?"

I said no, although she was in her own way,

"Damn right." She took a sip of her drink. "How'd you seduce her."

"I didn't. She seduced me."

"No!"

"Yeah."

I began an abbreviated version of a complicated story. I'd been hired to find the kidnapers who'd snatched the former King. His father-in-law, a prominent banker, paid the ransom, but his Majesty was never seen again.

"Oh, married was he?" Marcie interjected. "I suppose Miss whatshername lured him to his fate."

Hush, I told her, because the walls have ears at the Criterion.

"I'll tell'ya what happened if you swear you'll keep it under your hat.—I'm serious. If the so-called widow ever gets wind of what I'm about to tell'ya it would break her heart. I'm not gonna give you any names, but there are plenty of people who could put two and two together."

She swore she'd never tell a soul. I made her swear twice.

"I don't betray client's confidences," I said. "I'm not kiddin'. This is important to me."

"Ok, ok," she said.

I explained the trail of marked bills that led to Crane Lake up in northern Minnesota, and the supposed kidnapper. Who did I find? King Boreas himself, who'd connived his own disappearance and collected the ransom. He was off hunting. Jeannie invited me to spend the night before I went back.

"Ha," Marcie laughed. "Poor thing was stuck all alone in the middle of nowhere. No wonder she invited you to bed. She was scared."

I didn't bother explaining that Jeannie Hallgren was one tough cookie. I got back to the main point.

"Uh-uh, she was just lookin' for a good time. You gonna tell me somethin' like that never crosses your mind?"

She gave me a sly, sideways look.

"I told'ja it did, remember? But that doesn't mean we're gonna do it. Banish the thought."

"Why not?" I persisted.

"Because I have a good marriage, that's why.—Don't get me wrong. Dirk isn't a very *interesting* guy. I mean, he never was— never knew interesting people, never did interesting things. He'd talk about all these 'adventures' him and his friends had, but all they ever did was get blotto and speed around in their roadsters. I went with'em sometimes. There was always lotsa hooch, and you wondered if you were gonna get in an accident. Other than that it was—I don't know....dull."

"So how come you married him? Cake in the oven?"

"Uh uh." She didn't seem shocked that I'd asked.

"So—why?"

"Maybe I'll tell'ya some time, Martin. When we know each other better."

"Well, what better way to get acquainted -"

"Uh-uh." She shook her finger at me, but her eyes crinkled when she did it. She was most of the way through her Manhattan by then.

"And don't say my husband wouldn't find out. That has nothin' to do with it.—Well, almost nothin'. I mean if we were on a desert island..."

I reached across the table and took her hand. "How about if we were at the St. Francis Hotel?"

She looked deep into my bloodshot blue eyes, and said, "Forget it."

I ran my thumb over that rock of hers.

"Ok, a desert island. You can use this to signal ships at sea when we get tired'a foolin' around."

She smiled again, which was all the more fetching now that I'd seen that gap between her teeth. She wouldn't sit still for another Manhattan though.

"Until my next report," I said as we parted.

THE KEY MAN

The prospect of another meeting certainly speeded the probe. That very evening I wedged my way up to the bar next to the nefarious Eddy G, bought him one, and observed him carefully as we sipped our drinks.

He'd aged a bit, to put it mildly. Sallow skin, thinning hair, baggy eyes. *Corrupt* was an understatement. He appeared to be decomposing.

"How's it goin,' Eddy?" I inquired.

"So so."

"What'cha been up to?"

"Nothin' special."

Was it my imagination, or was he more taciturn than usual? I decided not to beat around the bush. He just shook his head wearily when I told him the subject of my inquiry.

I let him brood for awhile, and listened to Ruth Etting belt out Ten Cents A Dance on the Mighty Wurlitzer. A little too heartfelt for my taste, but her voice was so compelling that normal bar noise toned down as she sang. I suppose everyone was thinking about the same thing I was as they listened - all those newspaper stories about Etting's gangster-ex shooting her squeeze in a jealous rage. Eddy was still in a snit when it ended, so I had to sit through Peg' O My Heart, a scratchy old chestnut they kept on the machine for

sentimental reasons. The lyrics, sung by an old-time ham of a baritone named Shamus McClaskey, were forgotten as easily as they
were memorized, but the tune was lyrical in a way calculated to jerk
a tear. We'd had that very record to play on a Victrola when I was
a child, and hearing it made me think of my father, a topic I tried
mightily to avoid.

"That dame'll never leave me alone," Eddy finally said. "I wish
I'd never heard'a the case."

"What dame?"

"The deceased's daughter, of course. Who else would've hired
you? The rest of the family accepted it. Other day she chased me
down at the precinct. Called me a highbinder in so many words. It
was embarrassing fr'christ's sake."

"I had no idea you were so sensitive, Eddy."

"Ah, go to hell," he muttered.

He drained his drink and started to walk away, but, presto! I
was my normal cajoling self again. He didn't exactly cheer up, but
he succumbed to the point where he gave me the straight dope, in
detail.

"Deceased had a shop down the street by St. Albert's, a storefront with a big cooler where he kept some stock. He was usually
there by six A M, opened at seven, which I come to find out is how
it's done in the flower business. The retail florists do all their buyin'
early in the morning. He had an appointment at seven, a woman. She
arrives a few minutes before, thinkin' she'll knock on the door but
sees it's open. Walks in, finds Tuttweiler lyin' behind the counter.
Face looks like hamburger. Somebody put a twelve-gauge with a
load of birdshot right under his chin and let him have both barrels.
Little tiny BBs. Wouldn't'a killed him at ten feet."

Eddy was warming to his story. He was neglecting his drink.
Some color had returned to his mug. The redder he got the better he
looked, relatively speaking. On his best day he resembled nothing
so much as a stubbed toe. His puss looked like a normal face viewed
upside down—nose like a big square chin, underbite, little porcine
eyes too, but that beezer of his defined him. It looked like it had

withstood many a solid punch and about five shots of whiskey a day for decades.

He was a good investigator though, and the things he highlighted as he described the murder scene—the weapon, the fact that no money had been taken, the fact that the cooler was open and an armful of freshly cut roses lay on the floor next to the body—added up the same way for him that they did for me: Bobby Tuttweiler opened his door for someone before business hours, most likely someone who came under the guise of doing business, and that person killed him. His wallet was still in his pocket and the cash drawer was untouched, so robbery wasn't the motive. Nor was it a professional drop. Droppers don't lug shotguns around, especially if they're loaded with ammo that wouldn't be fatal unless you practically stuck the barrel in the victim's mouth.

"The way his mush was massacred, that tell you anything?" I asked.

"Jealous girl friend? Uh-uh. I talked to the dames he was known to be intimate with. Busy man, Mr. Tuttweiler, but they all had alibis and so did their hubbys. I did the basics, Martin. Talked to the deceased's business associates, checked the whereabouts of his family. Wife and daughter were home when it happened, coppers got'em outta bed to tell'em about the murder. Son spent the night at a friend's place. Him, couple guys, some rich gal who hung out with'em, all of'em cuttin'a rug after Kuby's closed. Coppers hadda wake them up too. Bobby Junior broke down an'cried when they told him. There's only one real suspect, and he got away with it clean. Betty and her other kids accepted it, and what's her name, Marcella, sooner or later she'll have to accept it too."

"His ex-employer, right?"

"Right. Mocky name'a Sheldon Slansky, owned Midland Wholesale Flowers. Deceased quit, opened his own shop, and took every nickel'a business with him when he left. Slansky was after him to come back, makin' offers, threats. He was desperate."

"Must'a been to come up with a plan like that. What's he gonna do, march him back to his old job at gunpoint? Follow him around with a shotgun while he called on customers?"

Eddy sighed. "I'm gonna tell you what I told the Chief, what I told the prosecutors. Then I never wanna hear about this again, ok?"

He explained that Slansky had taken out an insurance policy on Bobby Tuttweiler when Bobby first began talking about leaving. It was a type of insurance called a "key man policy." It paid Slansky ten thousand dollars if his star salesman died or became disabled.

"But he quit first, so it was worthless, right?" I said.

"No. Here's the strange thing. Once the company sells the policy they can't cancel it, as long as the policy holder pays the premiums. Agent told me the only rule is, he couldn't'a wrote it in the first place unless the insured was an employee at the time. The insurance company figures anyone who buys a key man policy will stop payin' premiums if the key man quits workin,' but Slansky didn't stop and nobody could make him. Deceased tried, deceased's wife tried, insurance agent tried. He just told'em, 'screw you.' Paid monthly, right on time. Even though his business was goin' under."

"And he collected all that do re mi?"

"All that and more. Double the face value because it was murder. Slansky's lawyer demanded payment. The insurance company asked the D A if Slansky was gonna be indicted. D A says no, company pays Slansky twenty thousand smackers. Now who d'you think killed him?"

"I see who had motive. What else you got?"

"Opportunity. Betty Tuttweiler tells me Bobby wanted to end the bad blood between him and Slansky. Says if Slansky knocked on the door and gave Bobby some song and dance about needin' roses for his business that day he'd have said ok. Bobby goes into the cooler to get the flowers, Slanksy pulls the shotgun out from under his coat and kills him when he comes back."

"Good theory. What else?"

"Nothin.' Slansky says he was home with the wife. She backs him up. They're both lyin.' No confession, no physical evidence. Haven't found the weapon. We got motive. We got opportunity. I've seen men convicted on less, but they won't even indict him."

As his story wound down Eddy deflated like a tire with a slow leak. By the time he finished he was pale as a ghost again. I asked him why they wouldn't prosecute, a topic he would've certainly discussed with the D A. He shrugged and mumbled something about Slansky's lawyer.

"You don't have any of that money, do'ya?" I asked.

"What the hell do you think?"

"Just touchin' all the bases before I slide home."

He sighed. "Don't think it's the first time I been asked," he said.

Before we parted he inquired if I'd been attending mass recently.

"Nah, I'm fallen away, Eddy."

"Go back to Holy Mother, Martin," he advised. "It's the only comfort we have."

That and his appearance led me to believe the iron crab had him. I made a mental note to remember Eddy the next time I prayed. If he lived that long.

At that point the murder of Bobby Tuttweiler appeared to be a routine case of know but can't prove. One thing bothered me though. As Eddy noted, stir is full of men convicted on motive and opportunity alone, so why wasn't Slansky prosecuted?

It wasn't exactly inexplicable. The D A doesn't want to lose a case, so he's loathe to go to court without a confession or some solid evidence. But the people who elected him grumble about the streets of St. Paul being full of gangsters who appear to be immune from prosecution, which they are. Given the popular clamor, somebody has to go to trial some time. A Mockey who murders a Kraut for money seems like a good candidate. Hotshot lawyer or no, why not put him in front of a jury and roll the dice?

I knew who to ask, and I wasn't going to run into him at Tin Cup's. Teddy Eccles and I were freshmen at St. Thomas together. Like me, Teddy entered college determined to follow in his father's footsteps. Difference was, his father was a judge and mine was a lush. Teddy was headed for law school, I was headed for the door but I did enjoy my year of higher education. My favorite course was Sacred Music, which baffled Teddy because I couldn't play a note on any instrument, still can't, nor can I carry a tune. Something—scales and melodic lines, the way sound evoked emotion —struck a chord in my impressionable young mind—but I digress. I lasted two semesters, during which Teddy and I spent a lot of time together, mostly in joints where they played dixieland jazz.

Teddy served a short apprenticeship in the D A's office, then made a career of defending guys the D A prosecuted. It was his idea that I become a private eye. I was contemplating joining the police force (actually, now that I think of it, Uncle Jerk was pressuring me to join the police force and I was contemplating whether I wanted to spend my life being a copper), but Teddy said that with my connections and my knack for using them I'd do better on my own.

"And it's a good way to meet women," he added, which cinched it for me.

Teddy was obviously my next move, but there's more than one way to prejudice an inquiry. I was determined to go after this case one step at a time, with frequent reports to my client. It was still the shank of the evening when I left Tin Cup's and headed for Kuby's joint to find Bobby Jr.

Mr. Kuby's horizons had expanded recently. It began with the installation of the Mighty Wurlitzer. The day time regulars like Jerk and a few other old gents grumbled, but it didn't change things much for them. After dark, however, Kuby's became a juke joint. First I heard there was live music was when Angie told me, but I knew it was hot spot for the young crowd.

A four piece band was blaring away when I walked in. They were set up on a little stage in back that was well lit compared to the rest of the place, and sure enough, they had a smoke piano player. There were couples jitterbug dancing on the sawdust covered floor. I grabbed the last empty stool at the bar and looked around for Angie, but couldn't make out faces. She spotted me though.

"MARTIN," she shouted to be heard over the music. 'WHAT BRINGS YOU HERE?"

She squeezed in beside me. Her hip rubbed against mine. I stood quickly, and offered her my seat without thinking. She took it and set her drink in front of her like it was the most natural thing in the world. Apparently Kuby's after dark was the kind of joint where a frail could sit at the bar. At least Angie could. I didn't see any others.

The stage lights dimmed. The band put their instruments down and drifted out to the murky dance floor, among them the smoke, who was practically invisible except for a derby hat that he wore with a fat red ribbon tied around it. A ceiling fan was stirring up enough breeze so the ribbon hovered and squirmed like the tail of a kite above the milling crowd.

I told Angie I was hoping to talk to her brother. "He was here a few minutes ago," she said. "Don't see him now though."

"Too bad. Gotta cross him off my list."

I tried to get the bartender's attention, which took awhile. By the time I turned back a couple of fellows were standing next to her.

"Martin McDonough, meet Danny Wegleitner," said Angie.

It was the rose peddler who'd stuck his beezer into Tin Cup's and got punched. We shook hands.

"And this's my brother Bobby," she said.

Even in the dim light and nothing to go by but the photo I'd seen, I could tell he was the spit and image of his father. Same nose, same black hair, same blue eyes, though his were gentle and melancholy, not full of snap like the old man's. He had a strange outfit on; creased black pants, red suspenders, frayed white shirt, and a bow tie hung loose around his open collar.

We shook hands, awkwardly for him, because a tomato was clinging to his arm, a real dish of a blonde.

"This's Amy," he said, jerking his head in her direction.

Amy nodded without tearing her adoring gaze from Bobby Jr. She was a gorgeous, dissolute-looking young thing, barely of an age to be in a saloon.

"Got a few bucks, sis?' he asked Angie. "I left my cush in my other pants."

"You'd leave your head home if it wasn't attached to your neck," said Angie— fondly, the way you'd chastize a beloved pet who'd just peed the floor again. She opened a little sequined handbag and pulled out a bill. I spotted a deck of Luckys in there. Angie was quite the bearcat, no question. She waved at the bartender.

"Allow me," I said, more out of self-interest than civility.

They ordered straight gin. Given the music and the general tenor of the joint, I took that as an homage to the late Bix Beiderbecke, a noted gin drinker, and if memory serves, the wayward son of a Kraut music teacher. Amy and the other kid (they called him "Wigger") attacked theirs with gusto. Bobby was a sipper.

"Told'ja about Martin, remember?" said Angie to her brother.

"Yeah. Marcie hired him to find out who killed Dad." It looked for a moment like he might weep.

"Aww Bobby," said Amy. She gave him a quick hug.

I waited to ask a few questions in private, but some gals began to gravitate around, a few fellows followed, and soon I could see there was no way to cut Bobby loose. Angie joined their conversation. She caught me glancing at her and shot me a smile. A pained look crossed Wigger's mug.

Dick Pranke, the guy who'd fingered Baby Face Nelson for Jack back in '34, was hovering on the edge of the crowd. He didn't look like he belonged there. He was older than the rest, more my age.

Pranke was maybe five foot five, but he had a big head crowned with a shock of reddish hair, a moon face, and great big hands that he waved around and gestured with constantly. He had a big, toothy smile on his mug that appeared to be meant for someone in particular, but I had nothing better to do than observe him and I could see that it wasn't. He was gassing with everybody at once, and he'd look from one to the other without ever altering that expression.

He had a big chin for a little guy too. The same kind of chin as that wop who'd been strutting around the newsreels lately. Pretty soon he recognized me.

"Hey, Martin, what brings you here?"

"Business.—This your hangout?"

"Lately. I try to keep movin." He gave me a little nudge, like that was a gag and I was in on it. "These kids come from all over town t'hear this coon music. Streetcars ain't runnin' by the time the joint closes. Some of'em buy used buckets from me."

He felt out my need for wheels. I told him my Model A was running ok, and would for a while because one of the guys at Mrs. Dunn's boarding house liked to work on cars. We gabbed a little about the fights, then he excused himself.—"Gotta see a man about a dog," he said.

The smoke from the band wandered over, a tall, powerful-looking guy, with skin so black it was blue. He might've been around my age too, but it's hard to tell with those people. I asked him where he was from. Chicago, he told me, but some friends who worked on the trains had told him about an opportunity here in St. Paul.

"You play in any'a the hot bands in Chicago?"

"Nosuh. I labored in obscurity, amongst the Oxford Gray."

I smiled. He smiled back. "What we grinnin' 'bout, my ofay friend?" he inquired.

"Way you talk reminds me of someone I met at a club over in Minneapolis. A horn player."

You could almost see his ears prick up. "Who?"

"Lester somethin', Lester..."

"You heard Lester Young?"

"Yeah, that's the name."

"Red's my man! Red's my idol! Tall kind'a gate, with light-skin, reddish hair, talks with a 'lithp' sometimes, got a ribbon 'round his hat like me?"

"That's him."

He smiled broadly, revealing teeth white as piano keys. I bought him a whiskey, a selection that made us a minority of two, and told him I was a private eye looking into the murder of Bobby Tuttweiler's father. He'd heard about it.

"Happened around the time I come here," he said. "That guy a friend'a yours?" He nodded in Pranke's direction, and referred to him by a nickname I didn't quite catch.

"Just an acquaintance. What'd you call him? 'Duce'?"

"'Dutchy.' Folks here call him Dutchy. —Man so crooked he could piss around a corner."

Turns out Pranke sold him a used Model T, said it was a runner, charged him a C note.

"First cold day, turn the crank, motor goin' 'ruhhh-ruhhh-ruh-hh' real slow-like. Never did spark. Told Dutchy, but he jus' say 'bad break.'—'Bad break' hell. Jack-roll is what it was."

We commiserated about car salesmen and cold weather. He told me in more detail why he'd come here. Some Pullman porter friends of his had tipped him that white youngsters in St. Paul were evincing an interest in hot music. The porters stayed in the Rondo neighborhood during layovers, and the white kids had been frequenting a blind pig across the street from their rooming house.

"The oxford boys came for the jazz. An' the muggles. An' the gash." He swiped the back of his hand across his beezer. "Not to mention the nose candy."

The porters made extra swag peddling the stuff, he explained.

This wasn't exactly news to me. The cursed Sunday closing laws in our state—a veritable sea of sanctimony dotted about with islands of honest self-indulgence—had driven me to the back door of that very establishment on several occasions. Along with the aforementioned goods and services they sold something that resembled whiskey after hours, and on the Sabbath day as well.

"Scares me the way these gray boys take to the snow," he said, in a confidential tone. "Personally, I wouldn't touch it with a barge pole. Catch a nigger with snow he'd be lucky if they give him life in prison. Mos' likely hang him from the nearest lamp post."

I told him I didn't know why the bulls should care what people snort up their nose, or who sells it to them. It smacked of Prohibition to me. To my surprise he took exception.

"Ain't like whiskey. Folks get all jingle-brain behind it. Costs big cush, makes 'em do all kinda dirt just to get some. An' they don't bunk when they get tootin' neither. They toot some more, an' stay up all night, runnin' their mouth." He nodded at the bunch gathered around Bobby. "Lotsa these kids are tooters. It's a now an'then thing with most of'em I guess, but see that one gal? The tall, skinny one?"

He pointed out a well-dressed, nervous-looking frail standing at the edge of the crowd, gnawing her thumbnail.

"They say she's the ritz, got'er a crush on Bobby, started buyin' snow t'show him how hep she is. Now she got the habit, bad.

"There's two hope-to-die-snowbirds hang out here," he added. "The rich gal an' Wigger. Used to be three, but one of'em went down for the count awhile back."

"Snow kill him?"

"Not exactly."

As you can imagine, I've developed an ear for the sort of tale that ends in death and this one was truly strange. The kid had gotten into the habit of stepping outside and sniffing nose candy a few times per evening. Inevitably, at some point during one of those tooters, a mood would come upon him, he'd let out a blood-curdling whoop, bolt across Front Avenue, scramble over the Calvary Cemetery fence, and spend the next while tipping over gravestones.

"He'd come back all outta breath and sweaty, big grin all over his map. Me an'the band be swingin'away, and we'd hear a cheer when he walked in. 'Yay Tipper. Attaboy Tipper.' But one night, maybe a year ago, he didn't come back. Next day they found him over in the graveyard, squashed like a bug under one'a them big old monuments."

He said the stone that crushed him weighed eight hundred pounds. There was some hooch-talk about the revenge of the stiffs, but the sober surmise was that he'd gotten to rocking that monument back and forth in order to tip it over, and it tipped the wrong way.

"Rocking a piece of stone that weighs eight hundred pounds?" I was incredulous.

"Snow give a man superhuman powers," he explained. "'Specially the oxford gray. They claim they go a week without sleepin', make love twelve hours straight, go down to the pool hall an' run the table—rack'em up, do it over again—sounds kinda suspicious to me too."

"Better tell those porter friends'a yours to watch out," I advised. "White kids whiffin' snow, dyin' under suspicious circumstances .."

"Oh, the porters ain't sellin' it no more."

"Coppers on to'em?"

He shook his head no. There'd been no local pressure, he explained, but the crew chief had taken all the porters and conductors aside, one crew at a time as they passed through Chicago, and told them to quit peddling in St. Paul.

"Man said it'd cost'em their job if they done it. Trainmen think the mob got after'em. Want it all to themselves."

"No mob here," I said. "We got a different set up."

He nodded as if he knew. "Some gal's sellin' it 'round town now."

I should get out like this more often, I thought. You learn things in these joints you'll never hear at Tin Cup's.

"She come in here?" I asked.

"Uh-uh. Nobody ever sees her. Dutchy's the man here."

I was eager to hear more, but Bobby Jr. tugged on his sleeve. Bobby was about to put on a performance, and he wanted everybody's attention.

The crowd around him hushed. He closed his eyes until a scratchy recording of I'm Comin' Virginia came on the Wurlitzer, tapped his foot patiently all the way through Trumbauer's saxophone opening, then mimed that entire Bix solo, swaying and fingering an imaginary coronet right through to the long fade at the end.

"Bobby's on to somethin'," my smoke companion whispered. "Can't play a note far's I know, but he understands 'bout the music."

"Understands what?"

"The real jazz ain't about dancin,' it's about tellin' a story."

The gals stared at Bobby in rapt admiration. The guys had envy written all over their faces, not of the performance, which was so corny it was embarrassing, but of the effect it had on the gals.

I told my smoke informant my name before the band reassembled to play, and he gave me his: Sean. Sometimes I feel like the modern world is passing me by.

My eyes were accustomed to the light by then. I noticed Slapper Doran and a couple of his fighters at a table near the stage. It didn't look like they'd come to do battle with the Hun. I couldn't picture them doing the Lindy Hop either.

Bobby and Amy drifted off when the music started, and took the crowd with them. Angie stuck around. A stool opened next to her, so I sat down. I had to lean right into her ear to talk, then turn my head so she could lean into mine when she replied.

"He's quite the performer, your brother."

"That pretend horn-playin' routine? I don't know. He's got a pretty good voice though."

"Piano player just told me about kid name'a Tipper. You know about him?"

"Sure. Neighborhood guy. Friend of my brother's. Terrible what happened. He knocked a big gravestone over on himself."

Her lips lingered after she spoke, and brushed my cheek when I turned to reply. I spotted Wigger out of the corner of my eye, looking ruefully at our tete a tete. It was pretty obvious he was soft on Angie. And just as obvious that Angie was vamping me.

"Kid had a headfull'a toot," I said. "Must'a made him crazy."

"It affects people different ways." She put her hand on my leg. "Makes some feel like jazzin' it. Want a little?"

"Nah, I'm strictly a hoocher, Angie. So, they think he pushed eight hundred pounds'a granite over, and managed to wind up underneath it?"

She wondered why I was interested. Force of habit, I explained. I hear about a murder, I investigate.

"What about dad. Figured out who killed him yet?"

"I discovered who everybody thinks killed him."

"You don't think it might be somebody else, do you?"

"Just tryin' to keep an open mind."

She didn't hide her disappointment when I said I was leaving. Angie clearly expected me to pitch some woo. I rarely hesitated when a gal gave me the come-on in those days, but something, the thought of her sister maybe, gave me pause.

I tried to say goodbye to Bobby Jr. but couldn't get his attention. He was out on the dance floor, cutting it up with Amy. Bobby was a smooth hoofer. They did a break out, and Amy's dress flew up to reveal a pair of knockout gams and some pink underwear. There were catcalls and wolf whistles.

I walked past Wigger and Slapper Doran on the way out. They were huddled together, deep in discussion.

***

Next morning I called Marcie to arrange a meeting.

"Mr and Mrs. Kirkwood are vacationing in Canada for two weeks," said the maid.

I considered putting everything on hold until our next meeting, so we could meet yet again after I got back to work. That seemed inexcusable, and besides it was always a pleasure chinning with Teddy Eccles. I wanted to drop by his office. Instead, he suggested lunch at the Green Lantern a few days hence. I prefer other venues when people take me to lunch, but didn't argue.

I visited Betty Tuttweiler again the next afternoon and had a nice, pleasant, uninformative little chat. Angie wasn't home. Bobby was asleep.

When it became apparent that I was settling in to wait him out, Betty started knitting her hands again, probably out of embarrassment. When Bobby finally came downstairs he was arm in arm with Amy.

Long engagements were common in those days due to the Depression. That loosened the premarital sex taboo considerably, but sleeping together in the parental abode was still pretty daring. So was the loving couple's behavior. Amy mumbled something about getting home. They gave each other a farewell buss at the door that lingered, escalated and threatened to turn into something best done in private. Betty cleared her throat, they broke it off and Amy said goodbye.

Bobby sat down to some warmed over coffee. He said he missed his dad every day, told me he'd tried to hold the business together after the murder but quit in frustration when he realized most of the records had been kept in Bobby Sr.'s noggin.

"I called on all his accounts. They bought a few times out of respect for dad, but after awhile they were askin' questions about seasonal buying, how many blooms they could move and when. Stuff like that." He looked over at Betty. "Dad learned it from the ground up. I'd have to be a delivery boy for five years to even begin—"

"Bobby, Bobby." She mussed his hair fondly. "You don't have to sell flowers. Sell bonds. That's where the money is."

"You don't get it, ma. Old guys sell bonds to the fat cats. Guys my age sell bonds to their relatives."

"Exactly,"she said.

"You wanna buy some bonds?" He laughed. "How's about Angie?"

"How's about the Ervines," she replied, and she raised an eye-brow.

It was an allusion to the well-known White Bear millionaires. Sounded like a long shot to me.

Bobby just repeated the common wisdom when we moved on to the murder. "Marcie knows who bumped him off," he said. "We all do."

"So you don't think it's possible anybody else shot him?" I asked.

He shrugged, torched a fag and took a deep pull.

"Well if somebody else did, who might it have been?"

"I can't imagine," said Betty.

Neither could Bobby, apparently. He was half-hidden in smoke, off in a dream.

"Hey, Bobby. You snort snow?"

He shook his head no, slowly. "Gin's my poison,—'Gimme a pig's foot and a bottle'a gin,'" he chanted, "'jazz me cuz I'm in my sin.'"

Now I'd heard a smoke gal singing something like that on the Wurlitzer, and Bobby's version was so self-consciously derivative that you'd have been tempted to laugh, except for one thing. He had the kind of growly, smoker's voice we liked in those days, and to the extent you could tell from such a short riff, maybe the gift for phrasing too.

"Why do you ask him about snow?" Betty inquired. She was working her hands a mile a minute. It was disconcerting.

"Just curious," I said. "I come to find out a lotta guys around Kuby's whiff snow."

"Bobby dear, you never told me that," she said.

"Don't worry, ma. I'm there for the sounds and a little taste'a hooch, that's all."

He blew a smoke ring, sat back and began fingering that phantom horn again. It seemed Betty was used to his eccentricities. She asked what he was playing.

"Goofin'," he said. "Bix called it 'correlated phrasing.'"

"You should take trumpet lessons, darling."

"Nah." He stuck the fag in his puss and closed his eyes.

"Maybe voice ," I suggested. "You could be up on that bandstand, Bobby. Right up front."

He blushed, and continued correlating phrases.

***

Next day I met with Teddy at the Green Lantern—a joint where the clientele told you all you needed to know about our city in the thirties.

Some gawkers showed up there in the evening, and of course the inevitable retinue of frails who get their kicks hanging out with gangsters, but during the day it was it was cops and robbers about fifty-fifty—strictly a place to exchange scuttlebutt and pass messages, spoken and unspoken.

I was making an effort to put off drinking until five P M in those days so I wasn't around the Lantern much, but when I was, it was in the company of Teddy or Jack Moylan. They were both good friends, and being seen with either served my purposes. The coppers were reminded that I had a direct line to the D A's office through Teddy, which kept them, if not honest, more honest than they'd be otherwise. The gangsters, who were sometimes inconvenienced by what I discovered, took note of my familiarity with Officer Jack. They might not care much for me, but they wanted to be on good terms him.

Whichever one I was with, I made sure the maitre'd walked us through to a back booth so everybody could see. Jack and Teddy were both big men, bigger than me and I'm six feet. Jack looked like he could knock your block off with a backhand slap. Teddy had a mane of thick, prematurely gray hair, and a ready smile for all, because all were potential clients.

The Lantern had drapes over the windows, lots of tables, booths along two walls, a long bar, and some nicely subdued light from a row of chandeliers with green-tinted bulbs. It gave the impression of class, which was dispelled once you tasted the food. Teddy and I nursed beers, and pushed our Salisbury Steak around in puddles of grease while we caught up.

A little scamp of a kid wearing patched pants and a worker's cap stuck a bouquet of roses in my face. I declined. Teddy bought one, gave him a buck and told him to keep the change.

Harry Sawyer, owner and proprietor, was seated in a booth along the far wall. He was in a heated conversation with Faennis Cuhulain, a man who seemed too gentlemanly to be what he was, a refugee from the Chicago gang wars. Capone had murdered his buddy Dion O'Banion, aka Gimpy, who'd run that city's North Side syndicate out of his flower shop.

Cuhulain was an oddity at the Lantern, neither a copper nor a wanted man. Rumor had it he'd simply been told to leave Chicago if he valued his life. Apparently he did, and the way he lived you could see why. He was fiftyish, a snazzy dresser, and said to be a connoisseur of food, music and other pleasures. He kept a suite of rooms at the St. Paul Hotel.

I had a notion of what Sawyer and Cuhulain's discussion concerned. Sawyer had inherited the Lantern and the sinecure it represented from his ex-boss Dan Hogan, who'd devised the layover system and made it work. According to the terms of the original layover a wanted criminal could come to St. Paul and live for up to a year under police protection, as long as he paid Hogan five thousand clams (it was a sliding scale; that was minimum) and committed no crimes in the immediate area. Hogan split the gratuity with the coppers, and his gang made sure the mugs behaved. It was a system that worked nicely as long as Hogan lived.

No one knew for sure who'd wired Hogan's bucket, but Sawyer certainly prospered after it blew up. Sawyer had no interest in disciplining gangsters. He preferred acting as their banker, and lately he'd been doing so in cahoots with Cuhulain. At least that was the rumor. I neither knew if it was true, nor cared. I'd been banking with Sawyer since the 1930 bank run, but it was the other side of that coin that really affected my life, and much for the better. After Sawyer went into financial services Eternal Tommy had to reach into the ranks and find someone to enforce the terms of the layover. My friend Jack Moylan was his choice.

"How's things," Teddy asked. "How's Jerk doing?"

"I don't see much of him nowadays."

"Why's that?"

"He double-crossed me."

I told him about the Margaret Thornton affair. Teddy said it didn't qualify as a double-cross, just a devious way of looking out for my best interests.

"That's one way of lookin' at it."

"Jesus, Martin. He's family."

"Which means of all people, he should know better."

"Know better than what?"

"Than to deke me into stepping out of character. Jesus, I get steamed just thinkin' about it! I felt like an organ-grinder's monkey. And here Jerk knew who was behind it the whole time."

"Did you learn anything?"

That was always Teddy's question. He was philosophically committed to the idea that no experience was wasted, because life was series of lessons about the human condition. It was a good enough theory that we chewed it over on many a drunken evening, during which, as I recall, I argued that life was just getting from one end to the other without tripping over your dick—but who knows?

"I heard some good music," I admitted.

"There you go.—So, what is it you wanted to discuss?"

I told him what I knew about the Tuttweiler case, and asked why the D A wouldn't try to nail Sheldon Slansky on motive and opportunity.

"Good question, but I've got a better one. How come that's all he's got?"

"Eddy claims he couldn't crack the guy's alibi, couldn't find the weapon, couldn't get any evidence at all. My client thinks he wasn't lookin' hard enough because some of the insurance money ended up in his pocket."

"I'm the DA, I'm going to check that out," said Teddy. "Unless the rest of it ended up in my pocket."

"Think that might've happened?"

"Martin, in a world where enlightened self-interest is the guiding principle we can never discount that possibility. Who's the client?"

He whistled when I told him. Turned out he knew her because he'd defended her husband.

"You probably remember," he said. "It was front page news. 'White Bear Youth In Sports Car Collision. Negligence Alleged.' That was Dirk Kirkwood. He was remorseful, I'll say that for him. He should've been. Him and his buddies used to get lit at the Yacht Club, and race their sports cars on the county roads out there. He was trying to pass another kid's Stutz in some kind of English roller skate when he sideswiped a horse and wagon. Dirk was barely scratched, but he killed the poor bastard in the wagon."

"He was lucky."

"Drunk. That helps. Keeps you loose while you're flying fifty feet into a swamp. We settled out of court for a pretty penny after the charges were dropped."

"Him and Marcie married then?"

"No. I went to their wedding a few months later. I suppose I must've met her father, don't remember. I remember her though. There was talk that Dirk was marrying down, and I wondered why. One look at the bride solved that mystery. She still a lulu?"

Must've been a certain expression on my mug when I nodded.

"I don't mind helping you out professionally Martin, but you're on your own when it comes to pokin' clients." He consulted his watch. "I have to run. You'll hear from me."

I watched him make his slow way out, pausing several times on the way to chat. He stopped at Sawyer's table, slapped Faennis Cuhulain on the back, and told a joke that left the two of them laughing. He waved when he reached the door, I raised my hand to wave back, and the waiter noticed.

That's how I found out lunch was on me.

***

A few nights later I heard the din of angry voices as I walked into Tin Cup's. A crowd of neighborhood guys had Little Mikey Bailey the beat copper surrounded. They were shouting threats. I spotted Billy Powell and Tim McKenna among them. Neither were particularly pugnacious fellows, but they looked grim.

"What's goin' on?" I asked McKenna.

He could barely contain his outrage long enough to explain. Then, just as he began, in walked Eddy Guilfoyle. The mob gathered around him, and started dishing out the same abuse only louder.

Eddy still looked awful, but being forced to defend himself acted as a tonic. He put his big nose right in their faces. Soon he'd shouted them down.

"That Kraut and the poison he was peddlin' corrupted the youth of our parish!" he said, when they'd quieted enough to hear him.

"Ya made a rat outta Slapper Doran," said someone in the crowd.

"That young man made a rat of himself," was Guilfoyle's rejoinder, "and if he rats under oath he might stay out of prison, which is more than he deserves.—G'wan, the lot'a yez!"

He pushed his way through to the bar. No one tried to stop him.

"Whiskey," he said. "And one for Little Mikey."

Mikey squirmed in beside him.

I didn't have the temerity to ask Eddy what it was all about, but Tim filled me in. Word had gone around that little Mikey had collared Slapper Doran at Eddy's behest, frisked him, and found a quantity of nose candy in his pocket. Then Eddy put the squeeze on Slap, and forced him to introduce an undercover bull to the Kraut he'd been buying the stuff from over at Kuby's.

"He got the Hun to sell some to the copper," said Tim. "Now the Hun's in the hoosegow, and Slap's gonna testify against him when he goes to trial to save his own bacon."

Tim didn't know the seller's name, but little Mikey confirmed my suspicions later that evening. It was Angie's friend, Wigger.

The list of things that I don't believe in is longer than a whore's dream, and coincidence is right there at the top—flower peddlers, nose candy, Eddy G and his mysterious lack of progress; they all fit together somehow, and the way I saw it, they had to be connected to Bobby Tuttweiler's murder.

I tried to approach Eddy about it. "I don't ever want to hear about that case again," he said, "ok?"

That was too bad, but it could have been worse. Eddy would get over it and meanwhile, each new twist was an opportunity for another meeting with Marcie. I was slowly pondering how to proceed a few days later when Teddy called.

"Find out where the insurance settlement went," he said. "I tried. All I could find out was where it didn't go, and that was interesting. It didn't go to bribe the D A, I can guarantee you that, and I'm ninety-nine percent sure it didn't go to Eddy Guilfoyle. Make that ninety-nine point nine. And the suspect doesn't have it either. So where is it?"

Teddy said the D A's office would have been glad to charge Slansky with the murder if they could've shown he'd profited by it, but they'd discovered the opposite.

"He's living like a church mouse," Teddy said. "His business is closed. His bank account is empty. He referees softball games for a living, if you can call that a living. They've been over his finances with a fine-toothed comb. The man has nothing. As far as they can tell he didn't even pay the lawyer who pressured the insurance company for him. Somebody else did."

"Who?"

"Well, that's good question. Attorney's name is Morris Fischbein, but I know Morrie. You'll never get anything out of him. The D A tried. He just said it was none of their business."

"So the D A's office doesn't have a clue where the money went?"

"Yeah, they have a clue, and a theory to go with it. Bobby Tuttweiler was a come-easy-go-easy type of guy, didn't have a pot to piss in when he died, but the widow is doing just fine near as anyone can tell. They think maybe the suspect gave the cash to the widow."

"Why?"

To prove to her at least that he didn't kill her husband in order to collect on that policy."

"Twenty grand? The whole thing?"

"Sounds excessive to me too, my friend, but it's the best anyone can come up with.—Thanks for lunch by the way."

"My pleasure."

"Let me know what happens," said Teddy. "I find it pretty interesting."

I found it interesting too, so much so that curiosity drove me out of Tin Cup's and over to Dunning Field for the Wednesday evening softball games.

There were five in progress. It was a regular league—uniforms, umps, the works. Slansky was easy to spot. He was a squared off fire plug of a guy, with the regulation Hebe beezer, and big sad eyes. The other umps yelled STEEE- RIKE! He just raised his arm and muttered, "strike."

I stood behind the backstop and watched from his perspective for awhile.

This was a few years before the advent of the Kitten Ball, which is so big it takes two hands to catch, and so light no mitt is required. A Kittenball game is mostly about lobbing the ball to the batter, who whacks it with all his might. The best players are middle-aged lunks who hit the thing so far that they can haul their beer bellies around the bases on their stiff old legs before the ball can be thrown back to the infield.

Softball, on the other hand, is an athletic contest, and I enjoyed watching it that evening. The pitchers whirled their arms around like aeroplane propellers three or four times before letting fly underhand. The ball—which, name notwithstanding, is not soft—came zooming in as fast as any major league pitcher could throw, that was how it looked to me. It took a brave batsman to stand in there and swing, but when they connected it went a long way.

A couple times foul tips almost beaned Slansky, but he pulled his head back between his shoulders just barely enough to avoid getting clunked. He reminded me of a turtle.

"Who'ya like in the series?" I asked him, between innings.

"Tigers," he replied, without bothering to turn around.

It figured. The Tigers first baseman was Hank Greenberg, the only Mocky in the game to my knowledge. The Tigers had won the series the year before, but Greenberg broke his wrist in game two, so it was a bittersweet victory for the people of the book.

I'd played enough sandlot ball to appreciate the finer points of the game, and liked to think of myself as above such considerations, but truth is I'd never warmed up to Babe Ruth, who'd retired the year before, or the Yanks generally. They were a team that featured Huns and Wops.

Which team you cheered for, I might add, was the least of the ethnic bias in St. Paul. A few years later, on Halloween Night, there was a radio drama on the air featuring fake news bulletins of Martians invading earth. The hysteria it caused is hard to imagine if you weren't there. People were piling into flivers and streaming out of town by the thousands, which, on our end of the city, meant heading through St. Albert's parish. I sat it out at Tin Cup's, preferring death at the hands of bug-eyed monsters to life without a drink. Later, when the refugees began straggling back, I heard that Rice Street had been lined with Krauts brandishing baseball bats, not to fight off the Martians, but to prevent something worse, Micks driving through their neighborhood unmolested.

After the games were over the players and umps gathered on the Central High School side of the field and drank beer. Slansky didn't join them. He plodded over to the sidelines on his thick legs and began slowly gathering up equipment. The sun was low and the heat of the day had eased. I watched him for awhile.

"You Sheldon Slansky," I said.

"Yes," he replied, quietly. "And you're a cop."

I assured him I wasn't but offered no further explanation. Nor did he ask for one.

"You're here to talk about Bobby Tuttweiler, whoever you are. I've been dealing with this long enough I can tell. I didn't kill him. Any other questions?"

"Yeah, what'd you do with the insurance money?"

"Oh, you're from the D A's office."

"Nope. I've been hired to find out who killed Bobby. If the D A won't charge you, that's good enough for me. I'd just like your help finding out who did."

He shook his head, as if to ask what kind of chump I thought he was. I could see his point.

"I'm in your shoes I wouldn't trust me either, but look at it this way. If I'm successful, the burden's off'a you."

He mulled that over long enough so I half expected him to start talking.

"You don't understand," he finally said. "You couldn't. I've been in the middle of it for a year and I don't understand. Who hired you?"

"Can't tell'ya. It's unethical."

"Nice talking to you."

He turned his back, stuffed a catcher's mask into a big canvas bag, and started picking up odds and ends—a bag of resin, a rule book. He went about it methodically, one thing at a time. I watched him for awhile then cleared my throat.

"You still here," he said.

"Gonna give me anything if I tell you who's my client?"

"I won't if you don't. We'll see otherwise."

I told him. It seemed to sink in.

"Marcella," he said. "I barely remember her. She was married by the time she was 18. Some rich kid."

He paused, scratched his head. A little smile inched across his puss, the first emotion I'd seen him show. After a bit he started talking again.

"Good thing Marcella left home when she did. Otherwise I'd have had to hire her too. The rest of Bobby's family was on my payroll at one time or another. Bobby always complained I didn't pay him enough, but as far as I was concerned every nickel I paid them was money he cost me. I had Betty making bouquets and wreaths out in front of the shop for awhile. She knew from nothing about flower arranging, but she wasn't a total write-off. There aren't many men in the retail flower business any more, but the few there were came around and bought from me, so they could try to get in her pants. Y'see, word got around that if you approached Betty at the right time, she might say yes. Problem was, she didn't just go have a quickie. She made a big production out of it, disappeared for a few days, wrecked homes. It was bad for business."

He shook his head as if he were remembering something painful, but he still had that little smile.

"Angie and Bobby Jr.? They were a complete waste of money. Angie was supposed to handle walk-ins. Showed up about half the time, and bitched if I didn't pay her for the days she missed. I tried Bobby Jr. in sales. Good looking kid, but he had his head in the clouds. Drew a salary for a year and never sold much."

"So why'd you hire'em?"

"Because Bobby wanted me to and I couldn't risk losing him, that's why. Bobby Tuttweiler was the kind who comes along once in a lifetime, if you're lucky. There'll never be another guy who can sell flowers like he did.—I also paid for a room he kept at the St. Paul Hotel. Told me he used it 'for business purposes' (now he grinned for real). You're not supposed to mix business with pleasure, but Bobby was the exception who proves that rule... Anyway, it's different now, that's for sure. He took all my accounts with him when he left, and then it got split up between three four wholesalers after he was murdered. Makes no difference to me. I went bankrupt. Had it all to myself for years, now I have nothing and everybody thinks I killed him. But damn it, I did not kill Bobby Tuttweiler."

"Must'a given it some thought. I would, if I lost everything. Eddy Guilfoyle said you were threatening him."

"That's a lie. You know Guilfoyle?"

"I know every bull in town," I said, in the ominous tone I use when I tell people that.

"He's quite the ladies man," Slansky said.

"Uhh, no. Not Eddy."

"Really? I thought he was a regular Rudolph Valentino. He slept with one of the most beautiful women I ever laid eyes on."

"We're thinkin' of two different people," I told him. "The Eddy Guilfoyle I know looks like Paddy's pig, and he's been happily married twenty five years to a woman who could pass for Fatty Arbuckle if she tucked her hair under her hat."

"That's him. Eddy Guilfoyle. Betty Tuttweiler found him irresistible. Must be that nose of his."

This was either a flat lie or the most interesting fact I'd unearthed since the key man policy.

"You certain?" I asked.

"Yeah."

"I don't believe it. How do you know?"

"My attorney told me."

"And how does he know?"

"It's his business to know things like that. After Bobby was murdered I went to somebody you've probably heard of, Leon Gleeman. Told him I needed help. He put me in touch with his own lawyer. 'Don't worry,' Leon told me, 'Morrie'll take care of it.' And he did."

That was certainly plausible. Gleeman had a better pipeline to the buzz than I did.

"Well, for arguments sake, let's assume Eddy did sleep with Betty Tuttweiler," I said. "What's the difference?"

"Betty and Bobby wanted me to drop the key man policy and I refused. When Bobby was murdered, Betty told Guilfoyle about it, and he came after me. He couldn't find any evidence, because there isn't any. I didn't do it, but she kept him comin' after me. Any way she could."

"You have to admit you were a good suspect."

"Doesn't mean he shouldn't look for anyone else, but he never did. My lawyer thinks Betty wanted to use his investigation as the basis for a civil suit, so she could get that insurance money. He figured she planned to sue for unjust enrichment."

"So why didn't she?"

"Maybe because she found out I didn't have the money. Also, she knows in her heart that I didn't kill Bobby. We go back a long way, Betty and me. She knows damn well I never could've shot Bobby. Truth is, I liked the guy. Everybody did."

"Not everybody.—If you didn't shoot him, who did?"

"I wish I knew." He pulled the cords tight on the canvas bag, and carefully tied a square knot.

He concentrates on details because the big picture doesn't bear looking at, that was how it seemed to me.

The long springtime dusk had begun while we were talking. The electric lights on Marshall Avenue hadn't come on yet, but the gas lamps on the nearby side streets were lit. Laughter and a few scraps of conversation drifted over from the other side of the field. I knew Slansky wanted to be over there with them, talking baseball, drinking beer. But he couldn't. It would've been hard enough just because he was a Hebe, but everybody thought he was a murderer too. That made it impossible.

"How's this," I said. "You tell me where the money went, I'll find out who killed him."

"If I tell you where the money went, I won't live to hear about it."

"Really? That sounds promising."

"What, the lead, or I won't live? Get me killed and the whole thing goes away. Shelly shot Bobby, somebody shot Shelly. Case closed."

"I'm not kiddin'. If the kinda mugs who kill people are connected to the money, I know I'm on the right track."

"That doesn't solve my problem. I'm the only person can tell you where the money went, and the man I gave it to knows that."

"Maybe he killed Bobby."

"I doubt it. They were friends, and besides, Bobby was worth more to him alive. Me, I'm worth nothing to him. Not now."

"But what were you worth in the first place? Why'd you take that policy out and keep on payin' while you were goin' bust?"

"Easy now.—You're asking the right questions, but you're way ahead of yourself.—I told you he'd kill me if he found out, and if you talk to him he'll know. There's no way around it."

"There wouldn't be if he stuck the money under his pillow. But if he used it and you tell me how, then I could claim I worked backwards and found out."

He thought that over for awhile.

"Why should I trust you?" he asked.

"My client and me, we're interested in the truth. Nobody else seems to be. We're your only hope."

He thought it over for awhile, sighed, and said, "He's one of your people. Name's Faennis Cuhulain. If I had to guess, I'd say he used it the same way I would've. He bought flowers.—Oh, and I kept the policy as an enticement. Told Bobby if he came back to work for me, the proceeds were his when he retired."

He threw the canvas bag over his shoulder and plodded off into the gathering darkness before I could ask him anything else. Didn't matter. What I'd learned constituted such a great stride forward that I decided to take a few days off. I wanted to meet with Marcie again before proceeding, and besides, I had to think things through. I needed to approach Cuhulain, but there was no obvious way to do it.

Officer Jack would be no help. Cuhulain didn't need anyone's protection as long as he stayed out of Chicago, and that was the least of it. Capone, who'd murdered Cuhulain's pal O'Banion, and several hundred other rivals, decided to make a deal with Cuhulain. Nobody knew the particulars, but he was a survivor and there was an air about him—part danger, part sophistication. Best be careful, that was my attitude.

I decided to call Teddy again. I told him my investigation had taken an interesting turn and asked if he could arrange a meeting with Cuhulain. That really piqued his interest, but I kept my trap shut about the reason. He asked if he could sit in. I agreed. Then I made the usual arrangement with Marcie.

***

The afternoon crowd at the Criterion was getting used to us. I suppose they filled in the blanks with lurid speculation. I could feel their eyes follow me to a back booth, and of course heads swivelled a few minutes later when Marcie walked in. She was sporting a golden tan, and wearing a sleeveless dress cut low enough so her pince nez rested on sun-kissed flesh.

She told me that she and The Lucky Dog had been to some island in Lake Michigan.

"I relaxed for awhile, but by the time a week went by your, um— investigation was on my mind again," she said. "So what've you found out?"

I told her that nobody, including me, liked Slansky for the murder. That didn't please her at all.

"Has somebody got a better idea?" she asked. "He takes out a life insurance policy on my dad, keeps payin' it after my dad quits on him, even though his business is practically busted, then collects double the face amount because my dad is murdered? That's some coincidence."

"I hear'ya, but according to the D A he doesn't have the money."

"Maybe he spent it." she said.

"If so, there's no trace of how. It's hard to spend twenty grand without leaving a trail of some kind."

"Not if you're a florist. Florists buy flowers with cash. I learned a few things growin' up with my dad.—More than a few."

"I suppose it's possible he bought flowers. I'll check into it. The D A thinks he gave that money to somebody."

"Well?" she demanded, leaning over the table, looking irritated— "who?"—The specs swung loose from her bosom. I averted my eyes.

"I can tell you one theory they're considering," I said. "Maybe it went to your mother."

"Who said that? I'll slap his mug, whoever it was."

"Easy. Want a drink?"

"NO!" She drummed her manicured nails on the table.

"Yes." She waved at the waiter, and ordered a Manhattan.

She calmed down after a few sips. I could tell she was getting ready to ask about my plan, which would require a reply. Which would move our meeting toward a conclusion.

"Tell me about buyin' twenty grand worth'a flowers," I said.

"You should go to someone who knows what they're talkin' about. What I can tell you is obvious. Florists buy as many flowers as they can sell before they go stale. Their price per bloom goes down as the volume goes up."

"Twenty large. That's a lotta posies."

She didn't respond immediately. I sloshed my whiskey and water around, watched her take a few more tentative sips, then guzzle her Manhattan.

"Another?" I asked. She nodded curtly, but in the affirmative.

"I once heard my dad explain the flower business to some rich men," she said, after the waiter brought her drink. "In one sentence."

"Remember it?"

"Sure. 'Men like to buy flowers from dames, and dames like to buy flowers from me.' Somethin' about the way they laughed made me feel funny, but I didn't know what. I was only fourteen. A few years later I understood. They knew his reputation, and he was bragging. They were impressed, can you imagine?"

"Yeah."

"I suppose you'd have laughed too."

I dodged that one, wisely, judging from her tone as she continued.

"My father-in-law was one of'em. What do you think of that, Martin? Come on, I want to hear if you know anything about *corruption*. Maybe you're not the man for this job."

"My, aren't we in a lousy mood.—Where were you and your father when this happened?"

"On a golf course. Probably the one we belong to now, the Dellwood Country Club. I didn't notice. I was too young to be wowed by that kinda thing back then. Now I'm too jaded. I went from too young to too jaded with hardly any in between time when I could, y'know—*revel*."

I liked the sound of that word, the way she said it. I'd had drinks with women in this state of mind before, and knew the possibilities—tears, flying glasses, sudden passionate kisses. She was well into that second Manhattan. I tried to think of a nice neutral question.

"Your father took'ya golfin' often, did he?"

"No, matter of fact that was the only time. He was talkin' with those men about some money for Midland Florists, but he always had a couple schemes in mind."

"Yeah?"

She sniffed back what might have been a tear, or the bourbon stinging her nose. Her eyes were kind of shiny, which certainly didn't detract from her appeal.

"'Yeah,' Martin. They were there to discuss money, but the other men were bringin' their sons along, so dad figured he might as well bring his daughter and see if anything came of it."

I didn't take her meaning for a moment.

"Ah. He wanted to see if their sons had any interest in his daughter."

She nodded, and took another gulp.

"Well, so? One of'em did."

"Oh, they all did. At least Dirk wasn't tacky about it. There anything wrong with that, Martin? Is it, oh, I don't know—*corrupt*?"

I sensed I was on thin ice, but forged ahead anyway.

"You've got a good marriage. That's what you told me, remember."

"Yeah."

"Yeah you remember, or yeah you've got a good marriage?"

"Both." Her eyes narrowed. "What's your point?"

"So, you used animal magnetism to get what you want. Nothin' wrong with that."

"Gallant of'ya to say so, Martin." She raised her glass. "Here's to animal magnetism. And usin' it."

I touched her glass, tentatively, ready to put my free hand in front of my face, but she just drained it and raised her hand for the waiter.

"Think maybe you've had enough?" I asked.

"Put it on the bill."

"That's not what I'm talkin' about."

She didn't respond, but after the waiter brought her drink she spoke more softly.

"I liked Dirk when I was in high school, but I never would've married him if it wasn't for an accident he had. A man was killed. Before that he was silly, but that accident changed him. I couldn't say exactly how, but he was different enough so I could marry him and get out of our house. That's the main reason I care for him to this day. Because he got me out. I was sick of it."

Suddenly she was crying. The waiter walked over and handed her a cloth napkin.

Pretty soon she'd composed herself enough to get into that Manhattan again, a worrisome development in itself.

"You ok?" I asked.

She teared up again, quietly this time.

"This is weighin' on me, Martin. Does my mother have that money?"

Her voice, her eyes, everything about her, was pleading with me to say no, which of course I did.

"How d'you know?" she sniffled.

"Because I know who Slansky gave it to."

"Who? Tell me." She wiped her eyes and took a sip of her drink.

"Uh-uh. Not yet. I'm gonna talk to him first and get to the bottom of this thing, like'ya hired me to do."

She didn't insist. She seemed calmer on the surface, but I could tell her mind was still churning. I tried to think of something to get her off track.

"When I was a kid we had a priest talked to us about corruption of the flesh and the promise of life eternal," I said. "He told us we'd wake up some morning, look in the mirror and realize we were corrupt too.—The Church, that's where you got this corruption thing on your mind."

She looked at me quizzically. "I hardly remember the Church. This is real."

"So's this," I said, pointing at my mug. "I earned these lines. Pretty soon they'll be honest to god wrinkles. We're all corrupt."

Her eyes crinkled. "You're still a good looking man," she said.

That didn't exactly address the issue, but I was flattered. I also thought things were pretty well defused at that point.

"And you're not a phony either, Martin," she continued. "That's what real *corruption* is. Those bankers friends of my father-in-law's with their one-track minds; all those gangsters that hide in St. Paul; Dirk and his—his silly drinking buddies. None of'em are saints, far from it, but they aren't hip—hip—"

"Hypocrites?"

"Kerrr—rect, and that's what Lt. Eddy Guilfoyle is. A hypocrite. He pretends to be a policeman. He should be ashamed to put a uniform on."

"He doesn't," I said. "He's a plainclothesman."

It seemed like a reasonable observation, but she glared when she heard it. "Screw you," she muttered.

She finished her Manhattan, then closed her eyes and shivered the way you do when the hooch catches up all of a sudden.

"No, screw me," she said louder, loud enough so a couple guys at a nearby table heard it. "C'mon, less go." She stood abruptly and wobbled in place for a moment.

"We're off to a hotel," she told the guys, in a confidential tone. "Martin n'me."

Their jaws dropped. She smiled a crooked smile. "C'mon, Martin. Whatter—whatter you... waitin'—."

"Uh, the bill—"

"Bills, bills, bills" she sorted through her purse, pulled out a handful of ones and dropped them on the table. "C'mon.—Wait!"

Slowly, still leaning against the booth, she crooked one long gam at the knee, and plucked off a high-heeled sandal. Her skirt hiked up her thigh in the process, revealing the snaps that fastened her silk stockings to her garters, which were situated above the tan line, well into the alabaster zone.

"Don't wanna fall," she confided with a wink to her audience, which by then had grown to include everyone in the place.

She did the same with the other leg. When she'd finally secured both sandals in one hand, and her purse in the other, I took her by the arm and walked her out the door.

The heat was staggering. The sun was blinding. Marcie began to hiccup.

"Where's your—HIC—your aut—auto-mo -

"Right down here," I said.

A girl standing on the corner with an armful of roses spotted us and came running over. I tried to brush her off but Marcie insisted on buying the whole bouquet, and handed over a sawbuck. That little gal must've thought she'd died and gone to heaven. She followed us down University Avenue uttering thank yous, then held the door of the bucket while I stuffed Marcie in, roses and all.

"I don't wanna—HIC—go to the St. Francis," she said. "Less'go to the—HIC—Sain'paul Ho—Hotel. Ok—Martin?"

With that, she slumped back, dropped the roses on her lap, and passed out.

I should've known. That's how my luck ran with classy dames. It crossed my mind to go ahead with it anyway. I knew I wouldn't, but I drove around awhile pretending that I might. She hiccuped a few times, and mumbled something.

I considered taking her to her mother's house. That didn't sit well somehow. I wondered how she got to the Criterion. Did she drive? Did a chauffeur bring her? Eventually I settled on taking her home, wherever that was, and headed in the general direction of White Bear Lake.

By then I'd looped back to Rice Street on pure instinct, so I decided to take it north as far as I could.

I looked at her sprawled all over the seat. Marcie was a little weird, but something real was driving her nuts and she was determined to track it down. More precisely, she was determined to make me track it down. I liked that about her.

Once we passed Larpenteur Avenue blocks of neat little bungalows gave way to newly planted farm fields and acres of cow pasture. Rice Street petered out into a nameless, bumpy, gravel road. I was hoping Marcie would rouse herself and give me directions.

She finally did wake up momentarily, when we banged over a particularly jarring stretch. "O god my head," she moaned. "Turn that off." She gestured weakly toward the sun.

Roses tumbled to the floorboard. She put a hand over her eyes, leaned against the door and was out like a light again before I could say a word.

If I stay on this road I can't get lost, I reasoned, but I knew White Bear Lake lay to the east. We came to several unmarked crossroads where I could've turned, but thought better of it. Instead I squinted against the sun, which was nearing the horizon, and pressed on. The air had cooled a bit. The smell of freshly turned earth mingling with the scent of roses was pleasant enough, once my nose got over the initial shock.

I could've just driven aimlessly awhile, but soon I felt a prod from a stockinged foot. She was out the door the moment I stopped. A few roses tumbled into the ditch with her.

Some cows standing by a fence at the side of the road watched while she threw up.

"Oh shit oh dear," she muttered.

She stayed there with the dry heaves for several minutes. Eventually she steadied herself against the fence, and patted one of the cows on the nose. It mooed sympathetically.

"Where are we?" she asked.

"I was hopin' you might know."

"Oh god I feel awful... You tryin' to find my house?"

"Yeah, I didn't know what else -"

"You're a sweet guy, Martin.—Here, gimme your hand."

I reached out and helper her in. "My head," she moaned again, as she stepped up on the running board.

She closed her eyes as soon as she sat down. I thought she was out, but eventually, without opening them, she told me she lived on Birchwood Lane, on the south shore. A few minutes later I came upon a beer joint, right there in the middle of nowhere.

The bar man gave me directions, whilst a few rustics in denim overalls looked at me like I'd just arrived from Mars.

It was dusk when we entered the circle driveway in front of the Kirkwood mansion, and stopped at a cobbled walk that bisected the vast lawn up to the front steps. Marcie grabbed her shoes, a few roses, and exited, leaving the car door open behind her. She traipsed past a fellow who was watering the grass, acknowledging him en route with a slight wave of the shoes. He nodded with an amused look on his face, and watched as she stumbled up the steps to the door.

He was a handsome fellow, one of those black-haired limeys with a permanent five o'clock shadow. He was barefoot, wearing knee length striped bathing tights, and a bathing shirt. After she'd made her way inside, he walked over, leaned into the bucket and extended a hand.

"Dirk Kirkwood," he said.

"Martin McDonough."

He gave me the once-over, thorough but not unfriendly. "Had a few nips, has she?"

"You noticed."

He chuckled. "This thing with her father's murder has her pretty well flummoxed. Sure hope you can get to the bottom of it."

"I'm makin' headway," I assured him.

"Good, good. Must admit I was taken back when Marcie told me your fee, but she said you're a fellow who gets results. 'Then tell him to go to it,' I told her. It's brought up all sorts of unpleasant memories, made her quite unhappy....So, how do you manage it?"

"Manage what?"

"To solve all those crimes."

I was relieved. I thought he meant how do you manage to get my wife drunk and try to put the make on her under the guise of professional inquiry?—Marcie had left the door to the house wide open. Faint sounds of wretching came from within. It was time to leave.

"You hafta know who to ask," I replied. "And what to ask'em." I put the floor shift in first, and slowly released the clutch.

"Fascinating. Take care old sport."

"You too."

He picked up his hose and sprayed his way back toward the Kirkwood manse. I navigated the long driveway on to Birchwood Lane, and headed for the city.

MOTIVE AND OPPORTUNITY

It was a beautiful Sunday morning in June, the kind that makes you glad to be alive even if you're hungover. I showered, dressed and made for the fliver, but Mrs. Dunn collared me at the door and browbeat me into admitting that I wasn't heading for Mass.

"Your immortal soul is in jeopardy, Martin," she clucked. "Have some breakfast, so's you don't start your shenanigans with an empty belly."

My plan had been to jump in the bucket, park downtown, grab a cup of coffee at the Town Talk, and take the trolley to Lexington Park. Teddy Eccles had arranged a nice venue for our meeting with Faennis Cuhulain; seats directly behind first base to watch the St. Paul Saints play the Minneapolis Millers.—Could I pause long enough to eat and make it for the first pitch?—Yes, if I took the Rice Street trolley and transferred at University. I followed Mrs. Dunn back down the hall and seated myself at the boarding house table.

Next to me sat the laconic Arthur O'Malley, a man several years older than myself and more confirmed in his bachelorhood. He had his nose in the Sunday comics. "Mind if I look at the sport's page," I asked.

He grunted something I took as affirmative, and almost missed his mouth with a spoonful of Mrs. Dunn's gruel, so engrossed was he in the goings on in Gasoline Alley.

The headline was startling: **Schmeling KOs Brown Bomber In 12th!**

I could hardly believe my eyes. I'd followed Joe Louis's career with interest, despite the melodrama the man inspired. Some sportswriter had actually written that he was, "a credit to his race—the human race." That's a tough read with your stomach in the condition mine normally is when I pick up the morning paper, but I'd absorbed the blow gamely and kept up with Louis's amazing record all that previous year. He'd fought thirteen times, and won them all.

His signature victory had come when he knocked out the former Heavyweight Champ, Primo Carnera. That didn't impress me. I'd always thought the 265 pound Carnera was a big stiff, but when Louis KOed another former champ, Maxie Baer, I was convinced. Baer had an iron jaw. I braced myself against the inevitable hyperbole, and read the tale of Louis's surprising defeat:

"The Dark Uhlan almost knocked out Louis in the fourth when he left his feet to deliver 192 pounds of dynamite on the Brown Bomber's jaw.... The Teuton's right eye was closed by the seventh, after absorbing jab after piston-like jab delivered by the meteoric negro, but the gritty German squinted and kept to his task... A right flush on the chin rocked Louis from head to heel as he came from his corner in the ninth. A glassy stare came to the negro's eyes. He staggered as if drunken but kept his feet. Another right sent him spinning..."

I couldn't finish. It was a TKO. Before I threw in the towel I took a peek at the end, by which time, "the Hun's mighty right fist was cocked with a patience known only to his Germanic countrymen as the bell tolled for the twelfth."

I grabbed the front section out from under O'Malley's nose.

Schmeling's countrymen seemed to be losing their legendary patience with the French, who'd been hoping against hope that their craven yielding of the Ruhr Valley coal mines would mollify the gritty Teutons. Fat chance.

I glanced around the table, where the likes of Frank Mullen, Robert Fogarty, and other men of draft age were polishing off their victuals so they could make eleven o'clock Mass.

"Pray for peace," I advised Mullen. "If y'want peace work'fr justice," he replied. "I do work for justice," I told him. "And what're y'workin' on now?" he inquired. "I think of it as the case of The Key Man," I surprised myself by saying, because I'd been referring to it mentally as the case of seeing how many times I could meet with Marcie. "You'll have to tell me about it one'a these days," said Mullen. "Not until I've solved the mystery," I told him, "and even then you'll need to ply me with drink." He assured me he would.

Another item in the paper was of some interest, in view of my pending engagement:

"Al Capone Stabbed By Convict—Al Capone was stabbed in the back with a scissors by a desperate fellow convict in Alcatraz prison yesterday, but the former Chicago gang overlord smashed his assailant with his fist and walked to the prison hospital. Ill feeling has been reported between Capone and other convicts since the mutiny of prisoners last January. The assailant, a leader in that fruitless movement, had been bitter against Capone because the latter refused to participate."

I could well imagine why he refused. Unlike many other inmates, Capone would be getting out soon if he behaved. He was doing a few years for tax evasion, of all things. According to my copper friends that was the G's new strategy. They planned to put every gangster in America in stir for filing false tax returns. The gangsters weren't exactly shaking in their boots at the prospect. A couple years on the rock was better than a date with Old Sparky, and implicit in the tax strategy was the admission that efforts to nail them for murder and other major felonies hadn't panned out.

I had to run half a block to catch the streetcar, which was full of people heading for Lexington Park. Newsies were hawking special editions of the Dispatch when we got off to transfer at Rice and University.

"STEADY LOU FETTE HURLIN' FOR THE SAINTS," they shouted. "GIT'CHER GAME DAY SPECIAL!"

There was a line of trolleys at the traffic light, and a big crowd queuing to get on. As soon as one streetcar filled, another crossed the intersection. "I NEED TICKETS," shouted a scalper. "I GOT TICKETS," shouted another. "GET YOUR TICKETS HERE!"

The buzz in the crowd was about two major league scouts rumored to be attending. "They're lookin' Fette over," a fellow Saints fan confided, as we boarded for the park.

This wasn't exactly good news for the home team, but I viewed Fette's ascension to the majors as inevitable. He was a big righthander who rarely yielded a walk, and threw as hard in the late innings as he did in the early ones. He was going for win number thirteen that afternoon, and the season wasn't half over.

The trolley was full by the time I got aboard. All the windows were open but it was hot nevertheless. I edged and shoved my way back to the open smoking area in the rear. It was cooler there, but not much. The car was moving so slowly that little breeze was generated. I leaned out and looked at an endless jam of flivers, trolleys, and horse and wagon rigs, including many a horse pulling an automobile for lack of gas money.

"We gonna make the first inning?" I queried my fellow passengers. "I dunno," said one. "I'm gonna get out an' walk pretty soon," said another. "Think they'll sell out?"

"Nahh," I replied. "They always squeeze in a few more."

The streetcar began to empty as it became apparent that a determined fan in need of a ticket, and unwilling to pay the scalper's premium, could walk faster. Untroubled by such mundane concerns, I seated myself and rode until we came to a complete halt a few blocks east of Lexington Avenue. Then I made my leisurely way to the Will Call window, where my ducat awaited me.

In those days you had to climb the stairs, enter the second deck, then make your way back down to the box seats near first base. The sun had reached its zenith and was proceeding toward the high wall behind home plate, which would serve to shade those of us with means after the third inning or so. No such salvation awaited the bleacher bums, a solid mass of beer-swilling, peanut-cracking groundlings, many of whom would pass out from the combined effects of alcohol and heat stroke before the game was over. Meanwhile, the din they created in their agitation and discomfort nearly drowned out the more subdued discussions of the finer points of the game being conducted in the choice seats.

I spotted Teddy's gray locks and slid into the empty seat between him and Cuhulain. Teddy introduced us, and Cuhulain in turn introduced me to the man next to him.

"Jack Doyle, friend'o mine from Chicago" he said. "Jack's scoutin' for the Cubbys, he is."

Teddy and I leaned in to hear Doyle fill us in on the Cubs' pitching woes. Their bullpen was anchored by the aging Charlie Root, whose four run-plus ERA was indicative of the problems they were having.

"But Fette's a starter if he's anything," I said.

Doyle agreed, but pointed out that their starters left little to be desired. The number five guy, Curt Davis, had won six games. "I'm thinking Fette could be a long reliever," said Doyle. "Later in the season, when our starters get tired."

Having established our respective bona fides, we settled in to watch the game. The first two Millers went down swinging, but number three, first baseman Joe Hauser, knocked Fette's first pitch out of the park. The roar that rose from the cheap seats was amazing. Half the rubes out there were from Minneapolis.

The dapper Cuhulain clapped hands in a restrained and gentlemanly way. "Credit where credit's due," he said, with a wink. "I admire the athlete, whilst largely ignorin' th' team."

I looked him over surreptitiously while Fette gouged the mound with his heel, and slapped the ball into his mitt in disgust. Cuhulain's hat remained on his head, cocked at a jaunty angle, despite the heat. He had smooth-shaven, olive skin, black eyebrows that grew together over the sort of Roman nose that certain sons of the old sod sport, and bright, intelligent eyes. His cravat was loosened, his starched collar was open at the throat. He put his elbow on his knee, rested his prominent chin on his fist, and watched Fette rear back and burn one down the middle for a strike.

What did that chin of his remind me of?—Ah yes, the Italian fellow, Il Duce. There must've been a legionnaire in Cuhulain's lineage. And a Celtic lass who knew which side her bread was buttered on.

The rhythm of the game soon established itself. By the time the sun passed behind the wall the crowd had quieted to concentrate on a pitching duel. Cuhulain and I shared some small talk while the batters whiffed or grounded out one after the other.

"See where Schmeling KOed Louis?" I said.

"Indeed, an' didn't I predict somethin'o the sort when I read that he was studyin' newsreels've the Bomber's minny triumphs last year," he replied.

He proceeded to explain his theory, which made perfect sense, as all theories about sporting events, politics, history, crime and anything else will, when presented after the fact. First of all, he pointed out, no boxer, least of all a heavyweight, has any business fighting thirteen times in a year. And since every move Louis made in all those fights was immortalized on celluloid, a boxer with the patience to analyze the film, and the skills to take advantage of what he learned, had a chance to beat him.

"The Bomber inntered the ring tired and flat, and Schmeling knew he dropped his left when he was fixin t'throw his right. I tuned in the fight, and every time Schmeling hit'im there came a great sound—WHACK! Ye'could hear it over the static. Tirrible noise, like a man smackin a side'a beef with a two-by-four. The Bomber was walkin' into those blows. He was a step late th'entire bout."

Suddenly the crowd rose to its feet and roared. Mickey Slade had walked while we were engrossed in conversation, and Fette himself had tied the game with a single that scored him.

"How d'ye like that, Jack," said Cuhulain to the scout. "A pitcher who can hit!"

"All due respect, we're lookin' for a pitcher who can pitch," said Doyle. "I heard yez discussin' the fight. Did you notice Tommy O'Rourke dropped dead in Schmeling's dressing room before it began?"

"Well, th'man was of an age t'kick the bookit," said Cuhulain.

I listened while they lionized one of the most controversial men in the fight business. O'Rourke, who was well into his eighties, had managed Joe Walcott, aka The Barbados Demon, back when whites and smokes were barred by gentleman's agreement from meeting in the ring. But O'Rourke was no gentleman. He saw to it that his fighter fought white boys, which earned him a certain amount of disapproval, although fans like myself generally thought of it as a good thing. O'Rourke had held many positions in the fight game over the years—boxer, trainer, manager, commissioner. He'd even been a judge at ringside when Jimmy McLarnin decisioned Barney Ross for the Welterweight title a few years back. He scored it for McLarnin, a dubious call that won back the hearts of his fellow Micks, many of whom had shunned him for managing Walcott.

I mentioned that I'd read of Capone's misadventure. Doyle hadn't seen that item, but Cuhulain had.

"I'll tell'ye this," he said. "If ye've the temerity t'stick a shiv in Snorty, ye'd be wise t'stick it in his heart. He's a bull of a man, and there's little forgiveness in him."

"That his moniker?" I inquired.—Among the initiated, 'Snorty' meant a darb and debonair demeanor back in those days.

He nodded in the affirmative. "Tis Alphonse's conceit that he's snorty," he explained. "It'd take a brave intrepid fillow t'tell him he's merely well-dressed."

"I've heard he doesn't like the Irish." I said.

"Nonsense," Cuhulain replied. "He cares not a wit whether a man were Irish, Eyetalian or Jew. What can'ye do for Snorty? is his question, and if the answer is nothin', then ye'd best give him a wide berth, regardless'a your origins.

"Tis a wonderful little burg ye'have here," he continued, and he tugged on Teddy's sleeve to make sure he overheard, "full of all the things that make life pleasurable an' fair burstin' with opportunity, but when it comes to talk'a th' Mick, th' Mocky, th' Hun, th' Dinge an'such, I find it a wee bit provincial. As for me, I'm aware that I'm reputed t'be a Mick mobster on the run from a crazy Wop, but nothin' could be further from the truth. Gimpy O'Banion was a friend'a mine, may he rest in peace, but we lived different lives. After his sad passin' I found Snorty t'be a sinsible, down to earth fillow, and not inclined t'let our rispictive allegiances get in th' way of an understandin.' St. Paul seemed th' best place fr'me, given th' particulars. Isn't that right, Teddy?"

"I've said it before, I'll say it again," Teddy replied. "You are the world's foremost authority on the affairs of Faennis Cuhulain."

"That I am, and we'll drink to it," said Cuhulain. He waved for the beer hawker.

Whilst we enjoyed our beers Cuhulain confided that Capone's successor, Paulie Ricca, had offered him the opportunity to "organize" St. Paul a few years back, meaning he'd be provided with some muscle to take over crime here.

"I declined, and advoised him aginst it," he said. "'There's a gang in charge here already,' I says, 'and ye'd have to go t'war with'em. 'They can't be much,' says he, 'I nivir heard of'em.' 'Oh yes ye have,' says I. 'They call themselves 'The Police.''"

I asked him whether Ricca let it go at that, or offered the turf to someone else.

"I thought it best not t'inquire," he replied.

Doyle left during the seventh inning stretch, with Fette still throwing, and protecting a safe lead. He'd walked one, struck out five and allowed two hits, both home runs. Doyle was noncommital, but I was pretty sure we'd seen the last of Steady Lou.

After the Saints batted in the eighth, and scored another run, Teddy suggested we leave as well, to avoid traffic. He was anxious to show off his brand new touring sedan.

Amazingly in this crowd of thousands, he ran into several fellows he knew on the way out, and paused to glad hand them. McGlaughin winked at me, as if to say, "that's our Teddy."

He'd parked a few blocks away on Fuller Street, which was lined with cars, but Teddy's was easily spotted. It was a royal blue Fleetwood, thirty feet long if it was an inch, featuring a vented hood topped by a winged silver ornament, and four doors that opened at the middle of the chassis, like French Windows.

Teddy opened the curbside rear door, and revealed opera-style back seats. There was enough leg room for Primo Carnera. He bade the two of us be seated.

"I'll just take us on a tour of our provincial little burg," he said. "You ride in the rear like gentlemen."

He drove down Lexington Avenue, and turned east on Summit. As we cruised past the brownstones, Cuhulain expanded on the concept of "snorty" as applied to Chicago gangsters. He confessed to a veneer of snortiness himself, and even conceded that his natty duds and ornate locutions were a relic of the snorty habits he'd acquired when he palled around with Dion "Gimpy" O'Banion, the snortiest of them all.

"Gimpy certainly provoked Alphonse's wrath concernin' business on minny occasions," he said, "but I'll always believe Capone had him murthered because he possessed a natural sophistication that got under our Eyetalian friend's skin."

O'Banion, he explained, had a ready smile, a beautiful tenor voice and a deceptively gentle manner. He was always impeccably dressed and carefully groomed, right down to the neatly manicured six inch long nail on the little finger of his left hand, the mark of a Chicago rosco who'd never stooped to hand labor more arduous than pulling a trigger.

"He was always smilin, Gimpy was, always glad t'see ye. He'd look a man in th'eye, tell him he was a fine fillow, and a minute later tell Hymie t' rub him out."

According to Cuhulain, this coldly elegant manner of O'Banion's became the sine qua non of snorty in twenties Chicago.

O'Banion's hit man, Hymie Weiss, had an odd snortiness of his own, grounded in an inexplicable quirk. A Catholic of Polack extraction, he took a Hebe nom de guerre just for the snorty hell of it. If you asked why, he might smile and say nothing, or he might pull out a pistol and shoot you.

"Hymie was the only man in Chicago Capone feared," said Cuhulain, "and that were his death warrant. Snorty is not the type t'live in fear, y'see, so he had Hymie killed. He's like Gimpy was in that respect. They'd both kill on a whim. As fr'me, God willin' I'll get through life without blood on me hands."

I told him that was my wish as well. Cuhulain was a spellbinder and could obviously go on forever about Chicago. I waited patiently for an opening while we descended Ramsey Hill and turned on to Smith Street. As we crossed the High Bridge Cuhulain was in the midst of explaining what a great lover of flowers O'Banion was, and how he took pleasure in operating the florist shop that served as headquarters for his rackets. He said that O'Banion personally designed the wreaths he provided for the grand funerals that were thrown for fallen Chicago gangsters.

From there he slid seamlessly into a recollection of his maiden Aunt's annual pilgrimage to Newgrange, twelve kilometers from their humble sod home in County Meath, to place a garland of wildflowers on the ancient cairn. That was the way the old folks celebrated the vernal equinox in that neck of the woods, he explained.

"She took a carriage there, didn't she, bless her old heart." A tear slid down his cheek. "She called the day 'The Alban Eilir,' in the auld tongue."

He finally paused in his narrative to admire the forested bluffs of the Mississippi.

"You're in the flower business yourself, I'm told," I said.

He squinted at me as if he were studying some rare plant.

"'Told,' are'ye? Now who'd be tellin'ye that?"

"To be honest," I lied, "I can't remember. I've been talkin' to so many people lately. I'm a private detective."

"That's what our mutual friend Mr. Eccles E S Q up there tells me. He didn't tell me ye were talkin' t'people about my affairs, though. But then he's a devious sort, aren't ye Teddy?"

He leaned forward, nudged Teddy, and repeated his query.

"I am" Teddy agreed, over his shoulder. "How else could I be such a roaring success in these hard times?"

"I'm interested in your business only as it relates to a case I'm working on, Faennis," I told him. "I've been hired to find out who murdered Bobby Tuttweiler."

"Ah." He was silent for awhile.

"A sad day that was, when Bobby fell. We won't be seein' the likes'o him again. I've no compunction about talkin' t'ye about that matter, McDonough. I'd like t'see the bastard who murthered Bobby hung by th' heels and flayed alive. As far as my affairs are concerned, ye've a reputation fr'discretion and ye'wouldn't want to go spoilin' it, now would ye?"

I assured him I wouldn't.

He explained that his relationship with Bobby came about as an offshoot of his deal with Capone. It had begun when the Feds started using the Internal Revenue Act against mobsters, and money laundering became a lucrative occupation. Gangsters on the east coast used the tomato business to legitimize their loot, but any form of produce purchased for cash in large, untraceable quantities would do.

"I'd been buyin' flowers fr'Gimpy fr'years by the time he were murthered," he said, "an' if ye've ever seen a flower market ye'll know why it couldn't be better for the purpose. If ye try t'give a flower monger a check they'll laugh in your face. I told Snorty I could make cash presentable to the revenuers by buyin' flowers. An' of course I took mine off the top."

He explained the process of money laundering. Most of it went in one ear and out the other, but I got the basics. Purchase something with funds illegitimately acquired, sell it for publicly circulated money and document the sale according to your specifications. Mobsters expected to lose something in the wash, which was why a man in Cuhulain's shoes stood to make plenty, but each method of laundering had its own peculiar problems. Produce rots, for example, so if you launder cash in New York by buying thousands of pounds of tomatoes, many will go soft before they're sold. The only recourse is to make sauce, which, according to Cuhulain, explains why hundreds of spaghetti joints had sprung up all over the five boroughs.

"I grew to envy those fillows," he said. "Meself, I was eternally dealin' with the same auld problem. A bloom is good for three days, maybe five in a cooler. Then there's nothin' t'be done. It was gettin' so I couldn't sell flowers fast enough to clean up Snorty's money, an' others were comin' t'me as well. Dillinger's roscoes had begun usin'

my services. I was at the end'a me rope when a florist I was dealin'
with put a boog in me ear. 'Get on the train and take yerself a trip up
to St. Paul,' he said. 'It's a wee little city, but they sell more flowers
there than we do here, an'there's but one man behind it'."

That man was Bobby Tuttweiler, and as Cuhulain explained how
he and Bobby prospered together I began to better understand the odd
dynamics of the Tuttweiler family.

Cuhulain had seen the numbers before he came here. What the
florist told him was literally true. There were more flowers sold in St.
Paul than Chicago, and most of them were roses.

"Bobby were the progenitor'a the industry," he said. "This happened before my time here, but it's my understandin' that the local
flower business sprung directly from his loins, so to speak. When
he started sellin' flowers there were just a few shops, all of'em
run by men, and other men come around t'buy when they had to,
fr'anniverarys an'weddings an' such. Bobby put women behind the
counter, because he figured men would come around and buy from
the ladies more often, an' right he were."

Cuhulain admitted that he'd arrived with a notion of simply taking over Chicago-style, but quickly realized he was dealing with a
one-man show. Nor was it necessary to muscle in. Bobby was in it for
romance. Money was practically an afterthought. His life revolved
around setting women up at florist shops, running their business for
them because when they were happy he was happy, and making love
to them. He serviced a few shops a day, a dozen or so a week, and
used his suite at the St. Paul Hotel as a place to enjoy long rendevous,
as opposed to the back room quickies that were his stock in daily
trade.

Bobby's customers were forever telling him he should go into
business for himself, but he was content working for Midland, where
he could expense his predilections and not bother with the intrica-
cies of wholesaling—with one exception. He used his charm to talk
wealthy men into investing, because he knew how to create demand,
but cash for supply was a recurring problem. Until Cuhulain came
along.

"Bobby could sell as minny blooms as ye'could provide him with," said Cuhulain. "I can tell'ye I were happy as a pig in shite when I seen how our interests dovetailed."

Cuhulain got to know Bobby well, and they began to pal around because of their shared taste in what he termed, "th' foiner things." He was soon introduced to Betty Tuttweiler, and noticed that she was one of those things.

"Bobby were a sophisticated fillow, an my relationship with his wife was somethin' we acknowledged, but rarely spoke of," he said.

He smiled as he recollected one occasion when they'd spoken of it.

"Betty'd often spent a night'r two in me rooms up at the St. Paul Hotel, an' one mornin' she bumped into Bobby and a lady friend of his in the hall. Bobby couldn't help laughin when he told me of it. They all rode the lift together, y'see, and it got a bit stiff. Bobby had quite a sense'a humor, he did. Told marvelous jokes, and not even a wee bit smutty they were."

He shook his sadly.

"Betty's a lovely woman," he added. "I still see her occasionally." He smiled, and continued his story.

Because Cuhulain's arrival in St. Paul created a new supply of money, Bobby, who was never at a loss, set about creating a new demand. Until then, florists simply dumped their stale blooms and factored the price of waste into the flowers they sold. It was Bobby's genius to see the potential that represented.

"Poets have observed that the beauty of a rose is niver more exquisite than the moment it begins to wilt," Cuhulain explained, in his, dare I say it, flowery fashion. "A fillow might buy that rose on impulse, whereras, given time to peruse at leisure, he'd be inclined t'select somethin' a bit less mature. Now Bobby knew flowers an' th' business of flowers as well as anyone, but he were a true expert—and a poet t'boot—when it came t'women. He was aware that unlike a rose, the beauty of a woman is niver more poignant than the moment it bursts from the bud, so t'speak, an' if a man were ever to purchase a bloom impulsively, twould be in the presence of such beauty."

Or, stated simply, it was Bobby's idea to put nubile girls on the street selling moribund roses in order to turn excess inventory into cash. Overnight a new market was created, along with a method for laundering thousands more per week. As Cuhulain proceeded to explain, Bobby stumbled on it in his own way.

"He weren't the kind'a man t'be gettin in the knickers of a sixteen year old lass, but he did succumb t'that temptation once. Twere a friend of his dotter's. Then in a proper fit'a remorse he went t'the priest."

"He confessed?"

"Of course not. The man wasn't daft. He had a scheme. Two of 'em. Absolution and business. He devised his own act'a contrition, an' got the priest in on it without tellin' him why, so's to make it legal and bindin' on the Lard."

He explained that Bobby devised a plan in which poor parish families, most of whom had many children, including at least one teen-aged daughter, could make some money. He started collecting roses on the verge of wilting from his retail customers, and giving them to the girls. They sold them on the street for a nickel each, and split the proceeds with Bobby.

"He'd give a little'a that back t'the florists. That made the florists happy, an' not shy'a orderin' more than they might sell. He niver took a penny from the lass he wronged though. Gave her as minny roses as she could sell. Told me layin' with her was the worst sin he'd ever committed in a lifetime'a philanderin'. His dotter never forgave him, even though the lass said she were none the worse for it."

"Sounds like that girl's family might've had reason to take a shotgun to him," I observed.

"I've pondered minny possibilities since he was murthered, includin' that one. T'th'best'a me knowledge, her's was a humble family, an' thought it a foin thing t'have their dotter sullied by Mr. Tuttweiler. No, there're more likely suspects."

"Coppers think it was the guy who owned Midland. You heard about the key man insurance?"

"Heard of it? I collected it," he said, without a moment's hesitation.

He explained that Slansky had pestered him to fork over set sums on a regular basis, ideally a quarterly investment, so he could plan purchases ahead. Cuhulain knew that this was not unreasonable, but he also knew that if Slansky lost Bobby, Midland Wholesale Florists was useless as a money laundry.

"Mr. Slansky and I came to an agreement," he said. "I gave him his quarterly invistmint, but he purchased a key man insurance policy, an' agreed that if anything happened t'Bobby the money were mine. Bobby didn't know that I were behind buyin' that policy, or that I had a financial interest in it. When he strook out on his own—which Betty'd been after him t'do, but I never thought he would—Slansky wanted t'drop the insurance. 'No,' I told him, 'Bobby'll come back, mark my words,' an' in my opinion he would've. Of course Betty and Bobby were angry at Slansky over him keepin' the policy. Too bad, but twere nothin' to be done."

"And of course you know that makes you a prime suspect," I said.

"I do indeed, but the theory rests on a false assumption. I were doin' business with Bobby after he left Midland, an' he were worth minny thousands more t'me alive than dead. Not t'mention the fact that I'd cut off me arm before I'd raise it against him.... After Bobby were made they broke the mold. What a lovely an'worldly fillow. An' t'think I run into him in a rustic little backwater like this one."

He took a handkerchief out of his breast pocket and dabbed at his eye. If you want to know what kind of man he was, the fact that it didn't strike me as a false gesture is as good a description as I can offer.

"Think Slansky killed him?"

"If he did it were fr'spite not money. Excuse me." He blew his nose, and returned the hanky to his pocket. "A'course, if I had a dime for every man in Chicago that were killed fr'spite I'd retire.— Nah, I don't think so. He isn't a killer."

Cuhulain said he'd paid Slansky's legal expenses on condition that Slansky push his lawyer to collect on the policy. I asked if he'd used the insurance to buy flowers.

"Nota-tall," he said. "I've slowed down the money washin' commensurate with the situation—Prohibition gone, Snorty in stir. Paulie

Ricca and I used to do quite a lot've business, but there's not so minny blooms sold nowadays, are there? The stale ones still go out on the streets, but the hawkers have t'make their own deals with the florists, an'there's hundreds of hawkers now, lasses, lads, ten year old boys, old gents, all of'em competin' with each other, so that's not so lucrative as it once was. Nor is th' market so lively. People have caught on, y'see. They want fresh blooms, not somethin' that fades two hours after they bought it. But if th' hawkers are sellin' fresh roses, then th' florists are competin' with themselves, aren't they?"

I asked him how he dealt with that.

"By retirin'," he replied. "I'm pretty well fixed innyway. Only one thing I needed t'take care of, an' that's done. The insurance money were paid out last March. Came in the nick'a time. I called Betty the day I got it, and told her I were comin' over t'give'er a gift of flowers on The Alban Eilir, accordin' to the old traditions.—Y'know, Bobby were the type'a fillow t'spend ivery penny without a thought for th'morrow, an' there weren't much left after he were gone. Betty was lookin' pretty tense by then, him in the ground ten months an' her not knowin' where t'turn.—I'll niver forget the look on her face when I handed her a bouquet all wrapped in florist's paper, and inside among the flowers were an envelope containin' the insurance money. Ivery penny of it."

After she'd collapsed in his arms and thanked him, he'd seized the moment to confess that he was behind the purchase of the key man policy. He explained why, and told her the money was rightfully hers.

My mind was reeling from revelation overload by then. I caught Teddy's eye in the mirror and signaled it was time to bring things to a conclusion, but Cuhulain wasn't ready to call it a day. He continued to praise the Tuttweilers, both the quick and the dead, as we headed for the hotel. When we got there he invited us up for a drink.

His suite was on the third floor overlooking St. Peter Street, which was empty except for a few poor souls on the bum who'd forgotten how seriously we take the Sabbath around here. Nary a bottle to be purchased, nor a working stiff to panhandle.

Cuhulain took a fifth of Jameson's out of a drawer, poured us each a glass neat, and busied himself tuning in a concert on the Philco, all the while bemoaning the sorry state of music in the U.S.A.

"What've we here?" he said. "Why it's the Blue Network, and the illustrious Victor Herbert inflictin' his sorry self upon our ears."

He fiddled with the dial nonetheless, and eliminated the static just in time for a Lux Soap ad.

"I hesitate t'ponder what pleasures await us on the Red Net-work," he mumbled, "Perhaps the mel-lowjious Lawrence Tibbets. Or God help us, Nelson Eddy ...." He turned the volume down to background level.

"Of course," said Teddy, "only the great McKormack -"

"Now none'a your wisecracks, Mr Eccles E S Q. I've yet to take'ye t'task for puttin'me together with a private eye who's probin' a matter that concerns me. I'm trustin' this man with me life."—He nodded in my direction—"I'm not just beatin' me gums either. I'm well acquainted with the minny ways death can sneak up, an' it often begins like this.—No offense, mind'ye."

"None taken," I said.

"What do you mean?" asked Teddy.

He pondered the question briefly, while Victor Herbert, whom a Mocky client of mine once described as "the divine schmalz her-ring," followed his secret heart.

"What I mean," said Cuhulain, "is that a man might say some-thin' fr'simple love'a tellin' a story, an' it comes around an' whacks him a tirrible blow from behind. A man such as Martin here might give his sources away inadvertently, fr'example. Let on he knows somethin' when there's only one way he could know it, an' that might put his source in danger."

I told him I understood. He rubbed his chin and looked me over.

"I believe ye do. So that takes care'a that. But, as each of ye' know from your own occupations, there're other ways t'set the fatal thing in motion. Ye might talk casually of people ye don't think of as dangerous, ye may even go ahead an'rub shoulders with'em, but if ye'd given it a moment's thought ye'd realize ye'd underestimated the danger they represent."

Teddy nodded. "I only take clients on reference from people I trust now. Too many 'bingers.'"

"Meanin'?" Cuhulain asked.

"Meaning men who spent time in solitary confinement, and came out 'binged,' in jailbird lingo. It doesn't take much for an inmate to be put in solitary nowadays. The penitentiaries have no budget, no staff, so they use the threat of it to keep order. Crack wise to a guard, try to sneak some food out of the mess hall, get in a fist fight, off you go for a long time. Fellows lose their minds in solitary, and most of'em eventually get out of the pen. Back a few years ago, when all you had to do to engage my services was walk in the door and give your name to my secretary, a few bingers ended up in my office telling me they'd done some foolish thing and were desperate not to go back to stir. You can't talk rationally to people like that, but you can't promise you'll save them either. One fellow took a swing at me. Another said he'd hunt me down and shoot me if I didn't take his case and win it."

Cuhulain nodded. "Well, there ye'have it. We all know t'watch who we're dealin' with.—So then, what do ye make of Bobby's murther?" he asked me.

"This is the first I've heard that Bobby was connected to gangsters. I gotta think about that for awhile."

"It'd be overstatin' the case considerably t'say he were cinnicted t'gangsters. He were cinnicted t'me, an'I were cinnicted t'gangsters."

I smiled amiably. "All due respect, you love to tell a tale. I imagine Bobby and the roscoes you wash money for got to know quite a bit about each other over the years you and Bobby did business."

"But I were always conscious'a the risks. And so was he. Bobby niver rubbed shoulders with the roscoes. It disgusted him th' way people around here talk about 'em, and point'em out on the street like they're somethin' grand. So ye'd be barkin' up the wrong tree."

I shrugged. "I'm always hearing someone is connected to gangsters. I check it out, they rarely are. This is different though. No one said Bobby had even the remotest connection to gangsters. Now it turns out he did."

He continued to insist that connecting the murder to gangsters was a dead end. I agreed it probably was, but who else did Bobby rub shoulders with that might commit such a crime?

We ran through jealous husbands and jilted lovers. He dismissed them the same way Marcie had. Everybody loved Bobby. They couldn't help it. We chewed over the fact that he was murdered when he opened the door for someone who must have come under the guise of doing business, hence the roses on the floor. That brought it back to Slansky, but neither of us believed he did it.

Then Cuhulain had a thought. He said that the priest that helped Bobby devise the rose hawker scheme suggested that the poorer parish boys be given a chance to sell flowers as well. Bobby was reticent, but the priest insisted.

"Some'a them lads were trouble," Cuhulain said. "I recognized the type from me Chicago days. Street scrappers, rounders, cannon fodder fr' the mob, that's how I viewed'em. Snorty n'Gimpy used t'keep ten or twelve of'em on the payroll just t'make life miserable fr'each other. After Bobby opened his shop, a few of those lads couldn't get it through their thick heads that the flowers had t'come from retail florists, an' then only when they were stale. Couldn't get the scheme straight! Or maybe they could, an' they didn't like it. They were fr'ever pestering Bobby fr' fresh blooms at a price. Could one'a them've come knockin' that mornin'? Who knows. I nivir give a thought t'that end'a the business, it were in such capable hands. Maybe if I'd paid more attintion he'd be with us today "

He dabbed at his eye with his handkerchief again.—"Ah, what's the sense in keenin' when the funeral's over," he said, raising his glass. "T'Bobby Tuttweiler."

We drank to the deceased, then sat for awhile, lost in our own thoughts. Gradually, a low howl from the Philco intruded on our musings. It sounded like a malfunction related to the vacuum tubes. Cuhulain patted the side of the machine firmly. When that didn't halt it he tinkered with the tuner, until he realized it was only Jeanette

McDonald, emoting the dread Indian Love Call—"When I'm calling youuu- hooo-hoo-hoo -"

He snapped it off in disgust. "So then, Martin, where'll your inquiries take'ye next?" he asked

"Maybe to the priest." I held out my glass for a refill.

"Ye're in luck," he said, as he poured. "He'll be presidin' at the weddin'."

"What wedding?"

"Ye hadn't heard? It come up kind of sudden. Bobby Jr. is marryin.' An well, I'm told."

"I forgot to tell you, Martin," said Teddy. "I only found out yesterday myself. He's marrying into the White Bear Ervines. Very wealthy family."

"Bobby often told me he wanted his children t'marry rich," said Cuhulain

"He's marryin' rich and beautiful if she's the gal I'm thinkin' of," I said.

"I've heard she frequents Kuby's," said Teddy. "Just between us, her family doesn't like that at all. Kuby's is a dive. The D A tells me they sniff nose candy there."

"They do indeed," I said. "Can either'a you gents wangle me an invite to the wedding? Otherwise I'll have to find another way to approach the priest."

"Ah, don't worry yourself," said Cuhulain. According to him the wedding was a private affair, but it was come one come all for the reception, which would be held in a banquet room at this very hotel. "Th' priest'll certainly be there, sociable fillow that he is."

Everything seemed to be falling into place. I'd talk to the priest. He'd give me the low down on Wigger, Tipper and sundry other scrappers, rounders and nose candy sniffers, all of whom Eddy Guifoyle had managed to ignore when he investigated the murder. Marcie would be there. I could set up another meeting. My only regret was that it might be our last.

The three of us spent the rest of the afternoon talking baseball, boxing, and finally the war that everyone feared was brewing.

"It doesn't concern this country," said Teddy."We should stay out."

"Maybe, but we'll get dragged in anyway," was my reply.

"What do you think, Faennis?" Teddy asked.

He didn't answer directly. Instead, he sang us a verse to the tune of 'O Christmas Tree', a ditty that he said was all the rage in the old country when he'd emigrated, twenty years past, on the eve of The War To End All Wars:

"Ah Germany, sweet Germany, why don't ye come set Ireland free?"

A MORAL FAILING

Next evening found me at Tin Cup's, in the unique position of being on speaking terms with both Eddy Guilfoyle and Slapper Doran. Eddy was at the far end of the bar by himself, staring into his drink. I made a point of greeting him. He muttered hello, but was in no mood to converse. He'd lost more weight, and looked like he needed ironing.

Doran was in his usual booth near the front door, whispering with a couple of his boys. They peered at me like I was interrupting an IRA meeting.

"Whadda you want, McDonough?" snarled the pride of Slap's stable, Myron "My" Sullivan, a welterweight said to be in line for a title shot at Madison Square Garden.

Normally you don't need an appointment to talk with Slapper, who came by his moniker by slapping you on the back to get your attention if he thought you weren't fixated on him. I ignored Sullivan and addressed him directly.

"Gimme a few minutes of your precious time," I said. "Maybe we can help each other."

He told his boys to take a walk. They complied in reasonably good spirits, and posted themselves at the bar where they could cast menacing looks at Eddy. He sneered back once, then ignored them. I ordered us a couple drinks.

"Heard'ya had some bad luck," I said.

"Luck had nothin' to do with it. Your friend over there trapped me. That's what my lawyer says."

"Really? I heard it was you that trapped somebody, after Eddy put the squeeze on'ya. One'a those Huns I saw you with at Kuby's."

He registered some surprise that I'd seen him at Kuby's, but not much. He was preoccupied with the injustice of his predicament.

"Same thing," he said. "Eddy sends Little Mikey after me, pretty soon I'm back to the wall. What choice do I have?"

"You can clam up. They can put you in the dock, but they can't make you talk."

"Yeh yeh yeh. Then I take the fall."

"Bingo."

"Jee-zus McDonough! I thought'ya said ya could help me! I can help myself do five years in the can.—Jee- ZUS!"

"Just drawin' the picture. Here's what I have in mind. You tell me a few things about that fellow you trapped, I talk to somebody who knows the D A."

Doran was no fool. He asked the obvious question.

"Uh uh, no guarantees," I replied, "just a bug in somebody's ear."

He blustered and whined, but soon adopted the right attitude— what do I have to lose?

He told me he'd met Danny Wegleitner, aka Wigger, on Rice Street one evening about a year ago, selling flowers. They got to talking. Wigger told him that along with the roses he had some candy that he might sell to a few special customers. Slapper decided to try some. Wasn't long before he'd acquired a sweet tooth, but not much of one according to him.

He asked me if I was investigating the so-called dope ring that Eddy G had smashed, which, he assured me, was a figment of Eddy's cop imagination.

"I'm not interested in dope rings," I told him. "This Wigger character is maybe involved in somethin' else I'm nosin' around about."

He was curious, but I let him know who was asking the questions, and put a few more to him. He said he didn't know much about Wigger, but remembered him saying that he'd been in stir for awhile, and would've stayed longer if not for the help of a pen pal.

"He told me they weren't gonna turn him loose unless he had work, which was pretty hopeless what with the Depression and all," Slapper explained, "but this dame, this pen pal'a his, got him a job."

"What dame?"

He didn't know her name, but he knew her father was in the flower business. Then his face lit up. "So that's what you're investigatin'! I heard the guy was murdered. You don't think Wigger—"

"Don't get ahead'a yourself," I advised him.

The mere thought of being connected, even peripherally, to something as exciting as murder made Slapper forget his troubles. Instead of me pulling information out of him grudgingly, he started racking his brain for more. Some of it was helpful.

Wigger had been out of stir for six months or so when he and Slapper met, and yes, he had been romantically involved with his former pen pal, but their love didn't blossom immediately. They'd started sparking about the same time Slapper got to know him.

"I see her with him at Kuby's," he said. "Told me he was gone on her. I don't blame him, she's a knockout, but a little while ago he tells me that just as sudden as she got a crush on him, bang—it's all over."

"And this happened when?"

"Few weeks, maybe a month ago."

"Name's Angie, right?"

"Yeh yeh yeh, now ya mention it. Angie."

I told Slapper he'd been very helpful, but he wasn't ready to let go. He commiserated about his situation, and told me yet again that the nose candy ring was malarkey.

"So I whiffed a little snow, what of it?" he said. "That son of a bitch,"—he pointed at Eddy, not surreptitiously, but with wagging finger and outstretched arm—"is tellin' everybody there's this big buncha people in cahoots, and I'm sellin' the stuff. Lies! I give some snow to a guy referees matches at the Auditorium. Once. That's it. Eddy says there's a gang operatin' outta Kuby's, claims I'm sellin' it around the parish, even arrested some dinge who's supposed to bring it over from Rondo -"

"What dinge?"

"Guy plays piano, can't remember his name. Hey hey hey, he in on the flower guy drop? Tell me, McDonough, c'mon."

"His name Sean?"

"Yeh yeh yeh Sean. God's my witness I don't know nothin' about dope rings, I -

"Nice talkin' to you, Slap. I'll see what I can do."

Slap's boys rejoined him as soon as I left the booth. They leaned in and conspired. I took one of the stools they'd vacated and kept an eye on the imaginative Mr. G.

Eddy was never a guy to close the bar down. Best I could recall from taking casual note of his habits, he was home in the loving arms of Mrs. G by ten p. m. After awhile I stationed myself near the door, next to the Mighty Wurlitzer, and watched for signs of his imminent departure.

"Fill your pockets up with some—sunshine and flowers," crooned Crosby. "If you want the things you love—you must have showers --ba-baboo..."

John O'Connor came over to strike up a conversation. I invented a headache to explain why I wasn't my usual garrulous self.

"Try Carter's Pills," John suggested.

"But that's for your liver, isn't it?" I couldn't help replying.

"Tis your liver," John explained. "Liver'n lights, they're all connected to the seat of pain, and that's behind your eyes, Martin." He tapped his own noggin for emphasis. "My dad explained it. Just before he died."

Had I been as eager to engage as I normally am, I'd surely have pursued that line of inquiry. His father, John O'Connor Sr., former chief of the St. Paul Police, had trod the same well-worn path I was treading and if anyone knew about the associated maladies it was him. Unfortunately duty beckoned. I massaged my temples and mutely feigned the throes of a thumper. John drifted away. Soon I saw Eddy wave the barman off when he came to check.

I slipped out the door and waited.

A fliver rumbled past, then another a few minutes later. Enough time passed so I wondered if I'd jumped the gun. I walked across the street and stood in a doorway so's I wouldn't bump into anyone I knew.

The two bulbs in the Tin Cup's sign that burned out the day after Prohibition was repealed still hadn't been replaced. Several more had dimmed noticeably. Nevertheless, there was enough light to see who came and went.

Bertie Crimmins, a belligerent hoocher even by Rice Street standards, staggered out and looked around for someone to insult. The street was empty and I wasn't visible, so he wove his way down the block toward Mooney's.

Having nothing better to do, I mentally reconstructed the previous few minutes of Bertie's evening—draining his glass, swiping the back of his hand across his flattened beezer, loudly demanding one on the house, cursing the bar, the bar man and everyone in the bar upon being turned down, and slowly revolving on his bar stool in search of an antagonist. His eyes would have fallen on Doran's booth, but he isn't that screwy. The clientele at Mooney's was older and more to his liking.

A few minutes later Eddy strode out, paused to spark a gasper, and started down the street. I caught up to him at the corner.

"Got a minute, Eddy?"

He wore his weariness of me, of the Tuttweiler case and the many new and different forms of corruption to which it had introduced him, of life in general, like an ill-fitting overcoat. It looked awful but it was big enough to duck in.

"New twist in the Tuttweiler case, Eddy."

"Told'ja, I never want to hear about that again."

He started to leave, but I caught him by the arm.

"You should listen."

"Get your hands off me," he said. "Talk. Make it quick."

"I'll make it quick as I can, but there's some things we gotta cover. Number one, the smoke you collared? Turn him loose. I'm gonna check down at the lockup tomorrow, and he better be gone."

A little of the old flash showed in his eyes. "Who the hell are you to tell me -"

I told him I was the guy who knew he slept with Betty Tuttweiler, so he should keep his best interests in mind. He took a drag, dropped his butt on the sidewalk, and carefully ground it out with his size 12 brogan.

"Whatta you care about that dinge?" he asked, without conviction.

I said I had it on good authority that the dinge in question wouldn't touch snow with a barge pole, and anyway I needed to talk to him. Eddy knew I had him by the short hairs, but he managed a feeble counter.

"They let'cha visit guys in the can. Talk to him there. He's key to makin' my case."

"Case? Y'mean that nose candy ring you dreamed up? Listen, I'm willing to assume, for argument's sake, that you might be pursuing justice for Bobby Tuttweiler your own way, and all things bein' equal I don't wanna wreck your life—but..."

I let it hang.

"'But' what?"

"But Marcie Kirkwood hired me to find out who killed her father and I'm just about there. Best thing you can do is make things easy. I'll take care of you if I can. Maybe you won't lose your job."

He claimed, not very convincingly, that he didn't need anyone taking care of him. What he'd done with Betty Tuttweiler was immoral, he admitted. And failing to confess it was worse.

"But it ain't unethical," he said. "No reason it should cost my job."

He was on shaky ground and he knew it. Not that the ethical duty of a St. Paul copper wasn't a fluid concept, but crimes against ordinary citizens were supposed to be pursued impartially.

"No reason you should lose your job?" I countered. "Betty Tuttweiler stands to collect twenty large if the murder is pinned on Slansky, you sleep with her, do everything in your power to put him in the dock, and that's ethical?"

"He had motive and opportunity. He's the obvious suspect."

"But we both know he didn't do it."

He didn't say anything for awhile, then asked what I wanted. I wasn't sure yet, I said, but step one was turning Sean loose.

"I can't just walk in and unlock the door. I told the D A he was part of a dope ring."

"Figure somethin' out."

"It'll take time, maybe a week."

I agreed to that. He hung around and talked a few minutes, told me that Betty Tuttweiler had been on him from the day of the murder to arrest Sheldon Slansky, and never let up. She called four-five times a week, wheedled and pleaded, met him for drinks, told him she'd lose her home, that she'd have to sell flowers on the street. But the more he investigated, the less likely it seemed that Slansky was the killer.

"Ever come up with another suspect?" I asked.

"Nah. I looked into some people. The gal who discovered his body, some associates'a his. Led nowhere."

I told him I was surprised an investigator of his caliber hadn't discovered anything in all this time, as much as called him a liar, but he didn't take the bait. Then, as we were about to part, he blurted out the confession he'd been aching to make for more than a year. It didn't take long, but it contained a detail that revealed why he'd have had a tough time telling a priest.

"It was Ash Wednesday," he said, "right after morning Mass. Betty left a message at the precinct, said come over soon as I could, she had some new information. But there was nothin' new, just more talk've the key man policy, her fear of livin' on handouts. She poured us a drink, cried. I tried to comfort her..."

He paused with a look on his face as if he would burst into tears himself. "The mark of the ash was still on my forehead when I laid with her, Martin. God'll never forgive me."

A JOYOUS OCCASION

Maybe not, but Father Krause would. I met the earthy prelate of St. Albert's a few days later, at the gala reception that followed the Tuttweiler/Ervine nuptials. He had a big grin, a goatee, and a fringe of razor-cut hair around the balding crown of his head. His charcoal grey vestment was trimmed with silver piping, and tailored to hang just so.

"Call me Russ," he said when I introduced myself. He laid an arm on my shoulder and nudged me along as he used his collar to buffalo our way to the front of the drink line.

"Come on over here where we can talk," he said, after we picked up a couple whiskey and waters. He led us to a dimly lit corner where the sound of the band (which still lacked its regular piano player) was softened, and we were unlikely to be interrupted.

"Bobby would have loved this," he told me. "Classy crowd, classy venue, good hooch, everything he wanted for his son. He prayed every day that his children would marry well. Such a shame he didn't live to see this. You know, he'd had his eye on this family and this very young lady for a long time."

I had my eye on her too, since I realized she was not the curvy blonde who'd been hanging all over Bobby. Kate Tuttweiler, nee Ervine, was the gal with the snow habit that Sean had pointed out at Kuby's. She was a tall, flat-chested, auburn-haired frail who appeared to be dazed by the proceedings, which, I'd been told by a fellow celebrant, had been planned and executed in such haste that he assumed she was pregnant.

If she was, it was too early to show. Viewed from the reception line, the bride was exquisitely groomed, expensively coiffed, flat-bellied and semi-beautiful. At handshake distance she appeared tense and run-over. The wooden smile pasted on her otherwise severe mug ticked a fleeting acknowledgment when I wished her the best. She kept swiping at her nose.

I told Bobby he could still be a crooner when we shook hands. That seemed to please him.

"Isn't she lovely," said Russ.

"No. But I'm sure she's suitable in all the important ways."

He acknowledged the truth of that with a fleeting smile. "So. Tell me more about yourself," he said. "I find detective work fascinating."

"What's there to say, Russ? I went to St. Thomas for a year, thought about joining the police and decided to become a private eye instead. It's worked out pretty well."

"Ever kill a man?"

"Uh-uh."

"Just curious."

"I get that question all the time."

"And the family hired you to find out who killed Bobby?"

"Marcella hired me. The others just want to put it behind them. They think they know who killed him, but they're afraid he'll never be convicted."

Russ ate up this kind of gossip, I could see that. He told me that Betty had never confided in him, but he'd heard through the grapevine that a Hebe murdered Bobby, for money. I said my inquiries led me to believe otherwise. He whistled softly and asked who done it.

"I'm not sure yet," I replied, "but I've got a theory. I'd like to tell you about it. Maybe you could help."

"Of course, of course, go ahead."

I said it would best if we discussed it in more private circumstances. "I'll call soon," I told him.

"Maybe a little hint about where your investigation is leading?"

I declined with a smile and excused myself.

I'd taken barely a step when I bumped into Amy, the gal I'd seen with Bobby not so long ago at the family home. She was luscious as ever.

"Amy?" I said.

She looked at me blankly until I reminded her where we'd met, and whom she'd been with. "This isn't a very happy occasion for you, is it, dear?" I asked.

She seemed confused by the question. "Why?" she finally replied.

"Well, you and Bobby seemed pretty tight, I thought -"

"Oh, I get it." She favored me with a wicked little grin. "I don't think I've seen the last of Bobby."

I noticed Russ staring at us with what might have been a lascivious look in his eye. I introduced the two of them and excused myself.

I caught a glimpse of Marcie and The Lucky Dog among a group I took to be the Ervine clan. Like the others in that crowd, Marcie looked more bemused than joyful on this joyous occasion. I was making my way in her direction when Angie took my arm, planted a kiss on my cheek and squired me toward the buffet table. I told her whiskey killed my appetite, but she was having none of it.

"C'mon, grab a plate, sit with me," she insisted.

She speared a few slices of roast beef for me, spooned on some salad and potatoes, filled her own plate, and found us a table on the Tuttweiler's side of the room.

The band was playing a rendition of Hold That Tiger, featuring a vigorous solo by a drunk trumpet player. Between the music and the din of voices it was hard to make small talk. Betty waved from a nearby table. Angie leaned in close so I could hear her.

"I haven't seen mom this happy since.. ..well, you know. I don't want to think about it. Not today."

I tried to find some way to bring up Wigger, but before I could the sound of spoons banging on glasses arose. Soon the band stopped playing, and the groom stood to give his speech. His bow tie was askew, his ruffled shirt open at the collar. He looked like a movie star poised to accept the Oscar for best marriage.

He waited for quiet, then began by thanking everyone for joining him and his bride on this joyous occasion, especially those who'd come from distant White Bear.

He nodded in the band's direction, thanked them for the music, and asked as a special favor if they'd refrain from stealing the silverware. Polite laughter. He said he hoped the best man got a chance to prove it. More titters. He looked a little embarrassed, like he had to say these kind of things but wished he didn't.

Then my heart, and the hearts of everyone there—even the stone-faced Ervines—went out to him, because emotion overcame Bobby as he spoke of his sorrow over the empty chair at his family's table (actually it wasn't empty, Cuhulain was in it).

"This is all for him," said Bobby, with a sweep of the hand that encompassed the food, the music, the marriage, in one gesture. The look on Betty's face was bittersweet. Her lips trembled as her son paused to compose himself.

"To Bobby Tuttweiler Sr." he said.

Cuhulain hoisted his glass and led a loud, unanimous "AYE!" Bobby left the dais to a round of applause, and went over and kissed his mother.

AN ECCLESIASTICAL MATTER

I slacked off after the reception. With or without Sean filling in the blanks I felt I could wrap this case up soon, but Eddy G assured me that his release was in the works. I used that as an excuse to let it ride.

Slapper Doran pestered me to join him every time I walked into Tin Cup's. Had I spoken to my pal? How was the case coming? "Siddown siddown, McDonough," he said. "Howsabout a drink?"

One evening I succumbed to his blandishments. It turned out to be interesting, because a couple of his boxers were discussing the finer points of the sport.

Myron Sullivan had a predictable take. I'd seen him fight once. He seemed to possess a barely controlled fury that built on itself when he landed a blow. Thus, his style was one of constant probing and sudden, vicious flurries.

"Ye're always attackin'," he said, "even when yer defendin' yer lookin for an openin', and then y'go after it."

He demonstrated, clenching his fists and his jaw, and bobbing back from a phantom blow with a snarl on his face that must have disheartened all but the bravest of opponents.

Doran's middleweight, Harry Cassidy, told him he ought to learn to counterpunch.

"I tried doin' that," Sullivan said. "Remember, Slapper, down in Omaha?"

Doran nodded with a sour look. "How could I forget?"

They told the tale of that fight, interrupting each other to embellish on a disaster that had begun with such great promise.

"I hit him with a right in the first round, his knees buckled," said Sullivan. "He was out on his feet," said Doran. "We rode the blinds down there," Sullivan explained, "took two days. I thinks to myself, 'I come all this way in a boxcar t'fight thirty seconds? 'C'mon, c'mon,' I sez to him, 'wake up!'"—"'Take him out,' I sez," said Doran, "but My, he wants to practice some moves, use this kid for a punchin' bag. Not smart."—"I couldn't get that feel back," said Sullivan, "couldn't get goin', must'a been the fourth or fifth, I thinks to myself, 'you could lose this one ye damn fool.'"—"It was too late by then," Doran said. "T'my mind it was a close fight but they home-towned us, gave the other guy every round but the first."

He wagged a finger at his boys. "If yez got it in yer hand, take it goddam it!"

I rang Russ the moment I woke up next morning. It had been days since the wedding reception but it sounded like he'd been waiting for my call ever since.

"Why don't you come by right now?" he said.

I gulped a coffee and walked down Rice Street to St. Albert's. Russ was outside the rectory waiting for me, puffing on a fag. "Come on in to the office," he said.

We trod the echoing granite hallway to his little sanctum. It was cozy and highly personalized, with a shelf full of poetry books and lots of plaques and framed photos on all the walls. Another shelf held softball and bowling trophies for parish teams. One plaque, from The Stahl House Winter League, was inscribed to Father Krause personally. He'd won a Turkey Tournament.

The wall behind his desk was devoted to photos of Russ with the great and near great—Mayor Mahoney, the late Governor Olson, Babe Ruth, Bronko Nagurski, some nobodies from local sports and politics.

He seated me in a leather chair and grabbed a bottle of whiskey out of his desk drawer. Over the course of the next hour we had a couple drinks, and a wide ranging conversation. He filled me in on Bobby, gave me lots of useful information about the case, and straightened out an ecclesiastical matter that helped make the pieces fit.

After that we discussed things that had nothing to do with Bobby's murder. By the time our meeting was over I'd decided Russ was an odd and interesting sort of cleric. When I told him I had to go we shook hands, and he wished me luck.

"One more question," I said, as we walked down the hall. "Do you have faith?"

"Not much, how about you?"

"None," I replied.

"Oh, come on. Don't tell me you're not a little intrigued by the mystery. Everybody is.—'tho' he is under, the world's splendor and wonder, His mystery must be stressed—A poet said that."

"I'm a little intrigued by the mystery," I admitted. "Sometimes."

"Then you're just exactly like me."

"That's not very comforting, Russ, you being a priest and all."

"There's not much comfort to be had, Martin."

THE FATAL THING

The temperature was close to 100 and the sky was ominous the next day, when I met Marcie to wrap things up. I parked, and looked down University Avenue. A great wall of cloud was advancing from the west, rolling and billowing, black as a thunderstorm but looming up from the ground, not down from the sky. A rim of sunlight was visible above, a stiff wind blew out ahead. There was enough static electricity in the air to make my skin tingle. I grabbed for my hat. Suddenly the air was thick with little stinging particles. By the time they started pelting me I'd reached The Criterion, and it was a good thing too. By then you couldn't see your hand in front of your face.

I had all I could do to pull the door open against the wind. It banged closed again loudly. A thick haze entered with me. I must've been quite a sight emerging from a cloud, puffs of dust rising from my hat as I whacked it against my knee. The waiter and the bar man both smiled. A few bar flies took note, but most of them never looked up.

It was hot inside, but the fans helped a little. The waiter seated me in a back booth, near one of the solitary middle-aged dames who frequented the place.

I was later than usual. Not as late as Marcie though. She'd sounded hesitant when I called, in sharp contrast to her eagerness to get together earlier. I ordered a cold beer and wondered whether she was just reluctant to close the coffin on her father, or if she didn't want our relationship—such as it was—to end. Or if she wished it was over already.

***

After a few minutes passed and no Marcie I started going through what I'd learned again. Just to make sure.

"I'm on pins and needles," Russ had exclaimed, as soon as I sat down. "Who killed Bobby?"

I told him that it appeared to be a young man he knew.

"Jesus!" He whistled softly. "Who?"

I told him I needed more information before I could be certain, which was why I had to ask him some questions.

"Ok, I'm all ears," he said.

"You knew Bobby pretty well, didn't you?"

He nodded, with a wistful smile. "I heard his confessions often through the years, but our relationship went beyond that. Bobby became comfortable with me as a spiritual advisor."

Russ explained that Bobby's confessions presented a challenge of rare directness, because along with the usual venalities he always had dozens of adulterous encounters to divulge.

"I don't mind telling you that, because I'm sure it won't come as any surprise," he said. "The first time I heard him, I thought this was a man who hadn't confessed for months, maybe years, but it wasn't so. He came back a couple weeks later with the same story to tell." He gave me a sly grin, and stroked his goatee. "The same count, as it were."

According to Russ, he and Bobby did the standard confessor/ confesser dance for awhile, pretending they didn't know who'd been on the other side of the curtain, but that didn't last.

"He had a kind of sparkle in his eyes when we ran into each other," said Russ. "Maybe I did too. I was curious. It wasn't long before he began dropping by and talking more informally. So we spent a lot of time together, right here in this office. I thought to myself, this is damned interesting, from a lot of different perspectives. It was a pastoral challenge, it was a glimpse into a unique personality. But most of all, he told some wonderful stories. Love stories."

That came as a shock to my delicate sensibilities. I'd scoffed when Eddy G told me Holy Mother was the only comfort we had, but I still occasionally took solace in the knowledge that something stood between me and the void, something personified by the priesthood and expressed in the ancient rituals, none of which included sitting around and shooting the bull about extra-marital affairs with your confessor.

It was about then that I noticed that the wall of photos behind Russ illustrated more than his meetings with celebrities over the years. It documented his evolution from Father Krause—a conventional-looking young priest with an innocent face and a beatific smile—to a middle-aged wolf named Russ.

"We talked a lot about temptation," Russ continued, "and of course my attitude was the Church's attitude: Temptation is simply there to be resisted, as a sort of moral exercise. I remember the time we first discussed it at length. He was sitting in the chair where you're sitting now. He'd just been to confession a few days before. He'd told me again about the liaisons he'd had outside his marriage. I'd chastised him about his adulterous ways. He took it in good spirit—Bobby always had a good spirit, God bless him—but that day I finally said, "you're just going to keep on doing this, aren't you?'— 'Yes, I think I am,' he told me. 'I can see the wisdom of stopping but I'm not sure I can. In fact I'm pretty sure I can't.'

"We just looked at each other and laughed," said Russ.

According to Russ, their dialogue went on until Bobby was murdered. Bobby asked the same questions I might have if I were in his shoes. If God doesn't want you to make love to women, why does he make them so beautiful? Why do they smell so good? Why do they squirm the way they do when you kiss their neck?

"These were things that, to be honest, I wasn't acquainted with," said Russ. "He made them sound pretty good."

"So what'd you decide?"

"I can't say we decided anything, not in the sense that we came to an agreement. I was the one who was supposed to have an answer, but instead Bobby put a question in my mind that I have yet to resolve."

Bobby, Russ explained, didn't agree that temptation always leads to sin. He admitted that some temptations might, but he wondered how you'd know which ones did if you never succumbed to any of them? In other words, how would you know right from wrong? He told Russ that he'd rarely felt wrong after he made love to a woman.

"He knew it corrupted his marriage," said Russ, "but he considered that his wife's failing, or perhaps a failing of the institution itself."

"But he personally never bumped up against a temptation that led him to mortal sin?"

"I didn't say that."

Hints and intimations were all he'd ever gotten from Bobby on that matter, but enough for him to draw some conclusions.

"If you can honestly tell me it would aid your investigation I'll tell you what he did," Russ said.

"Just tell me how you absolved him if he didn't confess."

Russ smiled. "I enjoy a good conversation, and this is about as good as I've had since Bobby was killed.—I take it you aren't observant, but think back to when you were. Didn't you have to ask forgiveness? Of course you did. Now Bobby never asked forgiveness for anything except the most mundane and venial transgressions. Certainly not for seductions and adulteries."

Nevertheless, Russ could tell that he felt pretty bad about the matter they were discussing, bad enough so he wanted to work something out. Not absolution maybe, but some kind of redemption.

And that was how the fatal thing was set in motion.

**

BANG!—The sound of the Criterion's door blowing closed interrupted my recollection. The bar flies' heads all turned. Marcie was wearing a billowy summer dress that fluttered in the breeze from the fans, and those same high-heeled sandals she'd removed the last time we got together. She had a straw sun bonnet in her hand.

She put it on the table, then sat down and fussed with the ribbons.

"Dust storm over?" I asked.

She shook her head no, and studied the bonnet. I studied the tiny beads of sweat on her chest, amongst which perched her pince nez.

"So, who killed him?" she asked.

"I guess we're gettin' right down to work then."

Her eyes crinkled a little. "Maybe I'll have a Manhattan. Just one."

"For old time's sake?"

She eyed me skeptically. "Jeez, Martin, we're not lovers."

"Almost."

She dismissed that notion with a wave of her hand, and ordered a Manhattan. I swallowed a pill with a sip of beer. She asked what it was. I showed her the packet.

"'Carter's Little Liver Pills'? Why not just drink less?"

I said I'd take that under advisement. She scoffed. "A gal would be a fool to get interested in you, Martin. You practically drink for a living."

"You're a little quicker to order a drink than you used to be, I've noticed."

"Huh," she sniffed.

"It's got nothing to do with you though," she added, in a tone that told me it had plenty to do with me, but I didn't know what. I was pretty obtuse in those days.

"I drink for lotsa reasons," I said, "but when I drink with coppers I'm drinkin' for a living. Remember the first time we got together, I told you most murder cases aren't solved? Not precisely true. Most murder cases don't result in a conviction, but the coppers know who the killer is, they just can't prove it. They're usually happy to tell me after a few drinks though."

"Does Eddy Guilfoyle know who killed my father?" she asked.

"Yeah, but he wouldn't say. I had to figure it out. Keep in mind what I just told you though. They know, but they can't prove it, meaning they can't bring enough evidence to the D A to make a case."

I let that sink in, then began to walk her through my investigation.

"The fact that you hired me put a lot of things in motion," I explained.

I began with Eddy's trumped-up cocaine ring. I discovered how completely that had fallen apart the evening I had to tussle to keep Slapper Doran and his boxers from hoisting me on their shoulders and singing, "For He's A Jolly Good Fellow."

It seemed the charges against Slapper had been reduced to misdemeanor possession, which meant that he might cool his heels in the workhouse for a few weeks, but hard time wasn't in the cards. I didn't bother mentioning that I hadn't yet spoken to anyone on his behalf. Thus grows the legend of Martin McDonough, string puller.

I looked for Eddy G amid the clamor of praise and the thrusting of drinks upon my worthy self, but he was nowhere to be seen, so I surrendered to the spirit of the moment.

The morning after I awoke with the usual headache, and the feeling that I should get downtown fast if I wanted to talk to Sean. Nevertheless, I'd arrived too late. I learned something I never would have guessed though. Turns out that the penalty for not being a member of an imaginary nose candy ring in the Saintly City is deportation. Maybe it just applies to smokes.

I told Marcie that Sean's departure left only one alleged conspirator under lock and key. She didn't know where all this was going, of course. She listened patiently, interrupting only to make a few remarks about Eddy's detective work. Corruption was the theme of those comments.

The way she brushed me off when I said we'd almost been lovers, then as much as called me a terminal soak, must've irritated me. I couldn't resist a rejoinder.

"I see now why you're so down on corruption," I told her. "Something pretty rotten led to your father's murder."

"What d'you mean?"

"This case is a strange one, Marcie. It was from the beginning. For instance, I've never been in an investigation where the people who claim to want the truth were so unwilling to give me information. You wouldn't even tell me who you thought was guilty, remember?"

"Yeah, and I told you why."

"The rest of your family wouldn't give me anything either. I barely talked to your brother. Your sister told me nothing. I didn't get much from your mother, just a little tip about roses when she described the funeral, unintentional but useful, because later I come to find out that your father's special passion was roses."

Her eyes narrowed. "He was in the flower business, Martin. He liked flowers."

"But roses best of all," I insisted. "Preferably clutched in the trembling hand of a sixteen year old girl.'"

Marcie sighed, and took a sip of her Manhattan.

"Her name was Trudy," she said. "She was so sweet and pretty. So meek."

"I heard you were a friend of hers."

She shrugged, just a little twitch of the shoulders that jiggled her pince nez. "Not really," she said. "She was a poor kid, went to St. Albert's, lived down by the shop ponds. I didn't pay much attention to her. I remember once in school she called me 'Miss Tuttweiler.' I said, 'you can call me Marcella, Trudy.' I suppose she thought that made us friends."

"How'd you find out?"

"She told me. She was proud of it."

"Did she tell other people?" I asked.

"No. I said it had to be our secret.—Why are we talkin' about this, Martin? It happened a long time ago. I hired you to find things out, so I can't complain if they're things I'd sooner you didn't know. But don't tell me Trudy killed him. I don't believe it."

I assured her I wouldn't, and explained how the act of contrition Bobby and Father Russ devised came to involve Danny Wegleitner.

Russ had been proud to tell me that he and Bobby had figured out a way to let some of the "less fortunate" kids in the parish earn some money. He'd directed my attention to the wall of photos behind me, and invited me to take a closer look at some pictures of outings Russ had taken, groups of three or four boys.

There were shots of them canoeing down Phalen Creek, seated in the bleachers at a Saints game, eating candy floss at Como Park, hunting grouse.

***

Those kids were fatherless for the most part," Russ said. "When they were youngsters I tried to give them some of the experiences they might have had otherwise, but by the time Bobby and I worked out the arrangement I'm speaking of they were older, and frankly, with the Depression on, poverty was their main problem. Bobby agreed to put them to work selling roses. You've probably seen them. They stand on busy corners and come around to the bars. There are lots of them now, but it began with just a few, and they were all from this parish."

"Most of the ones I see are girls, Russ. They're sixteen or so."

He nodded. "Correct."

We both knew what he meant.

I peered at the photos closely. He pointed out a picture of a crowded toboggan about to launch down a snowy hill.

"I took this a few years before Bobby and I got to know each other well. That's Bobby, kneeling on the back, under that parka. Bobby Jr. is one of the kids on the toboggan. I got Bobby involved with these kids early on. It was never any kind of quid pro quo at that point, just something I asked him and a lot of parish dads to do. Bobby was always willing."

I asked if there were any photos of Danny Wegleitner.

"Yes." He pointed to one of a boy on a playground swing. "That was about twelve years ago. Here he is when he's older."

I recognized him in that one, a tall, strapping kid, who'd just whacked a softball, and was watching it soar as he dropped the bat and began to stride toward first.

"That your suspect?" Russ asked.

"Yeah."

He sighed. "I was hoping that wasn't the case. He's been in trouble all his life. Bobby's daughter wrote to him when he was in prison, through a program we set up here at the parish. But why would he kill Bobby?"

"Just a guess, but I think Bobby knew he and Angie were getting cozy, and didn't like it."

He sighed. "He wouldn't have. He was determined his children would marry well." He shook his head sadly. "Much as I liked Bobby, loved him really, I feel sorry for Danny. He's in jail now, you know. At least he was until yesterday."

"He's out?"

Not exactly, Russ explained. He'd visited Danny a few times since his arrest, and he'd gone downtown to do so the day before, but was told that Danny had been transferred. They were holding him in the insane asylum, down in St. Peter.

That came as quite a surprise to me. Russ too. He said Danny had always been in one scrape or another, but he wasn't bugs.

Marcie was skeptical when I told her about Wigger. "Why would he kill my father if he's not nuts?" Marcie asked.

"Good question. I never could answer it. I first suspected him for the same reason Eddy suspected Sheldon Slansky. He's a good suspect. He's been in serious trouble. He did business with your father, could have come knockin' on his door. And he's a cocaine addict. That stuff makes people do funny things."

"Like murder?"

I put my finger to my lips and nodded in the direction of the lady in the nearby booth.

"Y'know, I wondered about that myself," I said. "It's one form of dissipation I have no experience with at all. I had to rely on a musician I ran into at Kuby's. He seemed to know quite a bit about 'snow birds.'"

***

The jailer told me Sean had been hustled out shortly before I'd arrived, with a ticket for the 9:30 train to Chicago and a police escort to make sure he used it. I made it to Union Depot with minutes to spare, risked life and limb flying down the long stairway to the platform just in time to see the bulls put him aboard.

I boarded as well, and caught up before he found a seat.

He was unshaven, and wearing a shirt that looked like it had been crumpled in the bin behind the booking desk since his arrest, but seemed none the worse otherwise. He didn't notice me approaching him, but the conductor did. He was a large fellow with a grin a mile wide and hard eyes that belied it.

"What'chu want!" he demanded. He put a powerful squeeze on my arm.

Sean looked up. "Ah my gumshoe friend," he said, beaming. "This man's ok, Jay-Jay," he told the conductor, who immediately loosened his grip and went about his business.

"Talk amongst the oxford gray back in the slammer had you strivin' to gain my release," he said.

"Simple justice, not to mention the fact that you might be able to help me out."

"ALL ABOARD," shouted the conductor.

I said I realized it was a longshot, but would he wrack his brain anyway, and try to remember if there was anything unusual going on the night before Bobby's murder? Of course he couldn't. He didn't even recall how long ago it had occurred. I told him Bobby was killed on May 25th last year.

"Night before would've been Friday," I said. "Did Wigger do anything special Friday nights? I mean to get ready to sell flowers on Saturday."

"Far's I can remember every night was the same. Wigger'd be around the bar, maybe sittin' at a table for awhile, an' sooner or later him'n Tipper, and that rich gal would go on out n'snort snow. Many nights I walked past'em after the joint closed, after the band had a drink. There they was, sittin' in that big Packard'a hers."

"You'd never talk to'em?"

"Hell no, they busy chinnin' an carryin' on amongst themselves. As is the snow bird's wont."

"What happened the night Tipper died?"

"Like I tole'ya, he jus' went away and never come back. Bobby went lookin' for him, said he wasn't nowhere around. Bobby wasn't into the snow, and he worried 'bout his friends who were."

"And that was after his dad was murdered?"

"Yeah, they was fireworks an' such goin' off. Musta been right roun' the fourth of July.—I heard Bobby married that rich gal. That true?"

"Yeah." I told him about the wedding. "That band needs you in the worst way," I said.

"Looks like they gonna hafta t'do without me." He grinned that tombstone grin of his. "Can't say I'm gonna miss this town."

There was a lurch, the cars banged together, and we were moving. I wished him luck and made it off the train before it passed the platform.

***

Marcie wondered what light my talk with Sean shed on her father's murder. Again, nothing specific, I had to tell her. "But that was a tight little group of hop heads, and there was another good suspect among'em."

"So you're not sure Wigger killed him?"

"Fact is, I'm sure he didn't."

When Russ assured me that Wigger was sane, I'd asked how he knew. He explained that he'd dealt with many troubled kids over the years. "You can tell when they're wrong in the head," he said. "Take this one, for example."

He pointed to a photo of three boys kneeling in a field of corn stubble. Russ and another man were standing behind them, holding a string hung with a brace of quail. One of the boys had a shotgun cradled in the crook of his arm. Russ tapped his finger on the kid with the shotgun.

"He was off his nut," Russ said. "An orphan. He lived with his aunt. She came to me when he was about eleven, told me he'd killed her cat, and she was afraid of him.—Eleven years old and a grown woman was afraid of him. I did what I could, thought maybe hunting might be a way to harness whatever screwy thing about animals was going on in his mind, but he just got odder and odder. Liked to hang around cemeteries, and eventually -"

"Wait a minute. Are you gonna tell me he died in a cemetery?"

"Yes, how did you know?"

"Heard about it at Kuby's. What was his name?"

"Kurt Terwilliger. The boys called him 'Tipper,' because he tipped over gravestones. That was how he died. Tipped a big monument over on himself."

"Sold roses, did he?"

"You could hardly call it selling in his case," Russ explained. "He'd just stand there and hope somebody would ask to buy one.—You're thinking maybe he killed Bobby?"

"Well, he'd have had the same opportunity that Danny Wegleitner did. In any case, I need to talk to Danny,"

According to Russ, that wouldn't be easy. He'd poked around enough to discover that anyone but immediate family needed permission to visit an inmate at St. Peter and it took weeks, even for a priest.

Before we parted we agreed that we'd both try to find a way to short circuit that process.

Marcie said she remembered Tipper the same way Angie did. Strange but harmless.

"Dad and my brother would go on parish outings with the poor kids, and he was one of 'em. He liked my dad. Why would he kill him?"

"Money? There wasn't much at stake, but this kid relied on those roses for whatever cash he had. They were supposed to get old roses from retail florists, but they were getting harder to sell. A source tells me they were always bothering your dad for fresher blooms."

I could see this didn't impress her much motive-wise.

"Tipper's hopped-up, he's not hittin' on all eight. Get it? Don't think of it as an ordinary knockover."

She was skeptical. I told her I didn't blame her, but if we assumed Tipper shot her father, some other things fell into place as well.

"One of them being an aspect of the case that I spoke about too soon," I said. "Your mother did end up with that insurance money."

She looked shocked, but she listened intently while I explained. She knew of her mother's relationship with Cuhulain, and seemed relieved when I told her the route the money took into her mother's hands.

"I suspected she got it," she said. "I asked her, 'ma, do you need some money?' awhile ago and she said she didn't. To be honest, that's when I decided to hire you. I was worried sick, thinkin' why doesn't she? It wasn't because dad put a bunch away, that's for sure. I didn't think she shot him, but —well, you know."

"You were worried she might've had him rubbed out.—No. It came as a complete surprise to her when Cuhulain gave her the money."

"You know that for a fact?"

"Yes."

She took another sip of her Manhattan, heaved a big sigh and relaxed visibly. But the wheels were still going around. I let them turn for awhile.

"But what does her getting the money have to do with that kid killing my dad?"

"Let's backtrack a little. We agreed that we don't believe in coincidences, right? Well, a couple of'em bother me still. For instance, there were two investigators who looked into this case, me and Eddy Guilfoyle. Your sister started vampin' me the moment I laid eyes on her, and -

"WHAT!"

The woman in the nearby booth turned with a look of frank anticipation on her face.

"Careful," I whispered.

"Why that conniving little flirt," Marcie muttered.

That rock of hers bobbed and sparkled as she drummed her fingers on the table .

"You're the only one gets to tease me, right?"

"I never— How can you say that?"

"Anyway, Angie wasn't teasin.' I know when a gal's struttin' some serious stuff." I leaned in and spoke softly. "She was tryin' to seduce me. And your mother seduced Eddy Guilfoyle."

I sat back and watched her reaction, which was sheer incredulity.

"That's right. Two investigators, your mother seduces one, your sister tries to seduce the other. Is that a coincidence? Don't get me wrong, I'm not one to minimize my animal magnetism, but the guy Angie'd been vampin' before we got together was more her age, more her type. That'd be Wigger, by the way. And as far as Eddy and your mother are concerned, what's goin' on there?—Sheldon Slansky thought it was Eddy's nose she couldn't resist."

Marcie's nose wrinkled in disgust. "Oh, this is from him, huh? He's still the best suspect as far as I'm—"

"I checked with Eddy, Marcie. He admitted it, gave me details. Wanna hear'em?"

She glanced over at the next booth. "No, unless it has something to do with the murder."

"It does. Why do you think she screwed him?"

Marcie finished her drink and sat quietly for a few moments. This was all coming a little too fast for her. Understandably. It had taken me a couple weeks to sort it out, with the information accumulating slowly, one piece at a time.

She took a deep breath and spoke quietly. "Because she wanted him to keep his mind on the case. She wanted him to arrest Slansky. She thought it would help her get her hands on the money, so she could age with some dignity."

"Want another drink?"

"No. That wouldn't be a good idea."

I said her theory of why her mother seduced Eddy was like a lot of things in this case. It made perfect sense until you probed a little. Then it fell apart. I explained that Faennis Cuhulain made sure he could bestow the cash upon her mother, along with a bouquet of flowers, on the first day of spring.

"Flowers and gifts on the first day of spring are a tradition in the part of Ireland he comes from," I said, "and Cuhulain's a sentimental ham. Eddy Guilfoyle, on the other hand, is not sentimental. He's religious. He thinks it's a sin to make love to a woman outside the sacrament of marriage, and a most grievous sin to do it on Ash Wednesday. He told me the mark of the ash was still on his forehead when your mother seduced him. See the problem there?"

"No."

"Should'a paid more attention to your catechism. Ash Wednesday is a moveable feast. I checked with Father Russ when it fell last year. March 28th, a week after Cuhulain gave her the dough."

I gave her a moment to ponder that.

"So what's your mother's motive?" I asked. "I told you Slansky's theory about his nose, but you're not buyin' it, right?"

"Stop playin' games, Martin. What?"

"Eddy might be corrupt but he's a good investigator," I told her. "I'd be a fool to think that he didn't find out everything I did, a long time ago. The reason it didn't come out is because your mother has been using her wiles on him ever since the murder. At first she really thought Slansky killed your father. So did Eddy, but the closer he looked the less likely that became. Your mother wheedled and pleaded and said she'd end up in the poorhouse, but Eddy knew Slansky didn't kill him, and so did your mother by a couple months after the murder. She persuaded Eddy to ignore what he'd discovered and pretend that Slansky was the only suspect. The longer that went on the more it wore on Eddy. Your mother could see that, and eventually, out of desperation, she seduced him, so she'd have something on him. She really needed him to keep his mouth shut."

"But why is she protecting Tipper?"

"She isn't. The coppers, the crowd at Kuby's, they all say that Tipper tipped an 800 pound monument over on himself, but how would a person do that? It's impossible. Eddy knows it, and if he was interested in solving Tipper's murder he'd know how to start. He'd look for somebody with motive and opportunity."

"Who?"

"Well, he knows what I know, that your brother went lookin' for Tipper in the cemetery the night he died. My guess, when Bobby found him he was workin' on that big stone. Bobby helped him, and made sure it fell the wrong way. Then he told his mother what he'd done."

That stunned her. She said nothing for awhile.

"My brother killed that boy because he killed my father?"

"Makes sense. It's the most common motive for murder."

"What is? Revenge"

"No, love."

There were tears this time, but they were quiet and discreet. The lady who'd been eavesdropping didn't even notice. After awhile Marcie dabbed at her eyes, and asked if I was certain.

I told her one loose end needed tying up, but I knew how we could take care of it. Russ had made some inquiries since we'd met. He'd discovered that a fifty buck bribe paid to the administrator of the St. Peter Asylum would buy the three of us an hour of privacy with Wigger. Russ would gladly hear his confession, and we'd be free to ask him anything we wanted.

"Even if he didn't do it, he knows what happened," I explained. "Otherwise your sister wouldn't have vamped him, and Eddy wouldn't have put him in the frame. It's up to you whether we talk to him. Far as I'm concerned, I've done what you hired me to do. Tipper shot your father. That's a mortal cinch. If I was in your shoes, I'd consider letting it go at that."

I knew she wouldn't. She gave me the cash and told me to set it up.

MYSTERY

I'm dredging up the trip to St. Peter seven years later, out of an impaired memory, so I can't vouch for the accuracy of my tale. I'm tempted to call that a sobering thought, but if so it hasn't worked yet.

I have a mental image of Russ seated in the front seat next to the chauffeur, gabbing over his shoulder at Marcie and me about the landscape. According to him, we were in the valley of an ancient river that was five miles wide, and hundreds of feet deep. Its' source, he said, was a gigantic lake formed by a melting glacier, with a massive wall of melting ice at its north shore, and a notch in the hills along the south shore that released the torrent he described.

It was the stuff of dreams, and I dozed as we bumped along a gravel road that mirrored the meandering of the Minnesota River, a placid stream that still flowed although the glacier that once fed it was long gone.

It seemed to me that Marcie was glad to be distracted from the task at hand. She was full of questions for Russ, about glaciers, rivers, geological time. He was happy to fill her in, although he admitted that much of what he described was the result of his own cogitations, inspired by a sense of mystery and a few facts that he'd learned from a book. He knew how to tell a story though.

The trip to the asylum—it was about sixty miles south of St. Paul—took more than three hours. We stopped in a small town about half way. The chauffeur removed a hamper that Marcie had packed for the occasion from the rumble seat, and we had a lunch in a park. She spread a linen cloth on a picnic table and poured us Manhattans from an insulated jug—cold, easy on the Vermouth, not too diluted by the ice cubes. When we finished those she passed around watercress sandwiches.

While Marcie and Russ chatted and put things away, the chauffeur and I took a walk around the park. I asked if he'd driven Marcie to our meetings.

"Yes sir," he replied. "I drive them everywhere. Madam does not drive. Mr. Kirkwood does, but prefers not to."

He told me that he'd routinely waited outside the Criterion while we discussed the case, although the meeting before last she'd sent him home when he dropped her off.

"She said you'd be bringing her back, and indeed you did sir. Earlier than she'd anticipated."

***

The asylum was situated on the bluffs outside town, three brick buildings of Victorian severity. After we parked Marcie took me aside.

"Before we go in there, tell me about this loose end we're tying up." She could see I was hesitant. "C'mon Martin, this is no time to hold out."

"Ok. Maybe it's nothin', but it bothers me. There's this little group of three snow birds, hung around whiffin snow, gabbin' and carryin' on, gettin' to know each other's business. Only one of'em killed your father, but whatever there is to know about that crime all three of'em knew it, and look what's happened to'em.—Tipper's dead. Bobby killed him. That's one."

"I guess so," she agreed.

"Then, months later, after I begin pokin' around, Wigger is arrested with a little nose candy. Not much of a charge, but Eddy claims he's the top guy in a dope ring, and starts arrestin' other people to make the case. Looks like Wigger's goin to the big house. But after I

242 BRUCE RUBENSTEIN

stick my nose in, that falls apart. Next day Wigger is whisked off to an insane asylum. Turns out he's bugs, so anything he might tell the coppers about your father's murder is easily discredited. That's two people who know about the murder and they're silenced, correct?"

"Well, yeah."

Two outta three, leavin' Kate Ervine, who's been vampin' Bobby without makin' any headway. Then, a few weeks ago, outta the clear blue sky, he proposes to her. So what does that sound like to you?"

She thought for a few moments.

"Well, it sounds to me like Eddy Guilfoyle made sure Bobby wouldn't go to trial for killing Tipper."

"And ..."

"And..?"

"C'mon, think about it. Why did Bobby marry Kate?"

"That's easy. To honor dad's wishes."

"Uh-uh. Bobby honored your father the only way he knew how, by imitating him. By makin' time with beautiful women."

She looked skeptical. "Kate isn't beautiful."

"Correct."

She still didn't get it. At first.

"Ahh," she finally said. "You think he married her so she'd couldn't be pressured to testify if he did go to trial."

"Yes. Bobby's head over heels over this gorgeous dame, they're practically livin' as man and wife under your mother's roof, then he decides to marry someone else, someone he isn't much interested in, but she's stuck on him, and might get vindictive and rat if she doesn't get her way. Makes perfect sense, doesn't it?"

She agreed it did, and turned to head for the nuthouse, but I stopped her.

"Problem is, it only makes sense until you think about the crime Bobby committed."

It took a moment for her to see what I was driving at.

"Oh, I guess it would be one of those 'know but can't prove' cases, wouldn't it," she said.

"Correct. There were only two people who knew what happened in that cemetery and one of 'em is dead. All your brother had to do is clam up. He'd be a very sympathetic defendant, not the kind a D A wants to put in front of a jury without hard evidence or a confession."

"Bobby doesn't know that."

"Maybe not, but Eddy does. So why did he go to such great lengths to keep Bobby outta the picture?"

She started to ponder that question, but Russ, who was waiting for us at the door, motioned for us to hurry.

We signed in at the administration desk. An officer with a night stick escorted us over to Building B, where Doctor Ecklund, a tall, bald-headed fellow wearing a white jacket and wire-rimmed spectacles, was waiting outside. The doc gave us a quick once-over. Russ's garb was priestly. No question Marcie was a woman. That left me.

"You must be the detective I spoke with," he said, and extended his hand for a shake. I crossed his palm with the agreed upon sum, and he ushered us through the heavy metal door without further formality.

We entered an area about the size of a high school gym. It had the same high windows a basement gym might have too, but these windows were striped with iron bars. Slats of sunlight poured through into an otherwise ill-lit and fetid space; hot, damp, and thick with unpleasant smells.

"Wait here," said the doctor. "Don't be afraid. They won't harm you."

"They" were about a dozen inmates wearing shoes without laces and loose blue shifts, shuffling around in a slow, clockwise circle. They stared at the floor as they walked, but somehow managed to avoid bumping into each other. Most of them were women. A few had tiny pointed heads.

Sounds drifted through the dense air, shrieks, laughter, other unidentifiable noises. The room was like an echo chamber.

A relatively normal looking fellow sat on a bench against the wall, counting imaginary money and piling it up beside him. He shuffled phantom bills off a thick wad, pausing occasionally to lick his thumb. When a pile got high enough to become precarious he'd pat it carefully, then start another. Suddenly he swept the piles to the floor and put head in his hands. His shoulders shook as he wept, but that only lasted a few moments. Then he sat up and started counting again.

One of the pin head women hoisted her shift, squatted, and pissed on the floor.

Marcie reached for my hand. Russ crossed himself. I fixed my eyes on a blackboard on the wall. It was full of "cranial measurements" and scrawled observations: "23 1/4 by 13 3/8—inordinate appetite; 21 by 11.9—wet, filthy agitated; 25.2 by 14—phrenzied, thinks family's been murdered."

The doc reappeared with Wigger, who was in shackles and handcuffs. He motioned for Russ, and the three of them went back down the corridor.

Soon the doc came out again, and engaged us in some small talk about his work.

"I'm a professor of phrenology," he said. "We're correlating symptoms with skull size here, and making great strides I'm proud to say. This is the exercise area. They all get an hour of exercise daily. Well, not all of them. The criminally insane are locked in cells, and in restraints. This is quite a privilege for Mr. Wegleitner, coming out and talking to you. He's been looking forward to it."

He gabbed on but I barely heard him. Marcie squeezed my hand. Soon Russ came out, looking grim. He motioned for us. We dodged the shuffling inmates, stepped carefully around the puddle of pee, and walked down the corridor to an open door.

Wigger was seated at a table, a gasper in his cuffed hand. He was inhaling it with the gusto of a hungry man eating lunch. He took a final drag and dropped the butt. His shackles rattled when he crushed it.

"How'ya doin?" I asked.

"You kiddin?" he replied.

I told him that he didn't strike me as nuts. He said he would be soon enough.

"Got a cigarette?" he asked.

Marcie volunteered to go get one from Russ. I tried a little small talk while she was gone. He was polite, but pretty subdued.

"You're Angie's sis, aint'cha," he said, when Marcie returned.

She nodded yes, and put the cigarette in his mug. I lit a match for him.

"What do you think you're doin' here?" I asked.

He said it had taken him awhile to figure that out. He was so used to being arrested on one thing or another—"suspicion" usually—that he put the whole thing off to bad luck, even after he heard that Slapper Doran was going to finger him, and Sean had been arrested.

"See, I figure Sean's a dinge, so that's why they jammed him. Didn't know about Slap, maybe somethin' between him and that copper with the beak. But after awhile I begin t'thinkin, it ain't got nothin' t'do with snow. It's all just a way to shut me up...."

He looked over at Marcie. "Bobby rubbed Tipper out y'know. Pushed that stone over on him."

Marcie bit her lip.

"Why'd he do it?" I asked.

"Because Tipper killed my dad, right?" said Marcie.

He took a few more drags and looked down at the table.

"Tell us why," she said calmly.

"Tipper'd fit right in here, y'know," he said. "'Bout half'a everything he said was just squirrel talk."

Marcie was looking at him intently. He paused and averted his gaze.

"We was all together up t'this place Kate rented, t'keep her snow at," he continued. "Me, Tipper, Kate, Bobby.—See, Kate was always after Bobby t'come up there after the bar closed, but he never would. Angie did sometimes, but not him, so I was kinda surprised when he came that night. Was a Friday, see, an' next morning me'n Tipper was gonna go get some roses from your dad, but we was up late sniffin' an' drinkin', an' Bobby got this idea that we should play a joke on his old man. See, we was always botherin' your dad for fresh roses, and he was always sayin' no. So Bobby sez, 'let's all go see him tomorrow morning, only Tipper, you bring the shotgun under your coat.

You guys ask him for the fresh roses, an' when he says no, stick the gun in his face an' get t'hollerin' at him, scare him good.' Sounded kinda squirrely t'me, but I didn't say nothin, just went along. So next mornin' Tipper was supposed to wake me up, but he never did. Just the two of'em, him and Bobby, went for the flowers."

He took a long pull on his gasper, and sat silently for a few moments.

"C'mon, Danny," Marcie urged. "Tell me what happened."

"So that's what they done. Least that's what Tipper told me. Bobby, he waited down the street. Tipper knocked on the door, an' when your dad opened it he pulls the shotgun an' says, 'go on now, get me some fresh flowers fr' a change!' Your dad musta been scared, so he goes into the cooler to get'em, and by the time he come out Bobby was right there next to Tipper, and he says, 'go on, stick that gun under his chin and shoot him.' An' Tipper says he just done it. Cuz he always done what Bobby said."

"You believe him?" I asked.

He shrugged. "Guess so. I didn't say nothin' for a long time, but when Tipper got squashed, I asked Bobby about it. He said it weren't true, that it was just Tipper talkin loony. 'Bullshit,' I sez. 'You told him to shoot your old man, then you killed him to shut him up, didn't'cha?' He sez to me, 'now it's you talkin' loony.'"

Marcie was surprisingly calm. "But why would Bobby kill dad?" she asked.

"Beats me. Your dad was a good man. Gave me a job, only one I ever had. I thought the world'a him. So'd Bobby. Didn't he?—I think that copper is takin' care of Bobby. I never would'a peached on him though. I ain't no rat."

Marcie sighed. She patted his cuffed hands.

"Does Angie know?" she asked.

"She sure does, maam. She was kinda givin' me the third degree one time, t'see if I knew. We talked about it. Then she was my squeeze for a bit. That didn't last though. I didn't wanna think she was doin' it to keep me quiet."—He looked over and gave me a rueful little smile. "But when you started snoopin' around she went right after you, didn't she?"

"Yeah. I guess she did," I said.—"One more thing before we go. Where'd you get the snow you were sellin'?"

"Cribbed it from Kate. We was always goin' up t'her place and snortin.' She had so much she couldn't keep track of it."

I told him I'd do what I could to get him out. He thanked me, but didn't seem optimistic.

None of us spoke until we were well on the way back, but when we did, we spoke as if the chauffeur wasn't there. I remember thinking how odd that was. I said that in my opinion what Wigger told us had the ring of truth. Marcie didn't argue.

"I thought my brother was a poet," she said.

"Nah, your father was a poet. Your brother's just a mimic."

We were silent again for awhile.

"Know any poems?" Marcie asked.

"How's about this," I replied: "'Love can make you drink and gamble, make you stay out all night long, love can make you do things that you know are wrong.'"

"That's more of a song," Marcie observed, reasonably.

"Songs are poetic," I said.

"But they're not poems. You know a poem, Father Krause?"

"Call me 'Russ,' dear. Yes I know a few:

'Come gather round me, Parnellites,
And praise our chosen man;
Stand upright on your legs awhile,
Stand upright while you can,
For soon we lie where he is laid,
And he is underground;
Come fill up all those glasses
And pass the bottle round.

"That's more like it," Marcie said. "That's a poem."

Later she wondered aloud how you could love someone and not love him, maybe even hate him, at the same time. It didn't sound that unusual to me. Russ called it a mystery. He said people spent too much time trying to solve mysteries.

"I've learned to cherish them," he told us.

"I hope that attitude doesn't catch on," I said.

Which made Marcie smile.

I was drafted six years later. Now I'm stationed at Camp Gil-roy, in California. We do a little drill, peel potatoes, police the area for litter. My buddy, Benny, a student of these things, is giving two to one odds that sometime next year we'll be heading for a well-defended beach on the coastal plain of Japan. Meanwhile, we rarely have that first drink until five P.M. and generally nod out before Taps. I spend hours reminiscing about old cases. My fellow soldiers are fascinated.

St. Paul seems far away. It won't be the same when I go back, I can tell from the only contact I have with the place, the Sunday paper that arrives in the mail the following Friday. No more gang-sters, no more bent coppers, lots of sanctimonious crooks who call themselves "public servants," and lots of low-paid divorce work for the likes of me. It's all there if you read between the lines. Times have changed.

The paper keeps me up on people too. The obituaries are good that way. I read where Leon Gleeman was on his way home from down-town when an odd thing happened. He drove directly into a bridge abutment under Kellogg Boulevard, and died instantly. Maybe he had a stroke or something.

Betty Tuttweiler died too, in '43, not young certainly, but she did love hard and leave a good-looking corpse, as the rest of that saying goes.

The Lucky Dog's luck ran out at Anzio, which saddened me, and prompted me to shuffle through the whole deck of might've-beens again.

Shortly after we visited St. Peter I got together with Eddy G. and the two of us decided on the appropriate penalty for not belonging to a nose candy ring, and not being nuts either. Exile solved everyone's problem, we agreed, and he arranged it the next day. I assume Wigger jumped the blinds, rode out the Great Depression and maybe even evaded the draft that way.

Bobby is living happily ever after, but he'll always be Junior.

Eddy admitted that he knew Bobby killed Tipper, and why. We discussed the tactics he'd employed to protect him, dispassionately, like a couple old pros.

"I hadda put the Wegleitner kid in the squeeze," Eddy said.

"He was born in the squeeze," I observed. "He told me he'd never rat, and I don't think he would've."

Eddy was silent on that point, which I took as agreement. He called Bobby a stargazer and a pretty boy, said he wanted to collar him for both murders, even got excited telling me how the D A might have convicted him.

"We wouldn't have stood a chance on either one alone, but using one as evidence for the other? Maybe."

In the end though, the hold Betty had on him stopped him. The conflict between that and his duty made him dread getting up in the morning. He said he felt like he was plodding through sucking mud all day.

"Ever interest you who was sellin' snow in Kuby's?" I asked.

"Not much."

As long as coppers like Eddy are in charge there will never be a shortage of drugs in St. Paul. They find such things so distasteful they ignore them. It's another form of *corruption*.

One afternoon awhile ago I got so bored waiting for the witching hour that I paged through the Society section of a month old Pioneer Press, and happened upon a small item of great personal interest. It said that the recently-widowed Marcella Kirkwood, White Bear, had funded a foundation and named it after her late husband. Among other good works, it would strive to better the lives of those confined to insane asylums. Her good friend and advisor, Father Krause, on leave from St. Albert's, would serve as chief executive officer.

Well, what could I do at that late date except commend Russ's initiative? And hope his service is satisfactory.

PART 3

CHANCE MEDLEY

argaret Thornton and Marcie Kirkwood, nee Tuttweiler, were the only women I ever considered jumping off the deep end with, and I never laid a finger on either of them. Pathetic as that sounds, maybe it's better that way. They roam my imagination unsullied, freeing me to pretend that what might have been could have been, while I pursue my real interests.

One thing it could have been is worse. Sometimes I imagine things working out so I was involved with both of them at once. I know about a guy who got in that situation and regretted it. Homer Van Meter wasn't a friend. I didn't even have much sympathy for him, but we both operated close to the line between the coppers and the crooks, so I heard a lot about him. I had to admire his boldness, if not the ends it served.

I was reminded of him in February, 1942, on one of the bleaker nights of my life.

I was standing on the platform at the Union Depot in St. Paul, waiting for a troop train. I kept my back to the cold west wind and looked for an engine light down the tracks. Eventually, seeing none, I meandered over to the long stairway up to the concourse and everything that was warm and familiar.

There was nothing to prevent me from climbing those stairs, but I didn't know when the train would arrive. I'd been warned that if I missed it I was 'subject to discipline,' so I ducked into the alcove at the bottom of the stairs and stood there, sheltered from the wind but shivering in the cold. I felt like a dumb beast in the chute. Out on the platform, snowflakes blew through a halo of light cast by a bare bulb swinging in the wind. It was almost midnight.

I'd aged in lockstep with the twentieth century, which should've put me beyond reach of the draft board, but it was barely eight weeks after Pearl Harbor and Uncle Sam was scraping the bottom of the barrel. Hence my second career as cannon fodder.

I was overdue for a change. That much was certain. The Layover, the system under which gangsters paid the St. Paul coppers for protection, which turned our sleepy little Midwestern burg into a world-class cauldron of corruption and intrigue, was a relic of the past. The gangsters who'd taken advantage of it were dead or in prison, except for a few has-beens spending their dotage in yesteryear's haunts, bowling alleys mostly. The Green Lantern had closed after Harry Sawyer retired to Florida. I was still a Tin Cup's regular, but my real chums were married and staying home nights. Coppers still frequented the joint, but now they were younger than me, and I didn't take the trouble to cultivate their friendship. Sometimes they gave me information anyway, for what it was worth, which was nothing to them. Wasn't even worth my buying drinks. I gathered they'd have gladly been on the take, but no one was giving.

Everything was falling apart. Grifters and gangsters were double-crossing each other left and right. The Italians could have muscled into St. Paul any time they wanted to, but they didn't bother. Time had passed me and the city of my birth by so thoroughly that I'd taken to sulking. I'd socked away plenty during my heydey, so I rarely troubled with the kind of low-end work that came my way. Instead of arriving at Tin Cup's at a civilized hour, say 4:00 p.m., I started dropping in after lunch and heading back to Mrs. Dunn's boarding house a few hours later. It was a routine I'd seen many an old-timer adopt. I might have sunk into it for good. Then my draft notice arrived.

That was a shock, but nothing compared to the blow my system took after I joined a few hundred other GI's at Fort Snelling for a hurry-up version of basic training. The sergeant, a loud little dago from out east, announced that there was no hooch allowed on base and he meant it.

By February 9, 1942, I'd been without a drink for a week. The shakes had calmed to the point where I could hit the target, if not the bull's-eye. After I regained the gift of gab (it surprised me how much of my personality I owed to hooch), I told my fellow draftees I'd been a private eye. From then on they peppered me with questions whenever there was a down moment. 'Meet a lot of beautiful women? How about gangsters? Ever kill a man?'

Answering helped me sort out the past. It even prompted me to ponder the future... assuming I had one. There was talk of our imminent deployment to England, where an army of invasion would be amassing, or to the Pacific, where bloody battles were about to be fought. Either way the odds looked bad, but it was out of my control. I would lie down on my bunk after drilling all day to the soundtrack of our brainless sergeant barking orders, and envision myself in a scene from a different movie: me and a bunch of other GI's at a canteen in a train station, some easy-on-the-eye WACs handing out donuts and coffee, a fellow hoocher passing me a flask—that first taste burning my gullet.

Imagine my surprise when Sergeant gate-mouth bellowed my name one evening while I was in the midst of that very fantasy.

"MAC-DONNA!" he screamed. "PUT'CHA KIT TUGETH-AH! YA GOIN' ALL DA WAY!"

"Where?" I managed to ask.

"TA DA STATION, YA DUMB BASTUD! WHERE ELSE?"

I threw a toothbrush and some clean underwear into a duffel, shook a few hands, and walked out of the barracks. My fellow trainees looked on in envy.

"They're gonna put ya in Intelligence cuz you was a detective," said someone. I just shrugged and climbed into a waiting jeep.

***

If the driver knew anything he didn't let on. It was as if a top-secret scheme to invade France had been hatched, and I'd been picked

to lead it. Later I learned that all over the country they were pluck-
ing men like me out of basic, in order to create a battalion of duffers
called the *Home Guard*. We would soon form into platoons and be
stationed near the coasts. Our duty was to protect the 'home front.'
If there was a softer assignment in the history of warfare I've never
heard of it, but as I waited for the train that night, I was heading toward an uncertain fate.

"Catch the westbound," said the driver when he dropped me.
"Don't know when it's comin', so you'd better stay on the platform.
If you miss it you're subject to discipline. Got it?

"And give this to the commanding officer on board," he added.
"Don't open it."

He handed me an envelope, which I tore open the moment I
entered the depot. It was an incomprehensible jumble of letters and
numbers. I pondered that word, 'discipline,' briefly. Our nitwit sergeant was always threatening us with the brig, and during the First
World War, when I was an impressionable youth, I'd heard that they
shot deserters. All things considered, a cold wait for the train seemed
best.

I'd been down in the alcove about half an hour when another
fellow joined me. He'd been jeeped in from somewhere in Wisconsin
with the same mysterious orders, but whoever sent him was a little
more forthcoming about the schedule.

"Train's due pretty quick," he informed me.

His name was Milo Bradich. He told me he'd left his wife and
two daughters behind on forty acres that they'd barely managed to
hang on to through the depression. Now, just when things were looking up, he'd have to rely on hired help to run it. He worried if the men
who were available, fifty and older most of them, would be able to
bring in a crop, and if they'd be honest with him if they did. He fretted about his fourteen-year-old daughter's welfare without a father
around, whether his wife could hold things together, if there'd be
anything left when he got back.

"You married?" he asked.

"Nah, gave it some thought once or twice. Never fit in with the rest of my life." I told him I was a private eye, worked nights, spent too much time in the joints and in the company of loose women.

"Private eye, huh." He nodded as if he understood.

We heard a whistle off in the distance. It seemed to be coming from the east, so we shouldered our duffel bags and walked out on the platform.

"Ever kill a man?" he asked.

"Yeah."

A light appeared in the east, became brighter, and turned the falling snow into a white glow that blotted out everything... the train yard, the depot, the city. The locomotive chuffed to a halt. Behind it we heard the ponderous thump of cars banging together one after another for what seemed like miles.

A smartly uniformed fellow with Captain's stripes all over his chest emerged from the first car, and said, "TENN-CHUT!"

Bradich had enough presence of mind to salute. I didn't, but the officer paid that no mind. "Let's see your orders," he said.

He examined our papers in the dim light, then gave them back. "You can board here," he told us, and nodded toward the first car. "You'll have to move back to find seats. Way back. There are more than a thousand GIs on this train. You'll both disembark in Sacramento... in three days, if the snow's not too deep out west."

He smiled, and motioned for us to follow. "C'mon. You're in the Army now."

By the time I got aboard we were moving. I grabbed the handrail and leaned back for a last look, but the stairway had already disappeared in the snow.

A MAN OF HONOR

It was atop those stairs, at the concourse lunch counter, that I'd met Tony Conforti, in the autumn of '36. He'd come from Chicago to hire me. I have to admit I took some pride in that. Back then, my reputation was such that people from distant cities came and spent real money for my services. He certainly did, but I'd pay ten times what he gave me to undo what I did for him.

Tony had just arrived when I walked in, and he immediately announced that he was catching the next train back to Chicago in half an hour, so we had to come to an agreement fast. Then he kept looking at his watch as we talked. Being away from his beloved 'Big C' made him nervous, he explained.

Let me count the ways I didn't like Tony Conforti. I didn't like the way he fidgeted and squirmed as if he had fleas; I didn't like the way he snorted like he had sinus trouble to emphasize some points, and poked me with his finger to impress me with others (not with the pinky-finger of his left hand, thankfully, because the nail on that one was six inches long and dirty); I didn't like the way he smelled, a mixture of cheap aftershave and flop sweat; I didn't like the way he hisssed his Ss; I didn't like the way he was in my home town but talked like we were in his.

"Ssee, I'm from da firsst ward," he said at one point in our negotiation, as if that explained something important and I was supposed to know what.

"So lissen McDonough, I want ya to find out who wass da so-nofabitch fingered Da Waiter," he said.

It just so happened I knew who he was talking about. Homer 'The Waiter' Van Meter had been ambushed and shot down in St. Paul two years before. I was puzzled by Tony's interest in finding the sonofabitch who shot him though. It was well-known that the mob had grown weary of the heat that front-page jug-busters like Van Meter generated, and when we'd arranged to meet by phone the day before, Tony told me that he worked for Capone's successor, Paulie Ricca.

People were always telling me they were connected in those days. Most of them had never rubbed shoulders with a gangster, much less a mobster, but thoughts that Tony might be lying were pretty well dispelled the moment I laid eyes on him. He might as well have been wearing a sign that said 'mobbed-up.' He was about my age, husky, with dark skin and a five o'clock shadow. He wore a tailored blue suit, a purple shirt, a yellow necktie, sunglasses, and a snap brim hat. The whole time we talked he chewed on an unlit cigar.

"Correct me if I'm wrong," I said, "but I thought you guys were glad to see mugs like Dillinger and Van Meter go down."

"Diss is perssonal," he said, and he explained that his sister, Marie, had been Van Meter's squeeze.

"Then we've got a problem," I told him. "I'm sorry for your sister's loss, but the coppers give me a lot of information, and they don't like it when people take revenge on the basis of what I find out. I'd be outta business if I let it happen."

The corner of his mouth twitched. "My experience, nobody gives a damn if a rat'ss rubbed out, not even da copperss."

"Where you come from maybe. Like I said, the coppers here don't want me usin' what I find out to get people killed. Sorry you came such a long way for nothin'."

"DAMN IT!" He bit the cigar and spit a little chunk of it on the concourse floor. He took a deep breath and snorted. He squirmed, and scratched, and pondered.

"Ok, ok den," he finally said. "I won't kill him, but I want every nickel da rat bastard got for finkin' da Waiter. He should not be allowed to profit from diss cowardly act."

I was dubious, but what he told me over the next few minutes, with many a pause for tics and grimaces (the man was a nervous wreck), did add up, given what I knew about Van Meter.

Homer had been the Layover's best customer until his untimely demise, which came at the hands of his erstwhile protectors, the police. Like most mugs he died intestate, but he was well-heeled, and, his many misdeeds notwithstanding, the real reason the coppers decided to snuff him was cash.

They'd nailed him at a time when Hoover had declared open season on bank robbers, especially Dillinger and his gang. Something in the neighborhood of $50,000 was said to have gone missing when Hoover's boys dry-gulched Johnny in Chicago. Roughly the same amount went unaccounted for when Baby Face Nelson was killed there several weeks later. Van Meter was a frugal fellow who was said to have upwards of one hundred Gs stashed in St. Paul, but there was no mention of his money in the reams of newspaper stories his killing prompted, and very little in the rumors that circulated for months after.

There was some talk of a brown paper bag containing six Gs that he'd been carrying when the coppers got him, supposedly to purchase a getaway car. No one ever saw that again. Also, an observant reporter took note of a curious fact when Van Meter's bullet-riddled corpse was put on display. Although he was known as a snazzy dresser, The Waiter had neglected to wear a belt the day he died. An early version of the front page story about his death made mention of this uncharacteristic sartorial omission, but it didn't appear in later editions. Those in the know assumed he'd worn a well-stuffed money belt, as was his habit, and it disappeared between the time he was gunned down and when he was laid on the slab.

But viewed in the worst possible light, those two mysteries accounted for but a fraction of The Waiter's net worth. Everybody assumed that the coppers got the rest. The best evidence for that was

Hoover's fury when he found out it was the St. Paul police, not his hit squad, that got him.

"You'd think he'd be rejoicing," Eternal Tommy Brown, who was then the police chief, was heard to say, and I'm told he had a grin a mile wide on his face when he said it.

Tony Conforti soon revealed that he was well aware that St. Paul's finest had inherited the bulk of Van Meter's estate, but he insisted that some of it must have gone to the finger man, and he wanted that for his sister.

"Homer was everything to Marie, includin' a meal ticket," he said. "I get da money, it goess for her care and feedin'. Udderwisse I'm on da hook for da resst of her life. Because she'ss family.

"And I love her," he added.

I'd have liked to have seen his eyes when he said that, but they were behind his sunglasses.

"The Geess arressted Marie same day dey shot Da Waiter," he explained. "She'ss been in da slammer ever since on some bullshit charge or another. No vissitin' privilegess... nothin'."

He paused and jammed a finger into his cheek. Was he was trying to put a hole in it? It must've hurt. He looked at the offending digit like it belonged to someone else. His hand began to tremble as he stared. He put it down on the table, and held it there against its will.

"Pretty soon dey're gonna let her out though," he continued, "den she'ss my problem. I figure..." He paused, then poked me in the chest with that rogue finger for emphasis. "No, I don't figure, I *heard,* dat da copperss here paid somebody twenty grand t' fink him."

He craned his neck to look over his shoulder, then stuck his fist up under his chin and pushed, gritting his teeth as he did so. His head trembled as if he were having a seizure.

"You ok?" I asked.

"I'm fine!"

I didn't want this job... not even for the two grand I was prepared to ask for.

"I have to get a few things straight if we're gonna go ahead with this," I said.

He chewed the ragged end of the cigar, and nodded.

"First, I find out who fingered Van Meter. Then what?"

"Gimme a call. I send somebody around t' assk for twenty Gsss."

I drew a quick mental picture of how that request would be conveyed. "That won't work," I said.

He sighed. "Ever kill a man, McDonough?"

"No."

"Ain't such a big deal like ya think. But I know what'ss on your mind. You're wonderin' I can trust diss guy he won't rub out da rat?"

"Right."

"Ok, ok, I understant. You don't know me, don't know I'm a proud ressident of da firsst ward, a voter in all electionss local and national... a man of honor. But I got an idea dat'll work. Talk to diss rat. Tell him dat I, Tony Sassich—dat'ss what people in da Big C call me—will personally sever his goddamn head off if he don't hand over twenty Gss."

He saw the look on my face, and thought I was disturbed by his bluster. I was actually reeling from the knowledge that he was a dago from Chicago with a Polack nom de guerre. Sassich indeed!

"Den *you* collect da dough," he continued. "Give it over t' me. I don't ever lay eyess on da guy. You don't even hafta tell me hiss name. Deal?"

"What if he doesn't have it?"

"Give him a week."

"And if he can't get it?"

"Jesuss!" He bit another chunk off his cigar. "Don't look for problemss, ok? If he don't get it in a week, we take it from dere."

"But he doesn't get hurt, right?"

He took off his sunglasses and peered at me.

"People don't get 'hurt' when I take revench, McDonough. Dey get snuffed. My experience, a man won't get up offa twenty large widout you touch him up a bit. But you convince diss rat to hand over da dough, and we don't have no problemsss. Dat'ss your job, understood?"

I sighed. It stunk.

"Who gave you my name?" I asked.

He shrugged. "Paulie got it. From who I don't know."

"Paulie Ricca? What's he got to do with it?"

His face contorted as if the corner of his mouth had gotten snagged on a coat hook. "Goddamnit! What'ss da difference? You're too fuckin' nossy, know dat?"

"Hey, I'm paid to be nosy. It's my nature."

We sat silently for a minute or so. He looked at his watch and twiddled his tie like Oliver Hardy.

"Did Ricca tell you how much I cost?" I asked.

"I'll bite, how much do you cosst?"

"For a job like this, four grand. Half in front. Plus expenses."

He smiled, baring two rows of yellow molars with what appeared to be a small diamond implanted in one of them.

"Fine. We got a deal."

I might've raised the ante again, but the loudspeaker called the train to Chicago, and before I could say another word he thumbed twenty C-notes off a thick stack of bills, then added an extra twenty bucks so I could bring his twenty grand to Chicago personally, by train.

"I don't like places like diss," he announced, and made a gesture that took in the atrium, the echoing concourse, and everybody in it. "C'mon, walk me to the track. I'll tell ya somethin' t' get ya started."

I put the dough in my pocket and followed him down the long, covered stairway to the platform. It was raining, so we stood in the same alcove I sheltered in on that freezing February night years later.

He said Van Meter had been stepping out on his sister. She was pretty sure his other sweetie fingered him.

"How does your sister know this?"

He shrugged. "She tellss me diss other dame wass a jealous bitch, wanted him t' break it off with Marie. Between you, me, and da lampposst, so's my sisster a jealouss bitch. Did the other dame drop the dime? I don't know, but she'ss mouthin' it around dat my sisster fingered him, and diss hass gotta end."

"End how?"

He managed a smile, despite his anxiety. He was itching to get aboard.

"Again you're worried? Somebody'ss gonna talk to her, dat'ss all. So you'll find her for me."

I didn't say anything.

"So you'll find her for me, right?" Tic. Grimace.

"Yeah right. I'll bill ya at the end."

"Couldn't throw it in?"

"No."

He smiled. "You're all about money, aren't cha?"

The conductor shouted all aboard. Tony relaxed visibly.

"Poor Homer," he said, as he headed for the car. "More balsls than brainss, dat'ss what I heard. Real cool when da fireworkss started. Know what I think? I think he didn't care if he lived or died, dosse two damess made hiss life so misserable."

"Know her name, this other frail?" I asked.

"Yeah. Opal Milligan. Stay in touch, tell me how thingss're goin'." He gave me a quick handshake. His palm was wet. "See ya in da Big C."

He bolted aboard like he'd been goosed.

I hung around the platform for a few minutes hoping he'd show up at a window so I could get a little more out of him. He didn't, but I had plenty to get started.

I'd known Opal Milligan since grammar school. I hadn't seen her in a few years, but when last I'd laid eyes on her she was quite the tomato. She could be troublesome, but as I recalled, 'bitch' was the wrong description. Missing a button or two was more like it.

I patted my pocket and the bankroll he'd just given me and walked back up the stairs.

**

Milo Bradich and I passed through one car full of GIs after another. The aisles were jammed with bags and boots and piles of rifles.

Knots of guys were crouched around dice games in a few cars. I saw a helmet full of cash inside the circle where one bunch was play-ing—fifties, C notes, maybe a thousand dollars. A kid picked up the dice while I watched, kissed his fist and rolled 'em— boxcars.

We'd passed through maybe twenty coaches before we finally found a place to settle, an old-fashioned car with wicker seats and long wooden benches. It must have been dragged out of a junk-yard for the war effort, judging from the thinning glass at the top of the windows and the dingy fixtures. The wheels didn't hum, they clunked, as if they'd been stationary so long they'd become oval.

We sat down on a half-empty bench. I leaned my head back against the frosted window. It seemed I'd walked a mile.

On the bench across the dim-lit aisle some guys were asleep sitting up, nodding and jerking as the train swayed. A couple more were curled up on their sides, taking up less than two spots but more than one.

A few men were prone in the aisle, duffels under their heads, khaki coats pulled up over their faces.

"I hope they have cots where we're goin'," I said.

Bradich shot me a wry smile. "My old man told me they just laid down in the mud in the last war. Couldn't tell who was dead and who was asleep until reveille."

"We've come a long way since then. Look around. This is a modern army on the move."

"Hey! Whistle-dick! Keep it down up there!" came a voice from the floor.

"'Scuse us," said Bradich.

We sat silently awhile. The train seemed to be moving at a de-cent clip. I caught a glimpse of a yard light through the frosty win-dow across the aisle and thought I saw snow falling, but it was hard to tell. It seemed warm when we first boarded, but now I realized that was only by comparison with the outdoors. If I turned to look out the window behind me I could see my breath. A cold draft came through the frame.

"So," Bradich whispered, "maybe it won't be hard for you then. Killin' guys, I mean. Seeing as how you've already done it."

"I didn't exactly put somebody in my sights and pull the trigger."

"What did ya do?"

"It's a long story. Started when this mobster from Chicago hired me. Tough guy, at least he acted like one, but it turned out he was afraid of the damndest things."

***

There'd been rumors about many people other than coppers profiting from Van Meter's murder, but I only knew of one who certainly did, Harry Sawyer. Word had it that Sawyer was twenty Gs up. He never denied it.

There was a perfectly logical reason for that, and it didn't involve dropping a dime. Sawyer handled cash for the gangsters who hung around The Green Lantern. He made small investments and paid a little interest—nothing formal, but it was understood that whatever was on deposit when the inevitable occurred belonged to Harry. Nevertheless, the fact that the sum was exactly twenty grand spurred me to invoke McDonough's theory of coincidence—*there ain't no such thing*.

Sawyer and his errand boy, Pat Reilly, were having words when I walked into The Green Lantern. At least Sawyer was having words. Reilly was standing mute at the end of the bar, arms open, palms up, in a what-am-I-supposed-to-do pose.

"Get outta here goddamnit," Sawyer said, "and don't come back until you bring me the money!" Reilly headed for the door. "Hear me? Every penny!" Sawyer hollered.

He turned to his drink, took a swallow and sat there muttering. I seated myself beside him.

"Usual?" asked the bartender, a guy named Frank Kerwin, who knew me from Tin Cup's, as well as The Lantern.

I nodded, started to greet Harry, and thought better of it. Waves of anger were coming off him. Being near him was like standing too close to an electromagnet.

I bided my time, looked around at the mostly empty joint. A few bars of a tune that had been haunting me ran through my mind—jazz on the slow side but hot anyway, if you can imagine that. There was something familiar about it, but I couldn't identify the song. I almost had it, then lost it, as usual.

That got me thinking where I might've heard it. Maybe right here at the Lantern, back in the old days, when there was usually something on the Wurlitzer, and the place was always at least half full, even at this time of day. You might have seen John Dillinger, Creepy Karpis, Chopper DeVol, maybe a St. Paul detective like the late Eddy Guilfoyle, or some of his shadier colleagues—Tom Philben, Jess Doyle. You'd always be rubbing shoulders with sexy gals too—Blanche Schuh, Billie Frechette, Indian Rose Rademacher. Now Billie was in prison and Rose was dead. Blanche was still around, but not around The Lantern.

Blanche was the last gal I'd slept with, months before.

Kerwin brought my drink. I cleared my throat.

"What the hell do you want, McDonough?" Sawyer said.

"Nice way to talk to a friend."

"Go screw yourself."

"You finger Van Meter, Harry?"

He looked at me with renewed interest. Then he shook his head and smiled.

"This isn't my day," he said. "First thing in the morning I hear Pat Reilly and Red Dupont held up a bank over in South St. Paul. How did I hear? Frank Cullen told me. Guess what he wanted."

I didn't have to guess. Frank Cullen had recently succeeded Eternal Tommy Brown as police chief. "He wants you to get the loot back, right?"

"Correct, and here's why that's nothing but a big pain in the ass."

Sawyer proceeded to tell me what I already knew. For years the police had relied on him and Jack Moylan to keep the thugs on the Layover in line. Harry handled his end by politely requesting them to refrain from criminal activity. If that didn't work, Jack had his own methods. That system was of such long standing that

I thought of it as eternal—just like Jack's former boss, Tommy Brown.

"Thing is," said Sawyer, "there ain't no more gangsters on the Layover. Ok, one or two maybe."

He named 'Lapland' Willy Weaver, and Alvin 'Creepy' Karpis, two guys who still paid something for protection and had some cash on deposit with him, but for the most part the good old days were over.

"Chopper DeVol was paying a C-note a month until a week ago," he said, "then he lammed for Chicago with some dame and went to work for Nitti. There might as well not be a Layover for the little money that goes through my hands. Nevertheless, and despite the fact that there is absolutely nothing in it for me, somebody robs a bank and who does Frank call? Yours truly."

"Well, Pat Reilly's your employee, isn't he?"

He peered at me as if I was a strange life form he was trying to classify.

"'Employee' is right, Martin. What the hell do I care what he does when he's not on the clock? What's in it for me to keep him in line? Cullen said he'd send Jack Moylan after Pat if I didn't get the dough back. I was ready to let him, and I will if he holds out a penny."

I didn't tell him, but it was probably an empty threat. Jack had gained weight since he and Maggie Quinn married and, it seemed to me, lost the keen urge to break a man's will that once defined him.

"So," Sawyer continued, "that's how my day begins, and just when I send Pat on his way you show up with a dumb question... an insulting question, now I think about it. Why the hell would I finger Van Meter? He was a paying customer."

I explained the odd congruence of the sums involved. He didn't deny that twenty Gs had come his way when The Waiter expired. By default, he claimed.

"I wasn't in any hurry to get his dough. It was going to be mine no matter what when he took the dirt nap and his day was coming fast. Anyway, I liked Homer. I sent his brother five hundred bucks so they could bury him back there in Indiana... even said I'd put up a grand for Opal's bail but—"

"Opal Milligan?"

"Yeah. That surprise you?"

He reminded me that Opal had been an off-and-on waitress at The Lantern. The Gees came in and made a big production out of arresting her after the cops shot Van Meter. They kept her locked up for a year, accusing her of aiding and abetting a fugitive, a ridiculous charge in Harry's opinion. Homer didn't need anybody's aid as long as the fix was in, and nobody could help him once the coppers decided he was worth more dead than alive.

Harry heard that the feds slapped Opal around, demanded detailed information about people she knew causally, like Creepy Karpis and his brother, and about people she'd never even heard of.

"Opal was ok in my book," he said. "So when I hear what they're doin' to her, I offer to go her bail. Soon as I said I'd put up a grand they make it five, so I dropped out of the bidding. They never did put her on trial. Held her as a material witness as long as they could, then turned her loose."

He told me where I could find her. I finished my drink.

"Got any idea who fingered him?" I asked, before departing.

He shrugged. "Maybe Pat. He was always jealous of Homer and Johnny and those guys, but he was always buddyin' up to 'em too."

He took note of the skeptical look on my puss.

"Think about it," he said. "The cops knew Homer was around town, where he hung out. What they needed was somebody to tell 'em he'd be at a certain place, at a certain time. Maybe even lure him there. Handy, how he had no place to run but up a dead end alley when they bushwhacked him. Yeah, come to think of it, could've been Pat."

**

I must have nodded off. I couldn't say for how long. What woke me was a prolonged hair-raising screech, like chalk scraping across the cosmic blackboard.

Once the train ground to a halt it was silent enough to hear the wind howling outside. I wiggled my numb toes. The rest of the men began stirring as well. First came the sound of hacking, then a few low voices, then the hackers started lighting cigarettes.

It was light outside... dim light, but enough to see where we were. It wasn't California. Snow blew horizontally across a white landscape that seemed to be flat as far as the eye could see—ten miles, ten feet, it was impossible to tell.

Soon the aisle was full of men stretching, sorting through duffels, stomping their boots to warm up. Bradich and I did likewise. It was the first time I'd gotten a good look at my traveling companions. They were kids.

"Anybody know where we are?" came a voice from the front of the car.

"South Dakota?" was someone's educated guess.

"The moon," ventured another lad, to general laughter.

I decided to enter the dialogue. "Anybody know where a man could get his hands on some hooch?"

Miraculously, my query eventuated in the passage of a bottle, and then another, so that within minutes anyone who so desired had a belly-warmer or two under his belt.

Word came from the car in front of us that we'd been halted by a blizzard, but we'd be underway shortly. By then the conversation had picked up a bit. The fact that I'd made the suggestion that resulted in such generosity and companionship propelled me to the center of a group of yakking draftees. Soon they all were spellbound by the tale of my quest for the man who'd finked The Waiter. Bradich had to listen to some of it twice, but he didn't seem to mind.

"How much dough you talkin' about?" one of my listeners asked.

"Van Meter had a hundred grand stashed," I replied. "And Pat Reilly was the kinda weasel who'd rat to get his mitts on ten cents."

THIRTY GS

At first I chalked up Harry's tip to his anger at Pat Reilly, but the more I thought about it the more sense it made. Harry had Pat pegged. He and his pals, Red DuPont and Frank Kerwin, were wannabe gangsters who'd been committing petty crimes around town as long as I could remember. Harry employed all three of them because they liked to act tough, and sometimes that came in handy. They could scare the hell out of anybody who scared easy. As far as the real gangsters were concerned, they were like mosquitos. No, make that flies. Mosquitos you swat... flies you just try to ignore.

I knew Pat hung out at The Stahl House on Rice and Como, a bowling alley where Van Meter had been known to roll a few lines. It was only a few minutes from The Lantern.

Pat was at the bar, chin propped in hand.

"Why so glum, Pat? It's only money." I turned to the barkeep. "Give this man whatever he's drinkin'."

Pat turned and gazed at me with a wounded look on his puss.

"Harry told ja, I guess. Bad enough I gotta give the dough back, now he's blabbin' it around—"

"He isn't 'blabbin' it around. He just told me."

The bartender brought him a drink. He took a swallow and got to brooding again.

"You finger Van Meter?" I asked him.

He looked shocked at the suggestion, but that's easy to do.

"Level with me and I'll take care of ya, Pat. Otherwise..."

He whipped off the corduroy worker's cap he wore summer and winter, indoors and out, and mopped his forehead. Back then that cap was a fashion statement and a good sign that you'd never done an honest day's work in your life.

"What the hell you talkin' about?" he asked.

"Somebody wants to know who fingered Van Meter. Somebody you don't wanna cross. Little bird told me you might be the guy."

"Harry?"

"What's the difference? Gimme a straight answer."

"Hell no I didn't finger him!" he shouted. "Listen here, Martin. Homer'n me was buddies! Why I—"

"Easy, easy." I nodded toward some turned heads over in the bowling lanes.

He whispered more denials, then stood and beckoned me to follow. We walked over to the Stahl House Hall of Fame, a bunch of photos on the wall next to the shoe rack. He pointed out a picture of him and Van Meter grinning at each other, bowling balls in hand.

"So you got him to pose for a picture. What's that prove?"

"Martin, you gotta believe me. I'd never fink Homer. I liked the guy."

"Yeah, yeah, you'n everybody else. What was so likeable about him anyway? He killed people, f'r Christ's sake."

"Coppers, G Men. Ordinary folks he was real nice to."

"Spare me, Pat."

He fell to denying again. Eventually I had to admit he was convincing. The clincher was a question he posed, by way of confession.

"How could I finger him anyway?" he asked. "We weren't really buddies. Truth is, he'd barely talk to me. He didn't even know my name. One time I says to him 'hiya Homer,' and he gives me a look like he wants t'shoot me. 'Get away from me,' he says. I ask Frank, 'is he sore at me for somethin?' Frank says, 'nah, he's havin' woman troubles.'"

"Frank Kerwin from Tin Cup's? Frank who tends bar at The Lantern?"

"Yeah, that Frank." He looked at his watch. "You coulda talked to him there, but his shift's over now. Probably catch him at Tin Cup's."

He told me that Kerwin had done some errands for The Waiter relating to the poor fellow's domestic difficulties. "You don't happen to be goin' over to Tin Cup's right now to give him the third degree, do ya?" he inquired.

He wanted to ride along in hopes of running into Red DuPont, his partner on the great South St. Paul Bank heist. I told him sure, why not.

Here's the kind of palookas that Pat Reilly and Red DuPont were. On the way to Tin Cup's, Pat explained that he needed to collect Red's half of the loot quick, before he spent it. I assumed that meant Red was about to embark on a monumental shopping spree— clothes, a new car.

Uh-uh. Turned out they'd pistol-whipped the bank dick, terrorized the tellers, and lammed out the door, risking decades in the slammer, with a bag containing $173 and change.

"Red was the jug man," Pat explained. "Claimed they had the stockyard's payroll on deposit, but we come to find out pay day was the day before."

We arrived at Tin Cup's in the nick of time. Red had just walked in, and was in the midst of buying for the house. Pat nixed the purchase, which elicited a chorus of complaints. I spotted Frank Kerwin amongst the complainers.

"How ya like that," he said. "Man says he's buyin' a drink and welshes. Hey Red—"

"I got it," I interrupted, and waved for the barman. "C'mon over to a booth and talk a few minutes, Frank."

Once we'd settled in I asked if he knew who fingered Van Meter.

Frank shook his head in the negative. "I got some ideas though. Who hired you?"

"Never mind, but he'd be grateful if you helped, and he's a guy whose gratitude you might appreciate someday. He's connected, if you know what I mean."

Frank's eyes lit up. He wanted me to promise I'd wangle an introduction to my client. I told him I'd consider it. He proceeded to give me the lowdown on The Waiter's love life, a rat's nest of subterfuge.

Frank had served as go-between, carrying messages to Opal Milligan, ferrying her to her rendezvous with Van Meter, and taking care of the chores that Homer used as excuses to get away from 'that dago bitch' he was living with.

According to Frank, he had evolved into Van Meter's de facto chauffeur by August '34, when the ambush took place. Van Meter had been sure the fix was in for so long that he didn't even own a car to get away in.

"He'd call me and we'd take mine when he had to go somewhere," he said. "Sometimes he forgot to pay for gas."

"Oh, so you're the guy that dropped him off?"

Anyone who read the newspapers was aware that on the day he was assassinated an unidentified person driving a Chevy had dropped Van Meter at the mouth of a blind alley. Van Meter had an appointment at a used car dealership more than a block away. The question was, why wasn't he dropped at the door? Maybe it was just normal caution for a guy like him, trying to make sure he wasn't being followed. Or maybe it was a setup. It certainly made cornering him easier.

Frank denied dropping Van Meter off and claimed he hadn't heard from him for about a week before he was killed. He said that after the Lincoln Court shootout that spring, Van Meter had gotten nervous enough to start thinking about buying a vehicle.

"He wanted somethin' high-powered. I've got an Olds, and he once asked me, 'how fast'll this bucket move?' I told him eighty on a downhill straightaway. He said that wasn't good enough."

I asked who Van Meter had been hanging around with.

Frank claimed he didn't know. "Last I heard he was shacked up at The Green Gables with Opal. More or less."

According to Frank, Van Meter had a terrible yen for Opal, but he couldn't spend the night with her. "That dago babe had him pussy-whipped into comin' home, can you imagine? Tough guy like him. If he wasn't back by eleven she'd come lookin' for him."

"How'd Opal take that?" I asked.

He shrugged. "You know Opal. A little stormy sometimes. Opal used to be my girl. She was waitressin' at The Lantern back then, and I was tendin' bar. Them was good times."

I heard a touch of practiced melancholy in his voice. He said he'd introduced her to Van Meter. I took that to mean he was pimping her. Not for dough… for proximity.

"Anyways, Opal could be trouble," he said. "She'd cry, throw scenes, come into the joints when Homer'n Marie was there, show herself around. Opal knew he was fixin' to lam, and she knew Marie would be right there with him when he did, on accounta she had people in Chicago could stash him. If you ask me, Opal dropped the dime."

"You tryin to get even with her?"

"Hell no!" He looked offended, but that's easy too.

"You ratted him, Frank, I can tell. Opal talked you into it."

"Hey, Martin, c'mon, you know I wouldn't—"

"Listen to me. This guy I'm workin' for is nobody to trifle with. You come clean I can take care a you, but hold out on me, even a little bit…" I raised a cautionary finger.

He blanched. "God's my witness, I ain't holdin' out," he said.

"C'mon Frank. You're his driver, but it just so happens you didn't drop him off the day he was ambushed? Why's that?"

He gave the matter some thought. I let him. I finished my drink and tried to listen to the Wurlitzer. That hoofer from the movies was singing about a fine romance with no kisses. Poetry, but another tune kept running through my head. I was beginning to understand that it was there constantly, but only audible, you might say, under certain circumstances. It was like my theme song but I couldn't name it. I was under a spell of sorts… the kind that music works.

"Ok, here's why," Frank said, breaking the spell. "Homer was so tired a those dames that he was hidin' out on da both of 'em. Didn't want nobody to know where, especially me, because he was afraid I'd tell Opal. Sometimes he'd still call when he needed a lift from the bowling alley or wherever, but one time he let it slip that he was sleepin' on a couch in an apartment over on Avon. Some guys he used to pull jobs with were rentin' it, but they weren't layin' over. They were in town on the sly. So he was pretty sure Marie and Opal wouldn't get wind a where he was, cuz even the coppers didn't know they were around."

"Oh, so he's layin' low, but he let it slip to you?"

"Yeah, he was kinda grumblin' to himself really, but tellin' me in the process. Then he realizes what he's done. Told me, 'breathe a word a where I am and I'll shoot cha.' Poor Homer, he used to be so happy-go-lucky."

It had the ring of truth. Not that there weren't some loose ends.

"How could Opal finger him if she didn't know where he was?" I inquired.

He admitted that it made it problematical, but in his opinion she'd found a way.

I asked him where the hideout was.

"On Avon, near University, by the creamery. That's all I know."

He said I could find Opal at The Green Gables. She'd been holed up there since her release from prison a few weeks before.

I excused myself and sought out Jack Moylan, who was entertaining some fellow coppers with the story of a mug he'd intimidated back in the days of plenty. He had nothing to tell me about my case though.

"Sure, a few bucks came my way when they got Van Meter, but I don't know the details," Jack said. "Didn't want to. It was Tommy and Frank Cullen ambushed him. They must know."

"Can't see 'em tellin' me, though."

Jack nodded his agreement. "Ya know, they killed Van Meter because they figured Hoover's lads would if they didn't, and then Hoover would get the money. A few of us didn't like it, double-crossin' him that way. Bad for the Layover. I said so to Tommy. He says to me, 'Jack, the Layover's finished anyway.' And it was. That was the last payoff. A bit here and there, but that was the last've the real money."

"How much, if ya don't mind my askin'?"

He said he'd personally gotten a grand, and every man down to the last beat copper got a C-note. "They divided up fifty thousand, kept half, handed out the rest."

That was interesting. According to what I'd heard, that meant there was still a nice chunk of dough missing, even if you added the twenty grand paid to the fink. Jack told me the twenty Gs Harry Sawyer was holding wasn't even counted in the total cash that came up for grabs when The Waiter bit the dust, which was rumored to be one hundred thousand plus.

"So that leaves at least thirty thousand unaccounted for?"

He agreed that it did.

"Where was it stashed?" I asked.

He didn't know. He hadn't heard of any mugs who were holed up on the QT around that time either.

"They must've been layin' pretty low," he said, "but this's two years ago. Might be I heard and don't remember. Who hired ye, boyo?"

"Guy from Chicago. A wop, but he calls himself Tony Sassich, like he's some kinda Hun."

"Sweet Jayzus. Why?"

I told him about snorty. I don't think he got it. By the time I was through explaining that it was an attitude and costume peculiar to Chicago gangsters, I wasn't sure I did either.

Slapper Doran came over and listened politely until I finished. He asked us if we wanted tickets for the fights that night. Slapper couldn't do enough for me since he'd finished his thirty days in the workhouse.

GILROY

I slept like I was dead after the last snow delay. That one halted us in the midst of a desert, but the snow came down just as hard as it had when we were stuck in the mountains. The wind was peppered with tiny grains of sand that tattooed the windows. It didn't howl, it screamed, and there wasn't a taste of hooch that anyone would own up to. I was too weary to talk and thought I was too cold to sleep, but apparently not. I vaguely recall the train jolting into motion. Next thing I knew Bradich nudged me awake.

"We're here," he said.

I shouldered my duffel bag and staggered off like a sailor with sea legs.

There were some other GIs disembarking from cars up front. By the time the train pulled out about thirty of us were on the platform, some even older than me, and of course we all looked like hell with our grizzled mugs and bloodshot eyes. It gradually dawned on us that we were overdressed. We began shedding khaki greatcoats, scratchy wool watch-caps, and mittens. It must have been sixty degrees out.

It was still a mystery where we were going, but the mystery was solved when a canvas-covered troop truck pulled into the parking lot and honked. The driver told us we were headed for a camp in the hills near Gilroy, the garlic capitol of the world.

That night about three hundred of us assembled in the mess hall and heard a speech about the Home Guard and how crucial we were to the war effort. It was delivered by a colonel. The significance of that didn't dawn on me for about two years, after I realized that I'd yet to see another officer of such exalted rank.

In fact, I never did. I rarely saw a captain. Only once did I see a lieutenant, and he turned out to be of but partial rank. Those in the know called him a 'half-looie.'

The colonel cautioned that we might be shipped over for one of the two great invasions that were being planned, but for now the homeland was our sole responsibility. There was a collective sigh, followed by a prolonged, spontaneous cheer. I clapped hands and whistled like I was at a Saints game.

They split us into thirty-man platoons, assigned each platoon to a barracks and told us to get some rest. Nobody felt like sleeping. Our weariness disappeared as soon as we heard that we weren't meat for the guns.

Bradich and I ended up in the same platoon, bunking next to each other. He and I, and another home guardian, Bendetto (Benny) Castronovo from San Francisco, gabbed until daybreak. Why the three of us got along so well I'll never know. Bradich was a likeable hick, smart about some things, but naive in the extreme. Castronovo was urbane and well-spoken, an opera lover who'd aspired to be an opera singer. He had the looks, and according to him he had the voice, with but one major flaw.

"I'm a baritone," he said, "not a tenor. That's the great tragedy of my life. A simple matter of pitch, a note or two of tone. Try as I might—and believe me I've tried—my voice conveys the temperate, the thoughtful."

"Is that so bad?"

"Yes. All the great roles are emotional. It takes a tenor to sing them. And that's just the beginning of it for me. Here's the real tragedy. Instead of consorting with artists and bon vivants, it's been my fate to mix with illiterates and petty hoodlums—mugs who worship the gun and eat spaghetti with their hands."

Like me, Benny had gone to college briefly. He'd spent the subsequent twenty years waiting tables and tending bar at his uncle's restaurant.

"Between that, the opera, and trying to sleep with every dame in the neighborhood, I stayed busy," he explained. "What did you do, Martin?"

"Well, I became a private eye."

SAUSAGE

Doran had given a couple of fight tickets to Teddy Eccles as well. He and Faennis Cuhulain were seated in the second row, right behind the press seats, next to Jack and me.

"I don't know why Slapper's so nice to me," shouted Teddy.

"Remind me to tell ya sometime when it's easier to talk," I replied.

The St. Paul Auditorium, where they held fights in those days, was full to the rafters. My Sullivan was the big draw on this occasion, but his opponent, a Polack from Gary, Indiana, wasn't given much of a chance. It was the last prelim that had the recipe for greatness—white versus smoke. It pitted an up-and-coming local heavyweight named Fritzy Schmidt against Sweet Potato Newcomb, an old pro from Minneapolis.

Schmidt's fans weren't there to sit on their hands until their boy made an appearance. They were so loud that the four of us barely exchanged a word through a couple three-rounders, during which a featherweight and a lightweight from Doran's stable both lost close decisions. The lightweight was robbed in my opinion, which didn't bode well for Sullivan if it went the scheduled ten. It looked like the Huns's night. That was how the smart money figured it too. Bookies were wandering down the aisle holding up fingers to signal the odds, which were down to eight-to-five on Sullivan. Schmidt was four-to-one to beat Newcomb, five-to-two to KO him. You could get ten-to-one if you bet Newcomb to KO Schmidt.

You couldn't hear yourself cheering, that's how noisy it was. The air was so smoky up in the cheap seats that it didn't seem possible they could see the ring, but they must have. They were shouting themselves hoarse, mostly at the appropriate occasions.

The penultimate prelim was five rounds, featuring Harry Kerry, a dumpling-shaped Harp who hung out at Tin Cup's. I'd seen him scraped off the sidewalk after so many losing efforts outside the bar that it seemed to me he made a better punching bag than a boxer. I leaned over and asked Faennis to join me in the corridor. "This guy's a bum," I told him. "C'mon, I gotta ask ya somethin'."

We elbowed our way to the beer concession. I bought a couple and we found a quiet corner.

"I want to thank you for sending that business my way," I said.

"Think nothin' of it, lad."

"You know the guy?"

"Niver mit 'em." He looked a bit sheepish. "Paulie says he's good for the fee."

"No problem there. He paid my advance without blinkin', and I didn't give him the neighborhood rate either. Thing I'm worried about, he wants me to find out—"

Faennis nodded. "I know what he wants, an' I know ye don't like t' involve yerself in such things. I found out what he were up to after I give Paulie your name. I'm truly sorry fer that, lad."

Faennis explained that Ricca had phoned and asked if he could recommend anyone. Faennis told him about me and thought the conversation was over, but Ricca started commiserating about the failing business opportunity known as St. Paul and the dud who ran it.

"Told me the man he put in charge up here were a bit've a jillyfish. 'Somethin's wrong with him,' he said. He simply will not leave Chicago. Sint his own sister here to take care a th' business, and she can do naught but sell th' nose candy. Paulie says th' money-makin' potential here were bein' wasted entirely. He almost took th' tirritory away from th' man. Gave him 'til summer's end a couple years back t' make some real money, and it took him 'til the last minute t' finally come up with some. Then they arrested his sister, and Paulie hasn't seen a nickel since."

"Lemme guess. This is Tony Sassich."

"Correct. Mr. Sausage."

"He says 'Sassich.'"

"That's how they pronounce it in Chicago, lad, but Sausage he is. Accordin' t' Paulie, he were a butcher by trade. Came t' th' attention of Capone back when he were a mere soldier, owin' t' th' unique way he disposed of his victims's remains. Paulie might be a wee bit frightened of him, that's how it seemed to me."

"Jesus! And this is the guy—"

"Tis indeed, lad, and agin... my apologies."

I took a swig of beer and contemplated this alarming information. Faennis kept an uncomfortable eye on me.

Loud boos from the arena suggested that Kerry had lived up to my expectations, and sure enough, the corridor was soon crowded with thirsty fans jostling each other to get at the beer.

A big, pug-nosed Hun wearing a bathrobe with 'Fritzy Schmidt' monogrammed across the front walked past us, with Dick Pranke behind him.

"Better take your seats, gents," Pranke said. "This bout will be over in a hurry."

Faennis winked at me as they entered the arena to loud cheers. "Villainous little rascal, is he not?" he asked. "We'd best go back."

"One more thing. Why does this Sausage really want to know who fingered Van Meter? He says it's because his sister and Van Meter were sweethearts, but somehow I don't believe him."

According to Faennis, it wasn't Sausage who wanted to know. It was Ricca.

"Yer aware that Van Meter's nickname were 'The Waiter,' are ye' not? Well so's Ricca's. Capone always called him 'Paulie The Waiter.' Him an' Van Meter were singin' waiters together at some beer hall, way back. Paulie liked Homer, an' when the word went out among the mob t' tip off the feds on Dillinger and his gang, Paulie told 'em to lay off Homer. He were furious when the man were murthered. He told Sausage t' find out who finked and make mince of him. This was two years ago mind ye. So when Paulie called me, he says, 'my own man don't know what's goin' on there,' that's how much control he has in his own little tirritory."

According to Faennis, Ricca had ordered Tony to come here personally and hire me, and said it would cost him his livelihood if he didn't find the finger man and kill him.

Needless to say, I found that disturbing. "He told me he won't kill the fink, but he wants the dough and he knows exactly how much it was. Twenty Gs. Says he'll use it to take care of his sister."

Faennis shook his head. "It's a mite late to take care o' her."

"What do ya mean?"

"Paulie were expectin' she'd be back here piddlin' th' nose candy when she got out've th' trimmer, but no sooner did they turn her loose, maybe a month ago, than she disappeared."

So, everything Tony had told me was a lie. In hindsight, I should've given him his money back right then, but the thought of parting with all that dough was painful, and I was confident of my ability to keep him in the dark about the finger man's identity.

I quickly told Faennis about the plan Tony and I had agreed on to shield the fink. Just as I was concluding my explanation the crowd roared.

"Be careful when ye bring the cash to Chicago," Faennis cautioned, as we hurried into the arena.

"I feel badly I've put ye in this situation," he added. "Don't hisitate to call on me if ye need anything."

"I'll be ok, and I'll make some good dough, too," I said, with more bravado than conviction.

On the way down the aisle we encountered Pranke heading in the opposite direction. His fighter was shuffling along behind him, head bowed. Up in the ring Sweet Potato was strutting around, hands raised in victory.

"Isn't he the lucky one," said Faennis. "Come in with a KO at ten to one."

At the opening bell of the next bout, Sullivan charged out with that look of fury on his mug. His opponent, a husky hod carrier with thick arms and a big square jaw, wasn't scared. He held his own for three rounds, but in the fourth he walked into a straight right and took an eight count. He started bleeding in the fifth, and the ref stopped it.

THE BATTLE OF THE PACIFIC

ergeant Weber, who drilled The Home Guard, Gilroy Division, was a man our age. Judging from his appearance he shared my fondness for strong spirits. However, first thing on day one, he told us that the no-hooch rule was in effect.

"Sorry fellas," he said with a shrug that endeared him to us, even as he conveyed the bad news.

Prohibition appeared to be total, but after a few days I noticed that while my demeanor improved along with my stomach, the sarge's deteriorated apace. After a week at Camp Gilroy, I felt better than I'd felt in twenty years, but Weber had the shakes every morning.

I mentioned that to Castronovo. He laughed.

"I walked into the latrine after the sarge puked yesterday and almost got lit on the fumes," he said. "There's a little roadhouse out by the hot springs that sells hooch, but so far nobody's found transportation. Some Okie is making jungle juice, though. That's what I've heard."

Turned out Castronovo's family hunted deer in the hills around Gilroy, and he knew the area well. He even knew some local women. He assured me that if he could get his hands on a jeep he'd run down a skirt and a bottle 'toot sweet.' So I lived in hopes of better days.

Meanwhile, he and I looked in on the Arkie, a guy named Jasper Hudspeth, who actually was an Arkie—a distinction that was lost on me but meant a lot to him. We tried a taste of his popskull. Castronovo spit his out. I didn't go that far, but declined to place an order.

I'd been sober for weeks when Castronovo finally got his hands on a jug of wine, from his uncle's vineyard, he said. After that he was rarely without, not even on our first deployment when they drove eight of us to an isolated stretch of seashore in Oregon. Supposedly a Jap sub had been spotted near there. It was an eight-hour ride.

On the way up we were mostly silent. We'd been warned that if the Nips thought they could kill some soldiers they'd rake the beach with so much 'millimeter pete' that there'd be nowhere to duck— and of course there was the off-chance that they'd already put men ashore who'd be lying in wait.

It was well after sunset, and a three-quarter moon was dropping toward the sea when we got out of the truck. I had a hollow feeling in the pit of my stomach.

"'The sea the sea the wine-dark sea,'" said Benny.

We patrolled in pairs, walking the length of the beach, looking for the silhouette of a sub's superstructure backlit by the moon. Benny and I would pass guys walking the other direction and ask if they'd seen anything. They hadn't. Neither had we. It was ridiculous, and we all knew it after about an hour. We gathered behind a big rock and passed the jug. Every once in a while somebody would climb the rock and take a peek at the ocean. Hudspeth almost fell off.

"Easy there, Jasper," said Benny. "You'll break your neck."

"Hell, I don't care," he said. "This here's the closest thing to action I'm gonna see. Maybe they'll give me a Purple Heart." He squinted out to sea and continued to teeter. We took turns making up speeches of commendation, just in case.

"This medal is awarded to PFC Jasper Hudspeth for performance above and beyond the call of duty," said Benny, "to wit, braving the mild chill of a coastal evening and, despite said chill, climbing a steep rock to a height of, oh eight feet."

"Ten feet if it's an inch, goddamn it."

"Ok, ten feet, then falling on his ass due to mild inebriation coupled with the treacherous foothold."

There was mild applause for his effort.

Somebody asked Jasper how long it took the troop train to get from Arkansas to Sacramento.

"Don't rightly know," he said. "I got on a bus in Bakersfield."

"What were you doing in Bakersfield?"

"That's where I fetched up. In '32."

"Tell us again what happened to that girlfriend of yours," said Benny.

"Went out t' shit and the hogs et her."

I wandered out on the sand and focused as best I could on the horizon. It was just a dim line behind the silvery moonlit water, but something, probably imaginary, poked above it.

"Hey, look," I said.

Some saw it, some didn't. Those of us who did started shooting. After we'd expended a few hundred rounds, I thought I saw a spark like that of a bullet striking metal. Either that or a trick of the moonlight and the spray.

"I think we sunk her," said Bradich.

"Let's drink to that," I replied.

We gathered behind the rock again. The talk soon turned to my former life.

***

The Green Gables was a down-at-the-heels resort on McCarron's Lake, north of town. It used to be an out of the way place, then the WPA paved Rice Street past the city limits and now you could hear automobile traffic through the windows of the faded green cabins.

Opal was in number five, a stone's throw from the water. It was dusk when I knocked. She opened the door a crack and peeked out. She was small and pretty and scared.

"Martin? What... what're you doin' here?"

"I need to talk to you."

I saw she was trembling. She really didn't want to open that door.

"You all right?" I asked.

She didn't answer, but she stepped aside and I went in.

She picked up a pack of cigarettes off the bed and fumbled for a nail, but she was shaking so badly that she dropped it on the floor.

"Hey, Opal, this is me. Martin. I'm not gonna hurt'ya, f'r Christ's sake."

She sat down on the bed and burst into tears. I let her cry a while.

"Jeez, I didn't mean to scare ya."

She nodded as if she believed me, but it took her a long time to pull herself together anyway. I figured I'd better wait before I brought up Van Meter.

"Wanna go out for a drink, or a bite to eat?" I suggested.

"I'm... I'm afraid to go out," she said.

I asked why. She dabbed at her tears and spilled her guts. It'd been a tough go for Opal.

She said she'd learned Homer was dead when the G Men arrested her, the afternoon he was shot. They put her in the city lockup, then beat her up. "They didn't even ask no questions," she said. "Just punched me around."

The St. Paul coppers put a stop to that after they heard her screaming, but next day she was whisked off to a woman's pen out east, and held 'pending trial.'

"Trial my rear end," she said bitterly. "They kept sayin' they was gonna charge me. What'd I do anyway? Homer'n me fell in love, is that a crime?"

She said they subjected her to periodic interrogations, which included slaps and threats, and incessant drilling about the Karpis brothers, whom she claimed she'd never even met.

"First they had me in a cell fulla daisies. Then, when they seen those gals weren't gonna do me no harm, they put me in solitary for months. It got so I wanted 'em to come around and beat me up or somethin'. She teared up again. "Just so's I wouldn't be alone."

I put my hand on her shoulder. "C'mon, Opal. Put some nice duds on... we'll go somewhere. Don't worry, I'll take care of you."

That promise, made casually and without much thought, settled my hash for the next five years.

She gathered up some clothes and went into the bathroom to change. When she came out she looked more like the Opal of old. Her dark hair was spit-curled. She'd penciled on some brows and rouged up her pale cheeks a bit. She had a nice figure, which she noticed me admiring. She smiled.

"Where we goin'?" she asked.

"Lantern?"

"Maybe not. I don't wanna run into nobody anybody can ask me about."

"Ok, let's head outta town, see what's there."

She was in a good mood, singing to herself as we glided over the newly poured concrete in my Model A, which had been the butt of many a snide remark over the past few years. In those days, if you had the bees you were supposed to signify it with a darb bucket. *What a thrifty fellow am I,* I reflected. My bankroll had grown steadily throughout The Great Depression, while everyone else's seemed to shrink, even the coppers's. My friend, John O'Connor, complained that he was struggling to keep up with the house payments since his recent marriage, a happy occasion that coincided with the wind down of the Layover. Me and a few remaining bank robbers were doing just fine though.

Out past the pavement, we found a chicken shack with a big neon sign you could see a mile down the road. It was just a little joint with a Wurlitzer, and maybe three customers besides us. We ordered a whole chicken and a couple bottles of beer. Opal didn't eat much but she was like a kid on a picnic, humming along with the music, dabbing at my mouth with her napkin when I got sloppy.

After the food was finished we had another bottle of beer, and she told me she could be of some assistance in my line of work. I agreed, and was about to tell her just how she could assist when she launched into an explanation of certain powers she'd developed during her stay in solitary. I decided to wait awhile before inquiring about The Waiter.

As it happened, I didn't get around to that until the next morning. First there were more tears and bitter denials.

"It was Marie! That's who done it," she shrieked. "She knew Homer loved me! She sold him out!"

"She claims it was you," I told her.

"That liar!" She burst into tears again.

Soon she calmed down and filled me in on Homer's last days. She didn't know where he'd been staying, but it wasn't with Marie.

"He was through with her, and it wasn't just on accounta he loved me. Frank Cullen told him to stay away from Marie. The coppers didn't like her."

"Why?"

"She peddled snow, and she wouldn't just go ahead and pay up when Frank and Tommy said she had to. She'd bargain. Anyway, that's what Harry Sawyer told me."

"Where was Homer stayin'?" I asked her.

"He was plannin' a job with some guys. Could be he was with them. I can't remember their names. Hey, Martin, I got a good idea."

She scrambled out from between the sheets, stuck her head under the bed, and commenced rooting around. She looked cute down there with her little rump sticking out, wrapped in a pink nightie.

"Here, this'll tell us," she said. She pulled out an oval wooden board, plopped it on the bed, and squirmed back under the covers.

I couldn't figure out what it was. Maybe a game of some kind. Fancy script letters of the alphabet were arranged in a circle around the entire board, so the Z was butted up against the A. HELLO and GOODBYE were written on top, and YES and NO on the bottom. A pointer was attached at the center. It was heart shaped, just like Opal's rear end.

"What is that thing?" I asked.

"A Ouija board, silly. Maybe we should wait until dark."

"Opal, c'mere."

We played Vatican Roulette again, then I walked around barefoot on that cold floor, picking up my clothes. I peered out the little front window that looked out on the deserted beach, and McCarron's

Lake, which was rimmed around with leafless trees. A lifeguard's boat was upside down in the sand. It was drizzling out. Droplets inched down the window.

"Y' hafta go?" she asked. That anxious tone had crept back into her voice.

I promised her I'd come back, which cheered her considerably. She was consulting the spirits in respect to The Waiter's betrayal when I left.

That tune kept running through my head as I headed for The Green Lantern—so persistent that I tried to pin it down. Had I ever really heard it? Maybe at that joint in North Minneapolis a few years back, but I couldn't consciously remember. It was a saxophone, four beat and bluesy with some kind of instrumentation, just a drum probably. The saxophone was what I heard, and it wasn't anything in the music that suggested a song. It was something in the silence between notes.

Eternal Tommy Brown was lunching with Harry Sawyer when I arrived. Otherwise the place was nearly empty.

"Mind if I join ya?"

Sawyer moved over so I could sit down. "Any luck?" he asked.

"Uh-uh."

The waiter came by. "Whiskey and water," I told him. "Easy on the water."

"The Salisbury steak is excellent today, sir," he suggested.

"No kiddin. You hire a new cook, Harry?"

"Very funny."

"Just the whiskey, thanks."

Tommy was busy finishing his chili. He crumbled a Ritz cracker into the bowl, spooned up the last of it, took off his glasses, and blew his nose.

"Jesus, that's hot," he said.

"So how ya like bein' a detective again, Tommy?" I asked.

"What're you up to, Martin? Divorce work? Peekin' in keyholes?"

"Funny you should ask. I'm breakin' my neck tryin' to find out somethin' you already know. I'd be very grateful if you'd tell me. Eternally grateful. And you know how long that is."

He registered mild amusement at what I considered to be sharp riposte. "What might that be?" he inquired.

"Who fingered Van Meter?"

"Nope."

The waiter put my drink down. "You guys want anything?" I asked.

Harry said he did, but he was lying. He just wanted to hear that cash register ring. Tommy claimed he'd quit drinking.

"I understand," I said. "I don't drink anymore myself."

"Then what's that?" He pointed at my glass.

"I don't drink any less either."

That elicited a laugh. I asked again for a name.

"Nix, Martin. I gave my word."

"So what? Everybody's double-crossin' everybody nowadays. Get with the program. Stand up and rat like a man."

"Who wants to know anyway?"

I told him. He became agitated. "You actually think I'd let some mobster murder the guy who got me Van Meter?" He shook his finger under my nose. "This is what I always worried about with you, Martin. One of my boys gives you some information and bang! Somebody gets killed."

"Yeah, I know. You like it when the coppers do the killin'."

The waiter brought Harry his drink. Tommy and I clammed up until he was out of ear shot.

"I'm a neutral observer," said Harry, "but I'm inclined to side with Tommy. You can't let informers get bumped off. It's unethical."

"And as far as justice is concerned, Van Meter was a thief and a killer," Tommy said. "So good riddance."

"I wouldn't go that far," said Harry.

"That's why you shot him?" was my rhetorical query. "Protect the banks, make it safe for ordinary Joes to walk the streets? Jeez, I'm glad you told me. I heard ya did it for money."

"A little of that too."

"Anyway, the guy who hired me says he won't kill the fink. He just wants the twenty grand he got."

I watched how Tommy reacted. He didn't, which told me about all I'd ever hoped to get out of the conversation anyway.

"You trust this Tony Conforti?" Harry asked. "I never heard of him."

"He calls himself Tony Sausage."

"Doesn't ring a bell."

"Anyway, I don't have to trust him. Deal is, I don't tell him who the fink is. I just give him the twenty Gs and collect my fee. Hey, know what I come t' find out? His sister, who was Van Meter's squeeze, was dealin' mob dope in town here. You know about that, Tommy?"

"Never mind what I know. You're on your own with this one. I was you, I'd watch my back. You don't know what those mobsters have in mind."

"Locate Opal?" Harry asked.

"Yeah."

"Opal Milligan? She doesn't know anything," said Tommy.

"So I discovered."

"Where is she?" Harry asked. "I was thinking of maybe lookin' her up."

I drained my drink. "Maybe Tommy can find her for ya," I told him. "He's a detective now."

***

Benny said, "So you'd more or less hit a dead end, hadn't you. It must've been difficult, trying to figure what's going on in the minds of petty criminals. I ought to know."

He explained that when he was a kid there were no mobsters in his neighborhood, just honest tradesmen—hard-working fishermen like his father, restaurant owners and wine merchants like his uncles.

"People loved good food, good wine, good music. The women wanted refinement in their men, and vice versa. Then the great experiment in forced sobriety began and everything changed."

Prohibition brought gangsters from the east coast to San Francisco to control the hooch racket. They found Benny's neighborhood to their liking. It reminded them of home. At first there were only a few of them, and they were well-behaved.

"Two problems, though," Benny explained. "People love to go out and drink in San Francisco, so they sold so much booze that they attracted competition. Then the local guys, people I grew up with, friends of mine, started working for them. Ralphie Malvese, a guy I went to the opera with for Christ's sake, became one of the so-called 'men of honor.'"

The first Don was Gerri Ferri from Philadelphia. He was murdered in 1928.

"After him, four or five more came and went. Genaro Broccolo was the only one with any class—went to the opera, tipped the cooks at my uncle's restaurant, drank Campari he had sent over from Rome. The man had taste. After they killed him, I lost track. Every six months or so you'd hear shots and shouts, and that was the end of another 'man of honor.' Some of my neighborhood pals started acting like the funerals were state occasions. Ralphie actually wanted me to put on my top hat—the one I wore to hear Claudia Muzio sing Tosca—and go to the service for some mug named Alfredo Sclariso. An animal! A murderous little cretin! He'd get drunk and sing 'Oy Marie' in his horrible croaking voice, while his soldiers stood around and 'oohed' and 'ahhed' like he was 'bel canto'! And I was supposed to care if they shot him! Why?"

He said his old friend Ralphie, who'd evaded the draft because his many arrests made him morally unfit to die for his country, now ran the show... such as it was post-Prohibition.

"He sits in the Del Monte Barber Shop on Columbus Avenue like he's some kind of royalty and tells his 'soldiers' what to do," said Benny. "I think he secretly longs to be assassinated there. He wants to wind up dead in the chair, with bloody shaving lather on his fat mug, because it'll make such a marvelous photo: 'Ralph Malvese, Don of North Beach, murdered by mob rivals.' Ha! He has no rivals. Nobody gives a damn. Marco DeCoco, a man of some refinement who will marry my beautiful cousin Marissa when he gets out of the Army, did errands for Ralphie before he was drafted."

He paused and shook his head in wonderment.

"It's not that they're up to such awful things, mind you. A whore-house in Chinatown, some tea they either sell to the Mexicans or buy from the Mexicans... I lose track. Otherwise they beat each other up and collect a few bucks protection from the merchants. They're not real gangsters— they play the role, you know? And how do they interpret it? By being purposefully déclassé. God! It makes me angry just thinking about it!"

The sound of gunfire startled us. It wasn't the Nips. It was one of our own who'd wandered off and was attacking the sub again, but erratically. We heard a bullet ricochet off something nearby, hopefully not a helmet.

"Careful where you're aiming," somebody hollered.

"My daddy useter say, 'don't never go huntin' with a man name'a Chug-A-Lug! Pass me that there jug, would'ja?" asked Hudspeth.

"Tell us about that steer of yours, Jasper," said Forsythe, a college professor-cum Home Guardian who found Hudspeth's regionalisms amusing.

"That ol' bull? He was an ornery sumbitch! Cut his horns off, but he was still ornery, so we cut his nuts off. Tweren't ornery then. Poor thang couldn't fight nor fuck. Couldn't do nothin' but beller'n shit."

"Think we dare build a fire?" someone asked.

We decided it wasn't advisable given the likelihood of enemy attack, although a vocal minority claimed it was ok since our rifle fire had probably sent at least one sub to the bottom, and the rest of the fleet must have fled for Tokyo by now.

We finished the jug, patrolled some more, and made our way to the troop truck just before dawn. Most of my comrades in arms fell into a deep slumber on the way back to Camp Gilroy. Not me. I sat up near the cab where the ride was smooth. A few Guardians gathered round.

"Tell me, McDonough," said Professor Forsythe, "this fellow you killed, how the devil did that come about?"

***

Traffic was moving at a snail's pace in downtown St. Paul or, more accurately, at the pace of a tired horse hitched to a fancy automobile. Most people who'd purchased the big buckets before the crash had them up on blocks by 1936, but there was always a parade of die-hards on Kellogg Boulevard, letting you know they'd seen better days.

I found a parking space in front of the recently shuttered Town Talk and hurried through the drizzle to the library.

John Howell was seated at his desk daydreaming. He told me business had slowed considerably since Nina Clifford closed her whorehouse.

"Those gals were my best customers," he said. "I'd retire, but what would I do? I'm gettin' old, Martin."

"How's your memory?"

"Not so good. A few bucks generally improves it though."

The deuce I slipped him was well-spent. John remembered letters verbatim that he'd written years ago. At least he did if they interested him. He'd found the one that concerned my inquiry pretty interesting.

"Van Meter never came to see me," John explained. "I think he learned to read and write in prison. Blackie Audette didn't though. The guy had a way with words, but he couldn't spell his own name." He tapped his noggin. "Somethin' wrong up here. Told me he sees letters backwards. Anyway, I used to write to his wife for him when he was in town."

Blackie had come in to get a letter written the day after the buzz nailed Van Meter, who'd been sleeping on Blackie's couch. According to John, Blackie seemed baffled by the turn of events. He was set to lam the moment he finished dictating.

John closed his eyes and recited, quietly, so the librarian wouldn't get after us.

Dearest Vi,

Enclosed you will find a couple C-notes from the Nebraska job, which dough being all I can spare. Me and Bobby Steele hooked up with Homer Van Meter

(you remember him—The Waiter) here in
St. Paul, and the three of us agreed
we'd live on what we had, which in our
case wasn't much, while we took our time
planning the next heist. Homer was bunking with us and we was all three laying low. Couldn't even send you a letter, because Homer did not want me going
downtown to get it writ by the scribe
here.

Mind you, all this is not because the
heat is on, but because poor Homer's on
the dodge from a couple dames. He's been
living with Marie Conforti from Chicago. She's here working for the mob some
way that's too complicated to explain,
but he's soft on another dame now. Marie
is jealous, but if he goes home to Marie
the other gal falls to crying and carrying on, and says she's putting spells on
him. He's about had it with the both of
them, but the thing is, there is a guy
connected with each of these dames that
he's involved with too. These two guys,
one of them works with Marie, the other
one is the other dame's ex-boyfriend,
they both drive Homer around because he
hasn't got a bucket of his own. Frank
is the second gal's ex, and he worships
the ground Homer walks on, but Homer
thinks he's a squirrel and avoids him.
The other guy, the one who works for
Marie, it's like him and Homer are in
cahoots on account of they both think
Marie's a bitch. So a few days ago Homer
takes it into his head he's got to have
a car of his own in case he has to lam,
on account of the G men are looking for
him high and low and the fix with the St.
Paul coppers is getting shaky.

So Homer tells us that Marie's guy,
Dutchy is his name, is setting up a
used car deal for him. Says Dutchy is

picking him up on the corner by the creamery near here at noon, and they've got an appointment at the car dealer. Homer's got a bag full of cash, and the two of them have a plan. Dutchy drops Homer a block away from the car dealer by an alley, so he can run if he has to. Dutchy drives right up in front of the dealer's place and parks. If the coast is clear Dutchy gives him the high sign. Homer tells us that if all goes well he'll be back in an hour or so with a twelve cylinder Duesenberg some sawbones used to own. Says it can outrun any copper in the country.

But the thing is, Homer don't come back. After a while we start hearing sirens, and we get itchy wondering what's going on. Just before supper-time Bobby sneaks out for a late paper. A few minutes later he comes runnin' in like he's been shot out of a cannon and shows me the headline: 'Dillinger Henchman Van Meter Gunned Down By St. Paul Police!'

That's right Vi, our old friend Homer is dead, dry-gulched just like Johnny and Jimmy Gillis. Did the system here come unglued? It must have. And this Dutchy character for sure set him up.

We're heading out of town the minute I finish this. Don't know what's coming next, but I hope two Cs tides you over for a bit.

Your loving Blackie.

So there it was, all wrapped up in a neat little package. Dick Pranke, a.k.a. Dutchy, ratted The Waiter, and all I had to do was convince him to hand over the blood money.

It took me a couple days to run Dutchy down. Meanwhile Opal and I settled into a routine. I'd come by after Tin Cup's. We'd go eat at out-of-the-way places. I usually spent the night. I worked her for a little information, mostly so we wouldn't spend the whole time discussing weejy spirits.

She knew who Dutchy was. When she and Van Meter were shacked up, he had a habit of dropping in. "I didn't like him," she said. "He was always whisperin' in Homer's ear. What do you want with him, Martin?"

"Never mind. It's nothin'."

I asked her what she planned to do when it got too cold to stay at Green Gables, which had already happened in my opinion. There'd been a sprinkling of snow the day before, and just thinking about that floor in the morning kept me in bed awhile.

"Charlie says he'll fix me up with some kinda heater."

***

The war was being waged in places we'd never heard of—Bataan, Ben-Ghazai, Leningrad. I think I speak for all Home Guardians when I say we woke up every morning hoping it wasn't the day we shipped out. Meanwhile we drank, drilled, policed the barracks, policed the yard, and went on patrols to guard bridges as far away as the state of Washington, where we unleashed lethal barrages at illusory subs we called 'bogeys.'

We maintained 'a state of readiness' at all times, which mostly meant marching in the hot sun, taking our rifles apart and putting them back together again. As the months rolled by, we became accustomed to the nerve-wracking status quo.

My main contribution to the war effort was peeling potatoes. I believe Sergeant Weber thought I was ethnically suited for the job. It wasn't so bad, except for a brief stretch when a captain honored us with his presence. He hung around a few days, devising 'efficiency tests.'

Here's how you peel potatoes: you sit down on a stool with a paring knife and three large pails, one full of potatoes, two empty; take a potato out of pail one, peel it so the skin falls in pail two, drop the peeled potato in pail three.

That's all there is to it. The routine puts you in a kind of trance, and as I dropped the last peeled spud in the bucket on the day I'm thinking of now, I heard a voice as if from a great distance calling, "Private. Private. PRIVATE!"

"Yes, SIR!" I finally replied.

"Private! Pick up those two buckets and follow me!"

I hauled the pail of potatoes and the pail of peelings over to the Admin building, where a scale had been set up outside the door. The captain—who would soon be dubbed captain pencil-licker because he was in the habit of doing that as he snooped around taking notes—ordered me to weigh the pails... first separately, then together.

I obeyed his command. He scribbled some figures and did a quick calculation.

"Just as I suspected, private," he said. "The bucket of peelings weighs fully ten percent as much as the bucket of potatoes."

He called that, 'massive waste,' the kind of thing that was 'sabotaging our war effort.' Henceforth, he proclaimed, the potato-to-peel ratio would be twenty-to-one or better, and I was to bring all my work to the scale to prove I'd achieved that lofty standard. He puffed out his skinny chest, which was full of fruit salad, and barked, "Failure will result in discipline! Do you understand, private?"

"Yes, SIR!"

"Dis-MISSED!"

I saluted and slunk off toward the mess hall, buckets in hand. Hudspeth, who'd been policing the yard for butts, witnessed the entire indignity. He howled and slapped his knee.

Hudspeth and I spent a fair amount of time on the shooting range together. He was a dead shot. I was pretty good, but I always wondered how I'd do if there was a fellow homo sap in the cross hairs, instead of a piece of cardboard. Hudspeth entertained no such reservations.

"I killed plenty'a critters," he said. "Cain't be no worser'n shootin' a hog an' listenin' to him squeal. Hell, that there Nip might-oughta be a hundred yards off. Won't even hear him grunt. How's about that feller I hear tell you kilt, McDonough? You put a gun to his head an' shoot?"

***

A few days after I talked to John Howell, I dropped in to the St. Francis Hotel. A ring was set up in the lobby. A couple young guys were sparring; a few others were banging the heavy bag. Sure enough, Dutchy was there. He and one of the boxers went in a corner and had a heart-to-heart between rounds.

"How's it goin', Martin?" asked Jimmy Brennan, who was resting his tired dogs after pounding the beat for maybe fifteen minutes.

I told him it was going well now that I'd located Dick Pranke.

"Why?" he wondered. "Lookin' for a tip? I'll give you one. Bet against the guy that son of a bitch is talkin' to."

"You don't like him?"

"If he was on fire I wouldn't cross the street to piss on Dutchy."

I asked Jimmy what made Dutchy so unpopular. He gave me a quick run-down on the man's many bad traits, which boiled down to fixing fights, one of the few forms of corruption the coppers didn't control. But they could profit by it nonetheless. When I said as much to Jimmy, he simply pointed out that Pranke was a Hun.

That settled that.

The bell rang. Dutchy patted the kid on the back and yelled after him to 'work that left' as he climbed into the ring.

I walked over and stood next to him. "You manage that guy?" I asked.

"Yeah. I'm a 'manager.' That's the new thing y'know. Pretty soon everybody's gonna be a manager or a chump. How's about you, McDonough?"

"Pokin' around. I didn't know you were a friend of Van Meter's."

He stepped back and frowned. "Who says I was?"

I took my time responding. I could tell that big noggin of his had suddenly filled with unpleasantness. He was wondering what I knew, and if the coppers told me, which meant it was no longer debatable, or if I dug it up some other way and he could weasel out of it.

"I got it from somebody who knows somebody who knows," I replied.

"Knows what?"

"Everything."

He grinned like that was a joke, and turned his attention to the kid in the ring.

"C'mon Ray," he said. "Jab him, jab him. Jab and run."

"That's no way to win a fight. The judges score for aggression."

He assessed my rigorously impassive puss in search of a strategy.

"Winning isn't everything. You bet on the fights, McDonough?"

"I don't want to talk about the fights. I want to discuss a case I'm workin' on."

The bell rang. His boy came over to the ropes.

"Hey Dutch," he hollered. "We need'a talk some more."

"Gimme a minute, Raymond. So, what about this case?"

"Fella hired me to find out who fingered him," I said.

"Van Meter?"

I gave him a look… one I practice in the mirror.

"Hey, listen… who told you? Hey, I bet it was Opal Milligan! That frail's nutty, McDonough. Don't pay no attention to her."

"We're not talkin' about who told me either, Dutchy. We're talkin' about I know." I put a friendly arm on his shoulder. "But don't worry, we can work somethin' out."

I guided him over to a leather couch by the window where we could chat confidentially, and laid it out for him. He complained but he didn't argue, especially after I told him who wanted the money and why.

"Tony Sausage… that's Marie's brother," he said.

I nodded. He whistled softly.

"How'd you know Marie anyway?" I asked.

He leveled with me about the nature of that relationship. He said he sold the cocaine Marie got from her brother, mostly at Kuby's and a few other spots, and volunteered that Marie was Tony's surrogate in St. Paul. He said he used to hear her on the phone with Tony. He could tell from her side of the conversation what was going on.

"He wanted her to open a whorehouse, or a gambling joint, something to make more money, but she'd tell him, 'If you need the dough so bad, c'mon up here and do it yourself.' I could hear him over the receiver, he yelled so loud. 'You do what I tell you or I'll sever your goddamn head off!'"

He looked worried.

"Don't worry," I assured him. "He wants the money. He said he wouldn't even ask who gave it to me."

"Ah Christ, twenty grand. That's everything for me."

"C'mon, you must've had some dough on Sweet Potato the other night. And what about the cash from the brown paper bag?"

He knew exactly what I was referring to. "Homer kept that bag," he said. "I heard the coppers had to pry it out of his mitts after they killed him."

"Anyway, you know how to make money. You'll be whole again in no time."

We walked down to the First National Bank together. On the way I asked him why he decided to sell out Van Meter.

"The money was good. Besides, Marie wanted me to."

I don't know why that came as a surprise. Maybe because Opal had already told me, but I chose to ignore her.

According to Dutchy, Marie didn't betray The Waiter out of jealousy. She did it because she was desperate. For years she'd lived off Van Meter and passed every nickel she made selling drugs on to her brother. But, after she and Van Meter split up, she had to pay her own way.

"That brother of hers was really lathered," said Dutchy. "He was always after her to bring in more, and here she was bringing in less. He put her in the squeeze... told her to come up with some money, and fast. Selling out Van Meter was her only option."

"You heard from Marie since she got out of stir?" I asked.

"No. I think she's done with the rackets."

Half an hour later Dutchy and I parted company, leaving me with a big manila envelope full of lettuce. I took it to The Green Lantern, got a receipt from Harry, then used his phone to call Chicago.

After some pro-forma congratulations on a job well done, Tony informed me of a change in plans. He was coming to St. Paul to get the dough personally.

That was a great relief to me. I didn't know what game he was playing, but I had home field.

***

We headed for Gilroy in any vehicle we could commandeer whenever they turned us loose for a few hours. It was usually a Jeep but sometimes a troop truck, or even a motorcycle with a side-car, which made for a hair-raising journey.

The area around there was beautiful, and to my eye, exotic. There were steep mountains nearby, but the road to Gilroy wound among rounded foothills dotted with cows and covered with the greenest grass I'd ever seen. The outcroppings of jagged gray rock that dotted the hillsides looked like they'd erupted through a green carpet. Clouds scudded by so close you could touch them. Mists blew over from the ocean, about thirty miles away.

The town of Gilroy, a mean little place full of scared Mexicans and guys who looked like strikebreakers, was quite a letdown after the scenery. The air smelled of garlic from early spring, when the crop was harvested, until late fall, when the last of it was shipped off on the little spur of railroad that ran through town.

Some weird Christian sect had a stranglehold on Gilroy. The townsfolk didn't like strangers, even if they were Home Guardians, and a form of prohibition was enforced because they frowned on strong spirits. There were two dingy joints on Monterey Street where servicemen and Mexicans could drink, which made it tolerable for an afternoon pass. But whenever we had a weekend, Castronovo and I headed straight for San Francisco.

That was a town more to my liking, even though there were thousands of sailors on the streets and if you wore your uniform they'd pick fights with you so frequently you'd think World War II was being waged between the US Navy and the US Army. After a few brawls we learned to wear civvies. Sometimes Hudspeth or Bradich came along, but usually it was just Benny and me. We'd arrive late in the afternoon, about the time Benny's father was due in with the day's catch, and try to make it to pier 39 in time to say hello.

I'd never seen anything like that pier. But I've seen it many times since, and it has gotten steadily bigger and busier… but it had a special quality during the war.

Soldiers, sailors, and teen-aged V-girls milled around the wharf, along with lots of chinks buying fish. 'Chinese chinks,' Benny informed me. 'The Nips are all in detention.'

Coast Guard ships hovered out on the horizon. Speedboats with big Coast Guard insignias swooped in, darted among the approaching flotilla of fishing boats, then sped out again. When the boats came in there'd be dozens of fishermen unloading their catch and wise cracking in Italian. Their wives would gather in little groups in front of the wharf restaurants to gab.

The wives all knew Benny. As we walked past they called out to him, 'hey Bettino.' If he paused to talk they'd pinch his cheek and run their hands through his curls.

'This is my friend, Martin,' he'd say, and they'd give me the same going over.

It was odd the way women treated us during the war. It was like we were young men. I suppose we were, relatively speaking. We'd hang around and talk to Benny's father awhile, then walk up the hill to a bar in the neighborhood where he grew up.

There were never any single gals in that joint. I don't think they were allowed, but those middle-aged dames we'd seen on the wharf would drift in and out. Some of them told us they had daughters who were sitting home alone, dying of boredom, while they waited for their soldier boys. The moms wanted Benny to organize some entertainment for those gals. Apparently they trusted him. Big mistake. He might've meant well—I certainly didn't—but women couldn't resist Benny. They flocked around him like pigeons… cooing, strutting, nudging each other out of the way.

The other guys from Gilroy would head down to the Mission neighborhood and contend with the rest of the servicemen for V-gals, but we rarely left Benny's neighborhood. He had a regular Lonely Hearts Club vying for his attention, and I was proud to serve as consolation prize on many occasions.

The most beautiful of them all was his cousin, Marissa. She was off limits for Benny, but she flirted with him mercilessly. She liked to walk down Lombard Street between the two of us, clinging to our arms, leaning her head on Benny's shoulder, then on mine. She had thick, soft, black hair that felt like a mink coat when it brushed your arm, and violet eyes under long black lashes.

'Hey Bettino, I think I'm fallin' for your friend here,' she'd say. 'Rescue me.'

One evening near the end of the war, Marissa blessed me with her sexual attentions. It happened in her own bedroom, with her mother snoozing down the hall. A framed photo of her fiancé, Marco, smiled at us from the night table.

She told me not to get any ideas. This was a one-nighter. "I'm no live wire," she said.

Later she asked me why I'd never married.

"I'm not husband material."

"You should've married that dame you told me about, that Opal Mulligan."

"Milligan."

"Yeah her. What became of her?"

***

It lasted five years between Opal and me, but there was never anything spoken. I just kept coming around. She depended on me. Not that I was the only guy in her life, but I took precedence.

That first winter Charlie installed a contraption called a 'space heater' in her cottage. From then on the place smelled faintly of kerosene. I didn't trust the thing. It sprang into action with an incendiary burst that made you jump, and the sight of those flames licking at thin sheet metal kept you on edge. Charlie claimed it was brand new, but if so it was flawed conceptually.

Much was asked of the space heater. You could hear it struggling at night. The metal made a banging sound as it heated up, then again when it cooled down.

Between that and the other I didn't get much sleep at Opal's, so I'd spend a few nights a week at Mrs. Dunn's.

During a cold snap in February '38, the bucket froze up outside Tin Cup's, and I couldn't get it started. By the time I got back to Green Gables I'd been gone for days. The space heater was banging away when I arrived, and Harry Sawyer, who'd obviously been doing the same, was sitting there in his undershirt. We exchanged barbs while Opal bustled about, humming and tidying up.

"Make yourself at home," I said.

"Don't mind if I do," he replied.

"You guys want some coffee?" Opal asked.

We shook our heads no.

"That's good. I haven't got any."

She didn't have a stove to cook on either. Charlie brought her one later that year, a one-burner, another fire hazard, but I'm getting ahead of myself. Harry said he was leaving for Florida the next week. He asked if I still had any money on deposit with him.

"Yeah, a hundred thousand smackers. Pay up."

"You've got three hundred bucks. You knew that, right?"

"Sure," I lied.

He went over to his coat, which was hanging from a nail on the wall, extracted a flask, and poured himself a shot into the screw top.

"You heard Charlie's selling these cottages?" he asked. "Wants five hundred a piece for them. Says he's too old to run the place as a resort any longer."

He passed the flask. I wet my whistle.

"What say we buy Opal's cottage for her?" he proposed. "Throw in your three, I'll make up the difference."

"Two-fifty. Half and half."

"Uh-uh. I'm leaving for good next week. You'll take the dirt nap right here in St. Paul, so it's only fair you should go more than half."

Opal continued to hum and tidy... quite a trick, since once she'd cleared last night's glasses off the table, dusted the space heater and made the bed, there was nothing left to do. Her smile was the only indication that she knew what we were talking about.

We didn't quibble long. I signed over the three hundred, and Harry said he'd put his lawyer on it. A few weeks later she got the deed.

That spring Opal spotted a gossamer curtain in a shop on Grand Avenue. She asked me to buy it for her, along with some peacock feathers, and a few strings of glass beads. I screwed hooks into the ceiling and hung the curtain so it divided the place in two. Opal stuck the feathers in the curtain, hung two strings of beads on the wall, and another one around her neck. That was how she became Madam Opal. Between consultations with the spirits, and whatever arrangements she made with her gentlemen friends, she began to get by.

One evening shortly before Pearl Harbor I made one of my increasingly rare visits. A young fellow I recognized from Tin Cup's was there, listening to the gramophone. He had his stocking feet on the table.

"Get your feet off the furniture, kid," I said.

"Who the fuck're you," was his reply. People were becoming coarser and coarser. Talk like that was common around women now.

"Watch your language," I said.

He laughed and we came to blows. I think he got the best of it. Opal's screams brought the fight to a halt. Neither of us had our hearts in it. He excused himself sheepishly, and I spent the night there.

"I think that was the last time I saw her," I told Marissa.

"Jesus, you're romantic," she said. "Make sure I don't become one of your stories, understand?"

I assured her I did, and meant it at the time.

"What're you going to do when the war is over?" she asked.

"I don't know. Go back home, I suppose. Look after my ma some. She's gettin' on."

"Same thing for a living?"

"Yeah."

"Martin McDonough, private eye."

She ran her palm over my stomach. I took that as a preliminary to the evening's second featured bout, which, beautiful as she was, I might have been up for. It was just an idle gesture though.

"You're getting a belly on you," she observed.

"Hey, I got a right… man my age. It's probably just that good Gilroy chow."

"I suppose you met plenty of dames when you were sleuthing."

"Sure."

She propped her head up on her elbow. Even in the dark I could see the wicked sparkle in her eyes.

"Ever get involved with one and sneak around with another? Not that I'd ever contemplate such a thing myself, but I sometimes wonder how people handle those situations."

"Not me. I knew someone who did though."

"Hmm." She traced a circle on what was now officially my belly. "How'd that work out for her."

"It was a him. A gangster. And it didn't work out so well."

***

Tony Conforti instructed me to meet him at the Lowry Hotel, right after the one p.m. train from Chicago arrived. I got there early. I could've just stood by the front desk, but I decided to lurk behind a pillar instead... just to assess things.

This will be easy, I told myself. Hand him the money and collect the rest of my fee. I don't even care if he holds out. I'll just leave and be glad I'm done with it.

Nevertheless, I had a feeling of dread.

At a few minutes after one, Tony made an impressive grand entrance, along with his four-mug entourage. Dummy that I was, I hadn't counted on that.

Somewhere in Chicago a haberdashery was sold out of camel's hair coats and snap brim hats. The four of them formed a tight circle around their boss, shouldered the bellboy and some guests aside, and swept through shouting, "Outta da way! Loogout!"

They paused at the desk. The clerk handed one of them a key, and they set forth again. I thought Tony might notice me, but there was no chance of that. He had his hat pulled down over his sunglasses, and his gang had to walk slowly to keep pace with him. He moved one lurch at a time, like a tin soldier winding down. I caught a glimpse of his puss as they waited for the elevator. He looked stricken.

I wandered around downtown for a few minutes, retrieved the cash from the trunk of my bucket, then returned to the Lowry and used the house phone to tell him that I'd arrived. Come up, he said.

It was a sunny afternoon, but the drapes were pulled and the lights were on in Tony's suite. He looked more relaxed now that the outside world had been obliterated. There was a bottle of whiskey, some glasses, and an ice bucket on the table where he was seated, drink in hand.

"Pour yoursself one, my shamuss friend," said Tony.

His gang was arranged around the room. They stood silently, pockets bulging with heat. I put a few cubes in a glass and poured a stiff one.

"Well, here it is." I laid the envelope on the table.

He extracted the cash, and counted it.

"Nice work, McDonough. Marie will be very happy about diss." He thumbed off a wad of C-notes and handed them to me. "Now we're square."

"Thanks."

"You're welcome." Then came a moment I hadn't expected, although it was something with which I was well acquainted. It probably doesn't happen in many professions. Doctors maybe. I'd done my job, nothing more, but it's the sort of job that makes a big difference in the client's life and many's the time they feel the need to express more gratitude than is signified by a mere exchange of cash.

I could tell Tony was summoning up all the control he could muster in an effort to be cordial. He gritted his teeth, and sighed.

My heart went out to the poor tortured fellow. Instead of bolting with the dough, I readied myself to reciprocate whatever little gesture he made.

"Ever meet Marie?" he asked.

I told him I hadn't.

He took some photographs out of his pocket and laid one on the table. "Dat'ss her. Pretty, ain't she?"

She was indeed. She had black hair, a big smile, and a short skirt that showed off her shapely gams.

Tony beamed. "Here'ss one a her and Da Waiter."

They were posed with their arms around each other. Van Meter had his hat on at a rakish angle. Marie's lips were puckered for a kiss.

"And diss here iss her bucket."

She and Van Meter were standing beside a big sedan. Somebody was holding the back door open. I peered closely. It was Dutchy. I must've registered something, surprise, maybe even dismay. But just barely.

I cleared my throat. "Nice flivver," I said.

It was no good. I could tell by the look on his face. The dread in my guts congealed into a cold lump of regret. Tony gave his mugs the high sign. Two of them put their drinks down and walked out the door. The other two stood by, impassively.

"Where they goin'?" I asked.

"Get some fresh air." He smiled. That diamond in his teeth flashed. "Maybe drop by a hotel called da St. Franciss. I hear da fight crowdss hangss out dere."

"Well, I'd best be goin'," I said.

He shoved the ice bucket toward me. "Stick around, have another drink."

"Sorry, gotta go." I pushed my chair back and stood up.

He took his glasses off. His eyes were cold as the ice in that bucket.

"Have another drink," he said.

One of his mugs came over and nudged me back into the chair, gently but firmly.

"Whattssamatter, McDonough, Richard Pranke also known as 'Dutchy' a pal'a yourss?"

"No," I replied. "But I gave him my word. That's why he handed over the dough."

"Some advice? If your word meanss dat much, don't give it so easy. You don't know nothin' about me."

"I know you're a man of honor. You said so."

"And you're a guy who don't give a rat-fuck about anything comess between him and a buck. Which, don't miss-understand, iss ok with me. I know where I stand wid you, McDonough. A word to the wise? Don't fret over what you can't control. I could maybe cut you in on some real dough here. Have you handle some businesss for me. Locate Opal Milligan yet?"

I was on the verge of saying that I wouldn't tell him where she was if he pulled my fingernails out one by one, but I caught myself and started thinking again.

"Maybe," I said. "What happens to her if I tell ya?"

"Ever think about diss? You don't ask questionss, you don't know nothin'."

I didn't answer.

"Give it some thought," he said.

One of his mugs turned on the radio. The three of them listened intently to Lum 'n Abner. Everybody had another drink.

The Guiding Light came on next. They weren't so interested in that. Tony started muttering into his glass and mopping his brow. Every now and then he jammed his fist up under his chin, gritted his teeth, and pushed against his noggin until he practically had a convulsion. He grew more uncomfortable with each passing moment.

"What'ss keepin' Jake and Joey?" he asked. He was trying to sound impatient, but it came out whiney.

One of his brunos opened the curtain, as if to see what was keeping Jake and Joey.

"CLOSE DAT THING! Tony screamed. HOW MANY TIMESS I HAFTA TELL YA!"

Two hours passed thus pleasantly. Then Jake and Joey came back.

"Take care of it?" Tony asked.

"Yeah," they said in unison, and I had a moment of panic, as if it were my own death I was facing up to.

"What'd you do to him?" I asked.

"Eh! Shamuss! Didn't I tell you? Sooner or later somebody'ss gonna ask what become a Dutchy. I wass you, I wouldn't wanna know. The look on yer face might give you away, huh?" He laughed. "We got one more little thing to discusss here you and me."

Tony wanted to pay Opal a call before he left, and he made it clear that the information had to be accurate and precise. Otherwise, it was time to make some sausage.

"It's gonna cost'ya," I said.

"Whatta ya wanna bet Jake and Joey can make ya tell me widout I give ya anudder nickel?"

"It'd take a while. How much time ya got?"

"Huh!" he snorted.

Tic. Grimace. The finger in the cheek again. Mild convulsion.

"So how much?" he inquired.

"I always give clients a little break the second time they hire me. One G will cover it."

"Yeah, ok, long ass it'ss where she'ss at right now. We're gonna be on the fisrst train out in the morning." He said that as if he were making a vow to himself.

"You'll be able to leave before morning," I told him.

That perked him up. "Whadda ya mean?"

I rubbed my thumb and forefingers together. He pulled the dough out of the envelope and counted off another thousand. I pocketed it, stood, and walked toward the door. One of his mugs stepped in front of me.

"Ixnay," I said. "Deal is, I tell you where to find Opal Milligan right before I step into the elevator. Alone."

He was wavering.

"C'mon, walk to the elevator with me. I'll tell'ya exactly where she is. You got my word."

"You two come wid me," he told Jake and Joey.

We proceeded down the corridor. I pushed the elevator button. Tony reached under his jacket and stuck a pistol in my ribs. I'd pretty much anticipated something of that nature, but I tried to act put out.

"No trust at all. And after I gave up Dutchy without a peep."

"Spill it," he said.

The elevator arrived. The door opened.

"She ran off to Chicago with a Thompson gunner name a Chopper DeVol," I put one foot in the car. "They met right after she got outta stir. DeVol was layin' low in St. Paul, but the two of 'em lammed a couple weeks ago, because DeVol went to work for a guy name a Ralph Nitti. You probably know who he is."

"Don't make a move," he said, trembling. "Get outta dat elevator or I'll shoot ya dead. C'mon. I know somebody I can call, see if diss DeVol iss workin' for Nitti. If he issn't, yer dead meat. If he iss, we're square."

He was. We were. Whoever he talked to even told him DeVol brought a dame from St. Paul with him, just like Harry Sawyer told me he had. Tony beamed as he gave me the news. He told me it was a pleasure doing business.

"Diss room'ss paid up for da night," he said. "Bring yer girlfriend, finish da whiskey. C'mon boyss, we can still make da train."

"Take good care a yer sister," I said, as he gathered his paraphernalia and put on his coat and hat.

"Huh? Oh yeah. C'mon, hurry," he told his mugs.

SNAFU

Benny's old man and I got along ok, and later on when I met his mother we hit it off too, but his uncles thought I was a bad influence.

Uncle Tomasso owned a vineyard across the Golden Gate Bridge somewhere. Uncle Eddy had a restaurant on Lombard Street called—you guessed it... Eddy's. It was a spaghetti joint with a Wurlitzer that played pre-war tunes. Eddy served Tomasso's wine for twenty cents a glass, quite a trick since you could buy it at a store down the block for a dime a gallon if you brought your own jug.

Tomasso was Marissa's father. Her fiancé, Marco, was interested in the vineyard. It was in the works to pass it on, but Eddy was a bachelor and he envisioned Benny taking over the restaurant. Sort of.

One afternoon we were sitting in his place sipping brandy and coffee Italian-style (tiny cup, strong bitter coffee, lemon and sugar, not bad), and listening to Eddy ramble on.

"You'll run the place, Bendetto," he told his nephew for the nine-hundredth time, "but you won't change nothin,' right?"

Benny had learned to ignore that question, which wasn't a real question, just another riff in the drone Eddy always lapsed into when he'd had a drink or two.

I felt kind of sorry for Eddy. He wasn't in good health, and I understood that his monologue was a way of coping with the inevitable. Nevertheless, it was a high price to pay for a shot of brandy. He had three or four stock utterances that came to the same thing. Everything had to be slathered in amber the moment he croaked.

"Maybe a paint job, and you could get rid've them corner booths but—"

"All due respect, Eddy, he's gotta change the name," I said.

"Oh, Jesus," muttered Benny. "Leave it alone for Christ's sake."

"No, I'm serious. Guy named Benny can't run a joint named Eddy's. Shouldn't name a place after the owner anyway. It's pretentious. All due respect."

"Oh, yeah, smart guy, what should he call it? How's about namin' it after his pal Martin? I can see the sign now—'The Mick Lush.'"

"Hey, that's pretty good, Eddy. I'm good for you, keep ya on your toes."

"Signing off," said Benny. He rested his head on the table while Eddy and I traded barbs for a few minutes. I do believe it got Eddy's blood moving for a change.

Both Eddy and Tomasso dwelt in delusion in regard to their nephew. Did he stay up all night drinking and making time? Blame it on McDonough. Did he, opera-lover, bon vivant, get into a fight with a sailor on California Street and wind up with a black eye? McDonough, of course. Did he buckle down and learn the ins and outs of a spaghetti joint as the war drew to a close, or take a half-hearted stab at the books and go about his wastrel ways? The latter, and down to McDonough again.

Actually, his tastes mirrored mine, which was why we were friends. We liked the hooch, but were trying to temper that by becoming winos. We liked a seaman's bar on Union Street that had stools with backrests, booths made of dark-stained oak, and a piano the customers sometimes played. We liked lots of dames, but not any dame in particular. We liked good stories, and we liked the kind of music we heard in some of the joints in the Mission, where the races mixed.

Servicemen frequented those places, sailors mostly, but as VE Day approached we began seeing more and more GIs, some on leave, some Section Eights—you could tell by the thousand-yard stare. They all wore civvies to avoid clashes, and they didn't shave every day.

Some of them wore French beanies called berets. Those guys liked the music as well as we did. It was different than the pre-war hot jazz. Sometimes it had a driving backbeat that sounded like a train. Often it called to mind that tune that had been haunting me since the mid-thirties. Nobody danced to it. They just listened. I began to understand that it appealed to a certain type of person.

"You should turn Eddy's into one of these joints," I suggested to Benny. "The kinda people come here would go over to your neighborhood. They'd like it there better."

"Maybe," he said.

That spring, the spring of '45, there was a picture on the front page of Il Duce strung up by his heels in front of a gas station in Milan. It was gruesome. That chin of his reminded me of Eddy Guilfoyle's nose, and certain other unpleasantries.

Things were clearly winding down in Europe, but they were getting nastier in the Pacific. In June, not long after VE Day, while the Battle of Okinawa was still raging, the entire Home Guard, Gilroy Division, convoyed over the mountains to an isolated stretch of sand on the far side of Golden Gate Bridge.

We arrived late on a cool, still, moonless night.

The sergeant, an earnest-looking kid who'd been waiting in the troop truck when we climbed in, had explained that this would be a dress rehearsal for the amphibious invasion soon to come. It would be precise down to the last detail, which meant total silence from the moment we jumped out of the truck. According to him, the tides where we were headed resembled those we'd encounter off Japan.

"Ok, this is it," he whispered, when the truck came to a halt.

He unzipped the canvas slit, put one leg on the bumper, and dropped to the road so softly his pack didn't rattle.

Our older, less agile carcasses followed. There were many a grunt, some muffled banging of equipment, but nary a deliberate sound. Soon all three hundred and fifty of us were lined up along the road, where we stood like statues.

We were high on a ridge. Between us and the ocean was a steep descent among jagged rocks and stunted trees.

We began moving slowly because we were converging toward the middle from both sides of the line to a spot where a draw led down to the sea. Later, when the fiasco was analyzed, we would learn that this strange mode of initial deployment was the result of mistake number one. The lead truck was supposed to park at the draw so the line could begin there. Instead, it drove another quarter mile.

There was some confusion when two lines of middle-aged soldiers met at the lip of the draw, but we soon organized ourselves into a single file and funneled through a notch between two boulders.

Our descent took us down a narrow, treacherous path. A steady wind blew up the draw into our faces. It was so dark that each of us was reliant on the man ahead not to walk off a cliff.

A dozen amphibious 'ducks' awaited us on the beach, enough to hold us all if we crammed in thirty-plus to a boat. There was plenty of time before boarding to listen to the waves crashing on the shore in both directions for what seemed like a very long way.

The cove we were about to embark upon looked relatively calm. But straight out to sea, you couldn't tell how far, there seemed to be a line of rocks with big swells rolling over them.

Every now and then a roller that looked about waist-high would ripple across the cove, run up the sand to where we'd assembled, and lick at our boots.

I began to hear chatter down the beach, then word was passed that we could break our vow of silence because what we were about to do, embark against the surf from the mainland, wouldn't happen when we invaded Japan anyway. On that not so distant day they'd simply open the hatches of a destroyer and dump us, ducks and all, into the ocean about one hundred yards offshore.

That was something whoever planned this precision rehearsal hadn't thought through. It was a 'snafu,' as the GI expression went—situation normal all fucked up. Some 'whistle dick' up the chain was responsible.

A few officers gathered near the shore, flashlights blazing. They got down on their hands and knees and spread a chart between them. An errant wave came along, and when it receded the chart was gone. The officers threw their hands up in disgust and ordered us to start boarding.

We climbed up the side of the ducks on ladders, jumped into the hulls one at a time, and knelt in the darkness shoulder to shoulder, chest to buoyant back-pack. As we waited to get underway, our child-sergeant told us that the dress rehearsal had resumed, and silence was again the rule. We'd soon be disembarking into chin deep water, he warned. There would be current to contend with.

"Not much current," he said. "A little, just like off Japan. Only thing that won't be the same… the Nips'll be shootin' at us over there."

Something in his tone told me that mortality didn't weigh on him as heavily as it should. We'd all heard about what had happened to our boys at Omaha Beach. Rumor had it that the casualty rate when we invaded Japan would be far worse.

This exercise, on the other hand, would just be a cold, wet slog. That was how we had it figured.

Our duck made a grinding sound as it scooted across the wet sand, nosed into the water, and crawled through shallow water over some rocky seabed. Soon we were afloat. A powerful marine motor kicked in. We made our way out to sea, rolling and bobbing.

In short order we could feel the duck turning, then the motor died and the front gate dropped. I heard splashing as the first wave of Home Guardians hit the water. Silence held for a few seconds, then the curses and shouts began.

By the time I got a whiff of what was happening, I was on the lip of the duck poised to jump, but it had reared back so I was fully ten feet above the water. Someone tried to shove me off. I resisted. Then we came crashing down on top of the men who'd just disembarked, drew water until the duck was half full, and reared up again. I was pinned to the stern, fully submerged.

The hull dropped with a ponderous slap, and every one of us was flushed into the sea. I poked my head above water, felt for the bottom with my foot, and stepped on a buoyant pack attached to one of my fellow Guardians.

At that point I must've intuited the broad outlines of the catastrophe. I know that I kept my noggin above water long enough to glimpse shore, and began making for it with all my might. A wave flung me face first into the water. As soon as I regained my feet the backwash knocked me over the other way.

I righted myself and made for land. There were shouts of warning. A breaker tossed one of the ducks into a line of men a few yards away. I threw off my pack and thrashed for dear life, swimming, crawling, making my way shoreward any way I could.

In the end, what probably saved the survivors was the steady surge of tide that wasn't supposed to be there. It kept you moving in the right direction most of the time. Soon—I couldn't have been in the water more than two minutes—everyone who'd made it had scrambled up the beach. We stood there shivering and looked out to sea.

There were a couple ducks aground about twenty yards offshore. The rest were riding the rollers out where they'd dropped their loads. Packs bobbed in the starlight. I saw a man tumble ashore on the crest of a wave, arms flailing so wildly that I expected him to get to his feet, but he didn't. The backwash took him before anyone could react. Later we agreed that he was DOA.

We lost more than twenty men that night, a mortality rate that didn't compare to Iwo Jima or Normandy, but it was our Armageddon. Everybody knew someone who didn't make it. Hudspeth drowned. So did our child-sergeant, a farm kid from Indiana, we learned.

Just before we gathered for a memorial service the next evening, the sky pilot took me aside and told me my mother had passed. "I probably can get you bereavement leave," he said. "We won't be shipping out for a few weeks."

So it was a time of mourning and decision, a good combination. By the conclusion of the hymns, the eulogies, and the exhortations to take it to those Nippon rats in order to 'give meaning' to our fallen comrades's deaths, I'd decided that there was no point in going back to St. Paul. Not then, not ever. The place didn't exist anymore. The only way I could visit it again was in my mind, and all I needed was a drink and an audience to do that.

For the next six weeks we waited for the order to ship out. We were told we'd be flown to a staging ground on some island and loaded on destroyers bound for the seas off Kyushu, the southernmost tip of Japan. Judging from the way the Nips fought for Okinawa, the chances of making it ashore were about fifty-fifty. Then the battle would begin.

We spent July contemplating what fate had in store. Then, on August 6, we awoke to the announcement that a bomb that 'harnessed the energy of the sun' had been dropped on Hiroshima and flattened the city. Two days later Nagasaki was similarly destroyed. Less than a week after that, Japan surrendered.

Benny and I shook hands and hoisted one when we heard. Unlike Hudspeth and several million others, we'd slid through unscathed.

We all listened to the VJ Day celebrations on the radio. People took to the streets of every city in America. According to the announcer, there'd never been such a throng in San Francisco. Sometimes you couldn't hear his voice because of the cheers, car horns, and shouts of victory. Market Street was said to be full of sailors, GIs, and civilians of all ages, including young gals kissing servicemen 'with wild abandon.'

We could picture them—short skirts, high heels, red lipstick, the works—but that's all we could do. We were sitting tight, awaiting discharge. It wasn't easy, but it was easier than invading Japan.

The celebration in Frisco went on and on. The next day, drunk GI's were still riding the roofs of automobiles and trolley cars up and down Market Street, passing bottles of Champagne. By then, most of the Home Guardians had heard enough, but Benny and I kept coming back to the radio, because every time there was a lull in the bedlam we could hear a saxophone, loud and insistent. It sounded good, and we wanted to hear more.

The guy with the microphone made his slow way toward whom-
ever was playing, because, he explained, it was, "at the very center
of the victory celebration, in America's great Pacific city."

"'Scuse me," he said, "can I get through, sir... maam, I'm almost there, now I'm squeezing through a big crowd of colored folks
gathered 'round a fellow with a horn of some kind. And here he is.
I'm tapping him on the arm... pardon me, boy... Say there, you with
the horn. Could I please—pardon me... hey, what—"

We heard rumbles of static, a series of loud bonks. Someone
must have held the microphone toward the saxophone, and we bent
our ears to an uninterrupted five minutes of pure joy.

We'd have listened all night, but the announcer got his mike
back and beat a hasty retreat.

EDDY'S

Benny said, "You're going home, Milo?"

"Oh no, I'm not. You see, God—" Bradich interrupted himself to take a sip from a shot glass held carefully twixt thumb and forefinger, got it down to manageable level without losing any to spillage, and tossed the rest back. "God spoke to me. He said, 'Milo Bradich, here's your life back. Now change it!' So I don't have to go home to Ione, and the kids, and the farm, and the cow shit, and one day after another behind the goddamn plow. That's not my—"

"You're starting to remind me of a clown, Milo." said Benny. "Not Pagliaccio either. He was sad and wise. You're giddy and stupid. A few more drinks, a few more days, then back to Wisconsin with you."

"Uh-uh. It's my life. Hey there!" Bradich waved a wad of mustering out pay at the waiter. "Three more."

I agreed with Benny, but I certainly understood why Bradich thought the Deity was personally involved in his affairs. Having been spared when millions weren't, tempted you to think you'd been spared by something besides blind luck, for a special destiny.

We'd arrived late to the party in Frisco. The VJ Day festivities had degenerated into a riot about day four, and the police cleared the streets. By the time we'd been formally discharged and got to town, the bars were where it was happening… all the bars, so people had begun sorting themselves out according to the kind of place that appealed to them. Those whose thoughts turned homeward were gathered for a last drink in the Mission, or near the train depot, but at The Gold Dust Lounge on Powell Street, every man you spoke to was at least toying with the idea of hanging around the Bay area.

All the chatter was about firming up the resolve to stay. Some fellows gabbed about high-paying jobs in the factories over in Oakland. Others said Frisco reminded them of Paris, or Hong Kong. Nobody said it reminded them of home. Most were younger than us by a decade or more. Maybe that's why they were so excited. I could see poets and rummies in the making, as well as eight-to-fivers.

Milo Bradich was none of those. He was a dawn-to-dusk farmer with a wife and two daughters. It was a mistake to bring him here, I realized. He was caught up in the mood and drunk to boot.

"Why the hell shouldn't I stay?" he kept asking. "All these guys are staying. You're stayin', Martin. Why's it so different for you?"

"I'm a single man, Milo… an only child. My father drank himself to death when I was a kid, my mother died a few weeks ago, and my only living relative, my uncle, double-crossed me back in '34. I don't have a home to go to. When I think of home, it's Mrs. Dunn's boarding house and a saloon called Tin Cup's, which both could've burned down for all I know. That's why it's different."

He mulled that over while we listened to the juke box. It was the same song some kid had been playing off and on all afternoon, about a gal waiting for a soldier—"waitin' for my life to begin, waitin' for the train to come in." The kid got drunker and drunker, and told anyone who'd listen that he was working up the courage to break the bad news to his girl.

He was making a soap opera out of it. But telling a gal who'd waited out the war that you weren't coming back was no small thing. I sympathized. So did the dames in the joint. They took turns comforting him with hugs and little pecks on the cheek. They'd smooth his hair back and give him long, 'screw me' looks. I wondered if they knew they were the reason he was staying.

Sadly, things were back to normal, frail-wise, now that the war was over. The gals had eyes for the young men… Benny too, of course. Me, they could take or leave. They looked at Milo like he was a bowl of cold oatmeal, which was a good thing in retrospect. If he'd gotten to first base with a dame we never would've been able to get him on a train, which we finally did a few days later.

Late in the afternoon a group of smokes came in. No one paid much attention until there was a pause in the music on the box. Then one of them, a tall, skinny fellow, with coffee-colored skin and the face of an Indian, got up on the bar and sang.

"Pardon me, MAN! Is dis da Chattanooga choo-choo—track twenty-nine, MAN! you can gimme a shine…"

His pals were snapping their fingers, and pretty soon there was a group of ex-GIs doing the same. Some gals joined them, and within minutes half the joint was gathered around listening to him 'scat.'

After he finished, one of his friends handed him a saxophone and he began to blow a jazzed-up version of a tune of the day—"My Dreams Are Getting Better All the Time." He had a way of playing with the notes that grabbed your attention. The place quieted down.

"Hear what he's doing?" Benny whispered. "He's breaking the chord up into tones and playing them separately instead of all at once." He tried humming it, but quit abruptly. "You know who this is, don't you?"

"Who?"

"He's the guy we heard on the radio."

He was right. It *was* him.

"Know what?" I said, "Eddy's isn't a bad name for a jazz joint."

He nodded, and tried humming a chord that way again.

"Solves everybody's problem," I persisted. "All we gotta do is talk to this guy."

He shrugged. "Ok, do it."

Easier said than done. He was a high-strung fellow. He wanted to punch me when I approached him between numbers, but his pals interceded. One thing led to another, Benny bought some drinks, and we began talking. They were from Louisiana, around our age. They'd come west to work in the weapons foundries over in Oakland… made good money during the war, but word was the plants would soon be converted to peace-time use and the jobs would go to white guys. They told us this in a matter-of-fact way, but the sax player—he was a little younger than the others—wore a look of undisguised disgust while his friends explained why they'd soon be out of work.

They all played instruments, but he was the only one who lugged his around. "Man's a genius," said Marcus, his pal and co-worker.

His name was Spartacus Bellerive. Months later, when I can honestly say we were friends, although he always had that edge on around white people, I asked him how he got such a moniker.

"Counta that's how they call people where I come from," he said. "How'd you get yours? Some kinda dumb-ass tribe thang from the Emerald Isle?"

I laughed when he said stuff like that. I couldn't help it. It was funny. At first he'd scowl, then after a while he'd nod. But he didn't often laugh.

THE DON

By the time the war ended Eddy was on his last legs, so most of the controversy the joint generated went right by him. He was glad his name was still up there, and he didn't have the energy to argue about anything else. He just went up to Tomasso's vineyard and sat in the sun.

The neighborhood fellows, on the other hand, were either skeptical or hostile. Every few nights a group of three or four guys, not always the same guys but the same type, the kind Faeniss Cuhulain called 'soldiers,' would stop in, stand in back by the bar, and crack wise with each other about the crowd or the music. They never started real trouble, but it was a constant worry that Cus would get into an argument with one of them.

That would've been too bad for everybody, especially the soldier. I never actually saw Cus fight, but he carried himself like a man who enjoyed using his fists. He once showed me a handful of pepper he kept in his front pocket to fling in an opponent's eyes. "Man can't do nothin' but cry and call for help if ya give him a face fulla pepper," he said. And in case those calls were answered, he had a razor in his shoe.

Daytimes were slow at Eddy's. One afternoon, maybe a month after the transformation, Benny and I were there by ourselves when Marissa's husband, Marco, dropped by. Benny made brandy and coffee, and the three of us sat down to talk. Marco kept stressing that he was simply an emissary, come to discuss the situation.

"Me, I can see both sides," he said. But he only presented the one.

Much of what he had to say concerned the 'mulle.' You didn't have to know what that word meant, you just had to hear him say it. Again, he claimed he was merely conveying an attitude that he didn't necessarily share.

"Musicians, ok, but now you got mulle come here and drink, hang out like they belong? Not so good, Bendetto, not so good." Marco shook his head and sighed.

"Jesus, Marco, get with it," said Benny. "It isn't 1939 anymore. We're out in front of something here."

"Maybe. Maybe you are. Marissa says so. She's on your side. Says, 'Bettino'—she always calls you that, like a pet name or somethin'—'Bettino's a smart guy. Him and his Mick buddy, they know what they're doin','" she says.

"Marissa's always had a soft spot for you," he added.

"Oh, you're wondering if I slept with her while you were overseas? No."

He let that go right by him and looked at me quizzically. "You a partner here now?"

"No, he's not a partner," said Benny. "He's a friend. He tends bar sometimes, handles things with the musicians."

"Just askin'. What do you do, Martin?"

"I was a private detective before the war. Thinkin' of gettin' back into it."

"Really? A private eye? So, Benny, I tell the fellas this is a… a jazz joint. And they got to live with it, mulle and all, correct?"

"Correct. And while you're at it, tell Tomasso I'm having a hard time selling his wine at twenty cents a glass here, because he's selling it a dime a gallon over on Filbert Street. I'll honor my agreement with him, of course, but just let him know, so he doesn't think I'm an idiot. And when you take over the vineyard, Marco? That'll have to change."

Marco rubbed the rind of the lemon around his glass and sipped the last of his drink. "Bendetto, Bendetto, don't start with the unpleasantness, please," he said. "I'm simply the messenger here. The fellas understand you got a right to run your place how you want. Their concerns are about the neighborhood. They don't know if they can keep people safe around here... with the mulle and all."

"Who says that?" Benny asked. "My old friend Ralph Malvese?"

"Yeah, him. Among others."

"Tell Ralph to drop by. We'll talk."

Marco took that as a good sign. "Ok, he'll be glad to hear," he said, looking very relieved. "You'll see him soon." He drained his espresso cup and left.

"We're going to settle this once and for all," Benny said, as soon as Marco walked out the door. He was fuming.

Of course, it had crossed my mind that the lovely Marissa might have let the cat out of the bag in a weak moment, or more likely a moment of pique, knowing her.

"Maybe I should make myself scarce," I said.

"Uh-uh. Stay put."

So we fixed another drink and waited, with our separate worries.

A few minutes later, in walked The Don himself, a portly fellow with hair as thick and black as Benny's, but the resemblance ended there. Ralphie lacked texture. There were big bruise-colored quarter moons under his eyes.

"Gimme one'a them, Benny," he said, pointing toward our little cups.

Benny raised a finger. "Manners, Ralphie. *Please* 'gimme one a them.' What's become of you my old friend? Remember when we used to go to the opera together?" He fixed another coffee and brandy. "One lump or two?"

Ralphie raised two fingers. Then, a third.

Benny dropped the cubes in, put a slice of lemon on the saucer, and placed it in front of The Don, along with a little lace napkin.

"So, Ralphie, Marco tells me I don't have to pay you fifty bucks a month anymore."

"What!" Ralphie sputtered. "What the hell! I never told him."

"Well, not in so many words. He just told me you couldn't protect the neighborhood on account of the mulle in my place. So I figure since the service is rescinded, I'm done paying."

"Hey, Bendetto, don't get funny on me now!"

Benny looked at me. "Did I just make a joke?" he asked.

"You must be the private eye," said Ralphie, with a sly little smile.

I nodded, but he'd already turned his attention back to Benny.

"We're gonna have to come to some kinda understanding here," he said.

"Well, if you can protect my bar I don't mind paying fifty a month. How's that?"

"Problem is, I don't know if music fits in around here." He slurped his drink, and wiped his mouth with the napkin. "Whaddaya want it for?"

"I love music, that's why. What do you love, Ralphie? Spaghetti? You've put on weight, my friend."

He held up a hand, as if to fend off a response.

"It's your business, your waistline. And the way I run my bar is my business. Thing is though, a gourmand like yourself has his pick of restaurants. Enough meatballs to feed an army around here, but jazz lovers like myself, and my friend Martin,"—he nodded my way—"and the hundred or more people who come every night that Cus's trio plays, we'd all be out of luck without Eddy's. And then the crowd wouldn't be stopping by Guardino's or some of the other spaghetti joints while they're in the neighborhood either. See how that works? To each his own, Ralphie. You know that tune?"

He stood and belted out a few lines in his tragic baritone. "To each his own, one and ooonly..."

"Another brandy and coffee, gentlemen?"

Ralph nodded yes, glumly.

I was beginning to get the drift. Ralphie didn't have any enthusiasm for screwing his old friend over. They'd trade wisecracks awhile and call it a day. I was about the only thing left to settle. While

Benny was up making the drinks, Ralphie asked if I ever planned to go back to 'West Overshoe,' or wherever it was I came from.

"Nope," I told him. "I'm settling down here."

"Right here in the neighborhood? That'll be a first. Well, not exactly. Guy name'a O'Doul has a joint around here, but generally it's Italian. You ever meet a man of honor before, McDonough? Or am I the first."

"You're the first. Met a guy who said he was a man of honor once, but turned out he was a double-crossin' rat."

Ralphie looked a bit startled at that. Benny brought our drinks over.

"Tell him about it, Martin," he said. "You'll be interested, Ralph."

BLOOD

A few days later I got a call from Detective Tommy Brown. "Meet me at the St. Francis. Room 508." He hung up before I responded.

He was standing in the hall when I arrived, with a handkerchief across his nose. He opened the door, and I had everything I could do not to gag.

"Come on in the bathroom," he said.

It really stunk in there, and there was no mistaking that odor, although I pretended to.

"Looks like somebody slaughtered a goat here," I said.

Tommy didn't bother correcting me. "Take a good look in the bathtub. I want you to remember this."

It was smeared—make that painted—with rust-colored goo. There were streaks where someone had taken a few swipes at it, probably with the washcloth that lay bunched up and stiff on the floor.

Clots of black junk clung to the bath mat. A plug of something greenish-purple was stuck in the drain.

"Remember when they made gin in bathtubs?" Tommy asked. "That was before these 'men of honor' came here. Look."

He picked up a bucket from under the sink, and held it to my face.

"Don't worry. This don't smell. Go ahead, look."

There appeared to be the remains of a skull inside.

"Those scum put it in lye so we'd have nothing to identify, but the maid found it first."

He plucked out a big, U-shaped bone, thinned-out but intact. Stubs of tooth poked out of it.

"Jaw bone," said Tommy. "Whose chin does it look like to you?"

"That Wop in the newsreels."

"Nobody's seen Dutchy around since some guys talked to him in the lobby the other day. Said they were from Chicago, had a fighter they wanted to bring here. He went up to their room to discuss it. Got any idea what happened?"

I shrugged.

"This stinks worse than what's left of him, Martin."

"It was inevitable. He fingered all sorts'a people, then somebody fingered him."

"Not somebody. You. You fingered him."

He gave that a few moments to sink in, then made me listen to Dick Pranke's life story, the short version.

"Know anything about Dutchy? Probably not. He was from a little town in North Dakota— Cavalier. Came here in '31 on the lam from some kind of beef in Winnipeg. He made a point of being useful to us, so I never looked into that. Said he'd had a few fights in Bismarck in the twenties, won 'em, but saw that he had no future. He wasn't much of a boxer, couldn't really punch very hard, but he had one advantage." He poked that damn bone in my face again. "Iron jaw. Easy to hit, hard to knock down. So he's on a one-way trip to Palookaville when it dawns on him how to make money in the fight game. Had his buddy in Fargo bet a bundle that some bum would KO him, and lo and behold, that's what happened. Took his winnings, came here. Probably has a mother back there in North Dakota, what do you think?"

"I think I was double-crossed, Tommy. Outsmarted. Sorry, but that's the long and short of it."

The smell was getting to me pretty bad. I started to leave, but he pulled at my sleeve.

"Some advice? I was you I'd keep this under my hat. Knowin' you, that won't be easy, but try."

SEAL BEACH

Cus's trio played weekends, and Monday afternoon late, billed as the 'Blue Monday Matinee.' Every time they took the stage the joint filled up. The crowd was like nothing I'd ever seen before. The guys were mostly ex-GIs wearing Army jackets and sunglasses. They made a point of going two-three days between shaves. Some grew little goatees. They didn't get into fights… they got into conversations. They'd argue with fierce intensity, then shut up and listen as soon as Cus and his band took the stage.

Benny practically rubbed his hands in glee when he overheard them talking. "That's music they're discussing," he'd say.

They discussed a few other things too. I'd often overhear the guys telling the gals about their battle-haunted souls, how they couldn't sleep at night because of the scrapes they'd had with death, or because of the men they'd killed. Of course, there was only one cure for that kind of insomnia.

The gals grew their hair long and wore tights, which had the curious effect of covering their gams and showing them off at the same time. They smoked in public, like chimneys. They were as passionate as the men in the confabs, but clammed up too when the music started, and applauded enthusiastically when it ended. They scandalized the neighborhood by simply being there for a while, but soon some local gals were coming in. The way they tied their dark hair up in bandanas and let it spill down their neck became the style.

Some of the gals came up from Los Angeles. According to Benny, who got to know them, they were in the movies. It seemed that in no time Eddy's had a reputation all over the West Coast. It wasn't long before the place was full every night, music or not.

When Cus soloed there were always fragments of melody to remind you where it began, but you never knew what it was when he started, or where it was going. If it was up-tempo at all there was a distinctive beat that was mindful of a train gathering speed.

Often he'd turn his back when he blew. That and his temper created a mystique, which didn't hurt with the gals. Many a lovely tomato had the hots for Cus, which had the potential to disturb our truce with the moblets. Benny had a way with Cus though. He took him aside one day and informed him that the neighborhood gals were off-limits. Cus immediately went on one of his rants, but Benny cut him off.

"Just stick to the dames from LA," he said. "I don't need the kind of trouble that would start if you were poking a neighborhood girl. Neither do you. We've got a good thing here."

That happened a few weeks after Thanksgiving, 1946, when the phenomenon that was Eddy's was really getting rolling. Cus let it ride at the time, but I knew that sooner or later he'd start an argument with me, just so he could get what he wanted to tell Benny off his chest.

I usually stood in back. Benny wanted me there for early warning in case the 'soldati' became troublesome. The bar was always full and clamorous. The tables were full too, sometimes seven or eight people seated, with a few more milling about as if a game of musical chairs was in progress.

The place didn't exactly clam up in reverence when Cus and his trio played, but you could hear them alright anyway, even from my vantage. Cus could only see the faces near the stage because of the spotlights, so he never knew that I listened until I told him, about the same time Benny told him it was hands off the neighborhood chicks.

"How come you like this kinda music?" he demanded out of the clear blue sky one Friday night, after the joint closed and emptied out.

It was almost Christmas by then, so this had been festering a while.

"I don't know. Because it tells a story? Maybe you noticed... I like stories."

He banged the saxophone into the case, snapped it shut and drained a shot of whiskey. He jerked his head toward the back, where Benny was counting receipts.

"Missus Castronovo's lil' boy Bendetto says these neighborhood chicks are off-limits f'r niggers."

"He called you a 'nigger'? That's a surprise."

"Might as well have."

A red-headed gal was waiting for him at a table near the stage. Her legs were crossed so her skirt hiked up her thigh. She wasn't wearing tights. It was enough to break a middle-aged bachelor's heart.

I nodded in her direction. "Too bad about you and the women, Cus."

He allowed himself the tiniest of smiles. "Yeah, Liz's nifty. Wish some brown-skin women would come in here though. They ain't allowed."

"First I heard about that."

As a matter of fact, some colored gals did start coming in not long after. Their style was so much like all the other dames that it didn't cause much of a stir, even amongst the moblets. To the best of my knowledge, Cus never exchanged a word with any of them.

Cus invited me to come along with him and the redhead that night. She had a convertible she'd driven up from LA. They were going down the Coast Highway to a beach where he could blow his horn.

I grabbed a jug of wine and the three of us got in the car. We didn't talk much on the way—the wind made it impossible. That was all right with me. I still hadn't gotten over the fact that you wouldn't freeze to death in an open car a few days before Christmas. The fog cleared a little ways out of town, and the temperature dropped a bit, but it was still comfortable.

There were seals sleeping on the beach, until we disturbed them. Then they squawked and honked, and waddled off down the sand. Cus walked behind, blowing his horn to shoo them along.

The gal and I sat down on some rocks. She told me her movie name was Lizbet —not to be confused with Elizabeth or Betty.
"There's already too many of them," she said.

She was under contract to a studio and knew a producer who was
interested in using Eddy's as a set. "Cus's group would be the background music," she told me. "They'd make some money, and it'd be
good publicity for the place."

Now and then the breeze blew a few ragged notes of a sentimental number Cus was playing our way, and it slowly dawned on me
that I'd heard it before, many times. Always in my head, except the
first time. It was my favorite song, the one I couldn't name.

Meanwhile Liz was explaining about the film, who'd be in it,
when it might happen. Distracted as I was trying to identify that tune,
it took me a while to figure out that she thought I was some kind of
impresario at Eddy's. I was on the verge of disabusing her of that notion when it occurred to me that it wasn't a bad reputation to have...
among the starlets.

Cus came back, scowling. "Yeah, well, you're right about the
music," he said, as if our earlier discussion had never ended, "but
it's the colored man's story. How you gonna understand? How them
white boys in the joint gonna understand? Ain't no ofay in the world
understands."

We drank some wine and listened to the waves crash.

"I beat a man crazy back in '35," Cus said. He looked pained
when he said it, but immediately began recounting the tale.

He told us that when he lived in Louisiana, he and Marcus and
a few other musicians used to play on a circuit that involved dance
halls and clubs as far away as Kansas City. It was there that he had a
run-in one night with a white guy.

They were standing outside a bar where they were playing, on
break, when the guy pulled up to the curb and waved a five dollar bill
out the window. "'Hey, boy,' he says, 'ah'm lookin' f'r a color-gal t'
have some fun with. Five for you, five for her.'

"Marcus and the others wanted to walk down the street and hope
he'd go away, but I hollered back, 'How you like 'em, boss, high
yalla? Black?'

"'Black,' the guy says. I told him there was a whore up the alley, waiting to do business. The guy hesitated, but I said, 'you gonna like her, boss.'

"Marcus, he told me, 'don't be no fool,' but I jumped that cracker and liked t'killed him soon's he turned into the alley. Would've killed him, kickin' on him and all, but the other fellas dragged me away. Then later on I heard he was off his chump, permanent... Couldn't play Kansas City after that."

"Never did feel too good about it," he added. "Anyways, that's my story an' ain't you or any other white man gonna understand it."

I must have shrugged, because he got right up in my face. "So what's it about then?" he asked. "C'mon, tell me."

"It's about doin' somebody harm and regretting it."

He said there was more to it than that. I agreed. "There always is," I said.

"Yeah, I know what you're thinkin', because I heard you fingered some fella who got killed. By accident. Ain't the same. I done what I done on purpose."

"You heard correctly, but you didn't hear the whole story. It was an accident fingering that guy, but I killed some other people and that was no accident."

THE FATAL THING

After Tony left, I hung around the hotel room until the coast was clear, then walked across the street to the St. Paul Hotel and knocked on Faennis Cuhulain's door. He was his usual gracious self, but I could see he was disturbed when I asked him to drop a dime on Tony Sausage.

"How do ye know 'twere him?" he asked.

"Had to be. You told me he was under the gun to come up with some money by the summer of '34. Van Meter was ambushed in August '34. No one ever found the rest of his cash because Marie took it, and I know Marie told Dutchy to set Van Meter up. Dutchy said so, and why would he lie? Tony put the squeeze on Marie, she gave him Van Meter's cash, and he gave it to Ricca."

"But yer guessin', lad. Ye couldn't prove any of it, if it came to that."

"This isn't a court case, Faennis. I know what's true. Tony used me to confirm his suspicions about Dutchy, then rubbed him out. Now he wants to snuff Opal Milligan just because she's hashin' it around that Marie fingered Van Meter. I suppose he's afraid if Ricca gets wind of it he'll put two and two together. But think about that. A dame with a screw loose makin' noise four hundred miles away, and he wants to kill her! I bet he killed his own sister as soon as she got outta the slammer so she couldn't blow the whistle. For all I know he'll sit and stew a while, then send somebody after me. I'm not gonna live that way, Faennis.

"He's on the train that just left St. Paul," I added. "Gets into Chicago tomorrow morning early."

"If I tell Paulie, ye know what'll happen."

"I do."

He put his chin in his hand and thought a bit, then agreed to make the call. "I got ye into this," he said. "Otherwise I'd niver do such a thing."

I paced around while the operator put him through. "That you, Paulie?" he said. He nodded to indicate it was time for me to leave.

He was still talking when I closed the door quietly behind me and headed for the Lowry, where I spent a restless night.

Next morning, I went down to the lobby for coffee, sat and read the paper a while, then went back up to the room and phoned The Real McKay.

"Anything interesting outta Chicago, Jack?" I asked.

I could hear him shuffling through the tape.

"Here's something," he said. "'Mob Murders At Union Station.' Want to hear the story?"

"Yeah."

"'Passengers exiting the overnight Zephyr from the Twin Cities and points west looked on in horror this a.m. as assassins shot down five men who'd just gotten off the train. Police identified one of the victims as Anthony Conforti, thirty-six, a former associate of Al Capone's, known to the underworld as 'Tony Sausage.' Conforti had been working for Paul 'The Waiter' Ricca since Capone went to prison, but was rumored to be on the outs with Ricca's gang. The killers fled the scene before the police arrived.'"

I thanked him and hung up, wandered into the bathroom and washed my hands. Then I sat in an easy chair for a while, staring at a slab of low sky through the window. It was the color of water in a mop bucket.

Ramsey Hill was hidden in the mist, but up above it, unmoored to anything visible, the brand new bronze cross they'd just placed high atop the cathedral caught some sunlight. It seemed to float in the air, looking grand enough to hang Jesus from.

Well, I told myself, it could've happened the other way. A quick scuffle, a gunshot, hopefully fatal. Wouldn't want to be conscious when they started making sausage.

After a while I called the desk. "I'm checking out," I said. "Any charges?"

"No sir, Mr. Conforti. You're all paid up."

***

After I finished my tale, Cus finished his.

"Thing is, there was an old gal up that alley, just like I said. Her, and her pimp standin' around keepin' an eye on things. Men at the bar where we was playin' were steady goin' out to visit her. 'Five an' two,' she'd say. 'Five fr'me, an' two for my man.' Truth is, I thought about takin' that five spot an' showing that cracker where she was, and that's what made me wanna kill him. Not what he did. What I thought about doin.'"

"But you did it for her too, didn't you?" I inquired, reasonably I thought. "To save her from further indignities, I mean."

He didn't answer right away.

Liz seemed to be cogitating on something. I guessed it was either what Cus did, or my interpretation of it. I caught her eye.

"So what do you think?"

"I think that gal in the alley would've wished she had that five spot. If anyone bothered to ask her."

Cus recoiled in mock horror. "That's a cold shot."

"I'm a practical girl. Can I have a swig of wine, please?"

I realized I'd been hogging the jug again, gesturing with it as I told my story. Sometimes I wonder why people are so patient with me.

"I wasn't exactly a saint before I arrived in Los Angeles, Cus," Liz said. "People come here to put the past behind'em. That's what you guys should do."

"That what you're doin'?" Cus asked me. "Puttin' it behind'ya?"

"I guess so. That's where it is, mostly."

"Some nights I can't sleep," he said.

"Me either. I dream about chins."

"I run into guys all the time who can't sleep at night. Because of the war," said Liz.

"I'll bet you're a great comfort to them, dear." I patted her copper top, and spied Cus laughing quietly, out of the corner of his mouth.

He stepped back, and blew a long, plangent note on his horn. "Thank God f'r small mercies. You believe in the Lord, Mc-D?"

"Sometimes."

"How come you gave up sleuthin'?"

"Mostly it was because things changed. I've been gettin' back into it recently."

I explained that Ralphie and the moblets had been recommending my services. They were usually under indictment for one thing or another. "The DA has his own investigators. These mob lawyers need somebody who can poke around, find things to trade for a reduced charge, or some leniency. Business is good."

"So where do you poke around?" asked the starlet, with the kind of sly smile so rarely directed at me nowadays.

"People in the neighborhood, people in the joint. It's easier than you'd think. There's always information. The trick is makin' it hang together so it's useful."

Cus blew a few bars of that tune he'd been playing.

"What is that?" I asked. "It reminds me of a tune that's been running through my mind for years."

"This here?" He blew it again. Sure enough, it was the very tune, note for bent note as best I could recall.

"That's somethin' I picked up in Kansas City," he said. "Some of them gates there, your age and more, played numbers they knew from way back. Picked 'em up from white bands, and such. A cat who played with Basie showed me that one."

"Remember his name?"

"Red's what they called him... Lester somethin'."

He blew a few bars, starting with a little overture that I finally recognized. After all these years. It was "Peg'O My Heart," pretty much as sung by Shamus McClaskey on the Tin Cup's Wurlitzer, and long before that, when I was a lad, on our old Victrola.

A fine bit of detective work. That and the wind made my eyes water.